I0628365

A Strange Little Band

By

Judith B. Glad

GCT, Inc.   Aloha, Oregon
2014

For my family.
Some I was born with, some I chose.
There when I need them,
there sometimes when I wish they weren't.
But always there.

"The family. We were a strange little band of characters trudging through life sharing diseases and toothpaste, coveting one another's desserts, hiding shampoo, borrowing money, locking each other out of our rooms, inflicting pain and kissing to heal it in the same instant, loving, laughing, defending, and trying to figure out the common thread that bound us all together."

~*Erma Bombeck*

Prologue

A Year Ago...

Margie Stennis waved a welcome. "Hi, Annie. Come on in the kitchen. Walter can watch the baby."

"No, I—"

"Go ahead," Ralph Stennis said, waving her toward the door where his wife stood. "We're going to take the kids out and run 'em ragged before supper."

She bit her lip, but said nothing. Walter still had little to do with Calvin, although he was getting better, now that Cal was starting to talk. "All right, but call me if he—"

"Annie, they're all daddies. They'll keep an eye on the kid," Margie said.

Reluctantly she followed Margie into the kitchen where five other women were engaged in various chores. "What can I do?" she asked, after introductions.

"Grab a glass of wine. Then you can help Jerri with the veggies. I should have picked up some already cut but I had all this broccoli, so I..." She turned away when her name was called.

Jerri Elliott was the slim woman working at a cutting board. "Our husbands share a secretary." She stepped to one side to make room for Annie at the counter. "Here, you can dismember this cauliflower. I never can do it without making an awful mess."

"Walter's talked about your husband. He's the one with the sailboat?"

"That's Bob." She grinned at Annie. "And Walter's the one who rides the Yamaha, right. Boys and their toys, huh?"

Annie smiled her agreement. As she cut up the cauliflower, she stole glances around the kitchen. Jerri was the only woman there even close to her age. The other four appeared to be in their late forties or fifties, but all were youthfully slim and dressed in designer clothing. She felt totally out of place in her denim pedal pushers and t-shirt, even if they had come from Nordstrom. She eyed Jerri's crisp chinos and polo shirt, noting that her sneakers' trim was the exact same shade of berry pink as her shirt. Obviously her idea of casual dress was an ocean removed from these women's. Well, she'd bet none of them had a toddler who was inclined to spill everything on his mother. "How old are your children?" she said to Jerri as she arranged white florets on the veggie platter.

"Five and nine. They're monsters. I'll do K.P. any time it lets me dump them on their dad." Reaching past Annie, she pulled a colander full of freshly washed snow peas toward her. "These need stringing. If you'll do that, I'll get the dips ready."

Once the appetizers had been set out for the men, the women returned to the kitchen. Annie would have rather stayed outside, where she could keep an eye on Cal, but Margie called her to join them. Inside, they gathered around the glass-topped table in a large breakfast nook. Margie refilled their wine glasses. The conversation turned to office gossip.

Walter had only been at Stennis Investment for five months, and this was the first company party they'd been invited to. She suspected, as she listened to the women's conversation, that she probably would be less than a perfect corporate wife, since she spent her days at a computer, instead of shopping and doing volunteer work.

Ralph stuck his head through the sliding door to the deck. "We can eat whenever you want, Margie. I think the natives are getting restless."

"We'll start bringing out the food in a bit then. Open another bottle of wine. That will pacify them."

Rising, Annie said, "I should check—"

"Now you sit yourself down and enjoy your wine, Annie." Ralph said from the doorway. "Your boy's just fine. Having a great time picking Margie's daisies."

"Oh no!"

"Never mind, Annie. He'll do no harm. You ought to see the damage our grandchildren do when they're here."

A quick look into the back yard revealed Calvin with the Elliott children. He was doing his best to catch a ball the older boy was tossing to him. She sat back down and allowed her wineglass to be topped off. It was delicious, a mildly sweet Oregon Riesling, very relaxing. The nervousness she'd felt at meeting Walter's business associates had all but dissolved. By the time Margie decided they should carry to food to the deck, she was enjoying herself.

Jerri's two and the three teenagers caused enough confusion that it took several minutes for the buffet table to get set up. At last Annie was free to join Walter. "Where's Calvin," she said, when she saw him standing alone by the railing.

"I don't know. He's around here somewhere."

"Walter, he's just a baby. You have to keep your eye on him every minute." She stood on tiptoe, trying to see the entire backyard. She couldn't. Clusters of shrubs and winding paths broke up the vast space. "I can't see him." Fear made her voice shrill.

"He was over there picking the heads off of daisies the last time I saw him."

Calvin had been picking daisies a half hour ago, when Ralph had assured her of his safety. He was only twenty months old. Nothing could hold his attention for a half hour. "Walter, we've got to find him!"

"Good God, Annie, will you calm down. You're making a fool of yourself." He did set his wineglass down and followed her down the stairs. "You go look around the play area. It's behind those tall shrubs."

"If I ever have a big yard, the play area is going to be in plain sight," Annie muttered as she strode across the lawn, ignoring the winding, graveled path. No matter how old the kids, they needed to have an eye kept on them. Witness some of the mischief she and her sibs and cousins had gotten into.

The play area was empty. With fear sitting in her belly like a block of ice, she walked along the elegantly landscaped border of the big yard. "Calvin, where are you? It's time to eat, darling. Please come out." She peered behind shrubs and parted tall ornamental grasses. The white wrought iron fence worried her.

Above the fancy scroll, its pickets looked far enough apart for a small child to slip through.

Walter met her halfway up the far side. He looked worried now, which scared her even more. "I'm going to ask the others to help. He's got to be here somewhere. Maybe he crawled under a bush and fell asleep."

"Yes, maybe he did." *Oh, God, please let that be it.*

Soon everyone was combing the backyard, peering under bushes, wading into the masses of flowering perennials. The incessant calls of "Calvin! Calvin, where are you?" made the lump of fear in Annie's belly grow, until it seemed to fill her whole insides.

The daisies were indeed decapitated. Some lay flat, as if someone had walked across them. A small pile of daisy flowers lay on the ground just beyond the fence.

"Calvin," she whispered. "Oh, my God. Calvin!" She was running by the time she passed through the gate. She dashed across the wide expanse of lawn between the houses. A brick path led around to the back, into the elegantly landscaped, white-iron-fenced yard.

The fishpond was landscaped in the Japanese manner. Her mind registered that much before it recognized the small shape floating among the lily pads.

"Calvin!"

Chapter One

A Friday Evening in August

HIS MOTHER WRINKLED HER NOSE AS A DRAFT OF STALE AIR enveloped them. "It smells musty."

"I'll open windows upstairs if you can get those on this floor." Ward set the bags of groceries on the oak commode in the entry. A good thing they'd come a day early. He could just imagine Joss's reaction to the smell.

"There used to be one of those box fans in the utility closet," she called after him. "If it still works, you could set it to exhaust out of the attic dormer."

He waved a hand in agreement, but continued up the stairs. His feet left prints on the dusty treads, another sign that they needed to find a better housekeeping service.

Or maybe they should simply sell the place. God knew, it wasn't paying for itself, even with the recent rent increase.

As he fought with stuck windows and dusty blinds, he considered what the reaction would be if he brought up selling what was left of the Floating Nought. Cecile was the only remaining heir, so it was purely her decision. But the rest of the family would have strong opinions, and wouldn't be shy about speaking them.

The air was already smelling fresher when he went back downstairs. His mother had set the box fan in the front door, blowing in. *Independent as ever, and still damned impatient.* He decided to leave it there while he unloaded the car. He'd already convinced her to sleep on the Hide-A-Bed in the living room tonight, so best clear the air for her before he worried about the upper floors. No one else would arrive until tomorrow anyhow.

Once Cecile had stowed the groceries they'd brought and he had moved his gear into the Blue House, they sat together at the long table in the kitchen. Ward had a beer and Cecile a tall glass of tea without ice. "I doubt anyone has refilled the ice cube trays since last summer," she said as she stirred in the contents of a blue sweetener packet. "The cleaners should check."

"The housekeeping service doesn't seem able to keep the floors clean, so filling ice cube trays is probably beyond them," Ward said. "I'm going to talk to the property management people, see if they can't find us a more dependable service."

"We need someone local. Someone who can keep an eye on the place." Her voice took on a querulous note, one he'd never heard until recently. She looked tired, too, even though they'd broken their journey in Baker City.

Ward thought back to his youth, when his father would think nothing of driving five or six hundred miles in a day—and that was before freeways. Ma had seemed tireless then, always ready to tell stories or sing, to keep him and his sibs from killing each other. She still had incredible stamina for her age, but at eighty-three she was slowing down.

No, she didn't have the energy she used to, but she wasn't about to admit it. He hoped this next week wouldn't wear her out. A family reunion where everyone got along would be tiring enough for her. This one promised to be hell on wheels.

Damn, but he wished he'd been able to talk her out of inviting everyone. Talk about an explosive mixture.

"I wish Annie had come over with us. I still don't trust her to come on her own."

"She's an adult, Ma. It's her decision."

Cecile picked up and put down her glass, leaving wet rings on the Formica tabletop. "She's still...fragile. It's been a year, and she's still blaming herself." Her mouth tightened. "If only she hadn't insisted on moving to Boise. She'd have been better off where we could keep an eye on her."

"That may have been why she moved. So you wouldn't be keeping an eye on her." He reached across and clasped her hand. "Stop worrying about Annie, Ma. When I called her last month, she sounded like she was in better spirits. Healing takes time."

"I know." Her eyes closed. "I know so well," she whispered.

He'd never known how to comfort her. Ward waited; she would conquer her sorrow as she always had.

"Will Frances come, do you think?" she said, startling him from his own dark memories.

"God, I hope not."

"Ward! She's your sister."

"A relationship she's done her best to forget. I can't believe you invited her, Ma. Talk about a disruptive force."

A disapproving shake of her head as she lifted her glass and drained it. "It's getting dark. I think I'll call it a day. I'll need all my energy tomorrow."

He stood as she did. "You can sleep in. Nobody's apt to arrive before early afternoon."

"No, I want to get up and watch the dawn. It's never the same in Portland." Gathering her tote and a paperback novel, she went toward the door, pausing only to set her glass in the sink. "I'll see you in the morning. Don't stay on the phone all night. You're on vacation, remember?"

He laughed. "Self-employed means you don't get vacations, Ma. You only get paid if you do work." He wasn't being strictly accurate. In the past year he'd been pulling back from active management and taking on more of an advisory role. The first steps to retirement. He hoped.

He bent to kiss her cheek. Still as soft and lilac scented as it had been fifty-odd years ago. "Good night."

Saturday

THERE WAS NOTHING LIKE TOWING A TRAILER ON A WINDING, mountain road to force a man into patience. What worried Clay was the driver ahead—an accident looking for a place to happen.

A woman. She'd passed him, just outside Mountain Home, and he'd caught a glimpse of an unmistakably feminine profile.

At last the road ahead straightened and the no-passing zone ended. Before Clay could make up his mind to pass, the green Accord slowed again, then drifted across the double center line, headed straight for the abrupt drop-off beyond.

He laid on the horn, without evident result.

"Damn woman! She *is* asleep!" The unwieldy combination of three-quarter-ton pickup and travel trailer swayed slightly in answer to his hand on the wheel. Wishing there was a guard rail between the other lane and empty space, he eased up close behind the small car. This time he hit the switch for the air horns. He winced at the blast of sound, knowing his ears would be ringing for a good long while.

The Accord jerked back into its lane, and then sped up, pulling away from him. Clay accelerated just enough to keep up.

By God, he'd give her a piece of his mind. *Some women shouldn't be granted driver's licenses.*

Again he switched on the horns. "Pull over, you dumb broad," he muttered, "before you get us both killed." A semi, loaded with bawling cattle, came around a curve ahead. Cold sweat beaded on his forehead as he thought about what could have happened.

A couple of miles down the road, the Accord pulled off onto a wide shoulder. Clay edged in behind it. He set the brake and climbed out, determined to scare some sense into her.

The driver was slumped in the seat, head resting against the steering wheel. He tried the door. Locked. He tapped on the window.

No reaction. "Damn it, woman, I know you can't be asleep. Open this door."

Her head moved, slowly. Turned.

"Get out." An edge of anger was still in his voice and Clay forced it down. "Ma'am, you need to get out, walk around a little. You almost went off the road."

She fumbled at her seat belt. As it slid open, her hand went to the door handle.

Clay stepped back, pasted a smile on his face. He hoped it was reassuring.

It must have been, because she opened the door and slowly, stiffly, got out. She moved like a woman three times her age. Two short, unsteady steps took her back to the rear quarter panel, where she leaned and stared vacantly across the gray-green sagebrush hills.

"Are you sick?"

A quick head shake. "No...no, I'm not sick. Just tired. So tired."

Crap. I can't leave her here. He pulled out his cell, checked the display. No signal. *What? You expected service out here in the boonies?* "Don't move."

She gave no sign she'd heard him, but neither did she move. When he returned, carrying his Thermos, she was where he'd left her, still staring across the hills. "Here. It's probably cold, but it's caffeine." He uncapped the stainless steel bottle, poured the last of his coffee into the lid.

She didn't move.

"Drink the coffee, God damn it!"

At last her hand closed around the cup. She stared down into it.

Clay held on to his temper. "Drink." He wrapped his hand around hers and forced the cup to her lips. Obediently she opened them. He was almost surprised to see her swallow. He'd half expected her to let the coffee dribble out of the sides of her mouth.

After a few swallows, she took hold of the cup and pushed it away. "Thanks."

When she wiped the back of her hand across her mouth, he noticed how richly pink and plump her lips were. "Move around now. You'll wake up faster with a little exercise. Give the caffeine a chance to work."

He pegged her age at mid- to late twenties. His earlier impression that she might be seriously ill strengthened. Her arms hung loosely at the sides of slacks that were obviously too large. They bagged at the hips, were gathered under the elastic belt cinching her slender waist. Her skin was unlined, her throat and chin firm. But there were dark lavender smudges under her tawny brown eyes and a sad downturn to her mouth. Despite the bagginess of her clothing, he found himself too aware of her slim curves, too close to drowning in those wide, haunted eyes. What was it his dad used to say? *She looked like she'd blow away in the first good breeze?*

Crap! I haven't got time for this. "Where are you headed?" he asked, hoping she lived in Fairfield or on one of the ranches hidden among these hills.

"The ranch...the Floating Nought." Her face seemed to light up a little, as if she'd made some connection to reality. "It's north of Rexburg."

"You're in no shape to drive that far, not without some rest." He thought rapidly, considering his options. "How about I follow you as far as Fairfield? You can get a room, rest up, before you go on."

"Oh, no! I've got to be there today. They'll worry."

"They'll worry a lot more if you kill yourself getting there. Let's go. I'll follow you, and if I see your car so much as wiggle, I'll give you a blast with the horns."

"Horns?" For the first time she looked back at his pickup. "Oh. That must have been what woke me. For a second I thought I heard a train."

He'd intended to remove the set of three bright, shiny airhorns from the almost new pickup he'd traded his BMW for, but hadn't gotten around to it. Getting ready for this trip had taken more time than he'd allowed, and he'd let a lot of nonessentials slide. Now he was glad he'd kept them. Instead of being a macho statement, they'd saved a life.

He mentally shook himself. "Move around. Get your blood flowing." The words came out more stern than he'd intended.

"I'll be fine, in a while. I just need a little longer to calm down." She buried her face in her hands.

"You don't look like you'll be fine." Despite the tension he could see in her shoulders and the tendons of her too-thin forearms, he was caught by her loveliness. He revised his first estimate of her age downward by five years. And she was not so thin that she had no figure, he realized, as his gaze followed the vee of her shirt neckline to the deep cleavage between generous breasts.

"No, really. I will. I'm better already." Pushing herself away from the fender, she took several steps, stopping when she rounded the hood. "Oh, my, that's glorious."

He had to agree. The morning sunlight slanted across the hills, casting deep blue shadows and turning the dry cheatgrass to a golden carpet. A dusty gravel road branched off from where they were parked and wound snakelike along a narrow ridge, dipped into a shadowy valley, and was lost in tall sagebrush. Beyond the nearby hills, a high, dark ridge extended across half the horizon, broken here and there by jagged black scars where basalt outcrops were slowly exfoliating into skeins of dark rockfields.

Clay looked down at her, wanting to thank her for making him pause and notice the view. He hadn't taken time to do that in a long time.

But I'll have time soon, he promised himself. *Very soon.*

"How are you doing?"

She started. "Oh. I'm fine. Awake now. No problem. I'll just—"

Clay opened the door of her car as she approached. "I'll follow you to Fairfield, just to make sure you don't fall asleep again." And to make sure she stopped and napped. He still thought she'd be wise to take a room and rest until tomorrow, but there was no way he could force her to. *She's not my responsibility. Once I've seen her safe to Fairfield, she's on her own.*

Yeah, but if anything happened to her...

I'd probably never know. Deliberately he pushed doubt out of his mind. Leaning down, he stuck his face into the open window. "Take it easy, and if you start feeling drowsy, pull off. I'll be right behind you."

At her nod, he straightened. Without a backward look—not that he wasn't tempted—he went to his pickup and climbed in. For the next thirty-odd miles he stayed on her tail. All the while he chafed at having to drive within the speed limit, something nobody ever did on this stretch of empty highway.

WADE STUCK HIS HEAD INSIDE THE FRONT DOOR AND CALLED, "Here come Joss and John."

His mother stepped out of the kitchen, a dish towel in her hands "Oh, good. I'm glad they got here first. They can get settled before the hordes descend."

He silently agreed with what she hadn't said, that they would make demands and complain about everything, and do all they could to be pains in the ass. John was about the stuffedest shirt Ward had ever met, and Joss was... Well, to be charitable, Joss was unpredictable.

But they were family, so he plastered a smile on his face and strode across the lawn to meet them as they got out of the cream-colored Cadillac.

BY THE TIME SHE REACHED FAIRFIELD, ANNIE WAS FIGHTING SLEEP again. Why was it, she wondered, that as soon as she lay her head on the pillow at night, she was wide awake. But let her get behind the wheel, and she was ready for a nap. She still wasn't sure why she was here, anyhow. No, that's wasn't right. She was here because Gran had commanded her to be.

"You'd think I would have grown out of the need to jump when Gran says 'Frog'," she muttered. The Floating Nought was the last place she wanted to be. So of course, that's where she *would* be, for the next week.

Walter hadn't liked the ranch, so they hadn't gone there after the first summer they were married. Instead they'd gone to

Hawaii, to Cozumel, and to Martinique. Last summer they'd been planning to cruise the Greek Isles, but of course...

No, don't think about last summer.

Gran said the whole family would be at the ranch this year, and she'd put a curious emphasis on *whole*. Did that mean Uncle Ward would be there? She hoped so. He never scolded her and he never judged. She was so tired of being told to pull herself together. To keep her upper lip stiff.

Even if he didn't come, Annie was looking forward to seeing Hetty, who was her favorite cousin. A good dose of Hetty's attitude might be almost as good as Uncle Ward's non-judgmental acceptance.

Trouble was, all the cousins and their kids would also be there. How was she going to manage a week of family? Living in each other's pockets, having no secrets, no silence. Not a moment to call her own. Gran would make sure she was kept busy.

"You spend entirely too much time brooding, Annie," she'd said when she informed Annie that she had no choice but to attend the reunion. "You need to get out among people, think of something besides your own troubles."

"Maybe I *like* thinking of my own troubles," Annie said out loud. "Maybe I don't want to forget." She looked in the rearview mirror. "Maybe I don't want people taking care of me. Why can't they just leave me alone?"

The pickup was still behind her. When she turned off the highway, he did, too. He followed her to the small park where she found a patch of shade to park in. She ignored him, and went to the rest room. When she returned, he was leaning against her car, just as if he belonged there.

"You don't need to follow me anymore. I promise I'll take a nap before I drive on."

"Good."

His quick smile made a tremendous difference in his looks. Scowling, he had been stern and just a little intimidating. "Look," she lied, "I really appreciate what you did for me back there. I hadn't realized I was so sleepy." She should have, though. She hadn't slept more than a couple of hours last night.

Or any night, for a long, long time.

HETTY SAW THE CADDY WHEN SHE PULLED UP NEXT TO THE Pink House. *They're here.* She leaned her head on the steering wheel, while she gathered calm and self-control.

Damn it! Something's wrong when you dread seeing your parents. When you wish you were anywhere, as long as it was a thousand miles away.

Yet she had looked forward to this week, had been excited. What a change it was from her usual trips. The co-owner of a travel agency rarely took a real vacation, even if she did travel to exotic locales and wear designer knockoffs. This week she would be able to kick back, sleep 'til noon if she chose, and read trashy novels instead of resort brochures.

She was looking forward to seeing her favorite cousins again, and to getting reacquainted with the ones she hadn't seen since the last Family Gathering she'd come to, back when she was in college.

And Frank. Let's not forget Frank. Just five more days.

A hot little tingle of excitement speared through her.

Clay was in a café in Arco when he saw a familiar green Accord drive past. He stared after it with relief. She'd had a good long nap.

He pulled out his wallet, tossed his credit card on the counter. Time he was on the road again. He'd wasted far too much time at Grove Creek Lodge, the first place on his list of properties to consider. As soon as he'd turned into the lane, he'd known it wasn't right for him. The place was big enough, yes, and it was located within reasonable driving distance of both the Big Wood River and Silver Creek. The half section of land it sat in the middle of was mostly in pasture, so there was a potential for some income in addition to what guests paid for lodging and food.

He'd run the numbers. The Grove Creek Lodge would be a good investment. An established resort catering to the fishing crowd in the summer, hunters in the fall, and skiers in the winter. Holden was eager to sell, would accept a reasonable offer.

Clay hadn't felt like he was coming home.

God! What the hell was I thinking? Was he thinking?

What a piss-poor reason for scratching the place off his list. After fifteen years in banking, he was still making decisions with his heart, not his head.

He let his mind move ahead to his destination. His appointment with Abe Wexler wasn't until Tuesday. He could spend the next two days on the river, reclaiming his soul.

Anticipation sizzled inside him. Only a few more hours and he'd be there. He had a feeling he'd find what he was looking for along the Henry's Fork.

Chapter Two

"Stop it, you two!"

Owen poked Char one last time, before folding his arms and doing his best to look innocent. He knew he was acting like a kid, but damn it, he was being treated like a kid.

"You'll enjoy it, sweetie," his mother had insisted when she and Peter had first brought up their plans for the summer.

"You've worked every summer since you were fourteen," Peter added. "Let us give you one last chance to be young and irresponsible."

Young and irresponsible. Ha! As if he even knew how. Ever since his real father had gone to...had gone away, he'd been the man of the house, mowing lawns and running errands and baby-sitting because he was too young to get a real job. Some of the guys had given him a bad time about doing a sissy-job, but his friends, who knew the score, had stood up for him. Even after Mom and Peter had gotten married, he'd kept working, mostly because he didn't want Peter supporting him.

Peter wasn't his father. No matter how great a guy he was, Peter just wasn't his father.

Mom used to tell him how much she appreciated his being self-supporting. Back then it had made the difference between them living in a decent house and having to move in with Grandma Chesney.

The old bat.

"Mo-om, he's crowding me!"

He jerked his elbow back before Mom got turned around.

Was Linda dating someone else? It wasn't like they'd been going steady or anything, but still, it really creamed him that she'd said she wasn't about to be faithful to him all summer.

"You'll be home a couple of weeks, then you'll go off to a new school. I love you, Owen, but not enough to give up having a life."

He hadn't even been able to argue. She was right.

God, I miss her. If I'd stayed home, maybe we'd have done it by now. He felt himself getting hot, so he started silently reciting the periodic table. It mostly worked.

I wonder if I'm the oldest virgin in the Science Club. Probably. He hadn't dated anyone before Linda, and it had taken him nearly a month to get up the courage to touch her breast. For a long time she hadn't let him do anything more than that. Her older sister had gotten an abortion last year and she said that wasn't going to happen to her.

She hadn't believed him when he'd claimed rubbers were safe.

"I'm gonna throw up."

Owen cringed away from his sister.

Peter slowed down. "Remember what I told you about looking straight ahead and keeping your eyes on a stationary object," he said. "I'll stop as soon as I find a wide shoulder."

Holy shit! Owen closed his eyes, shutting out the view from his window. Peter was driving really close to the edge of the road and the shoulder couldn't be much over a foot wide. Beyond it was empty space, straight down. If they went off the road, they'd roll, over and over, all the way to the bottom.

It seemed like forever before they stopped, but Char hadn't barfed. She scrambled out as soon as they were at a standstill and leaned against the side of the van, breathing deeply.

Mom dug out a Coke and told her to sip slowly. Peter came around the front of the van and leaned beside her. "Only a few more miles, Charlene. This is probably the worst road we'll have to face on the whole trip. It's the fastest route between Jackson Hole and the ranch, though. The other way would have taken us all day."

So who cares? What's so special about a dumb family reunion, when we're not even part of the family? "How much farther?"

Mom looked tired. Emma had been cranky last night, and Mom had taken her to the laundry room so she wouldn't keep the other campers awake.

Owen had offered to walk around with her, but Mom hadn't let him. She worried a lot about burdening him and Char with the brat, and he wished she wouldn't. Em was fun, even when she was fussy. He could always get her to smile.

"I'm okay now," Char said. "Maybe we could leave the window open or something."

Peter ruffled her hair. "Better yet, why don't you move up by Emma. She's going to be waking soon."

Owen could hardly wait. With the back seat all to himself, he could stretch out instead of having his knees jammed against the seat ahead.

Oh, God, six more weeks of this. I'm gonna go bonkers.

"I THINK I'M GOING TO REGRET THIS," ANNIE TOLD HERSELF AS SHE squeezed her car into the narrow space between her parents' Volvo and Louisa and Ben's battered, dusty Volkswagen bus.

"It's about time you got here." Hetty pulled the car door open. "My God, Annie! You look like death warmed over."

"It's good to see you, too, Het," Annie told her tall, red-haired cousin as she returned the hug. "And thanks a lot. You always did have the perfect compliment."

Hetty's reply was lost as Annie was enveloped in hugs from half a dozen people she knew, and a couple of perfect strangers. Her family's happiness and pleasure smothered her. They were so...*happy*.

Finally everyone scattered, leaving her alone with Hetty. "Where's Mom? And Gran?" She breathed in relief at the sudden peace.

"Up at the cookshack. They said to send you up as soon as you got unpacked. Want some help?"

"Sure. You can take the duffle. I'll get the rest." The tote bag holding her shoes was wedged between the cooler and one of the boxes. She tugged it free and set it on the ground.

"What on earth?"

"Oh, those are books. They've been in storage. I thought maybe someone might want them."

"What kind of books? I like a good mystery." Hetty reached in and started prying the top of one box open.

"They're all romances. Stupid stories about happy every after." The tote bag tipped over, spilling shoes everywhere. "Damn!" Annie snatched them up, stuffed them back into the bag. "Stupid shoes!"

"You said—" Hetty cleared her throat. "I'll take your bags in to our room while you go up to see Gran. You know how she hates to be kept waiting. We can catch up later."

"I suppose I have to." How she dreaded facing her grandmother, answering her questions, explaining why she had not yet, a year later, recovered from her sorrow. Talking to her on the phone had been difficult enough. Standing before her, like a little kid called in for a scolding, would be intolerable. For a moment she was tempted—really tempted—to aim the car the other way and go somewhere else. Anywhere else.

Would Gran remember what day tomorrow was? She got back into the car and drove along the unpaved road, around the copse of cottonwoods, to a small parking area between an old fashioned frame building—the cookshack now—and the Big House, the original barn that had been remodeled into a spacious rustic dwelling.

Would anyone even care what tomorrow was? Although her family had grieved with her at first, lately she wondered if they hadn't forgotten. Even her mother had been impatient with her excuses, when she'd tried to explain why she didn't want to come to the Floating Nought this year.

Her mother was waiting at the back door of the cookshack. "Annie, darling, I was beginning to worry. Did you get a late start?" She took the grocery bag in one arm and hugged Annie with the other.

Annie reached into the car for the second bag. "No, but I stopped a few times on the way. I was sleepy. How's Dad?"

"Your father is fine, as usual. He's out hiking with Ward."

"Uncle Ward came! I'm so glad. In his last letter, he said that he wasn't sure he could make it."

The screen door opened as they approached it. The tall, white-haired woman who held it looked Annie up and down. Her lips pursed as if she disliked what she saw.

"Well, miss, we were beginning to worry about you. And why haven't you been eating? You're skinny as a rail." She stepped aside, allowing Annie and her mother to enter.

"Hello, Gran." Annie put the bag on the counter and turned, tensing.

"'Hello, Gran.' Is that all you have to say for yourself? No smile, no hug, just 'hello, Gran?'"

Annie forced her mouth into a travesty of a smile. She went into her grandmother's arms, kissed her papery cheek. "I'm sorry, but it was a long, hot drive and I'm awfully tired. It really is great to see you, Gran."

"Still feeling sorry for yourself, I see." Gran stepped back, never releasing her hold on Annie's upper arms. "You look terrible. When was the last time you had your hair done? And you've lost weight. Too much. When are you going to accept that sorrow is part of living and go on with your life?"

Before Annie could snarl a reply, her mother interrupted. "Ma, please. Annie will recover in her own time and you won't help her by being unkind. Not all of us are as strong as you are."

"Strong? You build strength by fighting back, not by giving in."

"That's enough, Ma!" Thea's voice was sharp. "Now let Annie sit down and rest for a while. She's just driven nearly four hundred miles." She reached into the larger of the two refrigerators. "Would you like some lemonade, darling? It should be nice and cold."

Gran subsided into occasional mutters as she unloaded the sacks of food. Annie leaned against the refrigerator, sipping the tangy lemonade and watching her mother and grandmother move about the spacious kitchen. She'd forgotten how large it was.

This had been where the ranch hands were fed, back when the Floating Nought was the family's home. She wouldn't be surprised if some of the equipment was left over from those days.

The gas range had six burners and two grills, each about two feet wide. The whole appliance had to be more than six feet long. Two refrigerators stood against the inside wall, a restaurant-sized sink sat under the one window, and an oilcloth-covered island occupied the middle of the room. Yards and yards of cupboards lined the walls.

She carried her lemonade into the dining room. The eight long tables and their attendant benches were just as she remembered them. The white paint was fresh and clean but the benches still looked hard and uncomfortable. She sat where she could look out one of the side windows, toward the river.

Her mother slid in beside her. "Annie, you know I don't mean to pry, but Gran's right. You look as if you've lost even more weight."

"I've been trying to eat, Mom, and sometimes I can. But it usually sticks in my throat."

"Self-indulgence, that's what it is," Gran remarked from behind them.

"Gran! That's not fair. I have been trying to pull myself back together. It's just that tomorrow...it's been a year... Oh! Just leave me alone!" She set her glass down, hard. Some of the lemonade sloshed onto the table, but she didn't care. She had to get out, get away. *Oh, God, why did I come?*

Thea stood helpless as Annie stumbled through the kitchen and out the back door.

"Ma, you're carrying this tough love act too far. Have you forgotten that tomorrow's the anniversary of Calvin's death?"

Cecile had stepped aside to let Annie pass. Now she turned back. Shaking her head, she said, "Sometimes being hard on someone you love is kinder in the long run than being gentle and sympathetic."

"You don't seem very kind to me. I had to talk fast to convince her to come at all. If you don't let up on her, you'll drive her away."

Cecile's faded eyes seemed to be staring at some infinitely painful image. "Thea, if I've learned any wisdom in nearly eighty-three years, it's that only the fighters survive. The weak give up and let the world kick them around. I don't want that kind of existence for my granddaughter."

25

"No, you want to kick her around instead," Thea accused.

"Nonsense! You've been kind and sympathetic and supportive to Annie for a year. We all have. I don't see any signs that it's helped much. She's still wallowing in her misery when she ought to be getting back to living. Do you want her to mourn Calvin for the rest of her life?"

"How can she escape it? Does a mother ever get completely over losing a child?"

Cecile's lined face fell into an expression of unutterable pain. "No. Never," she whispered. "But," she continued, in a strong, no-nonsense tone, "neither do you let your sorrow control you. Annie is doing just that. I think in some perverse way, she's enjoying it."

Thea made a sound of disagreement, but her mother's lifted hand prevented her from speaking.

"What that young woman needs now is to be shocked back into life. She's been encouraged to hide behind her grief while the world goes on without her. This week, I'm going to do my best to give her that shock and, if you've got the sense God gave a goose, Thea, you'll help me."

"I won't. I don't agree with your methods, Ma. A year isn't very long to grieve, not when..."

"It's long enough for the worst of the pain to subside. Thea, Annie is sinking into despair. I've been there. I know." She slapped the counter. "I can't stand that. She's too dear to me. So I'm going to push, until she gets good and mad. Sympathy hasn't worked; maybe anger will."

"If you think for a moment that I'm going to let you hurt Annie..." Thea began, all her defensive maternal urges springing to life.

"I have no intention of hurting her. Just make her mad enough to bring her back to life. Now, are you going to help me peel potatoes, or are you going to stand there with your hackles up?" Cecile set a colander of washed potatoes on the table and handed Thea a knife.

Thea gave up. When Cecile Blankenship made up her mind to something, there was just no moving her. She did, however, resolve to protect Annie whenever she could.

What if Ma was right?

No, she was dead wrong. Annie was depressed. She needed medical help, not emotional battering from those who were supposed to love her. "I wonder if she ever saw that counselor," she said, and realized she'd spoken aloud.

"Counselor? As in a psychiatrist? Good heavens, Thea, Annie isn't crazy."

"No, of course she's not. Doctor Wilson recommended that she see a grief counselor. He recommended one in Boise, but I don't know if she ever—"

"A grief counselor? When she's got the whole family to help her? Why in my day—"

"Ma, your day wasn't all that long ago. I'm sure there were grief counselors then." Dropping the last potato into the big cookpot, Thea went to the sink to wash her hands. She turned, leaning back against the counter. "Sometimes a family isn't enough. You've seen how Annie has pulled away from us. I tried to talk her out of moving to Boise, but she was determined to get away from anything that reminded her of Calvin.

"I've worried about her ever since the move, even though she assured me she was getting better. Now I see..." She closed her eyes, picturing her daughter as she'd seen her for the first time in three months. She'd gained extra weight with her pregnancy, and it had been stubborn, still clinging to her slight frame at Calvin's funeral.

Now she looked even slimmer than she had during her last adolescent growth spurt, when she'd often bemoaned the fact that all her bones stuck out. Dark smudges under her eyes only called attention to the lack of color in her face.

"Maybe you're right. I don't know. I just want her to heal, to be happy again." She looked across the room to her mother. "I won't promise to be mean to Annie, but I won't try to stop you doing what you think is right. *This week.* Just this week, Ma. And if your method doesn't work, then I'll do what I can to get her to see a professional."

"Fair enough." Cecile pushed herself to her feet. "Good grief, look at the time. Let's get these potatoes on." She carried the cookpot to the stove. "Don't tell anyone, but I'm cheating. I brought gravy mix." After she had the potatoes on the burner, she bent over and peeked into the oven, where four whole chickens were roasting. "Almost done. I'll just turn this down and they'll keep until dinnertime."

ANNIE FLED TOWARD THE PINK HOUSE. HALFWAY THERE, SHE MET her younger sister.

"Hey, you can't leave your car at the cookshack, Annie. It's against the rules."

"Then you go get it," Annie snapped. She pulled the keys from her pocket and tossed them to Kristi. "I am not going back up there to face Gran again."

"Okay. Hetty's waiting for you inside. See you later."

A twinge of envy ran through Annie as Kristi went bouncing on toward the cookshack. Once she, too, had been that young and carefree, that happy. Not any more, though. Maybe never again. She trudged down the dusty road, shoulders bowed under infinite weight.

The house wasn't really pink. More of a rosy taupe. She wondered if making it the girls' bunkhouse and assigning the boys to the Blue House next door had been someone's idea of a joke. The last time she'd been here, everyone had bunked in the old barn, the adults in the curtained-off stalls and the kids in the central aisle. This was far better.

The living room was furnished with sturdy pine furniture, its upholstery a bright red and blue plaid. There were no curtains at the windows, which gave a view to the east, of rolling, pine-covered hills rising to distant mountains—the Tetons. Annie stepped close and leaned her forehead against the glass. Forest stretched as far as she could see, and beyond. Yellowstone Park was less than fifteen miles away, and everything between here and there was either Floating Nought land or National Forest.

What would happen if I walked out of here and just kept walking? Even as a child, she'd wondered. Now she found herself tempted to find the answer. Her life didn't seem to have any purpose, so why not?

"Annie? Back here."

Annie followed Hetty's voice to the farther bedroom, where her cousin lounged on a lower bunk. Besides two sets of peeled-log bunks, a rustic pine dresser and matching chest of drawers occupied the room. "We get the bottom beds," Hetty said. "I decided I was too old to be climbing around in the dark."

"Who else is in here?" The thought of sharing a room with three others, even family, made her want to run and hide. She'd hoped to have a bedroom to herself, or to share with no one but Hetty.

"Charlene and CeCe, which should make for an interesting week. Kristi's in the other room with the littles. She actually volunteered." Hetty shook her head, as if astonished.

"Littles?"

"Angela, Janice and Emma."

"I know I'm supposed to know who they are, but I'm drawing a blank. Is one of them Eric's daughter? She's awfully young, isn't she?"

"Gran says Angela's almost seven. The other two are two and three, but I don't remember which is which. I think Emma's Peter's daughter."

"I think you're right. God, Het, I should know more about my own niece. I've been so out of it." She turned to look out the window, not wanting Hetty to see the welling tears. Emma was just about the age Calvin had been last year... *No I won't think about Calvin. Not now.*

"One of those drawers is for you," Hetty said. "While this isn't the Ritz, there's a bit of closet and drawer space for all of us."

Annie sank down onto her bunk. "Het, I don't think this is going to work. I can't stay here. It's going to be too crowded, too noisy. And there's no privacy."

"Bull feathers! If you've gotten modest in your old age, you can dress in the bathroom. There are two besides the *en suite* master bath, one up near the kitchen, the other right across the hall. But I don't see what difference it makes. We're all family."

"That's not what I meant," Annie said.

"No, I don't suppose it is." Hetty sighed. "What you're really saying is that you want a place to hide. Look, Annie, I know you want to wallow in your misery, and I suppose you have a right to, if that's what you enjoy. But you're just going to have to wallow publicly this week if you feel you really have to." Hetty tossed a paperback onto her bed. "Gosh, who knows, maybe you'll even enjoy yourself now and then.

"Aunt Althea would be really hurt if you were to leave, and Gran would probably chase you down and bring you back. Besides, I thought you'd had to jump through hoops to get this week off. Are you going to waste it, just because our elegant accommodations aren't private enough to suit you?"

Annie smiled in spite of herself. "Elegant? Rustic would be the more appropriate word, I think."

"Perhaps you're right. Anyway, you're staying, if I have to chain you to this bed. Okay?"

"Okay," Annie agreed, reluctantly. She leaned back and closed her eyes against Hetty's level gaze. "I had a terrible time staying awake on the way over. Can you wake me when it's time to go to dinner?" To her surprise, the mattress was quite comfortable. Her pretense drifted slowly into real sleep.

Chapter Three

"WAKE UP, CHILDREN. WE'RE HERE."

CeCe kept her eyes closed and didn't move. Angela was a dead weight against her, hot and sweaty and sticky. She'd been pretending to be asleep ever since they'd left Idaho Falls. If she'd been awake, she'd have had to listen to more of Jennifer's opinions about neglectful fathers and girls who didn't act like ladies.

Oh, Daddy, why did you make me come? I could have stayed with Gretchen. Her folks wouldn't have minded. I could have raced today, instead of having to put up with Jennifer and Eric and their spoiled brats.

"Cecile, keep your eye on Joseph. Don't let him run off until he's met Aunt Cecile." Jennifer stopped gathering kids' toys into the big mesh tote and frowned at CeCe. "This is going to be confusing. It's unfortunate you were named after her."

"My name is CeCe. 'See-see'. There's nothing confusing about that." She pretended she didn't see Eric's disapproving glance. *Honestly!* Nobody ever called her Cecile.

The old lady who stepped down from the porch of the Big House opened her arms wide, like she was going to hug them all at once. Instead she cupped CeCe's chin. "You look so much like your mother, darling. So much." Her voice trembled on the last words.

CeCe didn't even mind the hug. It felt, somehow, like Mama's used to.

"Did you bring your bicycle? I know you missed some races, but we don't want you to let your practice slide while you're here."

"She brought her bicycle," Eric said, sounding just as grumpy as he had when he'd discovered he was expected to load the big box on the roof rack. "Silliest thing I ever heard." He stepped back and caught Jennifer around the waist. "Gran, this is my wife. Jennifer."

"No worse than bringing golf clubs or fishing tackle. Hello, Jennifer, it's wonderful to meet you at last. And your lovely children...?"

Jennifer clapped her hands, and the kids lined up like obedient little puppies, tall to short.

CeCe had never seen anything like it.

"Children, this is your Great-aunt Cecile—"

"All the kids call me Gran," the old lady interrupted.

"I'm afraid I can't allow that. So confusing, since they already have two grandmothers." She scowled at Joseph, who was inching out of line. "Norman is the eldest, then Angela, and Joseph and Bartram." She laid her hand on each kid's head as she spoke the names. "Say hello to Great-aunt Cecile, children."

They all muttered something intelligible.

Gran hugged each one like she really wanted to and wasn't being polite. Once she'd finished with the baby, she turned to where Tommy was leaning against the van. "Stephen?"

"I'm Tommy," her brother insisted. Dad still called him Junior, but nobody else did.

"Tommy, of course. I'll remember that. I'm so glad you're here." She sounded like she really was, too.

He didn't move. "Yeah."

"You didn't want to come, did you?"

"Uh-uh."

"Well," Gran said, not trying to hug him, "I hope we can change your mind. There's lots to do here."

Tommy shrugged, that *you can't impress me* shrug that drove Daddy wild.

A tall man emerged from the house. "Here comes someone else. I'll bet it's Peter," he said.

They all turned to look at the big van pulling a tent trailer up the hill from the main road.

"Charlene's just your age, CeCe," Gran said. "She's new to the family, so I hope you'll help us make her feel at home."

"Me? I mean, I don't know anybody here." She'd been about two the last time they'd come to a family Gathering. How'd Gran expect her to know anything?

"Yes, but you're part of us, and Charlene and Owen are brand new. They'll feel out of place unless we make them welcome."

CeCe remembered who they were. Uncle Peter, Mama's older brother, had married a woman with two kids. An older woman, Gran had said in one of her letters to Daddy.

Instead of unpacking her bike from the box it had traveled in, she waited beside Gran as the van pulled into the parking area. The back door slid open and a tall girl with long hair stepped out. Right behind her was a guy—her brother? *Oh my God. He's gorgeous!*

PETER STRETCHED. HE WAS STIFF FROM DRIVING ALL DAY, ALL several days. And not entirely comfortable. No one in the family had met Kenna. They'd decided against having family present at their wedding, mostly because she hadn't wanted to invite her in-laws. They still considered her part of the family, and she felt stifled by their possessiveness. Nice folks, but they seemed to expect her to devote the rest of her life to keeping her dead husband's memory alive.

Kenna was scared. He knew that, even if she hadn't admitted it. Slipping his arm around her waist, he pulled her with him. "Gran, here's the person to thank for us getting here. If she hadn't insisted on meeting my family..." Not quite the truth, but close enough to ensure her a hearty welcome.

Sure enough, she was snatched away from him, into the arms of his grandmother, his father, his mother, and his... His sister? "Kristie?"

"In person," she said, and released Kenna to envelop him in a bear hug.

He returned it, saying, "You're all grown up. How'd that happen?"

"The usual way. Clean living, healthy food." Grabbing his hand, she towed him out of the crowd. "They're not going to let loose of that baby or your wife in the foreseeable future, so I'll help you unload. You're in the pink house with me and Annie and Hetty. Think you can keep us in order?"

"I never could when you were little. How can I now?" He handed her Kenna's suitcase and grabbed two duffles. "Where are you putting Owen?"

"He's in the Blue House, with the other guys. Eric and his wife are in the master bedroom, but Ward's in a bunk, so Owen will be fine."

Peter wondered what she wasn't telling him. There had been something in her voice when she mentioned their cousin Eric.

Her relatives sure could make an awful racket. Annie shouldered her way between her father and Uncle Ward who were standing in the kitchen doorway. If the noise levels were going to be this high all week, she would have to buy earplugs. She was not used to people noise any more, not after six months in a pickup canopy assembly plant. The best thing about her job was that she didn't have to interact with anyone if she didn't want.

"Gib, Ward, move yourselves out of the doorway!" Gran raised her voice above the noise. "We'll never get the tables cleared unless you stay out of the way." She followed Hetty into the kitchen, carrying the ravaged meatloaf pan. "Annie, are you sure you and Hetty don't want to play Bridge tonight? Thea and I can do the dishes."

"Honest, Gran, we want to clean the kitchen," Annie insisted. "We haven't had a chance yet to visit. You keep the kids out and just leave us alone." What she really wanted to do was go and hide somewhere, but no one would let her. Kitchen duty was next best.

"And keep my mother out of my hair, please, Gran. I haven't told her yet that Frank's coming up on Thursday, and I know she'll worm it out of me if she comes in here and starts her usual prying." Hetty aimed Gran toward the door. "Let the old maids do the scutwork, will you?"

"I'm not an old maid," Annie protested, hurt at the appellation.

"Oh, shit, you know what I meant, Annie. We're both unmarried. I just wanted to get rid of Gran gracefully. I love her dearly, but you know if she'd stayed in here, we'd both get the rough side of her tongue before she was through."

"Don't I just? She lit into me as soon as I walked through that door." Annie quickly stepped back from the sink as water burst from the faucet, deflected from the bottom of the sink, and splashed over her midriff. "Frank? I though his name was Gary."

"Gary's old news. I met Frank in April. He's hot, Annie. Really hot. He's going to spend the end of the week here, before we head for San Francisco." She whirled around the room. "I've got three whole weeks' vacation. Freedom!"

"Good for you. But what will your parents say?"

"What they always say. That I'm devaluing myself because I'm sleeping with a man I don't intend to marry. That they've raised me better than this. That the whole family will be shocked." She grinned at Annie's derisive sound. "Right. As if no one in the family has ever had a lover before. Sheesh! Besides, Frank's invitation came from Gran."

"Gran? I can't believe it."

"That's because you and she are always at loggerheads. Gran is one foxy old lady, and don't you think different." Hetty stretched to set a stack of bowls on a high shelf. "She was the one who egged me on when I was trying to decide about the job in Seattle. Mother and Dad were so sure I'd be ruined if I lived there."

"Maybe in their eyes you were. Wasn't that the first time you lived with a guy?"

"The first time I did it openly. But it had nothing to do with my living in Seattle and everything to do with my not wanting to fight that particular battle as long as I was in Denver. My God! Can you imagine my father's reaction if I'd lived with a man and his business associates found out?"

"Umm," was all Annie was willing to say. Aunt Jocelyn and Uncle John were about as straight-laced as anyone she knew. She couldn't believe that all bankers were as upright and respectable as Hetty's folks believed they should be, but then she didn't know any other bankers. "I don't think the whole family will be shocked. Eric and Jennifer maybe, but no one else."

"Oh, Eric and Jennifer. I'd forgotten about them. Yeah, they'll be shocked." She looked positively gleeful at the thought.

Exactly the way Annie felt.

"My mother's just fooling herself, thinking the family doesn't know about me. She's doing her ostrich act, as usual. Pretend something doesn't exist, and Presto! It doesn't." Hetty stacked plates with unnecessary vigor. "Honestly, Annie, you'd think she'd learn someday that I don't give a damn what other people think."

"She knows. But I can just hear her say how your behavior reflects on her."

"After this many years she ought to have learned that I live my life as I choose and pay no attention to her Victorian ideas. Besides, I'm not the Bank President's little girl any longer." She slammed a cupboard door, rattling the dishes inside.

"Don't get excited. I'm not your mother. Now, tell me about Frank." Annie rinsed the last of the suds from the sink and squeezed excess water from the dishcloth. "Is he gorgeous?"

While Hetty was describing Frank's beautiful green eyes and magnificent body, Annie's mind wandered. It didn't seem fair that Hetty should have had such a series of interesting, handsome lovers while she had had only Walter, who had been thoughtful and protective, but not terribly exciting in bed. Or maybe it was that Hetty was more exciting in bed than Annie knew how to be.

She'd long suspected that she wasn't really very sexy, either in her reaction to love-making or in her appearance. Hetty, with her tall, willowy body, her wide, amber eyes, and her careless tousle of flame-red hair, was sexy and exciting. Annie, whose body never met a carbohydrate it didn't like, whose curly brown hair always looked as if she combed it by sticking her finger into a light socket, and whose eyes were the color of damp moss, was not any man's wet dream.

Certainly not Walter's.

Her parents had been less than thrilled with Walter. Gran had called him a pompous ass. Annie knew that what had really bothered them was Walter's constant references to how a wife like Annie could help him with his career. Upwardly mobile was an understatement when applied to Walter Abbott. But she'd been young and in love, so it hadn't really bothered her to quit work when she became pregnant. She was going to make a home for

Walter and their children, to help him advance in his career, to be the perfect wife and mother.

The trouble was, Annie had never been completely at home in the Country Club, nor in the Junior League. She would have preferred hiking in the hills to impressing Walter's boss. Cocktail party conversation was meaningless to her, and she'd spent too many evenings trying not to yawn in the face of Walter's associates while they boasted of their business prowess. And their wives! Some of them had been really nice, but Annie hadn't even spoken the same language as they did.

Walter had been excited, though, when she told him she was pregnant. Children were part of his career plan. Well-behaved, tidy children whose blameless behavior and outstanding accomplishments reflected well on their successful father. From the moment he knew he was to be a father, he'd dreamed great dreams for his son.

She'd been relieved when their child's sex was disclosed. Would Walter have forgiven himself for fathering a daughter? Or would he have found some way to blame her for letting him down?

"Annie! Annie, wake up!" Hetty was shaking her by the arm. "Where were you? I stopped talking five minutes ago and you just stood there, staring into space. Are you okay?"

"Sure, I'm fine. I was just remembering something."

"Well, you don't look fine. You look like your dog just died or something."

Annie's stomach heaved. "Not my dog, Het," she gasped. "My baby."

"Oh, shit. Me and my big mouth," Hetty said.

Annie pulled free of her cousin's hand and ran into the night.

HETTY HAD JUST HUNG THE DAMP TEA TOWELS ON THE CLOTHESLINE

behind the kitchen when light flashed across the yard. The approaching vehicle pulled into the parking area beside the Blue House, so she stepped into the dining room and waved her arms for attention. "Someone's coming."

Gib, Ward and Ben all stood up and headed for the door. Hetty stifled a chuckle. They looked for all the world like they were prepared to defend the homestead from invaders. When none of the other women seemed inclined to follow them, Hetty decided she would, mostly out of curiosity. She had no idea who all was coming, so any new arrival would be a nice surprise. Most of her relatives were nice people.

Too bad my mother isn't one of them. Immediately she reminded herself that she was far too mature to still be resenting her mother's interference.

She caught up with the men halfway down the slope.

"That's not a car I'd expect Frances to drive," Gib was saying. "Too small."

"Frances is coming? Francis, as in the mystery woman? Oh, I can hardly wait."

"I can," Ward said.

Gib grunted his agreement, and Ben snickered.

A tall, slight man climbed from the compact sedan. "Evan! I didn't know you were coming!" Hetty ran to embrace him. "Oh, it's *so* good to see you."

"How could I stay away, knowing you'd be here." He disentangled himself from her arms and faced Uncle Ben. "Hi, Dad."

Ben hugged Evan. "So you decided to come. Your mother will be pleased."

"They moved up my departure date. This will be the only chance I have to see Gran and all the cousins. I leave a week from Wednesday, so I thought I'd follow you and Mom home and spend a few days."

"Congratulations your new job," Ward slapped Evan lightly on the shoulder. "Quite a feather in your cap."

"It is, even if I am being sent to darkest Africa."

"Have you eaten?" Gib said, after shaking Evan's hand. "There's probably leftovers in the kitchen."

"More than enough," Hetty agreed.

"Thanks, but no. I stopped in Idaho Falls. Couldn't eat a bite." He opened the trunk. "Here, Hetty, this is for you." He handed her a bulky item wrapped in bubble packing.

"Oh! Is it—"

"The Embrace. I couldn't put it into storage, and knew you'd appreciate it."

Hetty hugged the package, torn between dashing back to the Pink House to unwrap it and spending this evening with Evan. Since Annie was probably sleeping in their bunkroom, she decided to stay. "Oh, I will. I know exactly where I'll put it." She had an inner vision of the fluidly carved, androgynous, embracing couple standing on the bronze-and-glass table in her entry. "When you settle..."

"Someday," he agreed. He pulled a suitcase from the trunk. "Let me take these in. Which bed is mine?"

"I'll show you. We're roommates," Ward said.

Not having been inside the Blue House, Hetty followed. It was decorated much like the Pink House, with rustic furniture and sturdy fabric. A woodstove sat in the corner of the living room under a dormer ceiling that gave an impression of spaciousness. It already looked like a male-occupied house, with a golf bag in one corner of the dining room and a tackle box on a kitchen counter. "Who's in the master bedroom?" She knew that a married couple was assigned to each master bedroom, but hadn't heard who went where.

The only unassigned beds were in the bunkrooms. *I wonder where Gran plans to put Frank.*

"Jennifer and Eric," Gib said. "Peter and Kenna are in your house, and Elaine and Stewart in the Guest House."

Hetty breathed a sigh of relief that she wouldn't have to live with Eric and Jennifer. She'd met Eric's wife just three hours ago and had already decided that the two of them would never be anything resembling friends. *He was such a nice little boy. It's too bad.*

Evan's car was unloaded in short order. The five of them strolled back to the cookshack together.

"So everyone's here, now," she said as they approached the door. "It promises to be an interesting week."

"Not everyone," Ward said, sounding glum. "There's still Frances."

No one replied.

Chapter Four

Sunday

NICE RIG YOU'VE GOT THERE."

Clay looked up from the frying pan to see an older fellow standing on the road just outside his camp site. He was holding a coffee cup.

"Thanks. It gets me where I want to go." He grinned, flipped the bacon out onto a plate, and reached for the eggs. "And it keeps the bugs off at night."

"Not many skeeters up here," his visitor observed. "Surprising, considering all the marshes upstream."

Clay lifted the coffee pot. "How's your coffee? I've got plenty."

"I'm a little low." He held out his cup to be refilled. "You up here for the fishin'?"

"Yeah. Any good?"

"So-so. Now, you shoulda' been here a couple of months ago, in June, for the mayfly hatch. Had to beat 'em off with a stick, practically."

"So I heard." The eggs were done, so Clay sat down to eat after giving his visitor an inquiring glance.

"I already ate. Just stopped by to be neighborly. That's my rig down the way there." He pointed to a large motor home parked in another campsite a short distance down the road, dimly seen in the half light of early morning. "Gotta be gettin' back. Let me know how you do today." He strolled away.

Clay grinned around his first mouthful of eggs. Fishermen were a friendly bunch, except when it came to sharing their favorite spots. He had noticed that his neighbor had not told him where he had to "...beat 'em off with a stick." That was all right, though. He had some favorite spots of his own whose locations he rarely divulged.

As he poured hot water over his breakfast dishes, Clay smiled at his idiosyncrasy. Why did bacon and eggs taste always better when cooked in the fresh air? The trailer had a perfectly good kitchen, but he always used his battered camp stove to cook breakfast outdoors.

With the trailer locked for the day and his fishing gear in the pickup bed, he pulled out of his campsite while the sky was still colored with the rosy glow of dawn. His mouth was dry with anticipation, just as it had been when, as a kid, he awaited Christmas. The first day of a fishing trip always found him excited, ready for something wonderful to happen, barely able to contain himself until he could get to the river. All other thoughts were banished from his mind, even his mild, residual curiosity about the woman he'd met yesterday. The river called.

Tuesday he would go look at the property in Last Chance, but today and tomorrow were his to spend as he wished. Even so, excitement wasn't solely due to the river's siren call. He'd driven by the properties, Abe's Fly Shop and Wexler's Cabins, yesterday before coming to the campground. They'd been even more run-down than he remembered from his last visit here three years ago. Abe Wexler must be in his eighties now, and it was obvious he was having trouble keeping the business up. On a Saturday afternoon in August, there had been a vacancy sign in the office's fly-specked window.

Tuesday. Today and tomorrow were for fishing.

THE WINDOW WAS A BARELY VISIBLE SQUARE IN THE ALMOST TOTAL darkness of the room when Annie woke. Her face was cold but, snuggled under the enveloping down comforter, her body was warm and cozy. She heard a door close with a faint thud, and someone shuffled past the almost closed door. Otherwise the house was silent. Pulling the flannel sheet over her face, she closed her eyes, hoping to recapture the dreamless sleep she had left.

Half an hour later, she gave up. With a sigh, she flipped the covers back, gasping at the iciness of the air on her bare legs. At least she could take advantage of her wakefulness to escape from her overly solicitous family. While dressing in the bathroom, she couldn't stop her teeth from chattering. The hooks beside the back door held an assortment of coats and jackets. She chose a down parka in a camouflage pattern.

The sun hadn't quite risen above the mountains when she slipped out. The air was crisp and cold, and carried the resinous odors of pine and sagebrush. Instead of cutting across the lawn surrounding the Big House and the cookshack, she followed the road around to where a narrow trail took off. She needed silence and solitude.

Especially solitude.

As she recalled, it was a couple of miles to the river, farther than she'd walked since...farther than she'd walked for a long time. By the time she crossed the highway and climbed over a style, her legs felt like jelly. *Good grief. I used to be able to run this far.* But that had been long ago, before Walter. Before Calvin.

Oh, God. Calvin. I miss you so much. Unable to avoid the children in the dining hall last night, she'd felt real pain at Emma's every giggle. Her arms had ached to hold little Janice. *I want to go home,* she cried silently. *I want to be far, far away from babies.*

At least there were no childish voices breaking the silence here. Only the occasional *flop* of a trout as it leapt after a low-flying insect. Only the infrequent rumble of a semi along the highway. Only a faint, low murmur of the river as it flowed past her, glinting in the morning light, moving the water plants in a slow, undulating waltz.

The river. How could she have ever forgotten it? As a very young child, she'd had nightmares about it. Caught in its slow current, tangled in the webs of waterweed that floated in huge mats on its placid surface, swallowed in its icy grasp.

Those nightmares had gone away, once she'd learned to swim, although that hadn't happened until she'd gone to Girl Scout camp the summer she was ten. As the only girl there who couldn't swim, she'd been laughed at, even shunned by some of the girls she'd known since first grade.

She'd overcome her fear of water then, enough to put her face in it, enough to go where it was deeper than she was tall. She'd learned to swim, had even passed the Red Cross Junior Lifesaver test. And she'd hated every minute of it.

Annie looked deep inside for the old fear, but it was just a memory. This morning the river gleamed peach and gold and silvery blue in the barely risen sun. Its wide, ever-changing surface, smooth as glass except where the patches of weed floated, was shattered here and there by surfacing fish. *Breakfast time.*

She could see why the Henrys Fork was considered one of the most beautiful rivers in America—according to her family, anyhow. *I've always taken it for granted, but it's really beautiful. How could I have not appreciated it?*

There was something almost hypnotic about gentle hint of current, the sparkling circles where fish poked their noses through the mirror-like surface. Peaceful. Tranquil. She was drawn closer by a hunger she hadn't know was there, closer to the bank, until she could look into the pure, transparent water, could watch an enormous silvery fish leisurely swim upstream.

It was shallow here, where it flowed through the state park in wide, sinuous curves, broken by rocky islets. Shallow enough that fishermen could wade in their pursuit of the legendary trout that made their home here. Shallow enough that glittering stones could be seen on the bottom, through water incredibly clear and clean.

For several minutes she stood there, on the grassy bank, watching the water flow past, her mind almost blank. There was still a residual dread, buried deep in her mind, of flowing water, but if she fell in, she'd be able to swim. Wouldn't she?

Or had she forgotten how? The last time she'd had on a bathing suit was in Cozumel. And then all she'd done was wade along the water's edge. She really didn't *like* to swim, wasn't comfortable in water deeper than a bathtub, wider than a hot tub.

Calvin didn't know how to swim. I could have taught him, but I didn't. I let my old fear of water overrule my better sense.

My fault.

Abruptly she turned away from the river and strode across the rocky ground toward the trail.

Hoarse calls broke the silence as she followed a dimly seen path beside the river. They seemed to come from Silver Lake, where a number of trumpeter swans made their homes Remembering how excited she'd been in earlier years to see the big white birds in their slow, majestic flight, she hoped to spy one. All she saw were a few swallows swooping silently over the water, hunting early rising insects.

She was so busy watching the swallows that she missed the rock in her path. It rolled when she stepped on it and she went sprawling. She tripped and fell, skinning the heel of one hand when she caught herself on a rough basalt outcrop. "Oww!" She pressed the abrasion to her mouth, sucking at it to relieve the stinging pain.

There was a patch of short, dry grass in the small depression where she had landed, inviting her to sit. Looking behind her, Annie could see the river and the lodgepole pines on the opposite shore. With any luck, here she would find the privacy she sought. She wriggled about, finally finding a comfortable position, with her back supported by a knob of basalt. Before her was a full view of the river, reflecting the colors of sunrise, the pastures through which it meandered, and the forest beyond it. She let the sounds of the awakening world envelop her, finding temporary peace in nature's music.

Annie woke with the sun shining directly in her face and trickles of perspiration making their way between her breasts. Her watch told her it was just after ten. The day was already too warm for a down parka. Her muscles told her it was time to stretch, to move from her cramped position. She slid out of the parka, tossed it aside, and extended her legs in front of her, her arms high over her head. She felt almost glad to be alive. Better than she had for a long time.

For a year. A year, today.

A gentle breeze stirred her hair, cooling her scalp and caressing her face. The scents of pine, of sagebrush, of crushed grass invaded her nostrils. Sharp, rough basalt prodded at her back, almost painful. The river murmured softly and birds twittered and chirped. She could almost believe that the world was fair, that life was good.

Almost.

"No!" *I've no right to feel this good. My baby is dead. If I'd only watched him more closely. If only...*

She sought deep within herself, seeking the pain, the bereavement and guilt that had consumed her for so long. She found them, but they were muffled. They did not take possession as they had done—should do. She pulled her legs against her chest and rested her head on her knees. Perhaps, if she concentrated hard enough, she could bring them back.

Oh, yeah, that makes sense. You know you should be recovering, not wallowing. Isn't that what Gran says? What everyone says, even Mom? Be honest, Anne Cecile Ogilvie. You've come to enjoy feeling sorry for yourself.

Well, maybe not enjoy. Maybe it's just easier to hold on to the self-pity and the grief so you won't have to start living again.

Why should I want to live again? My baby is dead. His father has gone on to a new life. My own mother thinks I'm crazy.

Besides, living hurts. It hurts so much.

Her thoughts were interrupted by a distant splashing. She stood and looked toward the river. Just downstream of her hiding place, a man was standing waist deep in the water. He held a long, whiplike fishing pole and wore chest waders. The bright red of his billed cap and plaid shirt contrasted with dark green chest waders and the tan, many-pocketed vest he wore. As he turned slightly away from her, Annie saw a net dangling down his back, its handle attached somehow to his collar.

A fly fisherman.

Even as she watched, the tip of the pole jerked. He had a bite. Occasionally, as a child, Annie had watched her father fish for steelhead and salmon in the streams of Oregon's Coast Range and Cascade Mountains, but she had never seen him move with the grace and sureness that this fisherman did as he played the fish until he could net it.

She must have seen fishermen on the river before, for she'd come to the Floating Nought often in her childhood. Considering that the Henry's Fork was world famous, she imagined it would be more unusual to *not* see someone fishing on any given day during the season.

Still, she watched, fascinated.

CLAY LIFTED THE NET FREE OF THE WATER AND LOOKED WITH admiration at the struggling trout. His first catch of the day and a real trophy winner. It was a good twelve pounds, if it was an ounce. The rainbows on its sides glittered in the morning light and its mouth worked as it fought to breathe.

"Oh, you beauty," he said softly as he lowered it again into the water. He tucked the rod into his waders and grasped the weakly struggling fish by the gills. Carefully he worked the barbless hook free from its jaw.

The fish grew quiet. He moved his hands to grasp its sleek, scaly sides, to hold it, lightly but firmly, in the water. His right hand stroked along the scales until it gave a convulsive jerk and tried to pull away. He continued to hold, waiting until he was sure that the trout was uninjured, and then he released it. With a flip of its tail, it swam away from him.

"Why'd you do that?"

Clay looked around. Not ten yards away, crouched on her knees on the high basalt bank, was the woman from the green Accord.

"Why did I do what?"

"Turn him loose. After all the work you did to catch him, why did you?"

"Why would I want to keep him?" Clay asked. Then he chuckled. "Oh, you thought I should take him home for dinner, didn't you?"

"Well, isn't that why people fish?" Annie rose to her feet "Why go to all that work if you're just going to let the fish swim away? It's dumb!"

"It's obvious that you've never fished."

"I have too! And I hated it. I don't like to kill things!" Her voice was strained, thin, just as it had been yesterday. She was under some terrible stress, Clay was sure. What was it?

Damn it, why should I care?

Calling himself ten kinds of fool for a pretty face, he attached the still dangling hook to the reel and made his slow way to shore. A short distance from where she stood, where the bank was lower, he climbed out.

He stripped off his vest and waders, while wondering what she thought of his getup. At least he'd put on a pair of nylon jogging shorts over his longjohns. He didn't usually. He pulled off gray wool socks and slid his bare feet into rubber flipflops he took from a large pocket at the back of his fishing vest. The cool morning air made him shiver. "Let's have some coffee, while I instruct you in the old and honorable art of fly fishing."

"Coffee? You have coffee?"

"I do indeed. Let's see if we can find a sunny place to sit."

"Follow me. There's a patch of grass that's softer than this rock." She led him through the open woods, to a sunlit, grassy depression. "It's dry. I was sitting here until I heard you."

Clay sat tailor fashion, facing her. The patch of grass was so small that their knees almost touched. The loose sweatshirt she wore was far too big for her, making her fragility all the more obvious. In the clear morning light, the violet patches under her eyes emphasized the lily-paleness of her skin, unlined except for faint smile brackets around her mouth. She wasn't a kid, but she was far younger than his first impression. He pulled the slim stainless Thermos from the back-pocket on his vest. "No cup, I'm afraid. But I guarantee that I'm not carrying any fatal germs." He offered her the bottle. When she'd sipped and had handed it back, he found himself turning it so he could drink from the same place she had. *You've been keeping your nose too sharp, Knight.*

They traded the bottle back and forth until it was empty. She went up in his estimation when she said nothing as she sipped, only made a little humming noise after each taste of the rich Sumatran blend. She shook her head when he offered her the last sip. "Okay, tell me about fly fishing."

He swallowed, took a moment to enjoy the aftertaste. "Fly fishing is a way of life. A fly fisherman would rather fish than eat, or sleep, or work."

"Particularly work, I'll bet."

"Well, yes," he said, chuckling. "But there are a lot of things people would rather do than work. Fly fishing isn't really something to do *instead of* anything. It's a way of life." He paused, trying to put his passion into words. For some reason, making her understand was important.

"We live to fish, not fish to live, like most other fishermen. Our object is not to fry the fish, but to outwit it. If catching fish to eat was all I cared about, I could do that without driving across two states. I come here because the Henrys Fork is one of the finest fly fishing streams in the country, because it has the smartest trout."

"Smart? Trout aren't smart."

"Want to bet? Why I've seen—" He broke off. "Never mind. Let's say that the challenge of fishing here on the Henry's Fork is worth the trip. It's not an easy stream to fish."

"That's all you came here for. Just to fish?" She was leaning forward now, her face more animated than he'd yet seen it.

"Well, not the only thing, but it was my primary reason."

"Where are you from?" she asked, before he could decide whether to tell her his primary reason.

"Beaverton. That's near Portland."

"I know; I lived...grew up in Portland." She paused, chewed on her lower lip for a moment. "My dad fishes, but he didn't even bring his fishing gear over here."

"He probably fishes for steelhead, then." At her nod, Clay grinned. "Steelhead fishermen are a breed apart, just like fly fishermen are. Not all do both." He held out an energy bar in a silent question.

Another shake of her head, the sun making bright glints of gold in her dark hair. "You were going to tell me about fly fishing."

"Right. Well, for one thing, a lot of fly fishermen don't often keep what they catch. Take here for instance—it's strictly catch-and-release along this reach of the river. If I had kept that fish, I would have been breaking the law. But I wouldn't have, anyway. He was too big, too good a fighter for me to want to kill him. Instead, I put him back to grow bigger. Maybe give another fisherman some sport someday."

He stretched his legs out across the depression, leaned back against a rock. When his foot brushed her leg, she shrank away from contact with him. Although he pretended not to notice, Clay admitted that her actions puzzled him. One minute she seemed young, alert and interested, and the next she was the lethargic, depressed woman he'd seen yesterday. He wondered why he was wasting his time. The fish were waiting for him.

"I guess the main reason I fish is that it's good for the soul. There's something inherently soothing about standing in the stream, hearing only the soft sounds of the water and an occasional birdcall. It wipes away all the stresses and strains of living in a world that's moving too fast." He leaned back and stared into the cloudless sky. "When I come out of the river at the end of a day's fishing, my soul feels cleansed and at peace with itself. Any problems I had when I started are in perspective and I'm mentally invigorated—ready to face the world again on my terms." He fell silent.

Annie, too, sat without speaking. Her mind worked, though. She had listened closely to what he had said—to the unspoken feelings behind his words. And she had watched his face. Such a strong, comforting face, masculine, attractive, yet full of compassion and gentleness. In spite of herself, Annie found her gaze traveling down the thick column of his neck, measuring the unusually broad shoulders, admiring the stocky legs. She found herself wondering what it would feel like to be held, closely, protectively in his arms.

Yeah, right. That's all you need right now. Romantic complications. Besides, he couldn't be less interested. *All he seems to care about is fishing.* She forced her thoughts back to what he'd told her. "A soul at peace," she said, quietly. "I would like that." She didn't believe it could happen, but she would like to find inner peace.

Clay looked at her from under lowered lids, seeing sorrow written in her eyes and pulling her mouth down at the corners. Was that the cause of her contradictory behavior, of her appearance of ill health? She wasn't the middle-aged woman he'd first thought, and she certainly wasn't naturally gloomy and sad. He'd bet on that, having seen glimpses of something youthful and bright, quickly hidden but unmistakable. He sat up, abruptly.

"Would you like to learn?"

"Learn what?"

"How to fly fish." He half reached out a hand, but at her involuntary retreat, pulled it back. "You'd be surprised at how many of your troubles stay on the bank when you climb into that river."

"What if I can't leave my troubles behind me?" she countered.

"Everyone can, once in a while. You just have to find something that keeps your mind occupied—or peacefully blank."

Her expression changed into one of terrible yearning. "I can't just walk away and forget everything I've done." Hopelessness was plain in her voice and on her face. "I know I can't. I've tried!" She shook her head. Flyaway strands of gleaming hair again caught the sunlight, glinting bronze and fiery orange on rich brown.

"I think you can. You know, once, in a fly shop, I saw a placard. It said something like 'God does not subtract from man's allotted time the hours spent in fishing.' It's like that, you know. When you're out on the river, it's as if you're outside of time. All the burdens, worries, anger, and sorrow that you usually carry around with you are gone. It's just you, the water, and the fish."

"The water..." she half-whispered. "It was water that took..."

A shout interrupted her. She rose to her knees and looked beyond him. Waved. "Look, I've got to go. They're probably worried about me. I snuck out before dawn."

"I'll be here tomorrow. Same time, same place." He watched her stride away, picking her way carefully across the uneven ground. Fragile and unhealthy she might be, but she'd once been in pretty good shape. She moved like an athlete—an out-of-shape athlete.

HER DAD WAS WAITING FOR HER ON THE PATH, HALFWAY BETWEEN the river and the fence along the highway. "You had us all wondering where the devil you'd got to."

"I came out here to...to watch the sunrise and fell asleep." *And to get away from the family's overwhelming cheerfulness.* "I really didn't think anyone would worry about me."

"Your mom did. Next time, tell someone where you are, okay?" He took her hand. "Look, kiddo, I know you're a big girl and can take care of yourself, but you ought to remember how Thea worries about you."

"I just needed to be alone for a while. I'm not used to so much noise and confusion." She tried to pull her hand loose. Even Dad, who'd always seemed to understand her better than anyone, was acting as if she were not to be trusted to take care of herself. "I didn't know that I had to check in with the whole family before I went for a walk!"

"It's always been the rule in this family," he said in a mild voice, "that children have to tell their parents where they're going."

"I am not a child!" She jerked free of his clasp and ran ahead, over the style, across the highway, and up the gently sloping path, not stopping until she was out of breath. Panting, she kept going, as fast as she could, earning cramps in her calves and incipient shin splints. By the time she reached the cookshack, she was regretting her childish reaction to her father's mild reproof. Even so, she resented the way everyone assumed she wasn't capable of taking care of herself. *I'm twenty-six years old, for Pete's sake. Surely they can give me credit for a little self-sufficiency.*

From somewhere in her mind, she heard her grandmother's voice. *Self-indulgence, that's what it is.*

Chapter Five

STILL SMARTING FROM HER FATHER'S REPROOF, ANNIE BURST through the cookshack door and slammed it shut behind her. She stood just inside the dining room and caught her breath. The breakfast mess had been cleared away, but her mother, Gran, Hetty, and Aunt Joss were sitting with coffee at the table closest to the kitchen.

"Darling, where have you been?" her mother asked.

"We would have appreciated your telling someone where you were going," her grandmother said, in a neutral tone.

Aunt Joss's face was set in its usual expression of mild disapproval.

Hetty merely said, "The coffee's hot." Her expression was as carefully neutral as Gran's.

Too full of resentment to respond to any of them, Annie went to the kitchen and got herself a cup. She stood beside the large coffee maker with it in her hand, staring out through the window. Four of her nephews were flying a Frisbee on the broad stretch of lawn which sloped down to the road. Joey's short, bare legs flashed in the sunlight as he chased, shrieking, after the red disk. The older boys cheered when he caught it, then applauded when he flew it back in Norman's direction.

"Calvin. Oh, Calvin, you'll never be five, like Joey," Annie murmured, feeling the tears well up, "and it's my fault." For a moment she hated her nephews. All of them.

Hetty stuck her head though the archway. "We're going on a nature walk after lunch. In the park."

"Enjoy yourself."

"You should go with them," Gran said. "It will do you a world of good."

"I'm going to take a nap this afternoon, Gran. I don't want to go on a nature walk."

"Darling, you need to get out with people more. After all, you came here to be with the family," Annie's mother said. "You can't keep running off and hiding."

"Mom, I came here because you and Gran forced me to. I don't want to go this afternoon."

"It seems a shame to be in a place like this and not take advantage of its opportunities," Aunt Joss said, "no matter how... primitive they are."

"Look Annie, you're outnumbered. If you don't go with us willingly, Gran will hogtie you and make us carry you. Give in gracefully." Hetty shot her a sympathetic smile. "Skinny as you are, you'd still be a load on a two-mile hike."

Annie bit back a swear word, knowing she owed her family some time with them, but hating the thought. She needed solitude, time to get her thoughts and emotions in order, not their smothering concern. "Oh, all right. But I hope you won't object if I go down and take a shower now?" She set the still empty cup on the counter. "I promise I'll be here for lunch, Gran, so you don't need to send someone with me to make sure I don't run away again."

"Get along with you." Gran waved a hand.

As she passed the boys, Owen called, "Hey, Annie, got a minute?"

Reluctantly she paused. "Sure. What do you need?"

"Peter says the barn down there belongs...is part of the ranch. Is it okay if we go down there?"

She looked down the hill at the barn and corrals near the ranch entrance. "I honestly don't know. We used to pester Charlie whenever we could, but I'm not sure he's still there." A shriek from one of the younger boys made her jump. "You could go ask Gran—"

"She might say no."

Annie had to grin. "Yeah, she might. Look, why don't you go down and find out for yourself. But don't take the little boys. Not until you're sure it's okay."

"Their mom wouldn't let them go anyway. She's real strict with them." He shook his head. "They mind her, too."

"Remarkable. And very un-kidlike."

"You said it. Thanks, Annie. See you later."

She watched him trot back to where the younger boys were still tossing the Frisbee. *Nice kid. Peter's so lucky.*

She didn't really envy her brother. Not really. She just wanted her own son back.

All the peace she'd felt this morning was gone, replaced by the familiar aching loneliness.

SHORTLY AFTER OWEN TOOK OFF ON HIS HIKE, TOMMY'S BIG SISTER called him into the cookshack. That left just Norman and Joey and their cousin Jeremy to play Frisbee. And the two little boys couldn't throw very well. "It's no fun with only three of us," Norman said. "Let's do something else."

"This place isn't any fun," Joey said. "No TV or swings or anything."

"We could ride a bike," Norman suggested. "I know where there's one."

"Where?" Jeremy looked interested.

"Over behind the Pink House. I saw Cecile—Tommy's sister—put it there when she came back."

"Came back? Where'd she go?"

"Somewhere." Joey shrugged. "Mom said somebody should tell her not to ride on the highway."

"Let's go," Norman said. "before someone comes." He knew he probably shouldn't touch the bicycle, but it was just sitting there, not being used. They wouldn't hurt it.

They ran around the Pink House. Sure enough, there the bicycle sat, leaning against the house beside the back door. Not locked or anything. It had those skinny tires and turned down handlebars like the *real* bike racers used. And it was a boy's bike, too.

He grabbed the handlebars and rolled it away from the house. The crossbar was really high.

"It looks awful big," Jeremy said. "Can you ride it?"

"Sure. Watch." Setting a foot on the pedal, he gave a scoot and swung his leg over the bar. He could reach the other pedal, but his legs were too short for him to sit on the seat.

"Oh, man, this is something," he cried and he swooped along the path. Unlike his bike at home, this one was light and easy to pedal, and it went really fast with just a little push. It was hard to steer, though. The front wheel wobbled as he rounded the corner of the house.

Joey and Jeremy came running after him. "Wait! Wait for us!"

Norman turned uphill on the road. He didn't see anybody on the lawn, and the trees in the Grove would hide him from the cookshack. Riding on the gravel was hard, though, with the skinny wheels. The handlebars kept wanting to jerk out of his hands.

At the top of the hill, he started to turn around, and the front wheel kind of tucked itself under. The next thing he knew, he was sprawled in the road, tangled with the bicycle.

"Owww!" His knees hurt and his hands, and he had something in one eye. He tried to turn sideways so he could get up. One of his feet was wedged in the front wheel spokes, and he couldn't get it loose.

"Oh wow, Normie, you broke it," Joey said, as he came to a sliding stop. Dust puffed up from his feet and came right into Norman's face.

"You're bleeding," Jeremy said. "Both knees."

"I know it. Help me up." He was the big brother. He couldn't cry in front of Joey, but he sure wanted to.

They helped him get untangled. When he stood up. he saw that that his knees were just skinned and the palms of his hands were only scraped a little bit. "How bad's the bike?" he was going to have to confess. Dad would scold, Mom would probably confine him to the house for the rest of the week, and the girl would probably kill him.

"It's not too bad" Jeremy stood it on its wheels. A couple of spokes were bent, and there was a long scratch on the part the seat stuck out of, but that was all they could see.

Norm took hold of the handlebars and walked the bike back to the parking space by the Big House. He leaned it against the big white car's back bumper. "I'm gonna go wash first, then I'll have to tell Mom and Dad."

"You want us to come with you?"

"No way." He hated it when the other kids saw him get scolded.

CeCe and Tommy were still in the cookshack with Gran when the stuffed shirt came in, looking like he was ready to kill someone. CeCe couldn't remember his name or how he was related, but she thought he was the father of Hetty, the cool redhead she'd liked on sight.

"If you cared enough about that silly bicycle of yours to bring it all the way from Denver, you should have put it somewhere safe," he said when he saw her. "I just ran over it. Ruined a tire, too."

"My bike?" CeCe couldn't move. "You ran over my bike? But it was—"

"Apparently you left it leaning against my back bumper. Now I'm going to miss my tee time." He glowered at Gran. "Cecile, I told you this was a ridiculous notion of yours, and I still believe it. These children's father should have come with them, or they shouldn't be here."

Released from the paralysis of shock, CeCe started toward the door.

"Wait," Gran called. "If he ran over it, there's nothing you can do. Now, John, do you make a habit of driving off without looking behind you?"

"Of course not, but how you can expect me to see a bicycle over the trunk lid? I ought to make you pay for my tire, young lady. Maybe that would teach you to take better care of your bicycle."

She wanted to throw up, and to cry, and to swear. It took all the discipline she'd learned in competition to say, with only a small quaver in her voice, "My bicycle was behind the Pink House. I left it there this morning, after my ride."

"A likely story. I know how you kids are."

"John, you're not making a bad matter any better. Sit down and be quiet until we get to the bottom of this.?"

To CeCe's amazement, he sat. But he didn't stop glowering at her.

"CeCe, will you see if Ward is in the Blue House?" Gran said. "Ask him to come over here. And then you'd better go see how badly your bike is damaged."

Her knees shook all the away to the Blue House. After she delivered the message to Uncle Ward, she went to look at her bike, now nothing but a tangle of titanium tubes and silver spokes caught under the side of a cream-colored Cadillac. She knelt and touched the handlebar grip, probably the only part of the bike that was still intact.

One more thing. Just one more thing that's gone.

Feet dragging, CeCe went back to the cookshack. She met Uncle Ward as he was coming out. He laid an arm over her shoulder and walked with her toward the Grove. "The boys took your bike, CeCe. Norman just confessed to his parents. It got scratched up when he fell with it. He left it leaning against John's car while he went to wash, and forgot to move it."

"Okay," was about all she could manage.

"All three boys will be punished, and Norman will probably be grounded for the rest of the summer. If that makes you feel any better."

She shook her head, knowing that saying one more word would start her crying like a baby.

"Eric will offer to buy you a new bike. I'm going to suggest that John chip in, too. He should have made sure there was nothing behind his car."

Another shake of her head. *What am I going to do all week? How can I stay in shape? The Criterium is in three weeks. I've got to keep training. What am I going to do?*

"Can you get a replacement in Idaho Falls?"

"No." She paused, cleared her throat. "My bike is a special build because I'm so short. Getting a new one will take weeks.

Maybe months." Sure, she had other bikes, but this one was the best. This is the one she'd hoped to ride to her first ever win.

"Well, then, can you get one to ride, while you're waiting for the replacement?" He gave her shoulder a little shake. "C'mon, CeCe, don't give up. I know you have a race coming up soon. You want to keep up with your training, don't you?"

"Yeah, okay. But how am I gonna get to Idaho Falls? I won't go with Eric. He lectures."

A short laugh exploded from Uncle Ward. "I'll just bet he does. I'll see if I can find someone who wants to drive down there tomorrow. If no one else, then I'll take you."

"Okay." She heard herself, and realized she'd sounded really grudging. "Thanks, Uncle Ward. I'll be okay, now."

"No, I don't think you will. Not right away. But you'll do, CeCe. You'll do." Another half-hug and he released her. "Why don't you and Charlene see if you can lure Annie out of her cave this afternoon? She needs to spend some time with family."

"I might." CeCe escaped into the Grove where she found a solitary bench, far away from family, far away from the boys she'd like to do something to. Something violent. Something mean.

WHEN CHARLENE AND CECE CAME TO PERSUADE HER TO JOIN THE nature walk at Harriman State Park, Annie found them hard to resist. If CeCe could smile despite her broken dreams, then Annie could do the same despite her broken heart.

Oh, yes, and don't we do pathetic well, she could almost hear Hetty saying.

Harriman State Park had once been a working ranch like the Floating Nought, although Annie rather imagined her family's ranch had never approached the luxury of the Railroad Ranch. The property was now part of the Idaho State Parks system, managed as habitat for the wild animals that made their homes there, among them moose, elk, trumpeter swans, sandhill cranes, and bald eagles.

The leader of the nature walk hardly looked old enough to be out alone. He was a shy young man, his face scarred by acne, his voice confident only when he embarked on the memorized spiel about the natural features of the park or when he was answering questions about its animal inhabitants.

"If you look carefully, you can see some trumpeter swans," He told the crowd standing along the path bordering Silver Lake. "Over there, just beyond that point."

Everyone obediently peered across the water. Sure enough, four white shapes were gliding across the mirror smooth surface of the water, too far away to be clearly seen. She'd seen them before, but Annie still wished for her binoculars, sitting on the windowsill beside her bunk. "Can we get closer?"

"Oh, sure. Just take the trail out past the old corrals, back up towards the hills." Their guide gestured. "If you go early in the morning, you might even see the moose."

"Moose? Do they really come in this close?" one of the tourists asked.

"Yeah. Sometimes they come right down behind the bunkhouse. Early in the morning, they're usually in the meadows on the north end of the lake. One of the cows has twin calves."

Everyone spoke at once. "Twins? Really?"

"Oh, how I'd love to see them!"

"I've never seen moose in the wild. How exciting!"

Hetty drew her aside when the tour ended. "Let's walk home by way of the corrals."

"Okay," Annie agreed, not particularly interested, but with nothing better to do. She wondered if Owen had found Charlie Jones still in charge of the horses. Charlie had seemed older than dirt when she was a kid, but she knew now that he'd only been in his mid-forties. So he'd be, what—sixty-something, now?

The younger girls decided to ride back with Ben and Louisa, who promised a detour to Island Park for ice cream. Hetty and Annie were silent as they took the trail back to the Floating Nought.

"I've never thought about it before," Hetty said, as they reached the highway, "but this must have been some operation in its time. Just imagine these two big ranches growing who knows how many cattle in these woods."

"I'd like to have seen it, back in 1922, when old John Blankenship homesteaded here. Do you remember Gran's stories of growing up on the ranch?"

"You mean the 'walking five miles to school through six feet of snow' stories?" Hetty chuckled. "Sure I remember, and I don't believe them any more now than I did back then. I'll bet they had school busses in the nineteen-thirties."

"Probably, but still... I think I'd like to live out here. There's something... Oh, I don't know...soothing about it. Last night I woke up and heard an owl."

"I can't imagine. Give me police sirens and landing jets any day. I'd go mad in this silence. My body went into smog withdrawal for the first three days. Now it's getting used to this clean air. I'll probably suffer when I get to San Francisco."

"City girl!"

"That's me. You, too, for that matter. You can't convince me you'd like to live way out here all the time. How would you make a living?"

"I don't know. I just..." Annie shrugged, unable to put her feelings into words. She wasn't sure of them herself.

Instead of going into the barn, they went directly to the corrals. Hetty climbed onto its lower rail, hooked her elbows over the top, and whistled. Horses lifted their heads and looked at her curiously, but none approached.

"Lost my touch, I guess," she said, when repeated whistles failed to lure the horses to them.

"With horses, anyway," Annie commented, "but you don't seem, to have the same problem with men."

Hetty looked over her shoulder, then jumped down. "That sounded almost envious, Annie. What's the matter? Don't you approve of Frank's coming either?"

"You can have fifteen lovers here for all of me. I don't care!" Sudden anger boil up within Annie. For some reason her favorite cousin's breezy manner was a distinct irritation. Learning that Hetty had still another gorgeous boyfriend hurt, like having a knife twisted into her gut. She'd done her best to ignore the pain, had tried not to think about how unfair it all was.

Hetty was the epitome of love-'em-and-leave-'em, while Annie had worked hard at being the perfect wife. Hetty was rewarded for her cavalier attitude with lovers waiting in line. Annie had failed to hold on to even one man.

"If you don't care, why are you yelling at me?"

"I wasn't yell—" Annie heard her strident voice. She took a deep breath. "I guess I was. Sorry, Het." Smiling ruefully, she slipped an arm around Hetty's waist. "Let's go. I'll try to explain." She knew that if she didn't, Hetty would bug her until she did. Het had never been one to tolerate unaccountable emotional reactions.

Somehow the peace and quiet, the barely audible background of bird calls and distant, childish voices made it easier for her to express thoughts that had been churning inside for a long time.

"I didn't used to feel inadequate, and I don't know why I started," she said when they were walking slowly up the road toward the houses. "When I was a kid I always figured I could handle anything the world tossed my way. Maybe if I hadn't fallen so hard for Walter..."

"He was a womanizing shit," Hillary said. "All charm and no substance."

"You never did like him, did you? No, don't deny it. He didn't like you, either. I never understood why."

"Maybe because I was immune to his charm. Look, Annie, we could talk all day about how Walter and I didn't get along, but that's not telling me your problem really is. Why on earth should you feel inadequate?"

"Because I was." The words burst from her like bullets. She took a couple of steps before she realized that Hetty had halted in the middle of the road and was staring at her as if she'd lost her mind. "I tried so damn hard to be a good wife, and I just never got the hang of it." Turning so Hetty wouldn't see the tears that had suddenly flooded her eyes, she said, "Do you know anyone else who's flunked a class in wine selection?"

"Somebody who prefers beer? You never have liked wine much, as I recall. Besides, who cares?"

"Walter did. It was very important to him that I know how to be a good hostess. It was important for his job that I know how to entertain his clients."

"Why? Aren't there any caterers in Portland?"

"Of course there are, but Walter would never—"

"Bullshit! What about Annie? You had a full-time job. Seems to me that hiring a caterer to do your social dinners would have made really good sense." Hetty draped an arm across her shoulders and squeezed. "You know what I think?"

Annie shook her head against Hetty's shoulder. "Uh-uh." The tears had receded, but were still caught in her throat.

"I think you forgot that nobody can do anything to us that we don't let them. Why didn't you stand up to Walter, instead of letting him push you around?"

"He never pushed me around," she said, pulling out of Hetty's arms. "He was always so understanding. He sympathized with me that my job was so demanding, and he always apologized when he asked me to entertain.

"When I found out I was pregnant, he was really supportive. He was the one who insisted I resign instead of taking maternity leave. And after...after Calvin was born, he suggested I stay at home and be a full-time mom."

Raising one eyebrow, Hetty said, "I'll bet he didn't stop expecting you to entertain, though."

"Well, of course not. It was an important part of his job. His clients expected him to entertain them."

"And you believed it was your job too?"

"Yes." When Hetty made a face, she snapped, "Well, it was, whatever you think."

A high keen from above caught her attention. Not fifty yards away a hawk swooped down upon an unsuspecting rodent. "Ohh, look!"

They watched in silence until the hawk bore its victim aloft. They resumed walking, speaking of scenery and weather and family gossip.

As were passing the Guest House, Hetty said, "Why are you so upset about my inviting Frank?"

"I'm not." She kicked a stone and it went clattering across the road.

"You could have fooled me." Hetty walked a few steps in silence. "Do you feel like a failure because you and Walter split? Do you want him back?"

Did she? The divorce had been her idea, but Walter hadn't objected when she broached the subject. He'd agreed to a no-fault decree and had been more than fair about the division of their assets. Not that there were all that many. The house had sold for a bit more than the outstanding mortgage, and she hadn't wanted the Mercedes. Walter had kept most of the furniture. Where on earth would she have put the Chinese rugs and the marble-topped commode, and all the other expensive and imported items he had insisted they buy? So now she had a nice stock portfolio and a three-year-old car that was paid for, instead of a house full of furniture.

"No," she decided. "No, I don't want him back. It's like..." Annie fluttered her hands helplessly. "We're like two strangers. I look at him and wonder how I could have ever loved him. How we could have made lo— had sex together." A small shiver of revulsion made its way up her spine. "Besides, I don't think he'd have me back. Not in a hundred years."

She fought the lump in her throat, but failed to prevent a slight tremble in her voice. "I don't know what I saw in him. Not now. I've tried to remember how I felt, and all I can think is that I must have been out of my mind. He's not the sort of man who appeals to me. So why did he?"

"I've always wondered that myself. Look, someone's coming."

The big car, a make Annie didn't recognize except that it looked expensive, pulled a rooster tail of dust behind it as it approached. Others had seen it too. She and Hetty joined a small crowd standing on the Big House's front porch as it finally came to a halt between Annie's Accord and the Cadillac belonging to Uncle John and Aunt Joss.

"Who on earth?" Annie heard her mother say behind her.

The driver door opened. A tall woman who could have been her mother's twin—her mother's evil twin Annie fancied, on second glance—got out and stood beside the car. "What are you all staring at?" she demanded. "I told Mother I'd be here if I could."

"Oh my goodness!" Thea said, just loud enough for those on the porch to hear. "It's Frances."

Before anyone could say more, the other door opened and a tall girl emerged. She glared at everyone.

"Oh, yes, it is indeed Frances," Uncle Ward muttered. He didn't sound happy.

Gran emerged from the front door while they were all still immobile. "Hello, Frances. I'm glad you could make it, although I would have preferred you'd let me know you were definitely coming."

Annie couldn't help but stare. This was her fabled Aunt Frances, the family black sheep? This elegant woman in clothes more suited to Rodeo Drive than an Idaho ranch.

"Who's the girl?" Hetty said in her ear.

"I've no idea."

"I often don't know from one day to the next what my schedule will be. As it happened, I was in Sun Valley, and found that I could make time to join you." Turning her back, she reached into the back seat and pulled out a small case. "Our luggage is in the trunk. Please have someone take it to our rooms."

"There are no servants here. And since I didn't expect you, I didn't allocate you a room. You'll have to sleep on the sofa in the study. Both of you."

Annie had never heard Gran sound quite so...so acid. She stepped back from the porch rail, dodging behind Uncle Ward.

Hetty followed. "Let's get lost. This is a battle I don't want to be in the middle of."

They slipped inside and went through the house and out the back door. "Do you know something I don't?" Annie said.

"No, not really," Hetty replied. "But I could smell a fight brewing. The tension was so thick you could slice it."

"It was, wasn't it? I've always wondered about Aunt Frances. Haven't you?"

"You mean why she never came to family Gatherings? I asked Gran once, and all she would say was that it was Frances's choice.

She got all tight-lipped and pissy when she said it, though, so I know there are some hard feelings."

"There must be. Nobody acted glad to see her. I wonder if the girl is her assistant." The sight of her bunk reminded Annie how early she'd arisen. She yawned. "I'm for a nap. Can you wake me in time for dinner?"

"Sure. I'm going to find a patch of shade and finish my book."

Curled up on her bunk, Annie found sleep elusive. She forced herself to lie still and pretend to sleep, even though she was alone, a condition she found entirely comfortable. She'd had enough of family togetherness for the day.

Except for tonight's command appearance. No one was allowed to miss dinner at a Gathering without a good excuse. Like fire, flood or nearly fatal accident.

Chapter Six

Y OU LOOK PERFECTLY CONTENT."

Hetty looked up from her book and smiled. "I am. Sloth and indolence is good, once in a while. I don't think I'd want a steady diet of it, though."

"Join you?" When she scooted over, Ward sat beside her on the rustic bench. He stretched his long legs out and leaned his head back, eyes closed. "You missed the fun."

"I'd rather hear about family spats second hand, thank you very much. I get enough of them with my folks."

"Uh-huh. I did hear you were planning on raising their hackles this week."

She saw the gleam of his eyes, nearly hidden under lowered lids. "Are you here to talk me out of it?"

"Not at all. In fact, it may be high time you stopped lying to your mother."

"Damn it, Ward, I do not lie to her. I just don't tell her everything."

"Well, you're the best judge of that. We can only hope for the best."

Hetty closed her book and slipped it into her tote. Was she doing the right thing, bringing Frank here? "I had this crazy idea that if Frank could meet my folks here, where he could see that the rest of the family is sober and respectable, he wouldn't think so badly of Joss."

"He doesn't know?"

She sighed but didn't answer.

"Was that wise? He may be expecting June Cleaver." At her raised eyebrow, he said, "I guess you couldn't very well tell him your mother's a drunk. Not if he's never met any of your family."

"Yeah, exactly."

They sat in thoughtful silence until the raucous cry of a magpie intruded. Without looking at Ward, Hetty said, "Who is the girl with Frances? She looks familiar."

"Serhilda? I don't know." Before she could speak, he said, "Mother chased me out, along with everyone else. I guess she figured they didn't need an audience while they sorted things out."

"I hope she's not what she looks like."

"A hooker? Probably not. I have a hunch her getup was carefully calculated for its shock value." He stood, but didn't leave. Instead he stared into the distance. "Hetty, be nice to her, even if it hurts. Help me keep things civilized this week."

She couldn't remember ever hearing Ward sound so... uncertain. "I can't imagine why I'd spend much time with her, but if the occasion arises, I'll be nice."

"And friendly?"

"Yes, Uncle Ward, I will be friendly."

He tousled her hair just as he had when she was ten. She hated it just as much as she had then.

"That's all I can ask," he said, and left her alone.

* * * *

The usual deafening confusion reigned once the family assembled for dinner. Annie tucked herself into the corner of the dining room nearest the kitchen, next to Uncle Ben and Aunt Louisa, hoping to be able to escape unobtrusively once dessert had been served. They talked international politics all through dinner. No, that wasn't right. Her uncle and aunt talked politics. Annie listened and nodded occasionally, trying to ignore the laughter all around her. Everyone seemed so happy. Did she envy them?

"Hey! Listen up, everybody!" Hetty, holding a plate in each hand, was standing on a bench at the middle table, amidst the younger kids. They were giggling hilariously.

"We have seen the development of a new art form tonight."

Catcalls and applause answered her.

Despite her determination not to join the fun, Annie felt a smile twitch her lips.

Hetty affected a pout. "All great artists are unappreciated at first."

Boos.

"Now I want you all to inspect this creation, by none other than Joseph Armstrong, Esquire." Hetty tilted one of the plates she was holding, rotating her hand so everyone could see its colorful contents. All Annie saw was a bright blob of the Jell-O that was dessert. Orange, strawberry, and lime, intermingled.

"Here, we have a strong, organic creation," Hetty said, "fluid and kinetic, exhibiting nature's unity." She tilted the plate still more and a bit of strawberry slid off, landing on Joey's head. He yelled when Kristi rubbed it in.

Annie swallowed a bubble of laughter. Jennifer, Joey's mother, appeared about to erupt.

"And this one," Hetty said, waving the other plate around, "is derivative of Mondrian. Strong lines and disciplined, geometric spaces." The Jell-O was cut into neat rectangles of each color.

Hetty waited until the noise receded. "It shows..."

"Gimme back my plate!" Tommy pretended to bite Hetty's ankle. She nearly lost her balance.

"...a rigid but mature mind. A well-developed sense of..." The plate slipped from her hand as Hetty tried to escape Tommy's clutch. Plate and Jell-O somersaulted in the air, miraculously remaining together. Kristi made a surprising catch, but her efforts dislodged the Jell-O. Most of it lit on Tommy.

"Great catch!" someone called.

Annie watched with something like envy. Once she would have been in the middle of the horseplay, happily slinging Jell-O alongside Hetty.

Hetty looked down at the boy, still pretending to gnaw on her ankle. "Good grief! Jackson Pollock."

Tommy swiped a blob of lime from his shoulder and smeared it across Hetty's bare foot, just as Owen flipped a spoonful of mixed flavors across the table at Joey.

Jennifer shrieked again and pandemonium broke loose. Jell-O, dinner rolls, and wadded-up napkins flew every which way.

Intelligent adults retreated to the end of the room and watched with varying expressions. John and Joss looked disapproving, Jennifer horrified, and Frances bored. The rest were cheering one or another of the combatants. Annie stood behind Gran and wondered when she had become a grown-up.

Ward called a truce when someone—Annie suspected Norman, but couldn't be sure—tossed a full cup of grape Kool-Aid in Kristi's face.

After the floor was mopped and the kids—along with Hetty and Kristi—were sent to the showers, the nightly Bridge game began at one end of a table. Annie sat and watched for a while. Not long, though, for Joss, John, Ward and her father took the game very seriously. Although she had been a rabid player in college, she had trouble following the terse bidding and rapid play.

Several invitations to cribbage came her way but she refused them all. Her mind felt stiff and unused. Even her teenaged cousins were likely to skunk her. And the last thing she needed was to get involved in Trivial Pursuit at another table. She found silence and solitude on the cookshack steps where she could stare into the darkness and be alone with her dark thoughts.

The door behind her opened. "Oh!"

She didn't recognize the voice, so there was only one person it could be. "I'm trying to decide whether that's a satellite up there, or just a jet."

"Who cares?" Serhilda—*what kind of cruel parent would name a child Serhilda?*—stepped past her and stomped off toward the Grove. Soon she disappeared in the dark.

Not terribly disappointed, Annie leaned back and propped herself on her elbows. Moving lights marked the few vehicles traveling the highway. She looked beyond, to where a few scattered lights marked the old ranch headquarters at Harriman State Park.

The far-off, faintly gleaming river reminded her of her encounter with the fly fisherman. Did she want to take him up on his offer, to learn to fly fish? If it could do for her even half of what he promised—bring her inner peace and forgetfulness—perhaps it would be worth the effort.

Besides, she wanted to see him again. He was so comfortable to be with, so undemanding. His warm, compassionate eyes had made her want to sink into their depths and find... What would she find? What did she want to find? A tiny flare blossomed in her belly as she visualized his broad shoulders and strong, stocky legs. A dangerously attractive man, she decided, examining her thoughts, recognizing faint stirrings of desire.

"No!" she whispered in the darkness. "No, I can't!" She wasn't ready to come alive again. Not that way. Desire, and all the attendant emotions, were too strong, too demanding. They hurt too much.

"What can't you do?" Uncle Ward said from behind her.

Annie took a deep breath, patted the concrete step beside her, and said, "Nothing, Uncle Ward. Just random thoughts." She gave him a smile, and felt her lower lip quiver.

Ward Blankenship was nobody's fool. He must have seen the tears on her lower lashes, but ignored them. "I came to see if you want to take my hand in the Bridge game. I'm too restless to sit still."

"I don't think so. I can't remember the point counts or the bidding conventions. And you know how impatient Aunt Joss gets with poor players."

"Then let's go for a walk. Work off some of that big dinner." He stood and extended a hand to her. "Come on, Annie, we haven't had a chance to visit."

Annie reluctantly let him pull her to her feet. He was her favorite uncle. Perhaps, if he told her about his latest construction project, she would forget for a while. Walking with him would get her away from the noise and confusion of the family. How could they be so happy in a world full of misery and sorrow?

They strolled down the gravel road toward the ranch headquarters. A nearly full moon sat just above the horizon, lighting up the landscape, casting long black shadows. As the sounds of laughter and conversation faded behind them, Ward finally spoke.

"You know, Annie, your mother and mine are right. You've got to stop grieving."

"Don't...don't you lecture me too, Uncle Ward. Please!"

"I'm not going to. I'm going to say this once, then leave you alone." He put his hands on her shoulders, gave her a small shake.

"When you were little, I never saw such an independent, stubborn kid. You insisted on doing everything Peter and Al did. 'Me, too!' was your favorite phrase. You were never belligerent about it, but you always managed to go your own way, do what you wanted to do. Thea used to worry about you, but Gib and I kept telling her that your instincts were good and you'd come to no harm." He paused, to tap his pipe out against his thigh.

"While other teenagers were giving their parents hell, you were single-mindedly getting straight A's, never worrying your parents, staying out of trouble."

He poked the stem of his pipe at her and Annie retreated. "Then you met that idiot, Walter, and you changed. You changed from independent, stubborn, and self-reliant into a helpless, obedient housewife who never had a thought that Walter didn't approve of. You were the perfect corporate wife."

Remembering all the times she'd retreated into a quiet corner at a cocktail party, her insecurity about menu planning and table décor for dinner parties, her lack of assurance... "Oh, no I wasn't. I really wasn't."

"You faked it well, then. When I visited you in Portland a couple of years ago, I couldn't see a trace of the old Annie. Just Mrs. Walter Abbott, helpmeet."

Ward bent to snap off a bit of sagebrush, crushed it between his fingers. Annie smelled its pungent aroma.

"Mother said Walter wasn't much help to you when you lost your boy. I guess he was pretty devastated himself, but it's a shame you couldn't have comforted each other. Of course, an egocentric bastard like him wasn't likely to think of anyone's needs but his own. Is that why you left him?"

"Mostly," she admitted. She wasn't sure herself of all the reasons. Just that after they'd buried Calvin, there hadn't been anything between her and Walter. No affection, no sympathy, nothing.

"What worries me, though, is that you're turning into a vegetable. Thea says you're working on an assembly line. Doing what? Putting together pickup canopies. Now that's a real intellectual challenge for a woman with a degree in microbiology. Why did you leave the DEQ anyhow?"

"I was pregnant. Walter wanted me to—"

"I thought so. Damn him! And you, too, for letting him turn you into a weak, clinging vine. What happened to the 'can do' kid I used to be so proud of? Where did she go?"

Annie shook her head, unable to answer.

"I think she's still in there somewhere, Annie, and I want you to look for her. Get a job that challenges you. Go back to school. Do something that will pull you out of this cycle of gloom and misery. But don't waste your life like this. Come back, Annie. Come back to us. We love you."

"And I love you," she cried. "All of you. But it hurts so much!"

"Of course it does. It always will, but eventually you'll grow a scab over the pain so that you can live with it. But not until you make an effort to let Calvin go." He shook her again, harder this time. "He's dead, Annie. He's gone, and none of your grief and anguish will bring him back. All it can do is kill you, inside."

Annie could find no response and Ward did not press her. They turned their backs to the moon and slowly retraced their steps in silence. When they were within a hundred yards or so of the women's house, Ward stopped again.

"You know, kiddo, your grandmother's advice to you may seem harsh and uncaring, but it's not. She's trying to help."

Annie made an incoherent sound of protest and disagreement.

"That mean old lady's my mother, you know. She's quite a gal. Wise, stubborn, and indestructible."

"And heartless!"

"Not a bit of it. You don't, you can't possibly know what she's lived through, following Dad to construction projects all over the world, while raising five kids. No, kiddo, your gran's trying, in her not too subtle way, to teach you what she learned the hard way—

to pick yourself up again and go on, no matter how completely life seems to have beat you down."

"Stiff upper lip and all that, you mean."

"Precisely. That may not be the easiest way, in the short term, to deal with heartbreak and sorrow, but over time it's the best way. Losers give in. Blankenships fight back."

"If you say so." Annie was too weary and miserable to argue. Hadn't she tried to fight back? Tried to shed the burden of sorrow, to resolve the guilt? Hadn't she?

He tousled her hair. "End of lecture. Now tell me about that young man Gib found you with this morning."

Annie swallowed the tears that threatened to choke her. "He was just a fisherman. I watched him catch a fish, then turn it loose. Isn't that dumb? All that effort and nothing to show for it."

"And so you told him what you thought?"

Annie nodded.

"Traces of the old Annie, after all. The eternal pragmatist. What did he say when you told him that?"

Annie related the gist of her conversation with the fisherman, but did not repeat his suggestion that she should learn to fly fish. She was still thinking about that.

Chapter Seven

Monday

L OUD VOICES FROM THE NEXT ROOM WOKE HETTY FAR TOO early the next morning. She pulled the pillow over her head, muttering, "I'm on vacation, damn it. Put a sock in it."

It helped a little. Not nearly enough. When Charlene's foot nearly landed on her elbow, she flung the pillow aside and sat up. "What the hell's going on?"

Annie was propped up on an elbow. "I don't know, but it sounds like someone's getting killed."

"It's Angela," Charlene said over her shoulder as she opened the door. "I'm going to see if Emma's all right."

"Maybe I should…"

"Enough!" The word came clearly through the wall.

"Never mind," Hetty said. "Kristi's in charge." She plopped the pillow back over her face, only to have it snatched away.

"Listen," CeCe told her. "It's that Serhilda. She's fighting with Kristi."

"Oh, God, I guess one of us had better go see." Hetty rolled out of bed, shivering in the chill of the room. She snatched her robe from the foot of the bed, but didn't bother with slippers.

Another scream rattled the windows.

"That's Angela. Sound's like she's being scalped or something." CeCe jumped down from her upper bunk. "I'm gonna go see."

"Wait—"

Too late. She was gone.

Hetty hesitated. The last thing she wanted to do was deal with Angela. One wrong word and Jennifer and Eric would be on her like steamrollers. Nonetheless, she followed Charlene and CeCe. Slowly. Hoping the altercation would be resolved before she got there.

Annie was climbing out of bed when she went through the door.

CeCe had hold of Angela, who was making a good try at imitating a calliope. Emma was huddled in her bunk, clinging to Charlene. Her thumb was in mouth, her eyes were big as saucers and fat tears glistened on her cheeks. Serhilda and Kristi were in a face-off in the center of the room, not quite nose-to-nose, but they might as well have been. As Hetty entered, Kristi was saying, "I don't care what Aunt Frances told you. There's no smoking in this house. Not in any of the houses. It's the rule."

"Fuck off, bitch. You're not in charge." A smoking cigarette bobbed in the corner of her mouth.

Angela screamed again, and kicked back at CeCe's legs. Fortunately she was barefooted, so she did no damage.

"As a matter of fact, I am," Kristi said. "It's a family rule that the oldest person in the room is in charge of all the kids present. Now put out that cigarette."

"Make me."

As Kristi hesitated, Hetty stepped forward and snatched the cigarette. "Kristi, get me something to put this thing in. Serhilda, it's possible Frances didn't understand the rules, but when Kristi told you there was no smoking inside, you should have paid attention. You're welcome to smoke anywhere outdoors, as long as you don't leave your butts lying around."

Serhilda turned her back. CeCe released Angela, who had stopped screaming, but looked ready to start again at the slightest provocation. "Charlene, take Emma out of here. In fact, all of you clear out. All but Serhilda."

She noticed then that Annie was staring at Emma, her mouth twisted as if she was trying to stop her own tears. For a moment she was moved to sympathy, then she remembered the promise Gran had demanded of her. "Annie, go see if there's any coffee. I can't be a peacemaker without caffeine."

Serhilda took a step toward the door.

"Hold it. Where do you think you're going?"

Serhilda strained against Hetty's grip on her upper arm. "Let go, God damn it! I'm outta here."

"No, you're not. Sit down." When the young woman resisted, Hetty applied force, pushing her into the nearer bottom bunk. "Kristi, you too. Sit over there."

When both young women were seated, glowering, on the lower bunks, she said, "Okay, here's the deal. Kristi, you're in charge of Emma. Serhilda, you're responsible for Angela. As long as those two little girls are in this room with you, they are your responsibilities. The whole enchilada. Tooth brushing, picking up toys, making beds, and anything else they need. Got it?"

"Go to hell!"

Kristi simply glared, her lower lip stuck out.

"Not only that," Hetty continued, ignoring their reactions, "you will be responsible for them getting along with each other and with everyone else. Serhilda, you've got the more difficult

87

task. Angela is spoiled rotten, and will do everything she can to get you into trouble with her parents. I'll back you if you deserve it, but if you're smart, you'll avoid any confrontations with Jennifer. Believe me, you'd lose."

"I don't know anything about kids," Serhilda said, sounding less belligerent with every word. "It's not fair, making me responsible for her."

"Life's not fair, kiddo, and the sooner you learn that, the better. Kristi?"

"Yeah?"

"Go get Emma and get her dressed. Since Peter and Kenna didn't come running when the screaming started, I imagine they've already gone up to the cookshack, so you can take Emma up there. She probably needs her mama."

When Kristi had gone, Hetty lowered herself to the floor in front of Serhilda. "I don't know what Frances was thinking of, bringing you here. She could have given you the week off, instead of— What?"

"The week off? What do you think I am, her fucking maid?" Serhilda said, voice cracking.

"Well, no, actually I figured you were her assistant. Her secretary, maybe."

"The bitch. The fucking bitch. I thought you knew."

All bravado was gone. Hetty revised her estimate of Serhilda's age downward by a good five years. "All I know is your name. Frances hasn't exactly kept in touch with the family. What is it? What should I...we know?"

Serhilda's laugh was harsh, humorless. "That I'm your cousin, that's what. The bitch is my mother."

ANNIE'S HANDS WERE STILL SHAKING WHEN SHE DROVE AWAY FROM

88

the compound. How she hated confrontation. Always had. As a middle child, she'd been a peacemaker, and she still had the urge to soothe ruffled feathers and shush raised voices.

When she reached the pavement, she turned north, but instead of going all the way to the highway, she headed toward the Harriman Park entrance. This early, the only people she was likely to encounter there were birders, and they were not inclined to be talkative.

She'd had about all the talk she could stand for one morning.

When she'd gone to the kitchen to start coffee, everyone had been jabbering at once. Everyone but Angela, who had still let out the occasional scream. Finally Charlene had threatened to throw a glass of ice water in her face if she screamed one more time, and she'd shut up.

How on earth did Jennifer and Eric cope with her? The little girl's voice grated on Annie's nerves like fingernails on a blackboard. As strongly as she felt against physically punishing a child, she had been tempted to slap Angela's face this morning.

Poor little Emma. Knowing her elder brother, Annie was sure his baby girl had never been exposed to shouting and screaming. No wonder she was terrified.

Calvin would have clung, just as Emma had. Would have clung and buried his face against her breasts.

Was that why she had this constant ache, just over her heart. Because Calvin was no longer here to bury his face against her? To fill her arms with his warm little body?

Stop it! You're supposed to be getting better, not making yourself feel worse!

She parked near the Visitor Center and took the trail that led to the river. When she reached the basalt promontory, she found the river empty of human presence, even though she had been hoping to see her fly fisherman.

Her fly fisherman. What a silly thought. *The* fly fisherman.

Hiking downstream, she soon spotted a red pickup at the fishing access. Beyond it he was standing on the riverbank, hands in hip pockets of baggy tan pants, hair shining golden in the morning light. She walked down to join him, resolutely ignoring the tiny bubble of excitement in her midriff.

"Good morning," he said, without turning as if he had known she would be there.

"How did you know it was me?"

"I saw you through the trees. Glad you came."

Now that he was before her, Annie was having second thoughts about the favor she was about to ask him. She scuffed the toe of her sneaker in the dry soil at her feet and stared out across the river, wondering if his offer had been meant seriously or if he had just been being polite.

"Yesterday you asked me if I would like to learn to fly fish..."

Clay's found her expression intriguing. What had made this woman so uncertain about asking a favor? The way she had approached along the trail spoke to him of enthusiasm, liveliness, a zest for life. Yet here she was, trying to ask him to teach her about his all-consuming interest, acting as if she expected him to refuse.

"And..." He gave her a sunny grin, hoping to put her at ease. Her full lips answered it tentatively, but she avoided his inquiring gaze, shifting her attention to the river.

"Well..." She bit her lip and took a deep breath, an effect that tantalized Clay. "Look, I don't even know your name. I feel... uncomfortable, asking you to do something for me when we're still perfect strangers."

He couldn't help but grin. Perfect strangers? Not exactly. Not after her visits to his dreams. "Clay Knight. And you are...?"

"Annie Ab— Annie Ogilvie." She held out a hand.

He took it, was unsurprised at its delicacy. One of the first things he'd noticed about her was her apparent fragility. Yet she'd walked along the trail as if she were at home on long hikes, as if she were reasonably athletic, not sedentary. "I'm glad to meet you, Annie. And yes, I'd enjoy teaching you about fly fishing."

"There's only one thing..."

"Yes?"

"Can I do it from the bank?" The swift glance she cast toward the river struck him as more fearful than hesitant.

"Sure. It's not as much fun, but it works."

Her expression reminded him of a puppy who knew it had done something wrong. "You're sure it's not an inconvenience?"

"It was my idea in the first place, wasn't it? You're here with your family aren't you? Do any of them have fishing gear?"

"How did you know— Of course. Dad, yesterday. Yes, I'm here with my family. It's like a reunion. But no, I don't think any of them have fishing stuff. Not like you do."

He had to shake his head at anyone coming to fly fisherman's heaven for a vacation and not fishing. *That's just bizarre.* "Well, we'll have to see if we can find some waders for you. I'll check this afternoon. In the meantime, I can explain what all my equipment is for, and maybe show you how to cast."

"Can't I just watch you today, instead? You came out here to fish, not give lessons. I can be thinking of questions while I watch you."

Clay wondered what caused her to be so unsure of herself. "Well, okay, if that's what you want to do. It'll be pretty boring, though."

"I don't mind. I sort of like the idea of doing nothing this morning."

Annie watched as Clay removed his pants, unable to look away from his hands. Underneath he wore running shorts and long johns again. Even so, she felt a shiver of something she did not want to acknowledge as his muscular legs were revealed.

She was almost disappointed when he pulled the heavy, shapeless chest waders on. Before he entered the river, he removed the Thermos from the back pocket of his vest and handed it to her. "Help yourself. Just save me a cup, will you?"

For more than an hour she sat on the bank, watching Clay slowly work his way upstream. It was difficult to ask questions when the source of your information was a hundred yards away, she acknowledged. But the experience of seeing him gracefully cast, whipping the rod over his head, laying the fly in just the right spot, was worth having her questions go unanswered.

He was truly an artist. Every motion was controlled, efficient, like a dancer's. When he cast, the singing of the line, as it curled through its loop into a silvery tendril above the water, blended with the soft murmur of the river and the distant, high-pitched bird calls. At last he reeled the line in and turned to wade toward the bank. Holding up the vacuum bottle, she waved. He grinned in response.

She'd found a small clearing about twenty feet back from the bank, where a log lay across a couple of rocks, at just the right height to be a comfortable backrest. He removed the chest waders and seated himself beside her. Slanting rays of sunlight shone through the surrounding trees, lighting him, turning him into something from her girlhood fantasies. *If it weren't for those raggedy longjohns, he'd look like a knight.* Then she had to giggle, because he was exactly that. A Knight.

"Something funny?"

"No. Nothing, really. Here." She handed him the cup.

"Ah, that hits the spot," Clay said, after taking a cautious sip. He leaned back onto one elbow. "You know, I think the fish must be taking their midmorning nap. Nary a rise."

"I noticed that you weren't having much luck. Is it always like this?" Annie sat tailor fashion before him, aware of tiny beads of perspiration dampening her upper lip. She picked up his discarded cap and fanned herself with it.

"No. In June, during the green drake hatch, I've caught six or eight within an hour."

"What's that? The green drake hatch?"

"*Ephemeroptera.* Mayflies. Great big ones. A lot of fly fishing success depends on the insects that are available to fish. You have to know what the fish are feeding on in order to choose flies that will attract them."

"In other words, you cheat." Desperate for something to distract her wayward mind, she poured liquid sunscreen into her palm. As she stroked it onto the other arm, she sensed Clay following her motions. Goosebumps rose along the path of his gaze. She saw him swallow convulsively before looking away.

"Cheat? Me?" he protested, with a little catch in his voice. "I never cheat!"

"What do you call it, then? Tricking the poor fish. You ought to be ashamed of yourself."

"Not a bit of it. A good fly fisherman has to know quite a bit of entomology or he'll never catch anything. This river is a good example. There are two hatches in June—green drakes and pale morning duns—that bring fly fishermen here from all over the world." He reached for the coffee. "They're both mayflies."

"What are they eating now? More mayflies?"

"Grasshoppers, mostly. I was using a Henrys Fork Hopper yesterday, when you saw me catch the big one. Today I'm trying something a little different." He showed her the tiny fluff of red and black attached to the end of his line. "But they don't seem to like ants this morning. I'll probably change it before I go back out. Right now I'm enjoying the sun." He lay back, closing his eyes and stretching out his legs. "And the company," he murmured, so softly that Annie barely heard him.

She was hard put to untangle her confused reactions to Clay. His very presence succored her, as if he possessed an inner source of repose that her soul responded to. No problem there.

She needed all of that she could get. It was this other elemental need she was experiencing that unnerved her. The inner warmth, the faint stirrings of desire—they were out of time and place.

His plaid shirt, brown today, was unbuttoned and falling open, exposing a muscular chest. Walter had been a hairy man, so much so that he had shaved well below his collar line. Clay Knight's body was relatively hairless, smooth, golden, and solid. Annie had a sudden vision of her hand spread across his hard belly, stroking up between the solid slabs of pectoral muscle.

She jumped to her feet. "You'll never catch any fish this way," she said when Clay started at her sudden movement. "Go catch another one so I can see again how you do it. I've got to be back at the cookshack in less than an hour."

Clay pulled himself to a sitting position. "Slave driver." He grinned, reassuring her that he was indeed willing to return to the river. "Hand me my vest."

Annie watched as he removed the colorful fly from his line, replacing it with one that looked for all the world like a fat grasshopper with its wings half open. "Where do you get your flies?" she said.

"Tie 'em myself. It's something to do on long winter evenings. There. If that doesn't appeal to a trout appetite, I'll eat it myself."

Annie chuckled. "Save it until I can watch. Are you still heading upstream?"

"Right. Say, how am I going to get word to you if I can locate some waders? Just in case you decide to come in the river, you understand."

The chances of her wading into that river were slim to none, but Annie didn't want him to think her a wimp. "How about if I meet you here tomorrow morning. About six??"

"Sounds good." He pulled on his waders and vest, slung the net over his shoulder. Annie handed him the rod.

"Good luck," she said, as he slipped down the bank into the river. "Catch a big one."

Clay waved as he waded into deeper water. Annie again followed him, moving along the bank as he waded upstream. She hated to leave when noon came. She called a good-bye to him and received a distracted wave in return.

Chapter Eight

"Hey, CeCe, you're wanted up at the Big House."

She put down the magazine and pushed herself out of the chair. *I feel like shit.* She'd missed her morning ride, and her body was complaining. She'd done yoga with Kristi, but it hadn't helped much. Running two miles hadn't worked either, mostly because she couldn't run flat out on the gravel road or the trail. And there was no way she'd run along the highway. It was dangerous enough riding her bike there.

Uncle Ward was waiting for her on the path to the cookshack. He wore a big grin.

"You rang?" She knew she sounded snotty, but she just didn't care. He'd promised to see that someone took her to Idaho Falls to shop for a bike, and so far he'd done nothing.

"More or less. Let's go to the cookshack."

"I already ate." She'd munched on an energy bar and washed it down with a Coke. Since she wasn't riding, she didn't need a big breakfast.

"Well, I haven't. We can talk while I do."

A UPS truck was just pulling away as they approached. *Didn't think they came out in the wilderness.*

They were all supposed to go in the front door and not cut through the kitchen, but maybe he could get away with it. Still, she was a little nervous. All the adults were staring at her. *Hey. He did it. I'm just following him.* But she didn't say it out loud, because Gran was smiling.

She'd already caught on that if Gran was happy, everybody was happy.

Well, everybody but Jennifer and Angela, anyhow.

Stuffed shirt and his wife were eating breakfast at the table closest to the kitchen, and Uncle Ben and Aunt Louisa were sitting clear across the room with the hot guy who'd come in yesterday. Evan was his name, wasn't it?

I wouldn't mind getting to know him better. He's not as cute as Owen, though.

Instead of stopping at a table, Uncle Ward led her all the way through. He stopped at the front door. "I did some calling yesterday, and couldn't find a bike your size in Idaho Falls or Pocatello. Not one you'd want to ride."

"Didn't think you would." She knew she sounded as bratty as Angela, but she figured she had a right to. It was going to be a week before she could train, and that meant—

"So I called Mrs. Winthrop."

"How—"

"Your dad gave me her name as an emergency contact. She said you have an old bike that you've been trying to sell. I know it's not as good as the one John killed, but at least it'll fit you." He opened the door and gestured outside.

Leaning against the porch railing was a big box. Big enough to contain a bike. She couldn't believe her eyes.

"CeCe, John's going to replace your titanium bike—his insurance should cover most of it—and I kind of twisted Eric's arm to pay the overnight freight on this one. It wasn't cheap."

She caught the twitch of his lips before he went real sober. "I hope you have what you need to put it together. I understand they had to take the handlebars and pedals off."

"You got me a bike? My own bike?"

"I hope that's what's in the box. Why don't you check and see?" He held out a big Swiss Army knife.

It didn't take her long. A few minutes later her trusty old Bridgestone, scarred and dusty, was lying on the lawn. She sat beside it, holding the handlebars in her arms. "I... Oh, God, Uncle Ward, I... Thanks."

He came down on one knee beside her. Funny how he suddenly looked all blurry. "Just be careful when you get out on the highway, huh?" His arms went around her tight, kind of like her mom's used to.

She nodded, knowing she was leaving a trail of tears on his shirt.

SIX VEHICLES EMERGED FROM A CLOUD OF DUST AT THE BOTTOM of the steep grade. They pulled to a stop in front of an elegant log building, gingerbread trimmed, with a wide front porch. Children of all sizes burst from five of them.

"We're here," Gib Ogilvy called to his passengers. "You all can wake up now."

Annie forced her eyes open, stretched a neck that was sore from her head's having fallen crooked against the seat back. Her spine was wet where it had been in contact with the upholstery and her face felt flushed.

"A fine thing, sleeping through all the scenery," her father commented with a smile at his wife, who stretched, yawned, and shook her head. "I'm nothing but a glorified taxi driver."

Her mother smiled sympathetically. "Take it as a compliment on your driving, love. We all felt so secure that we went to sleep instead of watching your every move."

"It must be the fresh air," Hetty said to Annie as they climbed out of the back seat. "I've slept more since we got here than I have in weeks."

"More likely the altitude. Air's thinner and cleaner than Seattle's."

"Could be, Uncle Gib, but I prefer to think that I'm having withdrawal symptoms from city air." Hetty spread her arms, took a deep breath. "No automobile exhaust, no seawater smell, just pure pine essence and whiffs of sagebrush. I hate it."

"Sure you do," Gib said, "and you also miss the noise, the crowds, and the concrete."

Hetty grinned and winked. Annie ignored their joking and headed toward an opening in the pine trees.

The road had only brought them halfway down the canyon. The lip of the falls was still a good distance below them, far enough that the roar of falling water did not completely mask the happy shouts of the children. Annie made her way down the steep path, climbing carefully over the rounded boulders that cropped out every few feet. "Oh, how marvelous!" She had forgotten how spectacular the view was from here. How long had it been since she'd seen it?

Too long.

The river, broad and tranquil at Harriman Park, here was rushing and alive. Upstream of the falls huge boulders broke up the water; downstream the white foam trailed away from the churning pool into which the river fell.

Several more bends in the steep, boulder strewn path brought her to a rocky platform overlooking the falls. Across the river, she could see the varied greens on a sheer cliff constantly wetted by spray from the falls. Mosses, ferns, and rock-hugging herbs and shrubs grew on every tiny ledge, from each crack in the basalt wall. She looked down, over the lip of the falls.

"It's a long way down there," she said to herself, feeling her body involuntarily sway toward the edge.

"About a hundred and fourteen feet," Hetty said, behind her. At Annie's startled glance, she grinned. "I did my homework. Your dad's got a Forest Service map of the area. I read about the falls this morning." She grimaced. "Come on, let's back off. I don't like being this close to the edge."

Annie, always drawn to heights, remembered that her cousin hated them. She followed Hetty back along another path which led them to a second overlook, this one well back from the cliff's edge, but still with a good view. They could see the whole face of the falls and farther downstream to where the river curved to the left and out of sight. There was a rounded boulder just big enough to seat them both in cool shade.

Annie sat, mesmerized by the movement of the water and its roar. How would it feel, she wondered, to throw herself into that churning cauldron at the base of the falls and let it batter her into unconsciousness? Would she have time to regret her action? Or would she fall into oblivion with relief at the end of pain?

Eventually a hand on her shoulder brought her back to the present. Hetty was shaking her gently. "Heads up. Here comes your mom."

"We wondered where you two had disappeared to," Thea said, gentle reproach in her tone. "Do you want to hike down to the foot of the falls with us? Everyone's going, even Gran."

Annie grabbed the first excuse that occurred to her. Her calves had been sore this morning, a reminder that she'd hiked four miles yesterday. "I don't think so, Mom. I'm not in the best of shape. I'll just sit here and enjoy the view. "

Her mother's mouth twitched. To Annie's relief, she didn't respond with the obvious remark about beneficial exercise. Instead she looked to Hetty.

"We travel agents only climb cliffs if we get paid to do it, Aunt Thea. I'll keep Annie company." A look of understanding passed between them.

Annie ignored it. Let them have their little conspiracy. She just wished Hetty would go with the hikers. Even her nonjudgmental company was more than she wanted this afternoon. She should have insisted on staying back at the compound.

As if Gran would have allowed that. Damn it, I'm a grown woman. Why can't I stand up to my grandmother?

The family streamed by them, even Serhilda, who wore a pair of borrowed sneakers and a billed cap with a John Deere logo on it. Somehow they made her look younger, less sophisticated. They didn't make her look happy about the hike, but Annie assumed that like herself, Serhilda had no choice.

As if reading her mind, Hetty said, "Want to bet she wishes she was back in L.A.? Poor kid."

"How old is she, do you suppose?" Ever since Hetty had told her who Serhilda was, she'd been dying to learn more about her. Usually secrets didn't last long at family gatherings, so she'd fully expected to hear more than she really wanted to know about Serhilda and Aunt Frances on the way up here. Had she slept through all the good stuff?

"Beats me. I thought somewhere around your age at first sight. After this morning, I'm thinking she's closer to Kristi's age—twenty or so." Leaning back, Hetty closed her eyes. "My turn for a nap."

"Oh, no you don't. I want to know more about this new cousin of ours. How come we never heard of her?"

"Maybe because no one knew. Your folks didn't even know she was Frances' daughter 'til I told them. Yesterday Ward was as surprised as we were. Maybe Frances never told Gran about her."

"Oh, right. That's pretty far-fetched."

"Everything I've ever heard about Frances is far-fetched." With a gaping yawn, Hetty pulled her hat low. "Maybe Joss isn't so bad after all. At least she claims me."

For several minutes Annie watched a hawk circle lazily above the falls. Her mind drifted, then fastened on something Hetty had said. She elbowed her cousin. "You're a terrible liar, you know. What about that week long pack trip you went on last summer?"

Hetty grinned. "That was different. I went with Simon, and that made up for all the exertion."

"Which one was Simon? The lawyer or the stevedore?"

"Simon is a lawyer. He started talking about marriage and a cottage in the suburbs, so I gave him his walking papers. I've never dated a stevedore. Vern was a construction worker. A real hunk."

"So when did you start seeing what's-his-name? The guy who's coming on Thursday."

"Frank? Oh, he's been around since May."

"Het, what's your problem with marriage? Don't you ever want children?"

Hetty stared at the falls and did not answer for a long time.

They hadn't seen much of each other the past few years, but growing up they'd been close. Closer than most sisters. Once upon a time, they'd shared dreams of the future, and then life had interfered. Neither had followed the path they'd so confidently planned, back when they were in their teens.

Now Hetty had a brittleness to her, in spite of the warmth Annie knew was at her core. She wondered what had caused it, but wouldn't ask. Still, she hated seeing that uncharacteristic, lost expression on her cousin's face. She took Hetty's hand and gave it a quick squeeze.

"Don't answer if you don't want to. It's none of my business. Besides, I'm the last person who should be giving advice about marriage or motherhood."

"It's nobody's business but mine," Hetty said, the cheerful breeziness back in her voice. Her expression softened into vulnerability. "Yes, I do want kids. I don't know if I'll ever have them, though. I'm not at all sure I'd be a good mother. The way I live is no kind of an environment to bring a kid into."

Remembering the times Hetty had been dumped on her parents while Aunt Joss had another 'nervous breakdown', Annie had to agree that her cousin's childhood had not been easy. Now she knew that Aunt Joss had been drying out during her absences, not recovering her mental health." I don't think you should let that stop you. You're not your mother. I've never known anyone as sane as you"

"I wasn't talking about Joss's drinking. I'm a travel agent, remember. I travel a lot."

"You're the boss. Surely you could let others do the traveling."

"Not really, at least not all the time. I can't sell trips to places I've never been."

"What you're really saying—at least what I hear you saying— is that you wouldn't give up your exciting, glamorous job for a family. Maybe you don't want children as badly as you say you do."

"Look, Annie, I don't want to talk about it, okay? Right now I'm not ready to make any commitments. Leave it at that."

"Sure. Whatever you say." Was Hetty subject to the same self-doubts and insecurities as she was? No, not breezy, self-confident Hetty.

The rest of their party came straggling back up the path by and by. All the little kids were bouncing, but Serhilda and some of the adults were puffing. Annie and Hetty fell in beside their grandmother, unobtrusively giving her support over the boulders in the path to the parking area.

"The trail was steeper than I expected," Gran admitted when they had opened the sliding door of Eric's minivan and seated her in the doorway. "Or I'm not as young as I once was." She nodded her thanks for the cup of lemonade Louisa handed her.

"You're ageless, Gran," Louisa commented. "I think you could out-hike me any day of the week."

"I doubt it. I don't go out and scrabble around the desert every weekend like you and Ben do. Where is he, by the way?"

"Here he comes," Annie said. She had to laugh at the sight of her uncle, his pockets bulging, his bald head glowing red in the filtered light through the pines, and his eyes looking somewhere far away from the path under his feet. When his foot struck a rock and sent it tumbling off the path, Annie said, "It's a wonder he doesn't break a leg. Doesn't he ever watch where he's walking, Aunt Louisa?"

"Of course. It just looks like he's somewhere else. Believe me, he never misses so much as a pebble in the path." Louisa tucked the plastic cups they had drunk from back into the wicker basket. "Look at him, bringing back another fifty pounds of rocks." She sighed, but it was a loving sigh. Annie felt a frisson of envy at their happy marriage.

The sun was hot, even here, halfway to the bottom of the canyon, and the cicadas were buzzing. Annie felt a great need to find a shady spot and take a nap. Instead, leaning mindlessly against the side of the minivan, she half listened to the conversation among her relatives as they drained the gallon container of lemonade. Finally Gran asked, "Did you see where the children went, Annie?"

She had not, but her father had. "They're all up at the Lodge, probably driving the docents crazy. Are we ready to go?" At their nodding assents, he whistled shrilly.

Children seemed to burst from everywhere. Ben's three and Adam and Jeremy came running from behind the Lodge. Kristi strolled out from the other side, accompanied by Owen. Her little sister had definitely made a conquest, although Kristi treated Owen no different from the younger boys. Poor Owen. And poor CeCe, who was so clearly smitten with him. Young love... Too bad its promises were so seldom realized.

The lower falls were not nearly as spectacular, even though they were rockier and the lip was more irregular. Annie joined the others in posing for photos at the viewpoint, but couldn't share their high spirits. She wanted to be somewhere else. Anywhere else, preferably alone, silent.

Silent. Like this morning beside the river, watching Clay's graceful moves. In his company all her troubles seemed to retreat. She was looking forward to tomorrow. How long had it been since she'd been this excited about anything?

Too long.

"You rode along here yesterday. No way!"

"Yes, way. It's only about thirty miles to Ashland. And it's mostly downhill." She shrugged, like it wasn't a big deal. "It was really early, so there wasn't much traffic."

Owen stared at CeCe. She was such a little bit of a thing, not even up to his shoulder. She had great legs, though. Sleek with muscle, but not bulked up or anything. But still... Thirty miles on a bike?

"So how'd you get back? We stopped in Ashland on the way up. There's a big hill just outside of town. You're not gonna tell me you came that way."

"Okay, I won't." Her elbow nudged him in the ribs. "I flew. Is that easier to believe?"

"Jeez, CeCe, I'm serious. Who brought you back?" Nothing was going to convince him she'd been able to ride a bike up that big hill.

Her eyes narrowed and she just looked at him like she was trying to figure out where to hit him.

They turned into the parking lot at the Lower Falls just then, and the resulting confusion almost made him forget how pissed he was that she was yanking his chain. The old guy with the pockets full of rocks was saying something about the Yellowstone Caldera. It was kind of interesting, so he hung around and listened.

CeCe and Char hung with Hetty and the sad one—Annie.

Fine with him.

THEY GOT BACK TO THE RANCH ABOUT FOUR. TONIGHT WAS AUNT Louisa and Uncle Ben's turn to cook, but Annie had volunteered to lend a hand, since she wasn't assigned to any particular night. She was shredding cabbage for coleslaw when her mother came into the kitchen.

"Did you bring your boots?" Thea said.

"Just my hikers. Why?"

"Charlie just called. His morning riders cancelled, so he can take us out tomorrow."

"I have other plans," she said, with some regret. She had not been on a horse since before her marriage to Walter and had looked forward to riding this week. Unfortunately no one had thought to ask Charlie to reserve time for the family. He'd been booked solid, morning, afternoon, and evening, for the entire week.

"We're going up on the ridge. Charlie says it's lovely up there this year." Her mother looked genuinely disappointed.

I do want to ride. She used to spend most of her time at the stables when they'd come here during her childhood. But she

107

would miss seeing Clay, would miss her fly fishing lesson. *I hate choices.*

If she left him a message, perhaps he would tell her where he would be in the afternoon. She hoped so. She really had been looking forward to seeing him tomorrow. "Okay. But I'll have to let my...my friend know I can't—" She shut her mouth just in time. If her grandmother found out she was meeting a man.

"I'm glad to hear you're getting out, Annie. It's about time you started making new friends."

Gran's words struck Annie as being almost automatic, sort of like an old-fashioned record with the needle stuck. She looked at her mother, who simply shook her head, as if in sympathy.

"He *is* just a friend," she told herself as she pulled into the Visitor Center parking lot later, an explanatory note to Clay tucked in her pocket. *I wish he'd told me where he was staying. But I didn't tell him, either.*

Walter had called friend only those who could help him advance in his career. She had lost touch with many of her childhood friends as a result. Since she'd moved to Boise, she'd kept to herself, not particularly interested in socializing with co-workers, not being neighborly, even though the young couple next door had invited her over for a barbecue just a few weeks ago.

Maybe that's part of my problem. Maybe I do need to get out more, like Gran says. Make new friends.

As she was looking for an open space on the crowded message board, she saw her name on a folded note. It was from Clay:

> Annie:
>
> No one, it seems, rents waders, and I haven't been able to find anyone who has your size to lend me. Don't despair, though, because I've got an idea or two. I'll see you at the Visitor Center tomorrow about six and tell you what I've found

out. We'll get you in the river yet. Take care.

It was signed with his initials. Annie sighed. She tucked it into her pocket and replaced it with her note to him. She had really wanted to fish tomorrow, but the trail ride was just too tempting to pass up. She hoped he would understand.

Chapter Nine

A TRAIL LED FROM THE COMPOUND OUT INTO THE WOODS. IT meandered through the recovering forest and into a fenced-off area that hadn't had cattle on it since the beetle-killed trees had been cleared three years ago. About a mile out, it ended on a small knoll, where a spectacular view of the Tetons was to be had. Hetty perched herself on a rock and patted the space beside her.

Her cousin Evan shook his head. "I've been sitting too much since I got here." He stretched and bent, twisted and stretched again. "So why'd you drag me way out here to talk? Deep, dark secrets?"

"I need your advice, and I wanted to get away for a while. Ordinarily I'd have asked Annie, but she's too wrapped up in her own problems. When I told her I'd invited my latest boyfriend up here, she got a little bitchy."

"Maybe she wishes she'd thought to do the same. I sure do."

"You're still seeing Richard? I thought the two of you decided it wouldn't work long-distance."

He grimaced. "It wouldn't. He resented it when I applied to Medic Corps, and matters went downhill from there. There's no one in my life right, now. I just meant I wish there was someone and I'd brought him."

"Your folks wouldn't have minded, but what about Gran?"

"When I got the email from her inviting me, she made it clear that I was welcome to bring Richard. I hadn't told her we'd split." The glance he threw her way was questioning. "Didn't she say the same to you?"

"Of course, but you know Gran. She's still trying to reform my folks. 'Joss and John need to realize this is the Twenty-first century. The trouble with them is they've forgotten that cohabitation without marriage is nothing new. It's just something they never had the courage to do.'" Hetty gave a mocking chuckle. "Can you imagine my parents ever committing such a social gaffe?"

Evan's laugh was genuine. "Honestly? No, I can't. It's hard to believe Uncle John and Dad are brothers."

"It's Joss's influence. She's the soul of rectitude. When she's sober."

His hand on her shoulder was comforting, his silence soothing. Hetty let herself indulge in a moment's self-pity before she said, "My parents are going to go ballistic about Frank. I almost wish I hadn't invited him."

"'I could create a distraction." He got to his feet and faced her. "Hey, listen up, everyone. I'm gay." As if responding to applause, he waved and bowed.

"Doesn't everyone know?"

"I'm pretty sure Eric doesn't. Even if he suspects, he'd deny it to his dying breath. And if Jennifer knew, well, can't you just imagine her reaction?"

"I see your point." Hetty mentally went down the list of family members. "I don't think my parents know either.

"Do you really want Eric to find out? Evan, he's your brother. Don't build a wall between you." Hetty pulled him down beside

112

her. "How did he come to be such a narrow-minded little prig? When you consider how liberal your parents are..."

"That may be part of it," Evan said. "Somewhere I read that each generation has to rebel against its parents' values. I think Eric's conservative streak was always there, but when he met Jennifer, he got way worse. Dad won't even talk politics or religion with him. He says it's the only way to keep peace in the family."

"Well, you need to do the same. Besides, I have a feeling there's going to be a blow-up before the week's out, the way Jennifer resents anyone else telling her kids what to do."

"Count on it. She's really touchy about them being influenced by others. I'll bet she chooses the kids they play with." He stood again, and pulled her to her feet. "For what it's worth, I think it's great that you've found someone you really care about."

"What makes you think that?"

"You've never brought anyone home before." Slinging one arm around her, he bumped her with his hip. "So tell me more about this Frank. Is he hot?"

"Sizzling," she said with a laugh. "And straight."

"Just my luck."

LONG AFTER DARKNESS ENVELOPED THE REST OF THE CAMPGROUND, Clay sat in a sphere of fading light, watching yellow flames consume the last log. *What the hell is wrong with me? It's not like tomorrow could be the end of the world.* He rammed a stick into the glowing coals. A cloud of sparks exploded upwards, and then quickly faded.

But it could be. If we can't agree...

Why wouldn't they? Abe wanted to sell. He wanted to buy.

The money's right, the location's right. None of the other places I looked at were good fits. This one is.

He pictured the shabby little cabins, saw them in his imagination as they could be. Still rustic, but comfortable, with peeled-log furniture softened with fat, squashy cushions covered in warm colors of denim or canvas. Efficiency kitchens, roomy bathrooms with tubs long enough for a tired fisherman to soak away the chill of the river. Shed-roofed front porches complete with swings and a couple of brightly painted Adirondack chairs.

The kind of place to make people want to stay a little longer. To relax, kick back, forget all the stress and strain they were trying to escape.

The vision in the campfire changed from a comfortable room to a sad face, framed by silky brown hair, dominated by wide, haunted eyes. Fragments of sentences sounded in his mind, spoken in a slightly husky voice. The words were unimportant. It was the timbre of her voice that got to him, making him think of silken sheets, romantic music, and sleek, warm skin under his hands.

"Shit!" He threw the stick into the fire, scattering coals outside the cement firepit. "Shit!" he said again, as he danced around, kicking them back in. A sharp pain in one toe reminded him that kicking live coals while wearing river sandals was beyond stupid. He kicked one last glowing fragment and looked around carefully for more. Although the ground surrounding the firepit was bare, he'd be stupid to take a chance. The fire danger was only moderate, but never completely went away in the summer.

Clay's last relationship had ended by mutual consent and without rancor nearly a year ago. Since then he'd been too busy planning and preparing for his new life that he hadn't had time for the dating scene. And even if he had, what sense would there have been in getting involved with someone, knowing he would soon be going away for good?

Still, it would be nice to have someone to share his excitement with. Someone who would say to him, "Well done." Someone with whom he could share his visions of a bright, successful, happy future.

Oh, God, now I'm getting maudlin. Disgusted with his descent into sappy sentimentality, he tossed the dregs of his coffee, long since grown cold, into the fire. After the eruption of steam had died down, he picked up the poker and stirred the remaining coals. Only a few faint glows remained. A couple of cups of water extinguished those.

His future was bright and filled with possibilities, he told himself, once he was lying in bed. So he would live, for a while at least, a solitary life. That was probably a good thing, because he wouldn't have time or energy to engage in any sort of mating ritual.

Later, he promised. *Starting tomorrow, I've a business to build, a future to shape.*

THE NIGHTLY BRIDGE GAME BEGAN RIGHT AFTER DINNER. ANNIE again refused to join, saying she couldn't give it the concentration it deserved.

After she helped clean up the kitchen, she escaped to the front steps with her binoculars. The sandhill cranes were grazing in the nearest pasture. Annie watched them until the deepening dusk drove her inside, to sit in a corner, as far away from the Bridge game as she could get, with a jigsaw puzzle, one that showed an angler pulling a fish from a mountain stream.

A mistake, because she should have known that no one would be able to resist helping. First Uncle Ward came by and looked over her shoulder as she searched for edge pieces.

"You picked an easy one," he said, after a while.

She didn't answer him until she'd got the upper right corner and a few inches of the right side locked together. "It was the best of the bunch. Some of the ones in the cupboard were there the last time I was here."

His arm stretched across and he picked up an upper edge piece and fit it to what she'd just assembled. "There, I've done my share."

Although he stood watching for several minutes longer, he said nothing more. Annie had most of the fish assembled, was concentrating on finding its tail, when two of the middle boys came to watch—Tommy and Norman, she thought were their names. The younger one bumped the table and some of the puzzle pieces fell to the floor.

"Now look what you did, you dork," Tommy said. "Don't worry, Aunt Annie. I'll pick 'em up." He crawled under the table.

Norman came closer. "Whatcha doin'?"

Although she knew he was Eric and Jennifer's eldest, she'd not paid much attention to him. "Putting together a jigsaw puzzle. Would you like to help?"

"I don't know how." His voice was close to a whine. "It's dumb, anyhow."

"Naw, you're the dumb one," Tommy said, dumping half a dozen pieces on the table. "Everybody knows what a jigsaw puzzle is. Everybody but you, dummy."

The whine became a shriek. "I'm not a dummy!" Norman struck out with both hands. "I'm not. You're the dummy. Dummy!" His skinny arms were flailing, doing little damage, but only because Tommy was deflecting most of Norman's blows. Not all, though, for blood was streaming from his nose.

Annie leapt to her feet as Tommy shoved Norman. She heard the sharp click of teeth. "Stop it! Right now!"

Before she could grab either boy, Jennifer was there, her arms around her son. "You little savage. If you've hurt Norman—"

"He hit me first." Tommy swiped a hand across his upper lip, smearing blood along his cheek.

"He called me a dummy."

"You're both to blame," Annie told them. "I don't see why—"

"I heard, you little savage." She turned to Annie. "I heard it all. My son asked a perfectly innocent question, and that little monster made fun of him. He needs a keeper. I don't know why his father couldn't be here to take care of him. I'd never let *my* child—"

"Oh, for heaven's sake, Jennifer," Aunt Louisa said from behind Annie. "The boys were both acting like kids. It's no big deal."

Since she agreed, Annie kept her mouth shut. The last thing she wanted to do was get into a fight with Jennifer. Besides, how could she know what was normal behavior for boys their ages? Her son would never...

"I disagree, Mother. Norman knows he's not to call names or get into fights with the other children. We do expect him to defend himself, however. Tommy, I believe you owe Norman an apology."

"He hit me first," Tommy insisted, with another swipe at his nose. It had stopped bleeding now, but he looked a mess, with his Spiderman t-shirt covered with red splotches.

Aunt Louisa shook her head. "There's no need for either one of them to apologize. You're attaching too much importance to a kids' spat, Jennifer. The less said, the better. Send the boys to bed and let that be the end of it."

"But—"

"Jennifer, you're making a mountain out of a molehill. Just calm down." Aunt Louisa clapped her hands. "It's nine o'clock. Bedtime for all middles."

Since that category included only Angela, Norman and Tommy, the problem seemed solved. It also meant that Jennifer would be going to the Blue House with them, because she refused to trust her children's welfare to anyone else—never mind that Eric was already there with Joey and Barty.

"Somebody had better go over and let Elaine know what happened. I can just hear Angela's version, can't you?"

Annie raised one eyebrow. So Aunt Louisa wasn't all that fond of her daughter-in-law. Interesting. And a little sad. "I'll go. Do you suppose it will be okay if I leave this here?"

"Sure, if you don't mind that the rest of us will all have to see how much we can add to it."

"If she does, she's living in a dream world," Gran said, as she approached. "Jigsaw puzzles are like solitaire—you have to expect kibitzers when you're doing one. Louisa, do you want me to butt in?"

"I'd like to say yes, but no. I'll have a talk with Jennifer tomorrow, when she's calmed down. She's just very protective."

"Balderdash! She's just afraid her children might learn to be less than perfect by associating with the rest."

A chuckle. "Yes, that too. But she's my problem. I'll deal." She seated herself next to Gran and poked at the loose pieces. "Tomorrow."

Gran sat down beside her. "Annie, why don't you take some of the cake with you to the Pink House? I think there's a fortune telling session going on over there."

So that was where everyone had disappeared to. "Sure. All of it?"

"Leave a few pieces. Enough for all who are here."

"Okay." There wasn't any hurry. Her nerves still jangled after the boys' fight. That and Jennifer's belligerent interference. What she needed was some time alone.

She walked past the Big House and seated herself on the big peeled log that lay where the lawn began its slope down to the bunkhouses. She was far enough from the cookshack that only a murmur of conversation reached her through the open windows. Occasionally a loud comment from the Pink House broke the silence, tickling her curiosity. When she was in a good mood, Aunt Joss didn't mind telling fortunes with an audience, and the family wasn't afraid to offer opinions on those fortunes.

Despite the cicada's song, and the far-off, melancholy howl of a coyote, solitude brought her no peace, nor was she able to find familiar refuge in her grief. *Wallow, you mean*, she heard Gran say. The ache in her heart was still there, but faint, like the dying memory of something once experienced but nearly forgotten. She looked up at the moon, trying to see Calvin's chubby face smiling down at her, as she had so many times before. All she saw was the mottling of lunar seas and mountains.

"Maybe," she whispered into the moonlit silence, "just maybe I'm healing. And doesn't it feel good?" She stood in the moonlight, trying to hold to this moment of peace, but it slipped away as guilt returned.

"It does. But do I deserve to feel better?" Annie asked the night. She felt less burdened tonight, though, as if a heavy load had been lifted from her shoulders.

She picked up the cake pan and walked down the slope to the Pink House.

The sofa and chairs in the living room were all full. Half a dozen people were sitting around the table in the dining room. Aunt Joss and Kristi were facing each other across it, fortune teller and hopeful sucker. Annie stood by the door, half listening to Joss's words, trying to decide if she wanted to go to bed this early.

"I see your wish, Kristi, within a two," Joss said, after examining the cards. "That's two days, two weeks, maybe even as long two months. And good news. Not much else. A pretty mundane fortune." She reached for the glass and took a long swallow.

"That's all I want, Aunt Joss. I don't have any craving for drama or excitement." She stood up, motioned. "It's your turn, Elaine."

They traded places. Annie decided to stay and listen, even though she knew she should go to her room.

"I hope my fortune will be a good one, Aunt Joss," Elaine said as she picked up the cards. "Tell me I'm going to have lots of money, travel to exotic places, and do exciting things."

"Tell her if she's going to have a boy or a girl," Stew said, with a laugh. "She's determined it will be twins this time."

Everyone laughed.

Everyone but Annie, who pressed her hands to her belly. Would she ever have another child? And would it matter? No one could replace Calvin in her heart.

She didn't hear a thing Aunt Joss told Elaine, but she must have said something good, from the smile on Elaine's face as she went to sit beside Stewart on the sofa.

Annie tried to slip past the group and go to bed, but Hetty stopped her. "Your turn."

Short of forcibly pulling free of Hetty's restraining hand, she was stuck for a while. "Oh, no, I don't think..." but Annie's soft protest was lost in the chorus telling her that, since she had listened to other fortunes, she must let them all hear hers. Well, at least Gran was not here, for if she had been, she would have surely found something in the fortune that said Annie was going to find a wonderful man and live happily ever after. Or something like that.

She took the deck of cards and, following her aunt's instructions, made a silent wish for a relief from pain. She cut them into three piles. Joss took the bottom card from each stack, put it aside, and then went through them one by one, occasionally removing other cards.

"Again." Joss shuffled again and handed the deck back to Annie. "Same thing again. And keep thinking of your wish." Annie complied, thinking that to be free of sorrow was the only wish she could have. She was tired of guilt, tired of sorrow, tired of dreading each new, unpromising day that dawned.

Joss had her cut a third time. By this time, at least half the deck was in the stack of discards at her aunt's elbow. Setting what was left of the deck aside, Joss sorted the discards into six piles.

Turning the first over, Joss looked at the five cards. "This is strange. I see a major change in your house, but it looks as if it has already happened." She looked up at Annie. "I think it refers to your divorce, Annie, because this card," she tapped one, "indicates the past, not the future. You moved to Boise when you left Walter, didn't you?"

Annie nodded. Something in her throat prevented her speaking. She had divorced Walter, with sorrow, but no regret about ending her marriage. Why did she still feel as if she had failed as a wife?

Joss turned over the second pile. "I see a great sorrow. Something devastating."

Annie tensed. She could not face another loss. Not now.

"But again, it looks as if it has already happened." A sympathetic smile. "Don't look so stricken, Annie. It really does, like the change, seem to be in your past. But here. Look here. There's another change coming that will, in some way, compensate. It may be a new job that keeps you so occupied that you don't have time to brood..." Another quick glance, a fleeting smile. "Or something else that will take your mind and heart off your sorrow."

Joss took up the third pile, fanned them out, frowned. "I don't see your wish here."

"I didn't think you would," Annie said softly, but disappointed in spite of her lack of expectations.

"I do see good fortune in connection with your wish." She tossed the cards aside, reached for the fourth pile. "Oh, my, this is interesting. I don't see anything major, but I see a lot of little changes, almost certainly for the better, and even more good luck that will occur within a three. No surprises here, I'm afraid."

"I've been thinking of having my hair cut," Annie said in a dry tone, not wanting to believe Aunt Joss. But her fortunes so often, so uncannily, came true.

"Concentrate," Kristi said, squeezing her shoulder. "Think about your wish."

Joss turned the fifth pile over. "Now, this is more like it!" She smiled broadly at Annie. "Here, a light man is going to bring about a change for the better that you haven't any expectation of. A great change. And it will make you very happy!"

"Have you been holding out on us?" her sister stage-whispered in her ear. "Is there a man in your life?"

Annie shook her head, now concentrating fully on Joss' words.

"Well! Here's more changes. And your wish! Something wonderful will happen to you, Annie, within a three—days or weeks, I think. It doesn't look as if it will be a long time, anyway." She tapped the eight of hearts. "And this is the best luck card in the deck. You're going to have things your way for a while, my dear, and you'll love it." She gathered the cards together, then spread them out on the table, face up. A quick glance at Annie and she picked up the queen of clubs.

"Shuffle again, and pick out five cards, without looking at them."

Annie did so.

Using the queen as a center, Joss wove the five cards around it so that they held together, one card behind the queen and at right angles to it, the others forming a square around them. She expertly flipped them face up and examined them closely. Annie remembered, from previous fortunes, that this construction was called a bed. She was represented by the queen of clubs.

"There, I said the bad luck was in the past." Joss tapped the seven of spades, mostly hidden behind the queen. "Your sorrow is behind you."

Don't I wish.

Joss was silent for a long time, studying the cards. No one else spoke either. Suspense crackled like electricity in the room. Finally Joss spoke.

"It's not common for the same important cards that were in the piles to show up in the bed, Annie. But here are two of them. Here's the light man—he's young, I think, about your age—again, linked with the best luck card in the deck." She pointed to two small clubs. "And here's more change. Your life looks as if it's going to be wonderful and exciting, starting almost immediately. I think you'll like it." She gathered the cards together and shuffled them.

Annie rose, and as if at a signal, so did everyone else. Some drifted to the bathrooms, a few went to the kitchen to get beers or sodas. Joss drained her glass and took it to the kitchen, where she refilled it from a bottle wrapped in a brown paper bag. *Just like a wino*, Annie thought, then was ashamed of herself. It was none of her business what her aunt did.

When everyone had reclaimed chairs and sofas, Hetty pushed Evan forward. Annie didn't stay to hear his fortune, but headed for the bathroom, the only place in the house she could be assured of privacy. She stared in the mirror, making faces, until the lump in her throat dissolved and the tears stopped stinging. When she felt in control again, she emerged, just in time to hear Joss say, "I see a long journey here, and a new adventure. Something involving an older man, light-haired, I think." She paused. "hmmm. This doesn't look like anything involved with your work, Evan. It's more personal. As if...no, that's not possible." Quickly she spread the cards across the table.

Annie was directly across the table from Joss, so she saw the color drain from her aunt's face as she held her hands just above them. Slowly her right hand lowered and one finger lightly touched the King of Diamonds, the same red king representing a man who would be involved in Evan's adventure.

Joss looked across at Evan. Her mouth twisted in an ugly grimace as she pushed the cards away with such force that they flew off the table's edge. "You're queer, aren't you? You're a filthy homosexual."

Her chair fell backwards as she leapt to her feet.

No one moved as Joss stormed to the door and out into the night.

The silence lengthened, until Hetty draped her arms over Evan's shoulders. "I thought I told you not to create a diversion, you dope. But I love you for it."

Chapter Ten

Tuesday

CLAY PULLED UP IN FRONT OF ABE'S FLY SHOP JUST AFTER NINE. His was the only vehicle in the graveled parking area. It wasn't hard to see why. The windows were flyspecked and dusty, so that the interior appeared dark and deserted. The board-and-batten siding probably had been stained at one time, but now it was the soft gray of old, weathered wood. A couple of shiny patches on the roof appeared to be flattened tin cans used as patches.

I must be crazy. Modernizing this will be a monumental task.

He sat for a moment, mentally reviewing his research. Abe owned the shop and the seven cabins, along with eighteen acres of riverfront land, free and clear. He was close to eighty. No one seemed to be sure of his exact age. People who knew his reputation returned to stay in the cabins year after year, despite their shabby condition.

Abe was looking for a buyer, but he was being particular. "I don't have to sell out," he'd told Clay in their one telephone conversation, "so I can pick and choose who comes in here after me."

Clay still wasn't completely sure he wanted to be picked, but he couldn't think of a place he'd rather be than here on the Henry's Fork. He grabbed his attaché case and stepped out of the pickup, remembering the excitement he used to feel on Christmas morning, just before he climbed out of bed.

Since Abe had always seemed older than dirt, he hadn't changed much since Clay had been here two years ago. He moved a bit slower, though, and thought a little longer before speaking. He still got around just fine, and insisted on taking Clay along the property boundary, including the six hundred-odd feet of riverbank. They looked into the single vacant cabin. "Feller's comin' in tonight, late," Abe said. "He flies in to Salt Lake from back East somewhere. I never can recall where. Stays a week, just like clockwork, every year since '68."

"You said you rent the cabins out to skiers in the winter. Have any problems with frozen pipes?"

"Naw. I wrap 'em up good, keep a little trickle runnin' when the cabin's empty. Worst problem is sometimes I get folks in here who want to party. They're likely to leave a mess."

Clay pulled the door closed behind himself. "All the cabins are the same size? Two beds and a kitchen?"

"Got one with two rooms. It'll sleep six, if they're real friendly. Here, c'mon in and I'll show you my setup. I don't do much tyin' any more. Eyes aren't what they used to be. But you're a young feller. You'll build the business back up right quick."

A prickle of excitement swept up Clay's arms and across his shoulders. *Does that mean he's willing to sell to me?* "I haven't a hope to do as well as you with the flies, but for the rest, I'd like to add some more cabins in time. It seems to me that two or three more for the family trade might be a good thing." He turned and looked back across the grassy area between the cabins, back toward the river. "What a grand place."

Abe opened the back door of the main building. As they entered, Clay said, "Did I tell you I've still got one of your flies my grandfather bought back in 1961?"

"Well, that does tickle me. A hopper, I'll bet." Abe chuckled. Gesturing at the tidy workbench, with its well-organized tools, he said, "You'll get better, when you're doin' it all the time. Best thing you can do is like I did. Come up with a special fly and convince people it's a sure-fire fish catcher."

"I've got a couple I'm working on. I haven't had much time to try them out yet."

"Plenty of time, when you're livin' here. I used to open at noon, just so I could be on the river all morning." He shook his head, frowning. "I haven't got the balance to wade the river anymore, and it just ain't the same, fishing from the bank.

"Now then, young feller, how soon you want to settle up on this deal?"

Clay could only stare. Had he heard right?

"Close your mouth, boy. You'll catch flies."

"Yeah. Sorry. I mean... Oh, hell, Abe. I never thought you'd agree so fast."

"You already made me an offer that's fair. Only reason I didn't take it right off was that I wanted to see how you took to the place. And you did fine. Didn't turn up your nose at the way it's so run-down. Didn't talk about how you were goin' to modernize it. Best of all, you look at the place and see how pretty it is. That matters to me.

"I'd like you to move in here soon as we get all the paperwork done. You can park your rig alongside the shop until I get myself moved out." He held out his hand. "It's all yours, boy. Take good care of it."

Clay took the old man's hand in a firm clasp. He swallowed, unable to answer immediately.

ONCE AGAIN ANNIE CREPT OUT OF THE HOUSE WHILE EVERYONE else slept. This time she didn't so much want to escape as to watch the sunrise. Alone. There was something soothing...healing about sharing the world's awakening.

A few stars still twinkled in the western sky when she stepped outside, shivering in the chill predawn air. She looked to the east, where a pale glow cast the Tetons into ragged silhouette. From the surrounding woods came the call of a bird, then another, until gradually she was surrounded by a chorus of chirps, squawks and trills.

She walked into the Grove, where the dawning light turned tree trunks into ghostly figures, bushes into faery shapes. Emerging on the other side, she turned and followed the road back past the two houses and into the compact stand of pines beside the Guest House, where she climbed onto an enormous boulder and wrapped her arms around her legs.

The rim of the sun emerged and turned the peaks to gold. Long, dusty streamers of light gilded the forests and woke their denizens. From far off came the bugle of an elk, and from above the shrill keen of a hunting hawk.

I feel good. Alive. Happy?

Yes, she did. She felt happy, for this moment, in this place.

Oh, I hope it lasts.

THE WHOLE BUNK SHOOK. SERHILDA, WHO HADN'T SLEPT SOUNDLY all night long, opened one eye just enough to see pale lines of light around the blinds. Morning, then, but nowhere near time for breakfast. She wrapped the pillow around her head and tried to ignore the jiggling. Maybe she could pretend somebody was rocking her to sleep.

It almost worked, until something thumped onto the floor and Angela started screaming.

She lifted the pillow just as the door flew open.

"What on earth?"

Serhilda barely heard Elaine over the siren-loud screaming. She started to rebury herself under the pillow, but then curiosity got the best of her. Raising on her elbow, she peered over the edge of the bed.

Angela was sprawled on the floor, legs stiffly spread, arms wide and hands knitted into tight fists. Her eyes were squinched shut but her mouth was wide open. *How does she do that, without taking a breath?*

Elaine knelt beside Angela and tentatively laid a hand on her chest. The brat nearly exploded, kicking and swinging her arms. One fist got Elaine on the chin, hard enough that Serhilda heard teeth click.

"That's enough," Elaine said, grabbing the girl's shoulders and shaking her. "If you can fight like that, you're not hurt." It was a good thing her arms were longer than the brat's, or she might have gotten scratched, because Angela's arms were still flailing, her hands now clawed.

"Need some help?" Serhilda wouldn't mind holding the brat down. Wouldn't mind tying her up and tossing her off a cliff, either.

"I've got her," Elaine said. "What happened?"

"She fell out of bed, I think. I was asleep until I heard her hit the floor."

"Angela! Stop that screaming. Tell me where you hurt."

Kristi came in behind Elaine. "Here, let me." She reached over Elaine's shoulder and dumped the contents of a sports bottle in Angela's face.

The screaming stopped immediately. Angela sputtered and squeaked, then opened her mouth again.

"Don't you dare," Elaine warned.

"I'll get a refill," Kristi said, and disappeared.

The brat stuck her lip out and frowned. "I fell out of bed," she said, in a quavery little voice. "It hurt."

"And just how did you get over the rail?"

Last night, when Elaine had made Angela move into the top bunk so Serhilda could have the bottom one, Angela had whined that she was scared. Elaine's husband, Stewart, had gotten a board from somewhere and fixed it along the outside edge of the bunk. There was no way Angela could have just rolled out of bed.

"I just did. And I fell," Angela whined. "I want my mother."

Sounding disgusted, Elaine said, "Get dressed. I'll take you to her."

Serhilda stayed in her bunk. Angela sniffled and made little sobbing sounds while she dressed. The little girls' bunk was empty, which meant that Kristi had probably taken them out to the kitchen so their giggles wouldn't wake her and the brat.

Kristi was something else. Serhilda wasn't sure she liked her, but she sure didn't hate her as much as she did some of the others. Or like her as well as she did Hetty, who was way cool.

"DID YOU KNOW ABOUT EVAN?"

Cecile set her cup down with a sigh. She'd come out here onto the front porch of the Big House to drink her coffee in peace. Even though there were no young people sleeping here, there was still far too much confusion in the kitchen of a morning. *I've been living alone too long.* Once she would have thrived on the morning chaos of her family all together again.

"That he finally got his overseas assignment? Yes, I knew that. Isn't it wonderful?"

"Cecile, he's a queer. You've got to send him away. All these children—"

"Joss, he is my nephew, and as dear to me as your Hetty. Why on earth would I send him away?"

For a moment Joss's expression went from determined to confused, then it set again into the hard lines of a woman who demanded her own way about everything. "It's not the same at all. I know Hetty isn't as respectable as she should be, but at least she is normal. Evan's not. And he's a danger to all the little boys. There's just no telling what he might do."

"That's enough! Joss, Evan is a fine young man. He's fond of his cousins and he has no unnatural feelings toward any of them. The children are probably safer from him than they are from that oldest boy of Eric's. He's a bit of a bully." As soon as she'd spoken the words, she wanted to take them back. "Please don't tell Jennifer I said that."

"But—"

"Jocelyn, I said that's enough. Evan is welcome here. If you have a problem with that, you can simply avoid him. But don't be rude or unkind to him, and don't you dare say a word to anyone else about how you feel.

"Now go away and let me enjoy the sunrise."

As Joss's footsteps receded across the porch, Cecile sighed. There was trouble coming. She could feel it in her bones.

Why on earth did I think a family reunion was a good idea?

THEY ALL LOADED INTO ASSORTED VEHICLES FOR THE SHORT TRIP TO the ranch headquarters. "Jennifer's afraid dear little Angela will get her dainty feet dusty," Hetty muttered under her breath. Waving Annie into the back seat of the Volvo, she climbed in behind her.

131

"That had all the earmarks of an unkind remark," Annie said, as she fastened her seat belt. "Did I miss something?"

"Oh, nothing much," Hetty said. "Angela fell out of bed and had a screaming fit. I'm surprised you didn't hear her."

Elaine turned around. "I told Angela last night she had to move to the top bunk. It's just plain silly for someone as tall as Serhilda to be up there. Why I'll bet she couldn't even sit upright."

"And then you took Angela to her folks," Hetty said. "You've more courage than I have. Who won?"

Elaine's smile was rueful. "I won't fight with Jennifer. Mother would kill me. I just told her we'd let Gran decide who got the lower bunk, and Jennifer couldn't argue with that."

"I'll bet she couldn't. I think she's scared of Gran," Annie said.

Tommy and Norman climbed into the back end of the Volvo. Stewart slammed the door.

"There's no seat belt," Norman whined. "Mama says I can't ride in a car without a seat belt."

"We're only goin' down to the big barn, dummy," Tommy said, with all the authority of his almost-thirteen years. "You don't need a seat belt for that."

"Do too."

"Do not!"

"That's enough, boys," Stewart said from the driver's seat. "Norman, we're not going to be driving fast and there's no traffic on this road. You'll be safe enough if you don't get rambunctious."

The argument from the back died into barely audible grumbles.

Annie hadn't been to the ranch since the first year of her marriage to Walter. She hadn't ridden a horse since then, either, and was not sure she remembered how. The dusty, musky smell of the horsebarn was familiar and welcome. A wave of nostalgia almost overcame her reluctance to make a fool of herself. When she saw the bowlegged, mustachioed wrangler, she felt almost like a kid again. "Charlie!" she exclaimed with delight.

"Hey there, Little Annie Oakley. 'Bout time you showed your face around here again."

"I'm almost ashamed to be here. You're going to think I've forgotten everything you ever taught me." For at least thirty years, Charley Jones had been teaching Blankenship kids to ride. During the summers when she had been going through her horse-crazy stage, Annie had followed him around like a little shadow. Now she wondered how she'd forgotten the man who'd enriched her childhood so much.

The children gathered around Charlie fell silent when he said, "Now, you oughta know that too much silly chitterin' makes the horses right skittish. And there ain't nothin' worse'n a skittish horse when you ain't a skilled rider."

Annie grinned at Hetty. Charlie's English was as good as theirs, but his cowboy voice was how he had charmed three generations of children.

The two little boys' eyes grew wide. "Will they buck?" Jeremy asked with a quaver.

"They could, if'n you get 'em excited," Charlie answered with a straight face. "Now, how many of you youngsters know how to put a saddle on?"

CeCe and Tommy stuck their hands into the air. After a short hesitation, so did Owen, but with less confidence.

"I'll oversee them" Uncle Ben said. "You go ahead and get the others matched up with their mounts. Owen, how much riding have you done?"

Annie didn't hear the boy's low-voiced reply because Charlie was saying, "Now Miz Thea gave me a list yesterday so I've got you grownups all matched up with your mounts. They're out in the corral."

"I hope he gave me a gentle horse," Annie whispered to Hetty. "It's been forever."

"It'll come back to you."

The horses were lined up at a hitch rail. Thea pointed to each as she read off the names. "Peter, bay gelding. His name is Socks. Kenna, you're on Sky, the blue roan. Annie, I've put you on Lady, since you've not ridden for a while."

She went on, but Annie didn't pay attention. She was too busy convincing herself that the long-legged pinto mare was friendly. *What's wrong with me? I've never been afraid of a horse in my life.* She approached Lady slowly, wishing she'd thought to bring an apple. A sugar cube. Anything to convince Lady she was a nice person.

Idiot!

With a deep breath, she took a last step and stood next to the mare. She reached out and touched a warm cheek, stroked. And fell in love as she'd done many times before, with many other horses, when Lady turned her head and butted a soft nose against her shoulder.

After they got to know each other, Annie decided she could probably saddle Lady. *If I can lift the darn thing that high.*

Lady really was as long-legged as she'd seemed. Annie couldn't see over her back, even standing on tiptoe. She managed to get the bridle on correctly. Even if her head had forgotten, her fingers slipped, adjusted, and buckled as if they'd been doing it every single day.

Leaving Lady tied to the rail, she went into the tack room, where two dozen wooden saddlehorses stuck out from one wall. A card bearing a handwritten name was taped to the wall above each one. As she approached, Tommy was struggling to pull a saddle from one of the lower ones. Annie grabbed the horn.

"Thanks, Aunt Annie. I've got it now," the boy told her, once he'd gotten hold of it with both hands. His little arms looked far too spindly to lift such a weight, but his chin was set. She watched him out the door, smiling a little at how the stirrups dragged on either side of his legs. *Calvin would have loved horses.*

Oddly enough there was no pain. Only a gentle melancholy.

She managed to get Lady's saddle off the saddlehorse, but not gracefully. As she carried it outside, the stirrups dragged just as Tommy's had. Her arms were trembling by the time she stood beside Lady. There was no way on God's green earth she was going to lift that saddle to the mare's back. She set it down, about ready to give up.

No, I'm not going to. One way or another, I'll saddle this damned horse. She put the blanket in place, looked down at the saddle. Took a deep breath.

"Lemme give you a hand." Charlie hefted the saddle and tossed it atop the blanket. "You're so skinny, it probably weighs more than you do."

She smiled her thanks. "I can get it now." she said, and hoped she was telling the truth. If Lady was one of those horses that swelled up, she might have a fight on her hands getting the cinch tight enough.

Fortunately Lady lived up to her name. When Annie gave a good tug on the saddle, it stayed in place instead of sliding to one side.

It took some doing, but eventually Annie managed to get one foot into a stirrup and to swing herself onto the horse's back. Lady stepped sideways. Without thinking, Annie pulled up on the reins and turned her to walking in a circle. Although Lady's ears still twitched occasionally, she behaved herself. Annie relaxed slightly. Perhaps she hadn't entirely forgotten.

She swung Lady into the line of nineteen riders heading east along a trail that meandered through open woods.

CLAY ASSUMED THE TWO LITTLE GIRLS IN THE SANDBOX WERE PART of

Annie's family. He wondered where their mother was. Or some adult. Surely they weren't left out here unsupervised.

"I'm looking for Annie ," he said, as they stared at him with big, round eyes. He had found her note on the message board when he'd finally gotten there. He'd stayed at Abe's all morning, and it had been time well-spent. Afterward he'd gone back to his trailer and typed in everything he could recall of what Abe had told him. Words of wisdom, like the proverbial pearls beyond price. Besides, he liked the old fellow.

"Annie," the smaller girl said. It wasn't a question.

The other child was regarding him suspiciously, her mouth tightly shut.

"That's right. Annie," he agreed with what he hoped was a reassuring smile. "Is she around anywhere?"

The littler girl babbled something, but the only word Clay caught was "horsey".

He frowned. "She went horseback riding?"

A wide grin. "Horsey."

The older girl frowned. "Go away."

"Can I help you?"

With relief, Clay turned around, to face the woman whose expression was every bit as suspicious as the older girl's. "I'm looking for Annie. I was supposed to meet her earlier, but I had a flat."

The woman came to stand between him and the two little girls. "She didn't say anything to me."

After a short pause, she said, "You'd better talk to Aunt Ce... to Mrs. Blankenship." Her gesture was vaguely in the direction of the long, low building across the lawn. "She's probably in the cookshack."

Without another word, she snatched up the smaller girl and grabbed the hand of the larger and towed them away, around the corner of the house.

Good grief. I didn't think I looked like a monster. Clay admitted he knew little about children, but he'd always gotten along with those belonging to his co-workers at the bank, on the rare occasions he'd encountered them. No one had ever treated him like a potential molester before.

He pounded on the cookshack door. There were voices inside, but no one answered his knock. He tried again. Finally he heard footsteps approaching. A tall, darkly tanned older man pushed the door open and looked down at him.

"I was looking for Annie," Clay repeated. "The little girl said she'd gone riding. Do you know when she'll be back?"

"And you are?"

He was getting damned tired of being looked at with suspicion. "Clay Knight," he said, pulling the screen open before the other fellow could hold it closed. "Annie and I had talked of doing some fishing. I came to see when she'll be available."

"Fishing? I didn't know Annie fished."

"I don't know that she does. She said she'd like to learn." *And she can damn well find someone else to teach her.* He turned to go.

"Hold on. I didn't mean to chase you away. It's just that Annie—" He extended a hand. "Never mind. I'm Ward Blankenship, Annie's uncle."

Clay hesitated, and then shook the other's hand. *Something odd here. As if they're afraid for Annie.*

Blankenship said, "They ought to be back soon. Care to wait?"

"No, I don't think so," Clay was aware of a twinge of disappointment. "Maybe I'll catch her later this afternoon."

"I'll tell her you came by." Again Ward looked Clay over. He nodded his head slightly. "She probably could meet you down at the park." His eyes sent a message that Clay was not sure he understood.

"I was going up to Box Canyon, but..." Just how much did he want to see Annie again, anyhow? About medium, he decided. Not enough to disrupt his day, but enough to adjust his plans a bit. "Look, I'll be parked at the fishing access, if she wants to find me there. Otherwise, if she wants to fish, it'll have to be Thursday. I've got business to take care of tomorrow."

As he turned to leave he remembered. "Oh, yeah. I found her some waders." He'd bought them after convincing himself that having assorted sizes of waders would be good business, once he opened *Fly By Knight*. "Tell Annie I'm looking forward to seeing her."

"Will do," Blankenship said, sounding a lot more friendly than he had at first.

Chapter Eleven

BY THE TIME THEY REACHED THE RIDGE IN THE NORTHEAST corner of the ranch, Annie had decided her grandmother was a fiend, bent on eliminating all her unfit heirs. Or something equally evil and painful. Why else would she have ordered a bunch of city slickers onto horses and sent them out into the wilderness? But as soon as she looked around, she decided the scenery was worth the pain.

She'd forgotten how spectacular the view to the west was. The Floating Nought spread out below her, patches of forest interspersed with open meadows of lush grass just starting to go from bright spring green to summer's gold. Here and there grazed placid cows, their calves gamboling nearby or tucked under a maternal flank, skinny rumps in the air while they suckled.

Beyond the ranch, the highway carried its constant stream of traffic bound to or from Yellowstone. *Nobody's said anything about going up to the park. I hope we do.* North of the ranch, the little settlement of Last Chance looked like toy buildings set in a carpet of gray-green.

But it was the river that drew her eye. The river, winding silvery and bright, calling her while at the same time reminding her of what she had lost. What water had stolen from her.

How ridiculous. The pond didn't reach out and grab him. It was my neglect that killed Calvin.

Why then, did she get this awful, sick feeling whenever she looked at any water bigger than a bathtub?

"Hey!"

She started, causing Lady to prance. "What?"

Hetty's horse had sidled up beside Lady. "I asked you if you're feeling saddle sore. I sure am."

"Oh, God, yes. I don't think there's any skin left on my thighs."

"It's my butt. I'll probably stand up for the next three days. That and sleep on my stomach."

"Wimps," Kristi jibed, as she walked her palomino mare to Annie's other side. "You're both out of shape."

"I am not," Hetty said. "My muscles are in fine tone. That doesn't stop them from bruising, or my skin from wearing thin."

"I am," Annie admitted, "but I'm working on it." She remembered the shin splints and aching chest after this morning's run. "I'm definitely working on it."

The three of them sat silently. As far as Annie was concerned, there was something restful about a landscape so lightly touched by development, so empty. Something healing. The heavy ache in her heart had grown lighter since she'd come here.

Only a little bit lighter, but anything at all was an improvement. She had grown so tired, so terribly tired, of hurting clear down to her very soul.

"Yellowstone is just over the hills there," she heard Charlie say. "And over there's the Tetons."

Annie, Hetty and Kristi walked their horses to join the children clustered around Charlie.

To the northeast, the wall of the ancient Yellowstone caldera rose steep and tree-clad up to meet a sky so blue it hurt the eyes. Closer and nearly bare of trees, jagged peaks emerged from lower, gentler hills, spearing through the slightly smoky air.

"I see them!" Charlene called out. "There!" All the children looked where she pointed.

"They're not as big as the mountains at home," Norman said.

"Are too," Jeremy said.

"Are not. Ours are really big mountains. These are just little bitty."

"These are a lot farther away," Uncle Ben said. "You live right up close to the mountains at home, Norman, so they look bigger. If you were that close to these, they'd look really big."

"But not as big as our mountains," Norman insisted.

"Well, actually, sweetie, I think they're bigger," Aunt Louisa said, "but it doesn't really matter, since we're here to look at the nice scenery, not to compare mountains."

"But Grandma—"

"Enough, Norman," Uncle Ben told him.

The boy fell silent, but glared fiercely at his younger cousin. Jeremy glared back and stuck out his tongue.

Charlie let them enjoy the scenery for a while before urging his horse forward. Annie swung Lady back into line, after taking one last look across the valley, seeing the winding ribbon of river glinting in the bright sunlight. Much to her surprise, she was enjoying this, despite the aches and pains in a body unaccustomed to riding. Still, the river called her—a strange ambivalence, considering her gut reaction to running water.

Did she wish she was there? In the river, standing next to a stocky man with warm brown eyes? Learning to fish? Yes, she did. Part of her wanted to be with Clay.

Party of her wanted to deny any such desire. She really didn't deserve to do anything that brought her pleasure.

Annie was still gazing at the river, when Lady gave a jump. Instinctively her legs grasped more firmly and she tightened the reins. The pinto mare hopped sideways.

"Here, Scout!" Owen's voice came from behind her.

Annie half turned, to see Owen's horse, the only other pinto in the string, nipping at Lady's haunches. Again Lady jumped, then kicked out with her back legs. Fortunately, Owen's mount was out of range.

"Hyah!" Charlie yelled. He shouldered his horse between the two, slapping at Owen's horse with the ends of his reins. "Move over there, you spotted bastard." He grabbed Scout's reins, jerked his head aside and forced him to move off the trail. Owen, who'd only been on a horse a few times before today, held tightly to the saddle horn while Charlie led his horse farther back in the string.

Poor kid. I'll bet he's absolutely mortified, having Kristi see that. His ears were red.

"You okay, Annie?" Charlie asked as he came back beside her.

"Sure. No problem," Annie said, full of a real sense of accomplishment that she had been able to keep her seat while Lady threw her tantrum. She hadn't completely forgotten what Charlie had taught her, so long ago.

The last half mile of the trail was on the level, through an open stand of lodgepole and aspen. Even though she hated for the ride to end, Annie's muscles told her it was time. She wondered if she would be able to walk naturally when she dismounted. How could only two hours of riding make her so sore—she who had been used to spend an entire day on Scooter's back, exploring the trails in the Cascade foothills up in back of Uncle Ben's place?

It would be nice to get back to riding again. Just one more thing she'd given up because it hadn't fit into the life style she and Walter had lived. Maybe she shouldn't have run away, after— No she'd done the right thing in moving to Boise. There had been too much in Portland to remind her. Of her failures. Of her losses.

Annie hobbled to the cookshack with all the other horseback riders, thinking longingly of hot baths and shaded hammocks. She was hungry, really hungry, for the first time since she'd arrived at the ranch.

Uncle Ward came over and stood next to her while she was waiting in line for the sandwich makings. "You had a caller," he said quietly. "A fisherman."

"Fish— Oh! He came looking for me? When? What did he say?"

"He's got some waders for you. He'll be down at the park fishing access about four." He almost sounded like he was asking a question.

"Yes, Uncle Ward, I am excited, and no, Uncle Ward, I have no intention of wading around in the river. He says he can teach me to fish from the bank."

"He didn't sound like that's what he had in mind." He tousled her hair. "Are you going to meet him?"

"I... I don't know."

"Well, if you decide to, let someone know. I'll cover for you if you're late for dinner."

She squeezed his hand. "I will. Thanks."

Most of the adults and all the kids gathered on the shady lawn north of the Big House after the late lunch. Annie joined them for a while before going to the Pink House. She was still undecided about meeting Clay. What if he wouldn't teach her to fish from the bank? She liked him, wanted him to like her.

Wouldn't he think she wasn't serious about learning to fish if she wouldn't climb into the river?

I could. It's not as if I can't swim. And it has nothing to do with...with Calvin. I just don't want to wade in the river. The very thought made her stomach churn.

The bunkroom was cool and dark and quiet. She curled up on her bed, but was unable to relax. She picked up a paperback mystery Hetty had recommended and found it boring. Going to the kitchen, she poured a glass of ice tea from the pitcher in the refrigerator, but set it untasted on the counter. She looked at the clock on the stove.

Three-thirty. If she was going to meet Clay at four, she'd have to hurry. *Maybe I won't go.*

There were a few dirty dishes in the sink. Instead of putting them into the dishwasher, she washed them, dried them, put them in the cupboard. At ten of four she finished wiping down the countertops and hung the dishcloth on the faucet.

I should go. At least to tell him I've changed my mind. Tucking her driver's license into her hip pocket, she grabbed a billed cap off a hook by the back door and headed for her car. At the last minute she remembered her promise to Uncle Ward.

Back inside. She found a scrap of paper, a pencil, wrote in a hurried scribble: *Gone fishing. I may not be back in time for supper— Annie* and stuck it under a magnet on the fridge door.

It was only five after four when she drove into the graveled area near Osborn Bridge. A familiar red pickup was already parked there.

After spending the last half-hour wondering if she'd show, Clay grinned when she parked beside him.

"Sorry I'm late," she said as she locked her car. "I—"

"Fishing doesn't follow a schedule. You're here now. That's what counts. All ready to conquer the wily rainbow?"

"Absolutely."

Her smile was far more alive than anything he'd seen before. "Okay." Clay unloaded the rods and other gear from the pickup. "How much fishing have you done?"

"Practically none. Oh, I've gone out with Dad a few times, but I just held a pole like he told me and once in a while I'd get a bite." Her shrug told him just how exciting she'd found that.

"We'll have you doing more than holding a pole this afternoon," he promised. "The hardest thing about fly fishing is putting the flies exactly where you want them. You do that with your cast and there are a lot of variations of the basic cast."

"Show me."

He showed her how to hold the rod, had her practice the basic cast without line for a while. She was so earnest about the whole thing he almost laughed. Not at her, but in pleasure at how her concentration had wiped the lingering sadness from her expression.

Once her movements had become smooth and automatic, he asked if she was ready for the next step.

"Oh, yes. This is fun."

"Isn't it? And it gets better. Now, we'll add line. Unlock your reel and pull about ten feet out and hold it loosely in your left hand." He watched her trying to follow his instructions. "No, not like that. Let it fall in coils and hold them loosely between your thumb and forefinger."

Annie did as instructed, her lower lip caught between her teeth as she concentrated.

"Now, work most of that line off the tip of your rod, using the basic cast."

Annie tried, but all she ended up with was a tangle of line piled at her feet. She looked at him with chagrin.

"Don't give up. Bring it back in and try again. Use your elbow more and your wrist less."

He stood behind her, his hand holding hers, and showed her how to use wrist action.

Annie's breath caught in her throat and her stomach did flipflops. Much as she tried to keep her mind on his instruction, she could not. His words went into her ears, but they were lost in the unnerving sensation of having his arms wrapped around her, however loosely.

"I think you'd do better if I showed you," Clay said after a few bungled casts. He sounded as breathless as she felt. Avoiding her eyes, he picked up his flyrod and demonstrated the proper motions for lengthening the line and casting. Again Annie admired his grace as he moved the long, slender rod through the air. "Okay, now you try it."

After an hour's practice, Annie felt she was making headway. At least once in ten tries, she was putting the fly in the general vicinity of where she wanted it. How could something that looked so simple be so difficult?

"Good," Clay finally told her. "You're ready for the river. Let's go fishing!"

Annie gave the chest waders hanging over the tailgate a dubious look. From her expression, they held about as much appeal for her as a dose of castor oil. Clay was pretty sure she wasn't real excited about putting them on. *I wonder why.* He smiled encouragingly.

If he hadn't been watching so closely, he might have missed the way she set her jaw, how her throat worked a she swallowed. *She's scared. That's it. She's scared to death.* He opened his mouth to tell her to forget the waders, that she could fish from the bank.

Before he could say a word, she'd slipped out of her jeans, revealing red nylon jogging shorts over dark green tights. The dark color emphasized the slim, delicious curves of her legs. "I guess I forgot how short you are," he said, handing her the waders. "But I can fix the length after you put them on." He helped her struggle into the bibbed and booted garment, remembering how clumsy he'd been the first time or two he'd worn them.

The waders, even with their suspenders pulled up tight, sagged. Clay pulled a webbing belt from behind the seat. "Hold them up as high as they'll go," he instructed. He slipped the belt around Annie's waist—or where he thought her waist must be—and pulled it tight. Even through the thick rubber, he was conscious of her body. *Watch it, man,* he told himself. *You're here to fish, not to monkey around.*

Annie frowned down at the waders. The suspendered top drooped over the belt. "I look like a clown." She took a few steps, her legs spread, her feet coming down clumsily. "They feel weird."

Clay contained his laughter. "You'll get used to them. And we're going fishing, not to a fashion show." She did indeed look clownish, in her red and white billed cap, loose t-shirt, and the baggy waders. Quite a sight.

He led the way to the river, choosing a section of bank that slanted down to the water. He stepped in and turned to lend a hand.

She hesitated, bit her bottom lip. Then he saw her mouth firm, her chin set. She took his offered hand and stepped into the shallow water. Slowly he led her out into the river, until the water lapped at her belt.

She shivered.

He pretended not to notice. Many people were nervous their first time in the water. He'd seen it before. "You may feel cold at first," he said. "but it won't last, once you start casting. Are you ready?"

"I guess so."

He handed her the rod that he'd carried out for her. Tongue caught between her teeth, she pulled out enough line for a first cast, went through the motions, too carefully, too slowly. The fly landed about fifteen feet upstream, in a tangle of line.

"Obviously I need more practice," she said, as she reeled in.

"Actually, that wasn't too bad for a first cast. Like anything worth doing, this takes practice."

On her second try, she made a creditable cast. The fly landed within ten feet of where he'd told her to put it. Clay watched her for a while before wading upstream to make his cast.

For nearly an hour they fished in silence. Annie had no luck, but she found that the soothing murmur of the river, the muted roar of traffic on the highway, and an occasional birdcall worked on her in a way nothing else had.

The belly-clenching fear she'd felt when she first stepped into the river had gone, borne away on the gentle current, lost in the silence. She cast and cast again, not really caring whether she caught a fish, but trying to put into practice everything Clay had told her. In her mind there was an echo of something Clay had said. What was it? *...my soul feels cleansed and at peace with itself.* Yes. That was it.

Right now, at this single moment, she had a glimmering of what he'd meant. She truly did feel at peace, without any of the usual compulsion to seek out her sorrow and suffer with it.

"Are you ready for a break?" Clay's voice cut through her concentration. Annie turned to him with a smile.

"Not really, I'm enjoying this too much."

"I need coffee. And you're probably more tired than you realize. Let's get out for a while."

Annie reeled her line in and followed him. Once on the bank, Clay dug the vacuum bottle out of his vest and offered it to her.

She took a quick sip, quickly handed the Thermos back. Unable to stay upright, she sank to her knees, and then rolled down to lay prone in the warm grass. "My legs are shaking."

"I know. Mine always do, the first time out every year. It's the tension of holding yourself against the current. You'll get used to it after a while. It also helps if you move around more." He

148

handed her the Thermos again. "Kick your legs. Loosen them up."

She did. "Y'know, there's a package of Oreos in my daypack, if you can make it to my car. I doubt I could." She dug inside her waders and eventually pulled out a set of keys.

"The magic words." He got to his feet and strode to the parking area. In a few minutes he was back with the cookies and another Thermos. "My favorite cookies," he said, as she tore the package open.

"Mine too. I don't know who they belong to, but they'll probably be mad when they can't find them."

"You stole them?" Clay pretended to be shocked.

Annie grinned. "Let's just say I borrowed them. They were in the kitchen and that made them fair game." She accepted the cup of coffee he held out. "This is nice. Good food, good company."

"Good fishing," he added. "There. Did you see that? They're starting to rise. Time to go back in."

Annie dropped her head onto her folded arms, letting the empty coffee cup fall into the grass. "Not yet, please. The sun feels so good on my back. I could sleep right here."

"Go ahead. The fish will be here another day." To his surprise, he didn't care whether he went back into the river or not. Just sitting here with her was about as good as anything he'd done for a long time.

"Not on your life. I came out here to catch a fish and that's what I'm gonna do." Annie stretched, feeling quietly content. Moving slowly, she got to her feet, picked up her rod. "Now we'll see if your teaching took."

Back in the river, she found that the brief rest had done her good. Casting was easier; it felt more natural. She became oblivious to everything but the gentle river sounds and the ever changing light on its surface as the sun slowly moved lower in the sky. Time was suspended, and the real world was far, far away.

Suddenly the tip of her rod dipped and line zipped through her left hand. She forgot what Clay had told her to do if she got a strike. All she could think of was landing the fish.

She grabbed at the line, felt it slip through her fingers. Her fingers fumbled on the spinning reel, finally caught it, slowed it. Despite her ineptitude, the fish stayed on her hook. She played it, following Clay's low-voiced instructions, until she had it reeled in.

"A big one!" he said approvingly, when the trout lay quiescent in the water. He handed her the net that had been hanging from the back of his vest.

"Now what?" Annie said. With the fly rod in one hand and the net in the other, how would she manage to find a hand free to release the fish? Or two hands, she wondered, eyeing the now-struggling trout in her net. She tried tucking the rod under her arm, as she had seen Clay do the first day. She almost dropped it.

She was still wondering how to find that necessary third hand when one materialized, taking hold of the net. "Slip your hand through the loop," Clay told her. "Or do you want me to release him?"

"Not on your life. He's my fish. If you'll just hold the rod, I think I can do it." She slipped the net around the fish and lifted it free of the water. It flopped about, nearly causing her to drop the net. "How big is he, do you think?"

"Three pounds, easy. Not bad for your first fish."

"What do I do now?" she said, lowering the fish back into the water, but still keeping it within the net.

"Just take hold of it right behind the gill slits," Clay told her, "and work the hook free."

"I never knew that a fish could be so...so strong." She gently pulled the hook from the trout's jaw. It had almost stopped struggling and she looked up at Clay. "Is it all right? I haven't killed it, have I?"

"No," he chuckled. "Just wore it out. Hold it still for a minute or two; give it a change to get its second wind."

The trout slowly moved under her hands and she let the net fall lower into the water. Finally it flexed its body and pulled free of her hands. One final flick of its tail and it was gone.

"Go eat lots of bugs and grow even bigger," Annie told it softly. "I'll see you next year."

"Your first fish," Clay said softly. "How'd it feel?"

"Oh, it was wonderful! I loved it. I love all of this." She gestured at the river, the open sky, the forest. "I could stay here forever."

"Not even come out for supper?"

"Now that you mention it, I'm starved." Annie rubbed her midriff. "But I hate to stop."

"We've got a couple more hours before sunset, but I think you've probably had enough. You'd be surprised how much work it is. Don't overdo it your first time."

Annie perched herself on the wide back bumper of his pickup after she'd pulled off the waders. Her legs felt like so much Jell-O, as if she'd run a marathon. "I'm starved," she said, in surprise. She hadn't been hungry for a long time, not like this.

"If you'll look in the cooler in the cab, you'll find a feast." He hung his waders over the tailgate beside hers and tossed her the keys.

"A feast? Real food?"

"Bologna sandwiches and potato chips."

"What time is it?" She'd left her watch on the bureau in the bunkroom.

He dug his out of one of the pockets on his vest. "Seven-forty. No wonder you're hungry. It's probably way past your dinnertime."

"It is, but we had a late lunch, so I shouldn't be this hungry." Her mouth twisted and her eyebrows drew together, as if she were thinking. "We're too late for dinner, but I'll bet there are leftovers. Do you want to come back with me and raid the fridge?"

Pretending to be affronted, he said, "You don't like bologna sandwiches and potato chips? I'm crushed."

"It's not that. I just don't want to take your supper. I'm really hungry." She felt like she could eat two sandwiches and half a bag of chips.

"There's plenty. I made extra, in case you showed up. And there are grapes, the rest of the cookies, and Cokes. That should feed us both."

"If you're sure..." She really wanted to stay with him, not to share him with her family. Not yet.

"I'm sure. I want you to stay for supper."

Chapter Twelve

Hetty handed the note to Gran, wondering what her reaction would be. Personally she was glad Annie had found something to do. She was also consumed with curiosity. Fishing? Of all things, that was the last she'd expected Annie to be enthusiastic about.

And enthusiastic she was, if her handwriting—a hurried scrawl—was any indication. The few notes she'd written Hetty this past year had been terse and written in a tight little hand that was scarcely recognizable as Annie's.

"Did you know about this?" Gran said as she folded the note and tucked it into her shirt pocket.

"Not a thing."

"Not to worry, Ma," Ward said, coming up behind her and draping an arm across her shoulders. "I told Annie I'd let you know she might not be here for dinner, but I guess I wasn't quick enough."

"Do you know anything about this fishing? Is she with someone?" Gran imbued the preposition with a whole lot of meaning.

"Not in the sense you mean," Ward said. "I met the fellow. He said he'd run into Annie in the park the other day and she'd asked him about fly fishing. He offered to teach her. I guess she decided to take him up on it." He sat down next to his mother and pulled Hetty with him. "He struck me as a good sort."

Gran raised an eyebrow but didn't comment. Instead she said, "So, Hetty, what is this problem of yours."

Hetty looked around. Her parents were sitting at the next table and Eric and Jennifer were across from them. "Can we talk about it after dinner? I need your advice." She hesitated when Gran frowned. "And your help. Please?"

For a good minute Gran gazed steadily at her, seeming to be searching for something. As last she sighed. "I don't have a good feeling about this, but yes, I'll listen to you. And I'll advise you, for what it's worth."

"Your advice is worth a lot," Hetty said, giving her a quick hug. "I'll never forget what you said when I told you I didn't want to be a botanist after all."

"Advice your mother still hasn't forgiven me for offering. I should learn to keep my nose out of other people's business."

"Nonsense, Ma. You know you'd never be able to do that," Ward said with a grin.

Just then the dinner bell sounded. And sounded. And sounded some more. Tonight Tommy had won the drawing, and he was making sure everyone heard him clanging the antique handbell. Hetty stood and held out a hand to help Gran.

"I can still get up on my own two legs, even if they don't move as fast as they used to." Cecile sniffed derisively. "Go on, now and save me a place in line."

The everlasting Bridge game started right after dinner. Tonight the players were Joss, John, Ben and Thea. Jennifer herded her complaining children to the Blue House, while the teenagers sauntered over to the Big House playroom, to play pool or watch one of the many videos on the shelves. There had been an uneasy truce among them all day, with Serhilda only occasionally sniping at CeCe and Charlene. Owen hadn't teased his sister once, and Tommy had apparently decided that hanging with the older kids was preferable to picking on Norman and Joey.

Ward and Hetty matched their pace to Gran's as they crossed the uneven lawn to the front porch of the Big House. It was a perfect evening, with the setting sun scattering color across the tendrils of clouds on the western horizon, a fitful breeze bringing an occasional whiff of sagebrush to the nose. Occasionally a truck sped along the highway with a far-off and faint snarl of tires on asphalt, but mostly the only sound was the occasional muted laugh from the game room.

Gran and Hetty settled in the swing. It moved gently, slowly, with a comfortable, low-pitched squeak. "I'll see you later," Ward said, turning to go indoors.

"No! Wait Uncle Ward. I'd like your advice too."

He raised one eyebrow, but said nothing as he pulled an Adirondack chair close and perched on one arm.

Squeak...squeak...squeak. Hetty listened to the night sounds, and sought the right words.

"Well?" Gran reminded her, after they'd sat in silence for several minutes.

"Well... Shit!" The word just sat there, waiting for someone to react. "I'm sorry," Hetty apologized, hating the necessity to do so. "This is hard."

"As long as she doesn't attack Evan publicly, I say you should let that particular sleeping dog snooze in peace." Gran's tone was sharp. "No one else is apt to say anything. Heavens, Hetty, He's a grown man. You don't need to protect him any longer."

"I'm not. That's not... It's mother's drinking. I'm worried—"

The faint sounds from the game room rose in volume as someone opened the door. Hetty leaned forward, but she couldn't

155

see inside. Nonetheless, she kept quiet until she heard one of the girls say, "There aren't any sodas in the fridge. I'll go down to the Pink House and get some. Who wants what?"

She leaned back and gave the swing another push. *Squeak... squeak...squeak...*in counterpoint to young voices raised in laughter.

Charlene emerged from the front door. "Oh, hi, Gran, Hetty, Uncle Ward. I'm going down—"

"We heard," Gran told her. "Will you bring me a Sprite, please?"

"Sure. Anybody else want anything?"

"Diet Coke for me," Hetty said.

"I'll come along and help you carry," Ward told her.

Hetty waited until they'd gone around the corner of the house. "I was hoping Mother was doing better."

"Might you be making a mountain out of a molehill?"

Unable to sit still any longer, Hetty rose and paced to the porch railing. She stared out into the night, watching the slight movement of the pine branches in the occasional puff of wind. The stiff, short needles sparkled, almost as if they were icy, yet the temperature couldn't be much under seventy. "Maybe I am," she said, at last. "Or maybe I'm just afraid that having Frank here will set her off again. Worse than last night, when she realized about Evan." She turned around, leaned against an upright post. "Gran, do you think Dad's still in denial?"

"I think this isn't something we want to discuss out here, where we might be overheard. Why don't we go up to my bedroom?"

"Okay, but would you mind if we wait for Uncle Ward? I really would like his advice too."

Ward and Charlene returned after about ten minutes, carrying between them a red-and-white picnic cooler. "We took all the ice, Aunt Hetty. But I refilled the trays."

"You can take some from the freezer here when you go back down. Ahh, this is nice and cold," Gran popped the top of the Sprite can. "Thank you."

She led the way up the stairs, climbing slowly. Again Uncle Ward aimed his raised eyebrow Hetty's way, but she just shook her head, mouthing *Wait*.

Gran occupied the largest of the four bedrooms, one with its own roomy bath and an enormous walk-in closet. There was a comfortable sitting area near the wide windows overlooking the lawn and the cookshack. Hetty and Gran took the two brocade wing chairs and Ward pulled the rocking chair close. "Okay, enough mystery. Let's have it, Hetty."

"I asked Gran if she thought Dad was still denying that my mother's an alcoholic. What do you think?"

Uncle Ward leaned back and scratched at his chin. "Hard to say. He watches her pretty closely. Last night he talked her out of having a third drink during the Bridge game."

"So far this week her drinking has been under control. Are you sure it's getting worse?" Gran said. "You haven't seen her since Christmas, have you?"

"She seems to be trying really hard to be on her best behavior." She leaned forward, elbows on her knees. "I think she's sneaking drinks, though, and sooner or later her control is going to slip."

Ward frowned. "Have you discussed this with your father?"

"I've tried to talk to him, but he refuses to discuss it. Last Christmas, after a really awful scene because he hadn't bought her the dinner ring she'd hinted about, I asked him point blank if he didn't think Mother was drinking too much. He looked me straight in the eye and said 'Your mother would never overindulge.' He was royally pissed.

"I haven't seen them since. They never come to visit me, and I've...well, I've avoided visiting them. Every time I do, Mother starts in on how I've wasted my education, and Dad asks when I'm going to give him a grandchild."

"Both are the sorts of things most parents would say, although I would think Jocelyn should have come to terms with your choice of career by now. Particularly since you've made such a success of it."

"Don't make excuses for them, Gran. They're both control freaks. I'm not living the life they laid out for me, and neither one of them is going to accept that it's my right."

"You know, kiddo, I'm hearing a couple of issues here," Ward said. "Which one bothers you the most?"

Trust a civil engineer to cut to the chase. Hetty took a deep breath and fought down the familiar sensation of choking that arguments with her parents always engendered. "Her drinking. I can deal with the arguments, the disapproval. God knows, I should be used to them, after ten years. But I'm really concerned about Mother's drinking." She opened her hands, reaching out, she realized, for help.

"And about your father's blindness, if he really is refusing to see the problem," Gran said. "But if she's controlling it, that makes his denial so much easier."

Uncle Ward shook his head. "There's more to this than her needing to drink, Hetty. I respect your dad, but I've always thought he did his best to repress Joss's natural high spirits."

"He does, but she never seemed to mind. In fact, he's often said she lightened his naturally gloomy disposition. The trouble is, she's not really *fun* anymore. At least it doesn't seem to me she is. Like the other night. When I was a kid, she'd have been egging me on, probably would have taken part in the food fight."

"You know Jennifer will never forgive you for that, don't you?" Ward said, with a chuckle.

"Oh, like I'm going to lose sleep over Jennifer's opinion of me. I'm sure she's a very nice person, but I can't stand her."

"She's a good mother, if over-protective," Gran said. "Eric seems very happy with her."

"Of course he is. She agrees with everything he says, and waits on him hand and foot."

"Is that what you think?" Gran sounded surprised. "That Eric rules that particular roost?"

"Of course. No, really," she insisted, as Gran and Uncle Ward both shook their heads. "She's always reminding those poor kids that their father wouldn't approve of whatever they're doing."

"It's not Hetty's fault, Mother. She's an only child." There was a hint of chuckle in Uncle Ward's tone.

"What's that got to do with it?"

"Just that you've not had a lot of opportunity to observe family dynamics," Gran told her with a smile. She reached across and took Hetty's hand. "Enough about Eric and Jennifer. Tell me what you'd like us to do to help."

"That's the trouble. I don't think there's anything you *can* do. Maybe talk to Dad, but only if the right opportunity offers itself. He's... He doesn't take kindly to outside interference in what he considers family business."

"We *are* family!"

"Well, yes, but not inner family, not to Dad. That's just Mother and me, and we're his responsibility. I'm not sure he'd listen to anything you say." Hetty made a fist and pressed it against her mouth. "I shouldn't have said anything. I don't think there's anything anyone can do. Not until Dad accepts what the real situation is."

"You might be the only person he'll listen to. Have you tried?"

"Ward, he won't listen to me. Maybe he would to one of you. I know he respects you both. He's said more than once that you both give the family's welfare priority."

"I'll do what I can," Gran said, patting her hand.

"And so will I." Ward stood up.

Hetty hugged them, first Gran then Ward. "Thanks." She was holding tight to her emotions. Tears were luring behind her eyelids, but she'd be damned if she'd let them show.

"Anytime," Ward replied, as he opened the door. "I'll go down with you. I want to get a book before Frances comes back. Having her sleeping in the library is putting a crimp in my plans to catch up on my reading."

"Wait—"

He paused, his hand on the doorknob. "Yes?"

She motioned for him to close it. "Frank. He'll be here Thursday."

"Frank? Your boyfriend?" Clearly Gran had not told even Ward.

"I...I guess you could call him that. Or maybe my partner. I don't know yet, but I feel more for him than I have for any of the men I've—"

While she groped for the right words, Gran chuckled. "You've slept with. Good heavens, Hetty, I know about sex—probably a good deal more than you do, for all of that. And I've never expected you to live a celibate life."

Gran was eighty-three. She wasn't supposed to be so...so open.

Uncle Ward had his hand over his mouth. Hiding a grin? She suspected so.

"There's this little matter of no empty beds," Hetty said, trying for bravado, but feeling her cheeks grow even warmer. "I was thinking I'd get a room in Island Park, or maybe up in West Yellowstone."

Apparently Uncle Ward couldn't hold it in any longer. His laughter covered Hetty's last few words. "You don't do anything the easy way, do you?" he said through the guffaws. "Your folks are going to have a fit, you know."

"It's not funny."

"No," he said, sobering, "it's not. I'm sorry, Hetty. I shouldn't have laughed, but if you could have seen your face when Mother said that about sex—" He quickly stifled his laughter. "Sorry again. What is it you want advice about?"

She looked at Gran, who was just sitting there, smiling. "How am I going to tell them? I don't want to send Mother into one of her tirades—or worse. I wish I'd never asked him to come," she said. "I wish I'd gone to San Francisco with him, like he wanted me to, and never come here at all."

"But you wanted him to meet your family, didn't you?"

The stinging in her eyes wouldn't go away, and now there was a tightness in her throat. "Uh-huh. Frank's different, not like any of the men I've...I've known before. He's calm and sensible and sexy and... I wish I'd met him a long time ago. Before I got so damn cynical."

"Cynical? That's the last word I'd use. I think you're in love and not sure how to handle it."

The words hit Hetty like a blow. "In love? Me? Not a chance," she said, without thinking. "Lust maybe. Yeah, I'm definitely in lust. Love's for romantic kids, and I've gone way past that."

Uncle Ward returned to the rocker and sat down. "Sure you have. That's why you haven't even considered putting this Frank into the Blue House with the rest of us bachelors."

"No way!"

He looked over at Gran. "He's coming Thursday, you said. so he'll only be here three nights, right? Mother, what would you say to trading beds with Hetty?"

"What an excellent idea. There's no reason for me to occupy this big room, and I certainly don't need a king-sized bed."

"Oh, no, I can't—"

"Of course you can. Besides, the thought of not having to climb these stairs every night is certainly appealing." She winked. "I'd rather enjoy being one of the girls anyway. Give me a chance to see how Annie's doing."

Feeling sort of like she'd been flattened by a steam-roller, Hetty shook her head. "Gran, you are really bad."

"Why thank you. Now, let's talk about how we're going to break the news to your parents."

"I REALLY SHOULD GET BACK," ANNIE SAID, WHEN THEY'D EATEN the last grape and were gathering the remains of their supper into a plastic bag for disposal. The sun had set, but the western sky was still aglow with color, long streaks of clouds glowing peach and gold and delicate pink. Mosquitoes whined around them, sensing their heat but held at bay by the repellent they'd both applied.

"It's not that late."

"No, but my family will be getting worried. I told them I was going fishing, not camping." As soon as the words were on the end of her tongue, she wanted to bite them back.

Too late.

Clay turned. His gaze moved back and forth across her face, as if he were trying to read her thoughts. "I wouldn't mind," he said, not moving.

"Oh, man, talk about opening mouth and inserting foot." She laughed, or tried to. "What I meant was—"

"Not to worry, Annie. I know what you meant. I meant what I said, too."

She turned away, unable to face him. "I'm sorry, Clay. I just—" Wrapping her arms around herself, she bent almost double. "Oh, God, I can't—"

"Hey, it's not a problem." He came up behind her and set his hands on her shoulders. "I'm not asking for anything. Just letting you know that if you decide—"

"I won't."

"Fine." Giving her shoulders a quick squeeze, he released her and stepped away "So, do you want to fish again on Thursday?"

With a shuddering breath, she pulled herself together. "Yes, please. I'd like that."

"Great! I'll meet you here about six, okay?"

"Okay." She looked around, trying to remember what she'd brought with her. Couldn't think of anything she hadn't already put into her car. "I've got to go. Good night."

Hands shaking, belly roiling, she opened the car door. "Clay, I—"

"Don't say anything," he told her, stepping forward, keeping the open door between them. He leaned forward, touched his lips briefly, lightly, to hers. "See you Thursday."

Before she could react, he'd turned away and was striding around the nose of his pickup.

Annie got into her car and pulled the door shut. She dropped the keys, scrabbled on the floor until she found them. Fumbled with the seat belt, managed to get it fastened.

The sound of the pickup's engine broke the stillness and pulled her out of her daze. She knew he wouldn't go anywhere until she did, so she started her car and, holding onto the steering wheel for dear life, guided it along the graveled road until she came to the highway. The lights of the pickup stayed in her rear-view mirror all the way.

She expected him to turn around when she pulled into the Floating Nought, but he didn't. He followed her all the way to the compound. When she turned into the parking area next to the Pink House, he slowed, came to a stop in the middle of the narrow drive.

Not until Annie was inside did he drive on. She knew, because she stood by the front window and watched his headlights circle the compound, then fade away down the hill toward the main road.

She was really glad the bunkroom was empty. Talking about this evening was the last thing she was interested in doing. With any luck, she'd be in bed and asleep—or pretending to be—before her roommates came in.

Chapter Thirteen

Wednesday

CLAY WAS STILL IN A STATE OF DISBELIEF AS HE DROVE TO ST. Anthony, the county seat. The lawyer his former boss had recommended had an opening today. Even better, Jim Larsen had already spoken to Abe's lawyer and they were working together to draw up the papers for the sale.

"I guess life is less complicated in small towns," he said, once he was settled in Jim's office, holding a cup of coffee.

"Not really," Jim said. It's just that Abe's been hoping someone like you would come along. He knew what he wanted out of the property and what kind of terms he'd settle on. Karla—his lawyer—pretty much had everything ready.

"You're making me feel like I walked into a baited trap. If I wasn't acquainted with Abe, I'd start holding onto my wallet." He smiled to show he was joking.

He hoped he was joking.

Jim laughed. "Abe's about the most honest fellow I've ever known. That doesn't mean he's a fool or naïve about money.

He knew exactly what the property was worth, but it was more important to him to find the right buyer than to get top dollar."

"So he said. I have to admit I was floored when he said he'd accept my offer. I'd figured we'd spend a month dickering."

"He remembered you from the last time you'd stayed with him, so he didn't feel like he was dealing with a stranger. Besides, Karla checked you out pretty well. She was determined to get Abe the best deal she could, given his stipulations."

"And they were?"

"Someone who loved fishing more than profit, who was willing to settle here and run the place himself instead of hiring a manager. Most of all, Karla said he wanted someone who'd last, and he figured you would. I think that's why he kept the price down for you."

"For me? Are you saying he sold me the property for less than it was worth?" Clay hadn't believed in fairy godmothers since he was about five. He kept expecting a nasty surprise or two.

Jim leaned back and propped on foot on the corner of his desk. "Let's just say he let you have it for low market. I know for a fact he could have gotten more if he'd held out for it. I had a resort developer in here just last month, looking for riverfront property, and he was willing to pay top dollar."

Clay could only shake his head. "I feel like I've fallen into a rabbit hole." He rose to his feet. "No sense in keeping you any longer. When shall I come back?"

Jim grinned. "How about three this afternoon? Can you stay in town that long?"

"Now I know I'm in some strange other dimension. Nobody gets legal papers drawn up that fast."

Jim shrugged. "It's a straightforward deal. You've agreed on the terms. The only question is how soon you want to settle."

"Abe said he'd like to stay on until Labor Day. How about we close the tenth of September? I don't want to rush him."

Jim made a note, and they parted with a handshake. Clay walked out of the office in a daze. He expected to see a white rabbit hopping down the street at any moment, watch in hand.

"WAKE UP SLEEPY HEAD. WE'RE GOING FOR A HIKE."

Annie rolled over and peered into the shadowy room. It was barely light, even with the blinds wide open. "Charlene? What on earth?"

"We're going for a hike. I woke up a little while ago and heard the swans. Or something. Geese maybe? Anyhow, it sounded like they were on the river. Come on. Hurry. Before it gets too light."

"I'll go get Kristi," CeCe said, as she pulled on her jeans.

"Serhilda," Hetty muttered from under her pillow. "Invite Serhilda, too."

"Aunt Hetty—"

"Do it," Hetty sat up and pushed off her covers. "Tell her I said I want her to come with us."

CeCe shook her head, without saying anything. She pulled a sweatshirt over her head, grabbed a windbreaker, and left.

"Do you really want her to come with us?" Charlene said. "She'll ruin it for the rest of us."

"Let's give her a chance. This is her first Gathering too, you know. And her mother isn't anything like yours. I doubt if she knows what a family is."

"I wonder why we never knew Aunt Frances had a child." Annie yawned and reached for her jeans. Now that she was awake, a hike actually sounded like fun.

"I think Gran knew," Hetty said. "She wasn't surprised when Frances showed up with Serhilda."

"I think Gran knows where every Blankenship and Armstrong body is buried. She just doesn't gossip."

Hetty grinned. "Which is really too bad. How are we to know all the dirt if she doesn't share it?"

CeCe and Charlene had water bottles and apples waiting for them in the kitchen. To Annie's surprise, Serhilda was with them and looking almost eager. Kristi staggered in last, wiping sleep from her eyes. "I don't believe this. There's just no excuse for getting up so early on vacation."

"It's good for you. Builds character." Annie pushed her younger sister toward the door. "Let's go."

They all piled into Annie's car for the drive down to the park. CeCe, who was the smallest, perched on the console between the seats. "Somebody else gets to dent her butt going home," she said as she climbed out and rubbed her bottom. "Mine's terminally bruised."

"We're going to walk out there?" Serhilda said as they stood by the interpretive sign marking the Silver Lake trail. "In the woods?"

"Sure. It's only about three miles. Let's go!" Charlene struck off through the trees, CeCe right behind her. The others followed, Annie making sure Serhilda was ahead of her. *Poor kid. She doesn't sound as if she's ever hiked in anything wilder than a city park.* Kristi brought up the rear.

The trail led them through stands of lodgepole pine where pink, yellow, and white wildflowers brightened the dappled understory. The first time Charlene asked if anyone knew what they were, Hetty replied, "Flowers. Pinks and yellows and whites."

"Aunt Hetty! That's not an answer."

"She's the botanist. Trust her," Kristi said, laughing.

"Well, I know that's a lupine," CeCe said, pointing into a sunny glade. "And those are sunflowers."

"Close, but no cigar. They're balsamroot," Hetty said. She refused to tell the girls what the flowers along the trail were. "Look them up. There's a picture book in the Big House."

Annie remembered how Hetty had done the same to her, and how she'd learned all the Latin names just to spite her cousin. She had to smile at the memory.

A boardwalk bridge crossed Thurman Creek where it entered Silver Lake. They came to a sudden stop at the sight of several trumpeter swans.

"So beautiful," Annie breathed, afraid of disturbing their serenity.

"They are magnificent, aren't they?" Hetty agreed.

The swans were not at all shy. They approached to within fifty feet of the bridge. "See the gray feathers?" Annie pointed at a trio off to the left. "They mean those birds are immature. They're probably a year old. Next summer they'll be all white." She was pleased she'd remembered. Bird watching was one more activity she'd put aside the past few years.

They continued along the trail, following the edge of a wet meadow. Once a mule deer bounded into the trees just ahead of them. Annie breathed deeply of the cool, moist air, listened to the silence. The empty meadow, bright green in the slanting morning light, showed glints of silver where streamlets meandered through it. In the lead, CeCe and Charlene chattered, but kept their voices low. Annie noticed that several times they tried to draw Serhilda into their conversation. She usually answered with a shrug, or in monosyllables.

Annie caught up with her. "Do you run?"

"Sometimes. I used to run with my...with Les." Her quick withdrawal told Annie not to ask who Les was.

"Oh, gosh, I was going to ask you to run with me, but you won't want to. I'm really out of shape."

"I guess I could. It's been a while."

"Maybe we could run back to the ranch. I tried the other morning and got about halfway. Maybe with someone to run with, I could make it all the way today."

"Maybe. And we wouldn't have to listen to CeCe bitchin' about her sore butt."

"There is that. Oh, look! Is that a—"

"Moose. It's a moose," Hetty said, her voice low. "Keep quiet. Don't alarm it."

The moose was perhaps a hundred yards away, lying at the base of a big pine. As they watched, it got to its feet and turned to face them.

"Shit, that's one big mother," Serhilda whispered. "Will it attack?"

"Probably not, but we're taking no chances. Let's go. Walk slowly and quietly. If it does charge, scatter. Get off the trail."

Annie kept looking over her shoulder as they walked away. The moose stood immobile, watching them. They'd nearly doubled their distance from it when she saw motion behind it. She gasped. Was some unsuspecting hiker walking into danger? She stopped walking. "Wait," she whispered. "Stop."

They all halted and turned. "Babies," CeCe said, in awe. "Baby mooses."

"Two of them," Charlene whispered. "Twins."

"Oh, my God!" Serhilda said, not a trace of the usual ennui or sarcasm in her tone. "They're adorable."

When the other girls turned to stare at her, she shrugged. "Well, sometimes ugly is cute."

Danger forgotten, they stood and watched as the two calves came to stand beside their mother. The cow stood where she was for a moment longer, glaring suspiciously, and then she tossed her head and herded her babies into the woods.

After that, everything else was anticlimactic. They finished the hike in high spirits, even Serhilda. When they reached the car, Annie tossed her keys to CeCe. "Serhilda and I are going to run back. We'll see you at the cookshack."

Kristi opened her mouth, but closed it again at Annie's slight headshake. "Don't be too long, or we'll have eaten everything."

"We won't. I could eat a horse."

"Or a moose," Serhilda said. "Race you?" She was off like a shot.

Annie didn't catch up with her until the highway crossing. They walked a while after they'd crossed, then, having caught their breath, they ran some more. The last quarter mile was uphill, and again they both slowed to a walk, panting.

"Keep this up and I'll be up all night with leg cramps," Annie said, as they reached the road around the compound. "I remember when I could run the whole distance at top speed."

"You're really lucky, having a place like this. Did you live here when you were a kid?"

"Oh, no, I grew up in Portland. We came here every summer, though, as far back as I can remember. Sometime I came with Gran and Gramps, when my folks couldn't get away. Hetty always came with them. I really resented that she got to spend all summer with Gran. I hated her every summer until I was about sixteen."

"How come you stopped?" Serhilda sat on the grass and reached for her toes, touching her nose to her knee.

"I think it was when I realized she was with Gran because her folks were too busy for her. Her dad used to work all the time. I don't think he ever came here when I was a kid."

They stretched in silence then, until Annie saw her car approaching. "They took long enough. I wonder why." She stood. "Let's go meet them. If we all descend on the kitchen at once, Gran's not likely to chase us out."

"I thought you could get food any time. That's what she told me."

Annie wrapped her windbreaker around her waist and tied it. "Theoretically, you can. But when Gran's cooking breakfast, she doesn't like interruptions. Let's go."

They met the others as they crossed the road from the Pink House. "We stopped to talk to Ejay," CeCe explained. "He's guiding a walk around Golden Lake this afternoon, so we told him we'd go."

"Some of us," Hetty corrected. "Personally, I intend to stake out the hammock and read until my book falls in my face."

As they approached the cookshack, Annie heard a chittering from above. She stopped, looked for its source.

"There." Serhilda pointed into the tall pine just ahead. "It looks like it's giving us hell."

"Not us," Hetty said, from behind Annie. "Look over there." She pointed to a stump about twenty feet away. On top of it a chipmunk was stuffing its cheeks with the sunflower seeds someone had scattered.

They watched while the squirrel made threatening runs down the trunk of the tree, none of which fazed the chipmunk. It continued stuffing until its cheek pouches were enormous, and then it sat up on its haunches, looked up at the squirrel as if to sneer, and scampered off. The squirrel dashed down the tree and across the lawn. Once on the stump, it eyed the humans suspiciously, but held its ground.

"Cool." Once again Serhilda's tone was full of wonder. "Way cool."

THE DOOR BURST OPEN AND SIX GIRLS TUMBLED IN, ALL LAUGHING fit to be tied.

"What's for breakfast, Gran? I'm starved!"

"Coffee, coffee, where's the coffee?"

"...the way he just sat there and scolded. I've never seen..."

"A ground squirrel, not a chipmunk..."

"Can I have some of this cheese?"

Cecile struck a big stockpot with a wooden spoon. The resulting clang cut through the noise. "Quiet! One at a time, please." She cast a quick glance at Thea, who was standing in the doorway smiling widely. She wanted to smile too, but was almost afraid to. Some situations were too delicate to take open notice of. "Charlene, get out of the refrigerator. Cheese is not breakfast food. Hetty, drink some orange juice before you rot your stomach with coffee."

Serhilda was the only one who hadn't come in. She stood in the doorway, almost as if she wasn't sure she was welcome. When she saw Cecile watching her, she raised her chin a couple of notches and swaggered forward. "I'll take some of the coffee," she said to Hetty.

Annie was rooting in the snack cupboard. "Cookies? I know I saw some..."

Cecile smacked her hand with the spoon. "Not before breakfast. Go sit down, all of you. I'll cook some eggs."

Serhilda poured cream into her coffee. "I don't eat eggs."

"Yes, you do. I'll scramble them with cream cheese and jelly." Reaching past her, Cecile pulled out a jar of grape jelly. "Go. Out of the kitchen."

Thea watched them as they trooped into the dining room. "I don't believe it," she breathed.

"I'm not sure I do either. Keep your fingers crossed it lasts."

Annie was clad in a royal blue parka, faded jeans and scuffed sneakers. She looked about sixteen as she laughed with her cousins. Although she still had a fragile air about her, this morning her face was blooming with health, glowing with the cold of early morning at six thousand feet above sea level.

Before she'd married Walter, Annie had tended to chubbiness. She'd never been fat, just well-padded. Cecile had always thought of her as voluptuous, even if it wasn't a grandmotherly choice of words. After her marriage, she had dieted to the point of emaciation, trying to please her husband's demands for an ultra-slim, chic wife. Cecile had never thought she looked as good in her size eights as she had when she'd worn size twelve. Nor had she found the slight hollowness in Annie's cheeks attractive.

Since Calvin's death, she had lost even more weight. Now translucent skin stretched too tightly over her cheekbones and hipbones protruded even under her baggy jeans. Cecile bit her lower lip and prayed that her appetite would stay good.

"We saw some pelicans!" Annie exclaimed, pausing in the doorway, "and a whole herd of swans. Oh, it was so wonderful!" She snatched an orange from the basket on the counter. "A moose and twin calves. They were humongous! We weren't more than a hundred yards from them."

"Where were you?"

"We hiked around Silver Lake," Annie said, gesturing vaguely. She followed the others into the dining room, while peeling her orange. The six of them sat in a noisy, laughing group at the far table.

Cecile turned to look at Thea, who had tears in her eyes. "Keep your fingers crossed," she said, "and pray."

Chapter Fourteen

TRUE TO HER WORD, HETTY LAID CLAIM TO THE HAMMOCK after lunch. Annie had always detested the Adirondack chairs, so she dug into the storage cupboard at the Big House and unearthed a ratty old sleeping bag. She spread it in a shady spot nearby and piled several pillows at one end. Armed with the newest thriller by her favorite author, a bottle of water, and a pocketful of jelly beans, she settled in for a totally self-indulgent afternoon.

The next thing she knew, someone was calling her name. She pushed the book off her face and looked up. "Serhilda. Hi." A jaw-cracking yawn. "Gosh, I didn't mean to fall asleep."

"I shouldn't have woke you up, but I wanted to talk to you while nobody was around."

Annie glanced over at the hammock. Empty. She checked the sun's angle and realized she must have been sleeping for a couple of hours. "Time for me to wake anyhow. Let's go find someplace more private. That hammock attracts people like a candle does moths."

They walked down to the north end of the compound, where Douglas-firs grew close together and the ground was covered with a thick layer of duff—needles, cone scales, dust. Someone long ago had rolled several log sections down here and stood them on end to serve as seats.

Once they were seated, Annie dug out the rest of her jelly beans. "Want one?"

Serhilda picked out the pink, orange and yellow ones. "Thanks." She sat chewing one after another, looking off toward the east.

Annie waited patiently, remembering how she'd hated to have adults demand that she get to the point when she was trying to make up her mind how to put something.

Finally Serhilda said, "How come everyone treats you like you're going to break? Are you sick or something?"

"No, I—" A child's laughter rippled through the warm air, sliced through her soul. "My baby drowned"

"Fuck!" Serhilda dug her toe into the duff, piled it up. Smoothed it out and dug again. "I guess that's rough if you really cared about him."

"I loved him."

"Why?" She raised her chin and looked straight at Annie, her expression earnest. "I mean, why did you love him? Babies are messy and smelly and noisy and they tie you down. You get a baby, you lose your life." Shoulders hunched, she turned to look out across the valley. "I'd hate a baby if I had one."

Annie opened her mouth to argue, but closed it again. Serhilda's statement had been from the heart. She said nothing. Wished she could get up and walk away. Felt guilty for wishing it.

Felt the lightness of spirit slip away like a forgotten dream. *Damn the girl!* "Is that all you wanted to talk about?"

The busy toe was digging another hole in the duff. "Uh-uh. I wanted to ask you about the old lady. You know. Gran." Her lip curled over the last word. "Is she for real?"

"What do you mean? Of course Gran is for real. She's your grandmother as much as she is mine."

"Oh, yeah, right. Like she ever gave a damn about me. I bet she didn't even know I existed until Frances brought me here."

"I'm not sure she did," Annie admitted. "Why don't you ask her?"

"Ask her! Are you out of your fucking mind? What should I say? Hey, Granny, didn't you know your own daughter had herself a kid down in L.A.? Right!"

"Serhilda, I don't know what happened between your mother and Gran. She never talks about it, not to me or Kristi or Hetty, anyhow. I do know that she's wished Aunt Frances would get over it, whatever it was."

"Don't call her my mother, okay?"

"Okay." Annie waited for her to say more, all the while wishing she could just get up and walk away. She was the last person to be giving this angry child advice.

"I've seen how she's all huggy-body, kissy-face with the others, but she acts like she's afraid to touch me. She doesn't even talk to me." Serhilda paused, and when she went on her voice was steady again. "Like this morning. She gave you all hell for getting into the food, but all she said to me was that I had to eat breakfast."

"She fixed it, too, didn't she? She gave the rest of us plain scrambled eggs, but you got jelly with yours."

"Yeah, like that's something special."

"It is, actually. The only time Gran ever made me scrambled eggs with jelly was when I was sick." There had been nothing like scrambled eggs with jelly to make her feel better, when she was a child.

"Gran always made mine with orange marmalade," she mused. "Hetty liked strawberry jam."

"The grape jelly was okay, I guess. Les always made me grape jelly and banana sandwiches when I had a cold."

For once Serhilda sounded like a child, not the hardened woman of the world she tried so hard to be. Annie decided to take advantage of it. "You mentioned Les before. Who is he?"

For a moment she thought Serhilda wasn't going to answer. The girl dug another hole and filled it in with a swift sideways motion, and then ground her whole foot into the duff. "He was sort of my dad, but he didn't want me anymore."

"Sort of your dad? Your stepfather, you mean?"

"I don't know. Maybe. And maybe he was my real dad. I just don't know." The last words came out in a shriek, as Serhilda leapt to her feet. She loomed over Annie, fists clenched at her sides, face red with rage, and screamed, "I don't know who my dad is, and I hate that bitch who won't admit she's my mother. I hate her!"

Annie reached out with both hands, wanting to soothe, to comfort, but before she could gather the girl into her arms, Serhilda had spun around and gone dashing off into the woods beyond the circle road.

When Annie caught Ward as he was going into the Blue House, he almost brushed her off.

"No, I haven't seen Serhilda," he said, in answer to her question. "I've been out riding."

"Damn. Okay, I'll keep looking."

"Wait a minute." He tossed his hat and boots inside. "Did something happen to make you worry about her?"

She wouldn't meet his eye. "Sort of. We were talking and I asked about her stepfather. She got really upset and ran off. I haven't seen her since."

"Which way?" Any direction but east would bring the girl to a road, eventually.

"Out between the houses. We were in the Grove, and she just took off."

"East, then. Damn." The land to the east of the compound gave onto thousands of acres of near-wilderness, with few roads. "Have you looked in the houses?"

"No, not yet. I didn't get worried until a little while ago."

"Okay, you check the Pink House, and I'll look in here. Don't forget to look in closets and under beds. She might be hiding." He didn't really think so. Serhilda wasn't a child, who'd crawl into a dark place and figure she was hidden.

When their searches of the bunkhouses yielded no results, Ward sent Annie to the cookshack to get others to help. He went to the Big House, where he started in the game room. Shortly his mother and John joined him.

"I'll start upstairs," his mother said. "Joss will be along in a few minutes to help."

"Evan and Eric are going to check down at headquarters. The others will fan out through the woods.," John added.

"Too damn many hiding places," Ward muttered as he opened yet another closet, this one filled with games and toys. He bent down to look under the bottom shelf, but all he saw were two open crates full of stuffed animals. He was about to move the sofa out from the wall when he heard his mother call.

She was leaning over the railing at the top of the stairs. "I found her. Send everyone else back to the cookshack. You come up here."

At the top of the stairs, Ward could see into his mother's bedroom. The bedspread was rumpled and wrapped around a figure, but no head showed its identity.

"I want you to tell everyone she's here," Cecile said. "Tell them she came up here to wait for me and fell asleep."

179

"Did she?"

"That's what you'll tell them. And when dinner is ready, would you make up a tray for the three of us and bring it up here? I think we need to decide how to handle this whole situation."

He did as he was asked, playing down any danger Serhilda might have been in. "She apparently circled around and sneaked into the Big House right after she ran from Annie," he said when Jennifer pressed him. "If you ask me, she overdid it this morning, running all the way from the park after the hike."

Annie opened her mouth, closed it again when he frowned at her. She gave a quick nod. Ward knew she'd be after him tomorrow for the whole story. Whether he told it or not would be up to his mother. And Serhilda.

When Ward returned to the Big House with the tray, his mother and Serhilda were seated in the wing chairs. Neither looked particularly happy. The thick silence sat there like it had taken permanent residence in the room. Ward set the food out on the small round table between the chairs and pulled the rocker closer. "Help yourselves," he told them. "It's getting cold."

Dinner tonight had been a joint effort among Evan, Elaine, and Stewart. Ward could tell Elaine was used to cooking for small children. The meatloaf and scalloped potatoes were bland, the green beans salt free, and the Jell-O was red.

"All right, Serhilda," Cecile said, when they'd finished their silent meal. "Suppose you tell us why you came here to hide. Annie said you were convinced I hate you."

The girl creased her lips together and closed her eyes. Ward was beginning to wonder if she'd ever speak when she said, "You made me scrambled eggs with jelly. Annie said you only did that when someone was sick."

"But you're not sick, are you? You're troubled, but not sick."

"I feel sick." The words were little more than a whisper. "I feel like I'm dying. Like...like Les."

180

Les? Ward mouthed.

Cecile shrugged.

"Did you know about me?" Serhilda said, instead of answering. "Did Frances tell you about me?"

"No, she didn't," Cecile said, surprising Ward. "I'd lost touch with your mother—she hadn't answered my Christmas and birthday cards for years, not since Tom—her father—died. But none of them ever came back. Not until last summer."

Serhilda nodded. "She sold her house then and moved into a condo in Malibu."

"I worried that something had happened. She is still my daughter, even if she doesn't want to be. I hired a private investigator to find her, and to let me know what she was doing with her life."

Ward looked at his mother with amazement. She'd not said a word to him.

"He did a better job than I'd expected," Cecile went on. "He told me that Frances had a daughter, that I had a granddaughter I'd never known about." A pause, while she stared out the window and breathed deeply. "That's when I wrote to her and invited her to this Gathering. I told her to bring you."

"You wanted to see me? Me?"

Ward heard a lifetime of neglect in those few words.

"Of course. How could I not? And now that I've seen you, seen how much you resemble your grandfather, I am so happy I did." She leaned forward, took Serhilda's restless hands in her own. "Oh, darling, I can't tell you how happy I am to have found you. And how sorry I am that I never knew you before this."

Serhilda's expression hardened. "Sure you're sorry," she said. "You're sorry because it looks really bad that Frances didn't give a damn about her kid. That she gave me away like she would a puppy that peed on her rugs. That she never came to see me, never even called to see if I was still alive for sixteen years. You're

181

sorry because it makes you look bad. What kind of mother were *you* to raise a woman like Frances-the-bitch?"

She jumped to her feet. "Well, you can just go to hell, Granny, because I can take care of myself. I don't need you or this family or...or anybody." She spun around and would have dashed out of the room, but Ward caught her in his arms. She was surprisingly strong for someone so slender, but he was bigger and stronger. He manacled her wrists when she tried to claw him, and wrapped his other arm around her. Despite her kicks and attempts to bite him, he managed to hold her while he dropped into the chair she'd vacated.

"Relax," he crooned. "Calm down. Come on, sweetheart, you're all right. Quiet, now. Quiet."

Her struggles gradually ceased but she still held herself stiffly in his arms.

"What the hell did she mean, her mother gave her away?" he demanded.

"According to the investigator, she was living with Frances's second husband and had been since she was about six months old. He had no legal responsibility for her, but the evidence is he provided her with a good home. Until March, when, for some reason the investigator couldn't discover, he sent her to live with Frances."

"He's dying," Serhilda whispered. "Les is dying."

Looking down, Ward saw tears streaming down her cheeks. "Les? Your father?"

"I wish—"

"He's not her father," Cecile said. "Her birth certificate says Rosenfeld is her father, but—"

"But he died more than a year before I was born." Serhilda laughed harshly. "I guess that's the longest pregnancy on record, huh?" She wiped her eyes with the backs of her hands. "Shit! I'll bet I look like a fucking raccoon."

"A little," Cecile said, before Ward could say anything about her language. "You'll wash. Now tell me about Les. You say he's dying."

"He's got AIDS. The docs say it's only a matter of time. I would have taken care of him, but he wouldn't let me.

"I wanted to take care of him. But he wouldn't let me," she wailed.

"Oh, my darling. "Cecile knelt before Ward and wrapped her arms around Serhilda. "How terrible for you. There's nothing they can do?"

She shook her head. "He's in hospice now. That means he's not gonna live more than six months. I wanted to go see him before we left L.A., but Les told them not to let me in." She lifted a tear-drenched face to Ward. "I want to tell him good-bye."

"And so you shall, if I have anything to say about it," Cecile said. "Tomorrow morning I'll have a talk with your mo— With Frances. And then we'll see what we can do about getting you to Los Angeles to tell your father good-bye."

"He's not my—"

Ward said, "He's your father in every way that matters. He loves you. I'm sure of that."

"You think?"

"I'm certain of it," Cecile told her. "Now, why don't you curl up here in my bed and see if you can rest. But first maybe you'd better take care of those raccoon eyes."

Serhilda stayed on Ward's lap a few more minutes before pushing herself to her feet. She moved like an old woman, stiff and aching, as she accepted a sleepshirt from Cecile and went into the bathroom to change.

"Will you take her to L.A. as soon as we can get more information?" Cecile said as soon as the door closed. "I'll call the investigator tomorrow."

"Of course. But what if this Les refuses to see her?"

"I'll speak to him. Once he hears what I have to say, he'll see her."

"Let's just hope he stays alive long enough."

Chapter Fifteen

Thursday

WHEN ANNIE WOKE, THE SUN WAS ALREADY SENDING ITS slanting rays into the bunkroom. There was something she was supposed to remember....

The air in the room was cold, her breath emerged in little clouds of vapor, making her snuggle down into her blankets. *Too early to get up—*

The door opened. She heard footsteps, a rustle of clothing. The mattress dipped as someone sat on it. "I thought you were going fishing," someone whispered.

Fishing. Clay. She sat up, flinging the covers aside. The cold air raised goose pimples on her bare legs. "What time is it??"

"A little after seven. I didn't notice you were still here until I came back in." Hetty yawned widely. "I slept like a log, never stirred all night long. My body must know it's not going to get much sleep tonight."

"I've got to go. Move!"

Hetty moved.

Annie scrambled into the clothes she'd worn yesterday. She'd told Clay she'd be at the fishing access at five-thirty. *Two hours late. Damn, damn ,damn.*

When she returned from the bathroom, CeCe and Charlene were sitting up in their bunks and Hetty was in front of the dresser, making up her eyes. "I've got to go," she told them. "Tell Mom—or somebody—I'll be back in time to go to Yellowstone."

"Tell her yourself," Hetty said. "She's probably in the cookshack by now."

"No time. I've got to go." Annie pulled her other sneaker on, left it untied. She grabbed a hoodie and dashed out the door.

All the cars' windows were coated with moisture. Annie swiped her forearm across the Accord's windshield, not wanting to take the time to squeegee it. She was about to climb in when she saw the red pickup just beyond Hetty's Corvette. A red pickup that didn't belong here, but down at the fishing access.

It was empty.

"Oh, no!" Frantically she looked around, but saw no sign of Clay. He hadn't come to the Pink House, so where— Of course. The cookshack. Even this far away, she could hear the faint sounds of conversation from its open windows.

CLAY HAD WAITED NEARLY AN HOUR FOR ANNIE, AND HAD ALMOST gone into the river without her. Only the memory of her glee at hooking her first trout had stopped him. He wanted to see, to share that glee again.

He'd driven up to the cluster of houses on the knoll, not intending to stop. Just to see if anyone was stirring. But when he'd slowed in front of the house where she was staying, he'd seen a couple of men crossing the road a ways ahead. One looked like the tall, older man he'd spoken to the other day. Blankenship? Yes,

Ward Blankenship. He parked his pickup beside a classy yellow corvette and followed the men to the long, low white house.

Blankenship came to the door when he knocked, holding a steaming cup. "Looking for Annie, I'll bet."

"I am, yes. She was going to meet me and never showed."

"Probably slept late. She got caught in a hot game of Monopoly last night. It didn't break up until nearly eleven. Coffee?"

"Sounds good. Is she around?"

"Here she comes." Blankenship grinned as he looked past Clay. "I'll get your coffee."

"I'm sorry," he heard Annie say, before he got turned around. She looked as if she'd pulled her clothing on in a hurry—shoes untied, hooded sweatshirt wrong side out, and hair a mass of tangles. The urge to kiss her was so strong he had to forcibly restrain himself.

"Not a problem. I've got weeks yet to fish." He wanted to tell her about yesterday, how everything had gone unbelievably smoothly. How in five short weeks he'd be the owner of *Fly By Knight*, Last Chance's newest and best fly shop and fishing resort.

Since he hadn't even told her he was considering the purchase, he kept his mouth shut. *Later,* he promised himself. *I'll tell her everything later.*

"Weeks? I thought you were on vacation. Don't you have to get back?" She motioned him inside just as her uncle approached with his coffee.

"Not immediately. I'm sort of between jobs." He'd have to go back to Portland one more time, just long enough to clear out his safe deposit box and arrange to have his stored possessions shipped. That would wait until after Labor Day. "I've got the rest of the summer free."

"Lucky man," Blankenship said. "Annie, why don't you introduce him to your folks."

"And to Gran." She grimaced. "She's over there giving you the eye. C'mon. I don't think she'll bite."

As he followed her across the room, he wondered at the change in her. Tuesday she'd been almost hesitant, and...well, vulnerable was the word that had come to mind. Now she seemed self-confident. Was she simply shy with strangers?

He didn't think so. She'd been the one to instigate their first conversation.

"Gran, this is Clay Knight, who's trying to teach me to fly fish. Clay, my grandmother, Ce...uh, Mrs. Blankenship."

"Cecile," the elderly woman said, holding out her hand. "We don't stand on ceremony around here. Have you had breakfast?"

"No, but you don't need to—"

"Nonsense. We've enough to feed an army here. Annie, go put yourself together better while I get acquainted with Mr. Knight. You look like you slept in those clothes." She gestured him to the bench behind them and seated herself beside him.

Clay braved himself for the third degree.

"I want to thank you, Clay, for catching Annie's interest. She's had a...a bad year, and we're all happy to see her find something that interests her."

"It was her idea," he said. "I do admit I've enjoyed it every bit as much as she has. You should have seen her the other day when she hooked a three pound trout. Talk about excited."

"I'm glad. And grateful. Now, tell me a bit about yourself."

Before he had a chance to say much more than where he was from, Annie returned, clothing on correctly and hair combed. "I'm bummed," she said, as she slid onto the bench on his other side. "We're all going to Yellowstone today, so I won't be able to fish this afternoon. And I ruined your morning, too."

"Not at all. I can fish anytime." *Did I really say that?* "There's always tomorrow."

"As long as you're back by ten," Cecile told him. "Ward's organized a raft trip from Big Springs. I'd hate for Annie to miss it."

"I wouldn't," Annie said, too low for her grandmother to hear.

Clay glanced at her, wondering what had put the quaver in her voice. Then he remembered how she'd obviously conquered her fear when she'd followed him into the river Tuesday. Why didn't she just refuse to go with them?

Too many mysteries. He was about to thank them for the coffee and leave, when a loud clanging sounded from the other end of the big room. Looking that way, he saw a tall girl on the porch, ringing a big brass handbell. Before the last *bong* had died away, the people in the room started lining up at a pass-through next to the door.

"You'll stay for breakfast, Clay?" Cecile said. It sounded more like an order than an invitation.

No, he thought. *I'm going fishing.* "Love to," is what popped out of his mouth. The seductive scents of someone else's cooking had no doubt damaged his brain.

Cecile kept him at her side while they ate. Between bites, she named the people in the room. "I'll never remember," Clay protested.

"Some will stick, and with practice you'll remember most. And if you don't, so what? I sometimes forget them myself."

"Gran used to call me Thea-Ann-Kristi," Annie added. "Or sometimes Hetty-Ann, if my mother wasn't around."

"Hetty's the redhead, right? You're cousins?"

"Second cousins. But they both resemble my mother-in-law, except for coloring." Cecile waved. "Hetty, come over here and meet Annie's young man."

"Gran!"

Clay shrugged and shook his head. "I've got a grandmother," he said, for her ears only. "Don't sweat it."

He met Hetty, three teenaged girls whose names he missed, a moody young man, and an assortment of boys from not-quite-teen to barely out of diapers. In between were more adults than he could keep straight. "You're going to have to make me up a cheat sheet," he muttered to Annie when everyone wandered off, having apparently satisfied any lingering curiosity.

As the big room started to empty, the noise level decreased. "Is it always like that?" Clay wondered aloud when the younger kids all disappeared at once.

"Oh, no, sometimes it gets noisy," Hetty said with a grin. "Gran, are you sure I shouldn't tell Mother and Dad about Frank before I go?"

"You know your mother's going to be upset. Why ruin the day for everyone?"

Clay gave Annie a questioning glance.

"Tell you later," she said, barely loud enough for him to hear.

"I'll hold you to that," he murmured.

"Okay, then, I'm off." Hetty departed after picking up a couple of bottles of water from a case near the coffee pots.

"As am I," Cecile said, getting slowly to her feet. "Clay, why don't you join us today? The more the merrier."

Since he'd been thinking the same thing, but from a slightly different perspective, he agreed immediately. "How about it, Annie? Shall we join the caravan? Or would you rather ride with your family?"

What he'd hoped for was an enthusiastic acceptance. What he got was a slow smile, and a soft, "I'd like to be with you."

Even better than enthusiasm.

* * * *

Yellowstone's roads were, as usual, full. Traffic was not quite bumper-to-bumper. Annie fretted at the slowness of their progress until she noticed that Clay was relaxed, one hand on the wheel and the other draped over the edge of the window.

"Doesn't this drive you nuts?"

"What? The traffic? Not a bit. The slower we go, the more I can see. We're here to be tourists, not to get anywhere in particular."

"Except Old Faithful, by one." Annie was relieved that the silence between them was broken at last. She had been aware of Clay throughout the journey, and had surreptitiously been watching him. They had not talked much, just inconsequential comments about the scenery. Annie had been content to enjoy his company. That let her have time to examine her feelings for him.

What were they? She was undeniably attracted to him. He was comfortable to be with. He was good looking, though not classically handsome.

"We'll make it. It's barely ten. Look. Is that an elk?" Clay pointed at a meadow just ahead of them.

"Or a big deer. Oh! I can see five...no, six. Can we stop?"

Clay obligingly pulled onto the broad shoulder. "Binocs behind the seat."

Annie reached back and pulled them out. They both got a chance to view the elk before a group of tourists headed across the meadow, frightening the animals away. "I can't believe how dumb people can be. Those are wild animals. They could attack just as easily as running away."

"To the average tourist, this is just another big zoo, I guess," Clay replied in a tone far milder than hers. "A lot of people who come here have never seen an animal in its natural habitat."

"I know, but it's still dumb to go running after them."

"Did I argue?"

They saw no other wildlife, and eventually they reached Old Faithful. The parking lots were packed, but Clay managed to find a space.

Several of her cousins were standing on the lodge's wide porch. Behind them, in a peeled log chair, sat Gran. "Eric and Jennifer are supposed to be holding a table for us. Shall we go before they eat everything?"

Clay held out his arm to her grandmother, totally abandoning her. She couldn't decide whether to be piqued or amused. She followed with Owen, who walked in his usual withdrawn silence. *Fine with me. I've got problems of my own. I don't need to worry about whatever's bothering you.*

She stifled a small twinge of guilt. This was his first Gathering. He probably was feeling overwhelmed. Had anyone reached out to him? Or were they all leaving him alone, put off by his deliberately keeping them at a distance?

A huge log picnic table awaited them. Annie helped distribute the contents of three picnic baskets and two cardboard boxes, laughing at the look on Clay's face when he saw the abundance of food. She noticed that he did his share at depleting it, though.

"He doesn't seem intimidated," Ward observed, once they'd all filled their plates and found seats. Clay had been hijacked by Annie's mother and Aunt Joss, while she was stuck between Evan and Uncle Ward.

Annie watched Clay, as he laughing replied to something Aunt Joss had said. "No, he doesn't," Annie agreed. She compared Clay's behavior to Walter's the one time he'd come with her to a family Gathering. Clay won, hands down.

In her usual commanding way. Gran organized the whole family to view Old Faithful after lunch. She took Clay's arm, once again crowding Annie aside.

Clay looked back over his shoulder, his expression a plea for help. She just grinned at him. There was no stopping Gran when she was on a roll.

"Looks like you've got some competition," Evan said to her as he draped one arm across her shoulders.

"Only temporary. Besides, why should I consider Gran competition? He's just a friend."

"I think he'd like to be more. Are you ready?"

His concern triggered the ever-imminent tears. "Oh, Evan, I don't know. Sometimes I feel as if I'm finally healing, and then... Oh, God, I miss him so much!"

"Crap! I'm sorry Annie. I shouldn't have said anything."

"No." She caught his hand as he drew away. "It's okay. Honest. I've got to get past this. I'd give anything to...to just stop hurting."

"I guess it takes time."

"I guess it does. How much time, I wonder."

Again his arm went around her shoulders. "As much as it takes. If you're starting to have times when you *don't* hurt, then I'd say you're on the road to recovery. When I was home in March, you still seemed like walking wounded."

"How'd you get so wise?"

"Me? I'm not wise. I've just learned a lot in the past few years. Some of my friends are HIV positive. I watch them live with that knowledge and I've seen a lot of them grow stronger because of it. They've taught me that life is to be lived every single day." He stopped walking, pulling her to a halt. "Annie, the other night, when Aunt Joss..." His voice, usually strong and confident, was thin, uncertain.

She looked up at him, her favorite male cousin. They'd been playmates, she and Hetty and Evan, when they were young. Walter had not liked him and had complained if she met Evan for lunch whenever he visited Portland. Eventually she'd found it easier to be too busy when Evan called. As a result, she hadn't seen him, other than at Calvin's funeral, for nearly four years. Now she saw lines in his face, shadows in his eyes, that hadn't been there before. She saw pain, but also a sort of peace. "You're not...?"

"HIIV positive. No. And I am being very careful, believe me. Ma asked me if I was seeing anyone when I got here. I could tell she was scared."

"She probably is. Even knowing you're careful, I worry. And now, with you going to Africa... Can you blame us?"

His shrug said he couldn't.

"Actually," Annie said after a few steps, "you may have more immediate worries. Aunt Joss isn't good at keeping things to herself."

"You mean Eric and Jennifer?"

Annie gave him a rueful smile. "I never have understood how someone like Eric could have been born in this family. Hetty and I used to wonder if maybe your mother had brought the wrong baby home from the hospital."

"Until he grew up to be the spitting image of Pa. Hard to figure, isn't it." He stepped to the side of the trail to let a gaggle of chattering girls go past. "We're going to miss the show if we don't hurry. Just remember, if you need to talk, a shoulder to cry on, or some really bad advice, I'm your man."

"I knew that. I've always known that. Thanks, Evan. I love you."

"Me too. You." He grabbed her hand and pulled her along the trail. They walked, swinging their hands as they had as children, and for a brief time, Annie felt almost as carefree as she had back then.

Chapter Sixteen

THE GROUP SPLIT UP AFTER THE OLD FAITHFUL ERUPTION. CLAY and Annie headed out along an unpaved trail to see Solitary Geyser, which Clay had never visited. When they arrived back at the Firehole River bridge, they decided to go on to Morning Glory Pool, stopping to see all the sites along the way. Annie found him good company, undemanding, easy-going, and not compelled to fill each moment of silence with chatter.

"When Gran and Gramps first used to come here there were no boardwalks or paved paths. People just walked anywhere," she commented, as they paused to watch Plume Geyser. "It doesn't look as natural now, but it's got to be a lot easier on the soil."

"I guess when you have as many people as this, you've got to manage them. But I'd have liked to see this place before it got developed."

"Me too."

Her hand slipped naturally into Clay's as they continued their stroll. How much brighter the world seemed today than it had for a long time. She was sure the difference came from within her, not from the vivid colors around her. Laughter bubbled in her throat, seeking release.

I wish I could hold on to this, she thought. *I wish it would last.* She knew it wouldn't. When the Gathering was over and she went back to Boise, when she was alone night after night, she'd start thinking, and slide back into the melancholy mood that had held her captive for so long.

Clay pulled her to a halt. She looked where he was pointing. A ground squirrel was being tempted by a peanut in a child's hand. The little boy was about two, with tousled brown hair and round, pink cheeks. About the age Calvin had been... She waited for the familiar pain.

Instead of overwhelming grief, delicious warmth suffused her body when Clay slipped an arm around her waist. Was this so wrong, this response to him? She returned his smile, even as she resolved to talk to Gran as soon as she had a chance. Maybe she could help in the sorting out of feelings that were at once exciting and confusing.

The chipmunk finally made his move, snatching the peanut out of the child's hand. The little boy jumped to his feet, crowing in joy, clapping his hands, chattering a mile a minute in a language only a two-year-old could speak. Clay laughed out loud.

"I know I should disapprove," Annie told him, as they walked on. "Feeding the critters is a bad idea. But he was so cute."

"The kid or the chipmunk?"

"Both, of course. Oh, listen! What's that?" The noise she was hearing was almost like an animal's roar, yet deeper and lasting longer.

A man just ahead of them turned around. "It's Lion Geyser. It's going to erupt."

It did indeed, and Annie and Clay stood, watching, until it had finished its show. After that, they strolled on, stopping at geyser after geyser. Some were sputtering, some were silent, inactive holes in the ground.

After duly admiring Morning Glory Pool, Clay suggested they go on to Biscuit Basin. Annie agreed, more because she didn't want this time with him to end than anything. She'd forgotten that her favorite thermal feature, the Fountain Pain Pots, were there.

"You know, women pay a lot of money in fancy salons for facial mud packs," Clay commented later, as they watched the mud, in all shades of yellow, boil and roil.

"We should get a concession to bottle this and sell it. We'd make a fortune." She wrinkled her nose as she caught a whiff of the steam. "All we'd have to do is tout it as being full of Vitamin S."

"What's vitamin S?"

"Sulfur, but we wouldn't tell them. It would be our secret ingredient."

"You are sulfur of nonsense, I ought to pot you one."

Annie wracked her brain for a pun to top his, without results. She pretended to ignore him for a few minutes, but soon her glance was caught by his twinkling eyes. She grinned in response, enjoying the mild glow that seemed to be a permanent state whenever she was with him.

I wonder how he kisses, when he's serious about it. Does he pucker, or is he more the nibbling kind? I'll bet he doesn't just shove his tongue in and out. He'd be more subtle.

Once again slipping her hand into his felt like the most natural thing in the world. All the way back to Morning Glory, they walked in silence. For her, at least, there was also peace and contentment.

They had just crossed the Firehole River again when he pointed. "Hey! Look at that geyser!" A huge spout of water was erupting from an irregular cone.

"Who are you calling a guy, sir?"

Clay grabbed her and tickled, until Annie begged for mercy. By the time she escaped him and conquered her giggles, the geyser had stopped spouting.

On their way back to the parking area, Annie said, "I think I'm suffering from geyser overload. At first it was a thrill, but now—"

"Now it's sort of 'you've seen one geyser, you've seen them all', isn't it?" Clay shook his head. "I hate to admit it, but that's sort of how I feel too."

"You know what would be fun? To live close enough that you could come up here often and see just one or two of the geysers each time. Then the wonder wouldn't turn into ennui."

He turned to stare at her. "You'd like to live nearby? It's a long way from the city."

She paused to pick a candy wrapper off the boardwalk. "I wouldn't miss the city if I could go for a visit every six months or so. These past few years I've had my fill of city life."

"Let me have that." Clay took the wrapper and stuffed it into his shirt pocket. "Have you ever lived in the country?" He felt like holding his breath while he waited for her answer.

"We never actually lived in town when I was growing up. Our place was a little over five acres, along the Tualatin River south of Lake Oswego. It wasn't exactly country, but it sure wasn't city. What I'd like, what I'd *really* like, is to live somewhere there are seasons besides wet and dry. That's one reason I moved to Boise, after...after my divorce."

"Boise isn't country, either." Unsurprised, but pleased that she'd actually told him something about her past, Clay wondered what else he would discover about her today. The next instant he told himself firmly that he wasn't in any position to care one way or another. *I've got enough on my plate. I can't let this go beyond a summer romance. If that.*

"I'm working on that." She didn't say anything else as they walked the last half mile to the parking area. It was nearly five and time to head back. Clay opened the tailgate and dug a couple of sodas out of his cooler. As he handed her one, he said, "What time does the dinner bell ring?"

"I think it's just sandwiches and fruit tonight, since folks will straggle. Whenever we get there, we'll find food."

The car next to his pickup sat crooked in its space, and he had to do some fancy twisting to get into his door. Once seated, with his seatbelt in place, he said, "Or we could stop for dinner somewhere on the way."

"Gran and Mom know I'm with you, so I don't think they'll be concerned if we don't go directly home. But only if you'll let me buy."

"No way!"

"Clay, you did the driving, provided the gas. The least you can do is let me buy your dinner."

"I invited you. That makes it my treat."

WARD WAS WAITING FOR HIS MOTHER ON THE FRONT PORCH OF THE Big House when she returned from the Yellowstone expedition. He motioned her inside, and she followed him down the hall and through the kitchen. "I haven't much time. I want to get moved while Joss is in the shower," She chuckled. "I'm excited, It's been years since I've been to a sleepover."

"Tell me that again in the morning."

He opened the door to the sun porch for her and waited until she'd seated herself on the wicker couch. "I found Les," he said. "It was easy. Getting to talk to him might be more difficult."

"Oh? How so?"

"I didn't make the connection", he said, lowering himself into a chair facing her. "Serhilda just called him Les, and I'd forgotten his last name. Even when she told me, it meant nothing. Mom, Les is Les Champion."

She frowned in thought. "I've heard that name...oh! The actor." The frown deepened. "Oh, dear, that does complicate matters, doesn't it? I imagine his privacy is well protected."

"It sure is. I've been trying all day to get through the wall of protection. No dice." Swiping a hand across his mouth, Ward grimaced in frustration. "His partner—Brian Silverman—wasn't available. Or wasn't taking calls. I've decided the only way she is going to see him is if I take her down there. Together we may be able to storm the walls."

"Frances will have a fit."

"Frances doesn't have much to say about it. It's a little late for her to start making mothering noises. I'm going to see that Serhilda get a chance to say goodbye to the man who's been her father in all but blood "

His mother's smile was all he could have hoped for. "Go for it then. I'm behind you every inch of the way."

"ELAINE, WAIT A MINUTE. I WANT TO TALK TO YOU."

Elaine waited while Jennifer caught up with her. "Problems?"

"Oh, no, not really, I just wondered..." She chewed her lower lip, not quite meeting Elaine's gaze. "Well, what Gran said. I was wondering how you felt about it." The last sentence came out in a rush.

"How I feel about it? Why should I feel anything about it? It's Hetty's life, and it's not as if she's a kid. She must be getting close to thirty." Janice whimpered in her sleep. Elaine's arms were starting to ache from holding her. "Look, Jennifer, it's late and she's heavy. If you've a problem about Hetty bringing her boyfriend here, take it up with her. It's none of my business."

"I will. It may not matter to you, but I certainly don't want my children exposed to that kind of immorality. It seems to me that the least Hetty could have done was take her lover to a motel somewhere, instead of imposing on her family like this."

"Whatever. Look, I'm tired and Janice weighs a ton. I'll see you tomorrow." Without waiting for Jennifer to reply, she headed down the path to the Pink House. *That kind of immorality, indeed. What would she say if she knew that Ma and Pa had lived together for two years before they got married? I'll bet Eric never told her about that.*

ONCE THEY WERE ON THE ROAD, CLAY SAID, "I PROMISED YOUR father I'd have you home by ten tonight."

"Oh, no! Did he come on all protective father with you?"

"A little, I suppose. Can't say that I blame him, though. I'd probably feel the same way about my daughter."

He heard her indrawn breath. "Your daughter? Do you—"

"Not yet. Someday, I hope. I'd like to have a bunch of kids, raise 'em out here in God's country."

Annie shifted so she was leaning half against the door. "Do you know, I still don't know much about you, other than you love to fish. Oh, yes, you live in Portland. You've met most of my family and I don't even know if you have one."

He kept his eyes on the road as he said. "My parents are both gone. I was an only child. One grandmother is still living, but in frail health. I work... I used to work in a bank. Right now I'm between jobs."

Clay decided, as he inched along with the slow traffic, that it was safe to share his dream with her. Would she call it irresponsible, as others had?

"My granddad taught me to fish. His dream was to live somewhere he could step out of his back door and cast his line. Give him a long weekend, he'd be off to a trout stream. He fished the Deschutes a lot, because it was close to Portland. But when his vacation rolled around, he'd come here, or to Silver Creek, or maybe up to Montana, around Three Forks." A memory came, one that made him chuckle. "Granny always went with him, bringing her knitting. She kept the whole neighborhood in sweaters, all knitted while Granddad fished."

"She never fished?"

"Oh, sometimes she would, but it wasn't a passion for her. Just something to do with Granddad. She always went with him, though. I remember her sitting on the bank in her folding chair, cooler full of sodas on one side of her, knitting bag on the other. She always wore a wide-brimmed sunhat, usually decorated with bright flowers."

Annie smiled at the love in his voice. "So he taught you to fish?"

"He taught me to love to fish, encouraged me to choose a career that would give me plenty of opportunity to do so. Dad never quite approved, even though he was an avid fisherman himself. He urged me to get an education, to do something worthwhile with my life. So did everyone else." Clay grimaced, remembering the sense of loss he'd experienced when he'd made the decision to relegate fishing to hobby status and gone straight from college to the bank.

Annie's pat on his knee told him she heard the regret in his voice.

"Don't get me wrong. I worked hard and never gave less than a hundred percent to my job. But Annie, I died a little, inside, every time I walked through those imposing bronze doors, into that impressive lobby. For thirteen years, I did something worthwhile with my life."

Annie made a soothing, sympathetic sound. "So what do you really, truly want to do, Clay?"

His heart did a flip at her question. She hadn't told him how secure and respectable it was to work in a bank.

"I want to fish. And to live where I can fish, not just visit once a year."

"Good for you. Everybody should follow his dream." There was a curious sadness in her words, as if she had given up her own dreams.

"I've bought a place," he blurted, although he hadn't planned to tell anyone about *Fly By Knight* for a while. Like a new toy at Christmas, he'd wanted to keep it all to himself until the new wore off. "A fly shop and motel. It's not much to look at, but it has a steady clientele and I can build it up. I'll have to work hard, and I'll be in debt for years, but I know I can make a go of it."

"It sounds marvelous. I'll keep my fingers crossed for you." Annie was quiet then. He glanced over and saw her blink, nod.

"Sleepy?" he asked.

"A little. Are we there yet?"

"Not for another hour or so. Go to sleep if you want. I'll expect you to be wide awake and on the river at six tomorrow."

"Slave driver!" But she grinned. "Are you sure it's okay for me to sleep? You've been driving all day. Will you be all right?"

"I'll be fine. Lay your seat back and relax."

She was still sleeping when Clay slowed and pulled off the highway about eight-thirty. The slanting evening light showed the fragility of the bones in her face and the perfection of her skin. Looking at her peaceful face and slightly parted lips, he felt an overwhelming surge of protectiveness and desire. He unbuckled his seat belt and moved across, sliding from under the steering wheel. His fingers stroked lightly along her cheek, trailed down the shadowed column of throat, while he marveled at the delicacy of her features. Annie stirred under his touch, but her eyes remained closed. His fingers stole under her collar, crept around so that his hand cupped the back of her head. *I've got to taste her. Just once.*

Annie came out of sleep, feeling a feather touch across her lips, then down her neck. She figured that if she pretended sleep, Walter would leave her alone. She wanted nothing to do with him—not any more.

But his touch was leaving a trail of burning flesh in its wake. She could not move, so delicious was the warmth exploding in her belly. But she must! She would not let Walter make love to her. She forced her eyes open as she felt warm breath on her lips.

The face before her was not Walter's, not classically handsome, not wearing a practiced smile. In her relief, she relaxed, leaning into Clay's kiss, returning it with fervor, parting her lips under his and boldly meeting his questing tongue with her own. She arched her back, trying to get closer to him, to feel his chest against her suddenly taut nipples.

She felt Clay's hand on her belly, heard the seatbelt release. His arms enfolded her, his mouth covered hers. *A nibbler. Oh, yes, that's good.*

How good he smelled. And tasted. She licked delicately at his lips, flicked his tongue, pulled her mouth away to press a line of kisses along the firm angle of his jaw. Although she felt his hands roving over her back, she ignored their distraction, intent on biting gently at his earlobe and probing his ear with her tongue.

"Annie, I think we had better look up some supper before we do something we regret," Clay whispered against her hair.

She ignored him, her questing tongue and nipping teeth sending shivers through her body.

He took her face between his hands, kissed her lightly, almost impersonally. "Whoa. I'm hungry." Reaching across her, he opened her door, gave her a little nudge.

Annie scooted out of the pickup, knowing her face must be red enough to light a cave. *My God! I've known him less than a week! What must he think?* She sought the right words to explain herself to him.

204

He dropped out of the cab behind her, slid his arm around her and pulled her close. His kiss this time was somehow comforting, protective, and almost brotherly. He gathered her close to him in a quiet, soothing embrace, with no hint of passion. She relaxed, letting the embarrassment fade. She knew he somehow understood her confusion, her chagrin.

From then on, they were like a couple of old friends, comfortable with each other. Their conversation over juicy, elbow-dripping hamburgers was limited to small moans of contentment as they devoured the burgers, munched on fries crispy-hot on the outside, soft and mealy on the inside.

Even after supper, the tension was in abeyance. He drove her to the ranch, pulled up before the Pink House. Only then did he reach for her.

"I hate for today to end," she murmured, when his lips finally lifted from hers.

"I know. I hate to let you go. But if I don't get some sleep, the fish will catch us tomorrow, rather than the other way around."

She stood at the window, watching the taillights of his pickup disappear down the road. Wondering if the tiny glimmer of peace she'd found today might, with his help, grow into enough to sustain her as she rebuilt her life.

Chapter Seventeen

Friday

T HERE'S A WOMAN IN MY BED."

The voice in her ear was deep and warm and sent shivers down her spine. Hetty didn't move, but she did breathe deeply, inhaling the faint spiciness lingering from yesterday's aftershave, the musky reminder of their silent and frantic lovemaking last night.

"Hey, woman, wake up. I'm horny."

She turned in his arms, her hand going unerringly to his cock. "So'm I," she said, and put her open mouth against his neck.

His hands were practiced, hers were persuasive. This morning the hunger was muted, and they moved slowly, teasingly. Although they hadn't been lovers long, they already knew what worked. Had known since the first time.

When he finally slid into her, they moved together in a slow, sensuous dance, content to let the passion build slowly, fully.

All Hetty knew was the feel of his seeking mouth, the clasp of his work-hardened hands, the rhythm of his lithe, strong body as he drove her higher and higher toward the kind of mind-blowing climax only he could give her.

So close. She felt the first tingles in her toes, the first kindling heat in her face.

The noise in the hall outside seemed distant, until the door flew open.

Until a woman shrieked, "You tramp! You filthy little tramp. How could you!" Her voice shattered into disjointed curses.

Frank yelled and fell to one side, pulling free of her. Before Hetty could react, he'd thrown himself across her, his big shoulders covering her face. She felt him jerk, heard his breath whistle between his teeth.

His body stiffened, jerked again, and he kicked, hard. "Cut it out!"

"Joss!" A man's voice—not her father's—cut through the now incoherent shrieks.

"Grab her," someone cried.

Something hard thwacked against her thigh, sending an explosion of pain from foot to belly. Frank rolled to that side, putting himself even more between her and her mother.

"Get the rolling pin!"

A high scream, then Ben's voice saying, "I've got her. Damn it, John, help me."

"Don't move, Hetty," Thea yelled.

Hetty saw the edge of a blanket flip over Frank's shoulder, felt him relax minutely.

"Shit," he muttered between clenched teeth. "I hope to hell she didn't break my arm." He eased off of her, moving slowly, holding his left arm with his right hand.

She stayed still until he rolled onto his side next to her. Grabbing the edge of the blanket, she attempted to scoot under it, but nearly screamed herself as she put strain on her throbbing thigh. "Oh, God, Frank! Let me see—"

"Get her out of here," Louisa said, from somewhere behind Hetty. "Take her downstairs, if you can. I'll tend to this."

Frank looked up at her, his mouth twisted in a half grin. "I thought you said your family would love me."

Hetty let out a breath she hadn't known she was holding. "What I said was that Gran would love you. I don't think my mother does." She looked toward the door as it clicked shut. "Aunt Louisa, can you come and take a look at his arm?"

"It's fine."

"The hell it is." Hetty flipped the blanket back to his waist. "She's an EMT. Let her decide."

Her mother screamed again, somewhere downstairs. Hetty heard her father's deep voice and Uncle Ben's weathered baritone, both sounding strained.

While Aunt Louisa was poking and prodding Frank's arm, Hetty got dressed, moving slowly and favoring her leg. The muscles of her thigh were knotted, sending sharp knives of pain into her pelvis with every movement, but she was reasonably sure it was only bruised. She'd worry about showering later, she decided, and if anyone complained about how she smelled, she'd tell them—

Oh, shit! I can't believe this. My mother, the drunk. She glanced at the clock. Seven twenty-two. *Something set her off.*

"Without an X-ray, I can't be sure it's not cracked," Louisa told Hetty a few minutes later. "You'd better plan on driving down to— I can't remember where the nearest hospital is."

"Ashton," Aunt Thea said, as she came back into the room. "Hetty, has your mother ever behaved this way before?"

"I've never seen her this bad," Hetty told her, "but I haven't been around much these past few years."

"I've wondered..." Aunt Louisa said, "Ordinarily we don't see Joss and John unless we're here at the same time, but we ran into them a few months ago at one of those outdoor things in Portland. I had the feeling she was...nervy. As if... Never mind. There, now, hold that arm still while I go get something to splint it with." With a gentle pat to Frank's shoulder, she left the room.

Hetty sat on the edge of the bed, feeling a hundred years old and as tired as if she'd walked ten miles. "I'm going to drive Frank to the emergency room, Aunt Thea. While I'm gone, will you look and see if you can find where Joss is hiding her booze? If Dad won't let you search their room, talk to Gran. It's time for him to stop denying there's a problem."

"Booze? You think your mother's drunk?"

"I'm pretty sure she is, although I hadn't realized she was starting to drink so early." She refused to look at Frank, not wanting to see his disgust. If he had a brain, he'd be on the evening plane back to Seattle. *Damn! I had such hopes for him.*

Aunt Louisa splinted Frank's arm and Aunt Thea fed him. He went along with whatever they told him, not saying much. Hetty decided to shower after all, since they were likely to be gone all day.

Her thigh was already swelling and turning purple, a long, almost rectangular bruise perpendicular to its length. The force of water hitting it was enough to make her cringe. She gritted her teeth and kept going. By the time she slid into the driver's seat of her car, she was damp with sweat and wondering what they did to people who killed their mothers.

"So your mother's a drunk, huh?" was the first thing Frank said, once they were on the highway. "Is that why you don't drink?"

"Part of it. The rest is that I just don't like the taste of liquor. What's your excuse?"

"I'm an alcoholic."

Oh, shit. That's all I need. Hetty watched the road, locked her hands firmly on the wheel. Kept her voice light. "Oh? You don't seem like one. I've never seen you take a drink."

"You won't either. I haven't had a drink since I was twenty. But there's no such thing as an ex-alcoholic." He held up his left hand, showing her the stub of a little finger she'd often wondered about. "This was the wake-up call. I figured the next time it could be my whole hand. So I quit."

"What happened?"

"I worked in a shop that made cabinets for tract houses then. Plain, birch-faced plywood doors. Nothing fancy or expensive. That day I woke up late, hung over, so I didn't pack a lunch. I went out to lunch, had a couple of beers. I didn't feel them. It took more than a couple of beers to make me drunk. Never thought a thing about it. That afternoon I was using a table saw to cut cabinet doors from sheets of plywood."

He rubbed the stub with his thumb. "I didn't even notice this until blood sprayed onto my safety glasses."

"It didn't hurt?" Hetty couldn't decide if she wanted to be sick at the picture his words had painted or to grab and kiss his poor, mangled hand. She settled for reaching across and holding it.

He returned her squeeze. "Not right then. Later it hurt like a son of a bitch. I couldn't work for a while, and it gave me plenty of time to think."

"I'll bet it did." She drove in silence for several miles, unable to imagine her mother having the strength of will to do what Frank had done. Jocelyn Armstrong had been indulged all her life, had never had to scrimp and save, had never had to deal with any real adversity. *Well, neither have I,* she admitted silently. *But I'm stronger than she is. I always have been. I wonder why.*

They were over the ridge and on the long descent into Ashton when she said, "I should have told Joss right off, as soon as I got to the Gathering. But I wanted you to meet the family, and I knew she'd have a fit if I told her you were coming. I didn't want to ruin the week for everyone. I wouldn't blame you if you went back to Seattle and never wanted to see me again."

"That's not going to happen. I'll stick it out if you will."

"But she's apt to make a big scene when we get back."

"If she does, we'll move into a motel. I was pretty impressed with the way the rest of your family rallied round and took care of everything. I'd like to get to know them better." This time it was his hand that took hers and squeezed. "Besides, didn't you say something about a raft trip this afternoon? I'd hate to miss that."

"You probably will anyhow," she told him. "I've never been in an emergency room for less than half a day. It's already after nine."

"Think positive thoughts."

Hetty nodded. The last thing she wanted to do was sit in a raft all afternoon. *I hurt.*

"JOHN, STOP BEING AN OSTRICH," CECILE TOLD HIM. "HETTY SAYS she's been trying for a long time to get you to admit that Joss's drinking is out of control."

"Nonsense. She's just upset about Hetty's deception. I'm amazed, Cecile, that you'd be a party to such underhanded dealings."

"She was drunk. At seven in the morning. That goes beyond upset."

John paced the length of the living room and back again. "Impossible. She'd just gotten out of bed—"

"No, she hadn't," Ben said. "I heard someone coming downstairs about three. My back was bothering me, so I came down here to see if I wouldn't rest better in the recliner. Couldn't figure out who'd be wandering around then, so I took a look. It was Joss, heading for the kitchen." He shrugged. "I figured she was looking for something to relax her, after that scene she made at dinner."

"Did you hear her go back upstairs?" Cecile asked.

"No, but I fell asleep before four. She was still downstairs then. Cecile, why didn't Hetty tell her mother about her young man herself? Why'd she get you to do it for her?"

Cecile grimaced. "It was my idea, Ben. John, I'm sorry. I thought... I thought not giving her time to stew about it would be best. And I wanted to protect Hetty. She has never wanted to bring a man to meet the family before."

"I should hope not. Good lord, Cecile, do you have any idea what the people I work with would say, know that my daughter is living in sin? And not just once, but one man after another. I don't know how many there have been. It's shameful."

Unable to contain her laughter, Cecile did her best to moderate it. "Oh my, if you could just hear yourself. You sound like something out of a Victorian novel. Times have changed, John, they've changed drastically. I'll bet that a good many of your colleagues at the bank are either 'living in sin'..." She made quote marks in the air with her fingers. "...or they have children who are. Traditional marriage is just one option today. It's not like when I was young, and a woman who opted to stay single was automatically assumed to be either wanton or homosexual."

"You can say that. All your children are respectable. Hetty... Well, I confess, I've never understood her. Neither has Joss."

"My children's sins are many and varied," Cecile said with a small chuckle, "and so are my grandchildren's. How about you, Ben? I doubt yours are any better."

"Well, there's Eric," Ben said, grinning. "He's pretty upright."

"A son you can be proud of," John said. "But Hetty—"

"Look, John, this is getting us nowhere. You won't listen to anything we say about Joss's condition, and you're not ready to accept Hetty's right to live her life as she chooses. I hate to say this, but I think you'd be happier if you took Joss away before Hetty and Frank get back."

John visibly donned his substantial bank CEO dignity. "I'd already decided to do so. We won't be able to get into the condo at Jackson Hole until Sunday, but I'll find us somewhere to stay until then. No sense wasting my vacation time." His shoulders slumped just a trifle. "Joss will be much better there. It's quiet and someone's usually looking for a good Bridge game."

Cecile sighed in defeat. "I still wish you'd talk to someone about her drinking."

His mouth firmed and his brows drew together, but he said nothing. He didn't need to. His expression said NO all too well.

After he'd gone upstairs, Cecile leaned back and sighed. "That went badly. My fault."

"My brother is as blind as a bat and as stubborn as any Missouri mule," Ben said. "His only saving grace is that he doesn't hold a grudge."

"Is there anything you can do?"

"I'll talk to Louisa. We'll see what we can come up with. Maybe John will listen to her, once he's over his mad."

"I hope so," Cecile said in a tired voice. "I hope so."

THIS MORNING ANNIE CARRIED HER OWN NET, HAD THREE FLIES OF her very own in a small plastic box in her shirt pocket. Clay had handed them to her before they donned their waders. "I'm not sure what they're biting today, but you can try these. The big brown one's a hopper, the one with white wings is a mayfly."

"I'll bet this one's an ant," she said, gingerly touching the minute tuft of red feathers.

"It is. You won't be using it today. I just thought you'd get a kick out of it."

She did. While the tiny fly didn't really look like an ant to her, a fish might be fooled, if it were hungry.

Annie and Clay fished until about ten. Neither of them spoke of the previous evening, although she often felt his gaze on her. She stole glances at him, too, when she was sure he wasn't looking her way.

Clay was not a particularly handsome man, she decided. Certainly nothing like Walter, who was extremely good looking, in an austere way. Clay's hair was light brown, his eyes the color of dark chocolate. His face was the sort to be forgotten, except that she hadn't been able to put it out of her mind last night. She loved his smile, the way his eyes gleamed when he spoke of fishing. She also liked the fact that he was only a few inches taller than she was, probably around five-eight. Kissing a very tall man had always made her feel awkward, as if she needed a box to stand on.

Her pole dipped as something took her bait. She reeled in, discovered that her catch was probably a bit of water weed, because instead of fighting her, it just sat there. After a few firm tugs, she managed to pull the hook loose. Sure enough, when she'd reeled it all the way in, there was a strand of slimy green stuff attached.

Despite this minor setback, she managed to hook several good-sized trout. Each time was as big a thrill as the first. During the quiet periods between fish, her line drifted with the current, or she practiced her casting, Getting it to form that perfect S-curve was her goal, and sometimes she came close.

Time meant nothing on the river. Her awareness narrowed, enclosing her in a globe of peace and serenity. The river sang to her, with the occasional call of a hunting hawk or a lonely meadowlark a bright counterpoint to its pensive melody. Her lifelong fear of water no longer controlled her, at least not here. She moved with confidence, feeling her slow way across the uneven river bed, holding herself against the current. When Clay called to her that it was time to quit, she had to force herself to make her way to the bank.

"I wish the fish didn't take siestas," she complained as she shucked her waders. But when she tried to stand, her legs shook, forcing her to plop back down onto the log. "Wow! How long were we out there?"

Clay glanced at his watch. "More than three hours. Too long for a beginner. I should have kept better track of the time."

"It was wonderful. I did great! I caught four fish. Did you see that last one? He was enormous." She held her hands about a yard apart. "Really, really enormous."

"I saw him." Clay held his hands about half as far apart. "Pretty good sized."

"Enormous," Annie insisted. She yawned. "Gosh, I could really use a nap."

"There's a quilt in the gear box. We could spread it in that little hollow where we sat the other day. It's shady."

"I can't." She stood again, this time managing to stay on her feet. Although her legs still quivered, they held her up. "I've got to get back. It's ten of ten." A thought struck her as she reached for the waders. "Why don't you come rafting with us? I'm sure there's room."

"I don't think so. Not today." He turned away, to stow their gear in the back of the pickup. "How about tomorrow morning, though? Same time?"

"I'll do my best," she said, disappointed at his refusal. Puzzled too. Last night he'd acted as if he wanted her. This morning he was treating her like a sister.

As far as Annie was concerned, she had all the brothers she needed. Brothers didn't kiss like he had, and she wanted more.

How much more? A question she had no answer for.

Chapter Eighteen

Annie found Gran in the bunkroom, lying down. "Hey, are you all right?"

"Perfectly fine. Just snatching a bit of peace and quiet before we go to Big Springs. It's been a busy morning."

"Oh? Did Aunt Joss make a scene?"

"You might say that, yes. I'm sure someone will tell you all about it." Gran closed her eyes, a hint she wanted to be left alone if Annie had ever seen one.

Not feeling particularly cooperative, Annie sat on her bed and propped her elbows on her knees. "I can't get out of this, can I?"

Gran sighed. "If you're talking about the raft trip, no. I know boating is not your favorite activity, but there's no reason for you to be uncomfortable this time. You've done this before, so you know the river's gentle, and fairly shallow."

"I'm not afraid." But a familiar hollowness was in her belly, the tightness in her throat. "I don't see why I have to. I thought this was supposed to be a vacation. Vacations are for enjoying yourself." Even to her ears, her voice had a whiny stain to it.

Another sigh. Gran could do long-suffering better than anyone. "Annie, I arranged this for my pleasure. I want my loved ones around me as much as possible this week."

Despite her amusement, Annie suddenly realized that this could be Gran's last reunion. She was what? Eighty-one? Eighty-two? It was hard to remember she was that old, because she was healthy and vigorous. *She could probably out hike me even now.*

"Yes, ma'am," she said with false meekness. "Whatever you say."

"Oh, go away and let me rest. I'm an old woman, you know."

Annie went, laughing.

Hetty's Corvette came snarling up the road as she was heading to the cookshack. She waved and decided to wait so she could meet the infamous Frank.

Hetty climbed out of the car with difficulty, favoring her left leg. She hobbled around to the other side of the car and opened the door. Curious, and a little alarmed, Annie recrossed the road. "Is something wrong?"

A very large man unfolded himself, with Hetty's help. He had a bright yellow cast on his right arm. Once upright, he said something in a low voice to Hetty.

"Everything's fine now. This is Frank." She slid her arm around him. "Frank, my favorite cousin, Annie Ab— Annie Ogilvie."

"Welcome to the Floating Nought."

His smile seemed strained, as if he were in pain. "Thanks. I'm glad to be here."

Hetty made an indeterminate noise.

"Yes, I am, Het. I've been looking forward to meeting your family. And this raft trip sounds like a good way to get acquainted."

"Don't be silly. You can't—"

"The cast is waterproof. Besides, I'm going to be riding in a raft, not swimming." He ruffled her hair, something Annie knew Hetty hated worse than anything. "What am I supposed to do? Sit on my butt and waste my vacation?"

Hetty's expression indicated that she thought his idea a very good one, but she didn't say anything. Together the three of them strolled toward the cookshack. Hetty still favored her leg, but it seemed to loosen as they walked.

The cookshack was filled with a loud buzz of conversation. Annie went to get a cup of coffee and Hetty took Frank around the room, introducing him. Most of the conversation she overheard was people talking about the planned raft trip. "Ask Uncle Ward," she said, each time someone asked her about it. She didn't even want to think about it, until she was forced onto the raft.

Finally Uncle Ward climbed up on a bench and waved his arms for silence. "For those of you who haven't been here before, the reach of the Henrys Fork between Big Springs and Macks Inn is great for rafting. It's fairly shallow, not too swift, and clean enough to drink. There's a landing, about a quarter mile below the springs, where we'll get in. It takes around three hours to float it. Access to the river is limited along there, so floating is the only way you'll see it."

Jennifer had a worried frown on her face. "Surely you're not planning to take the babies along."

"Why not?" Gran demanded from the doorway. "My children went with us when we canoed that river before they could walk. We just put life jackets on them and tied them to our belts. It didn't matter though. None of them ever fell in. They'd better sense."

Aunt Louisa said, "I thought you told me the children had swimming lessons this summer, Jennifer."

"Only Normie and Angela. The others are too young—"

"Nonsense, Jen," Elaine said. "Janice learned to swim before she was two. None of yours are that young."

Jennifer gave her sister-in-law a dirty look. "I don't think I should risk myself in a raft, either. Do you, Eric?" She patted her rounded belly.

"There's no risk. Heck, Ma took us kids on the river about a month before Elaine was born, didn't you Ma?"

When Aunt Louisa laughingly agreed, Jennifer stuck out her lower lip and sat down.

Kenna reached across and patted her hand. "Don't worry. Peter says it's perfectly safe. The kids will love it. Emma's so excited she's practically hysterical."

"I still say three is too young to take on a rubber raft," Jennifer said, sounding petulant.

"She's not real happy, is she?" Hetty murmured into Annie's ear. "And I shouldn't be amused, should I?"

"No, but I think it's hilarious that Eric didn't indulge her about this," Annie replied, equally low-voiced. "We're really wicked, you know that? We shouldn't laugh at her."

Still keeping her voice low amidst the tumult, Hetty said, "Can we take your car? I don't want to drive, and I'd like an hour or so of relative silence before we get stuck in a raft with the family."

"Sounds good to me." She wanted to ask Hetty why she was limping, and knew she'd never get an answer in this crowd.

Together they packed a lunch for the three of them. Hetty wanted time to show Frank Big Springs before meeting the rest for the float trip. They drove away as the rest of the family was still deciding who was going to ride with whom.

The parking area was empty when they reached the springs. After reading a nearby interpretive sign, Frank said he wanted to walk the nature trail.

"Are you sure?" Hetty said.

"I'm fine," he said. "Stop worrying."

"If you're not back in fifteen minutes, I'm coming after you."

"Make that a half-hour. I may want to stop and look around the cabin." He checked his watch. "We've plenty of time. Your uncle said the rafts would be delivered at the launch at one-thirty. It's not one yet."

Hetty looked after him as he walked away, a frown on her face.

"Okay, let's have it," Annie said. "Something happened this morning and I want to know what it was. Gran said your mother made a scene."

"She did more than that. I suppose you noticed that she and Dad weren't around."

"I wondered." They leaned over the bridge railing. Below them, in water so clear that they could see the plants on the riverbed clearly, were five huge trout, idly moving their tails just enough to stay in one place.

"Good grief! I'd forgotten how big the trout grew here!" Annie said. She watched the fish for a moment, wondering how it would feel to hook something that size. "Okay, spill it."

"And will you look at that water! I didn't expect it to still be so clear."

"Hetty—"

"Apparently Mother built up a good head of steam after Gran told her about Frank last night. Uncle Ben said she went to the kitchen about three, and we figure she started drinking then." She went on to tell Annie of the morning's events.

"My God!" Annie whispered, when Hetty concluded with the visit to the emergency room in Ashton. "It's a wonder she didn't break his arm."

"A cracked ulna is bad enough. He's not going to be able to work for a month, at least not if he has to handle anything

221

heavy." Turning her back on the river, she leaned against the bridge railing. Her voice trembled as she said, "Oh, Annie, I'm so scared. He says it's not my fault Mother tried to kill him—don't shake your head. She was totally out of control. Maybe she wasn't thinking murder, but if she'd hit him just right..."

"On the head..."

"Yeah. Scary thought." Turning back, she leaned over and stared at the water. "This just boggles the mind, doesn't it? More than two million gallons of water a day, just pouring out of the earth. Enough to supply a small city. I guess I didn't pay attention to this when we came here as kids. Now I'm impressed."

The message was clear. They weren't going to talk about this morning's events any more.

"What are those weeds down there?" Annie pointed to the mats of floating and submerged plants in the water.

"That one looks like a *Mimulus*," Hetty said.

"Right. Sure. What's a *Mimulus*?"

"*Mimulus* is monkey-flower. See those yellow flowers over there." Hetty pointed. Two small flowers floated in the tangled midst of matted leaves.

"So you haven't forgotten everything you learned in school," Annie said. "How come you never did anything with your botany, Het?"

"Oh, Annie, don't you start in on me, too. I get enough of that from my folks," Hetty said, wearily. "I'm doing very well financially, thank you very much. Far better than I would in academia. Besides, look at all the travel I get paid to do."

She hadn't meant to sound critical. Apparently Hetty was still touchy on the subject of what her parents called her wasted education. "Sorry. Shouldn't we be going? It's nearly one-thirty."

"We should. And here comes Frank, just in time."

The rest of the family was assembled and four large rubber rafts were waiting in the water when they arrived at the landing. Uncle Ward was assigning places.

"I forgot my sun screen," Annie said as she waited to be told where to go. "Did you bring yours?"

"In here." Hetty lifted her arm, in which swung a big tote. "I'll share."

Ignoring the confusion, she eyed the rafts with some reluctance. She truly didn't want to board one of the bright yellow boats. *I don't have much choice. Not unless I want to create a scene.* She picked up a flotation vest that looked about the right size, but didn't put it on.

Joey's shrill voice cut through the confusion. "No! I won't wear that dumb thing! I won't! I won't!"

She looked over. Eric was trying to get his middle son into a bulky orange flotation vest, without much success. The boy was writhing and twisting, doing everything he could to make the process difficult.

Nearby, Jeremy, already wearing a similar vest, watched the contest. He seemed puzzled. But then he'd been rafting on this river since he was a baby.

Uncle Ward came over, squatted down in front of Joey. "You want to go on the raft, don't you kiddo?"

The boy stopped struggling. "Yeah. But I won't wear that thing!"

"Then stay here."

"Huh?" Joey's eyes went round and his mouth dropped open. He was obviously used to having his tantrums result in his getting whatever he wanted.

"Look, Uncle Ward, I'll keep my eye on him." Eric said.

"He'll wear that vest or stay on shore."

"But he can swim," Eric protested.

"Vest or shore," Uncle Ward insisted, looking not at Eric but at his son. Annie didn't doubt that Joey would wear the life vest if he wanted to get aboard a raft.

"Eric, maybe it would be better if Joey and Bertie stayed behind. I wouldn't mind—"

"Jennifer, we are all going on this raft trip together. Put on the life jacket, Joey."

"Da-a-a-d!"

"Now!" After a short, stubborn silence, Joey sullenly allowed his father to slip the vest over his shoulders, buckle it across his chest.

"Do I have to wear one, too, Uncle Ward?" Serhilda asked, her tone mocking.

"You're a big girl. It's up to you. But you'd better be able to swim like a fish. Anyone who can't isn't going out on that river without one."

Frank stepped forward. "I guess I'd better wear one, then. Not many fishes with one of these." He brandished his cast.

Annie slipped into her vest, and saw that both CeCe and Charlene had done the same. She smiled, because she knew CeCe had earned her Red Cross Lifeguard certification last summer.

Ward had them all gather next to their rafts. He counted noses. "Okay, folks, let's get this show on the road." He shoved the first raft into the water, then the second.

Annie told herself she'd be perfectly safe as she clambered aboard the raft holding Owen, her parents, Gran, and Kristi. Ward followed her and they were away. The other rafts were slowly floating downstream just ahead of them.

The river flowed serenely between banks covered with lodgepole pine, sagebrush, and other, greener, shrubs. At first Annie held herself stiffly against the side of the raft, no more comfortable than she'd ever been in a boat. Within a few minutes the gentle motion and the warmth of the sun relaxed her. *This isn't so bad. Not like actually being in the water.*

If only she had gotten over her fear of water sooner. Much sooner, in time to send Calvin to the Water Babies program as Aunt Louisa had recommended.

A touch on her arm roused her. She looked over to see Kristi's arm pointing at something in the water. A small black head was coming straight toward the raft, long ripples trailing out behind it.

"Muskrat," Ward whispered. "Look, there's another." He pointed to the bank. Sure enough, a second vee of ripples spread behind another half-submerged animal face.

Annie elbowed herself upright, determined to waste no more of the trip in drowsing. Soon her vigilance was rewarded by the sight of three sandhill cranes grazing in a marsh along one low bank. The birds were so close that she could see their fierce yellow eyes and their bright red topknots.

She watched them as the raft floated onward, until they were far behind. She turned forward again when Owen cried, "Look! A woodpecker."

I wish I'd brought my binoculars.

SERHILDA WISHED SHE WAS IN THE RAFT WITH WARD. HE TREATED her like she had a brain. "Stop kicking me," she told Angie. *Excuuuse me. Angela.* The kid was the farthest thing from an angel Serhilda could imagine.

"I'm not."

"Well then, stop pushing on my leg with your foot."

"You'd have much more success with my children if you were polite," Jennifer said to her, from the front of the raft. "Rudeness only begets more of the same."

Fuck off. She only thought the words though. She could just imagine dear, sweet Jennifer's reaction if she'd spoken aloud.

Everyone in the boat just behind was staring and pointing at the shore. She looked that way. Three great big birds. They looked as tall as she was, but totally bizarre. Like something out of a SciFi flick. "Cool. Hey, Tomás, look at those cool birds."

Tommy rose to his knees, making Angela let out one of her fire-engine screams when the raft bobbled, just the tiniest bit.

Sheesh!

Pretty soon someone else pointed out a dark brown something in the water. Serhilda watched it and its buddy swim by. Maybe this rafting wasn't such a drag after all. She decided to see if she could be the first one to point out something, and leaned over the edge of the raft. Something in the water. Like a snake maybe. A great big snake, big enough to swallow Angela.

If she didn't actually see one, she'd make one up. Just for Angela.

Chapter Nineteen

THEA LAY RELAXED AGAINST THE SIDE OF THE RAFT, HALF ASLEEP. Sunlight warmed her face, birds sang in the woods along the shore, and the laughter of her family told of their enjoyment. It had been a good Gathering, for the most part. Annie seemed to be mending, at last. That young man, Clay Something-Or-Other, had been good for her. Who'd have thought she'd get interested in fishing. With her fear of water...

She heard a splash, louder than a fish would make. A shriek. She whipped her head around, looking for the source.

Someone was in the water beside the middle raft. Her first thought was that one of the older children had jumped in, as hers used to do, to swim alongside the rafts for a ways. But who was screaming? Not Angela...

No, it was Jennifer. She was crouched at the side of the raft, holding out her arms and yelling for all she was worth.

A small arm appeared in the middle of the splashes, a dark head, child-sized. Disappeared under swirling water. "Oh, my God!" Thea whispered. It was happening again. She would drown. Just like Annie. Like Calvin.

Memory replaced the present....

Only three children played at the water's edge. The narrow sandy beach was dented with small footprints, furrowed where childish engineers had dug a canal, built a dam. Nearby Annie's red plastic bucket lay half in the water. Beyond the quiet eddy, the white water of the Sandy River flowed noisily over and around rounded boulders.

"Annie? Where's Annie?"

Sandy shrugged. "I don't know, Thea. She was here a few minutes ago." She went back to diapering her baby.

Thea hardly heard her. She was scanning the scattered trees and brush, looking for the bright flash of Annie's yellow playsuit. She called again and again, while the other adults, alarmed now, helped her search. With each call, she became more frightened.

Annie was fearless. The white water didn't scare her, no matter how often Thea told her to stay close to shore.

She stumbled along the shore, feet bruised by the big cobbles, bare arms scratched by stiff shrubs at the water's edge. "Annie! Annie, where are you?"

Her voice was lost in the bellow of the creek, narrower now, running between rocky banks.

A shout came from farther downstream. Thea ran through the trees, through branches that whipped her face, left more stinging scratches along her bare arms. She burst from a clump of brush to see Stan, Sandy's husband, holding a limp and dripping form.

Annie was unresponsive, her face bruised. Before Thea could snatch her from Stan, he had laid her on the ground and was breathing into her tiny mouth, pumping her small chest between his big hands. Thea fell to her knees and reached for her child, but someone caught her, held her away while Stan worked.

Sandy stood behind her husband, holding her own baby, and saying, over and over, "Wake up. Wake up. Oh, please, wake up!"

Thea had no voice for pleas or prayers. She clutched at the strong arms that held her, never looking away from Annie's face, all but hidden under Stan's.

She is so small. So very small. Oh, God, what if she's...

Annie's legs suddenly spasmed, and then began kicking vigorously. Her thin little arms flailed. His big hands still wrapped around her chest, Stan sat back on his heels. "She's breathing," he said, almost a whisper. "Her heart's going. Thank God!"

Sandy gently laid a towel over Annie. It flew off again as Annie continued to kick wildly. She hiccupped, coughed, and began crying, a pitiful, thin little cry.

Thea pulled free from the restraining arms, crawled to her daughter. "Annie. Oh, Annie."

Stan held her off when she would have picked her daughter up and hugged her tightly. "We need to get medical attention. Sandy, you take over here. I'll drive Thea and Annie into town. Meet us at the hospital."

Thea never knew how they got her into the station wagon, nor did she remember anything of the journey to the nearest hospital, twenty-odd miles away...

WARD JUST HAPPENED TO SEE JOEY GO OVER THE SIDE. IN AN instant he'd rolled into the water. With a few quick strokes, he reached the boy, who was still threshing around, still gasping. Ward grabbed an arm, used it to pull the boy close to his chest. "Stop it. I've got you."

Another gasp, then a yell, choked off when Joey coughed. Ward wrapped both arms around him, felt for the bottom with his feet. *Wouldn't you know, the kid would pick the deepest part of the river to fall into.* He kicked his way toward shore, was soon able to stand, leaning into the gentle current. "Damn it, Joey, hold still. You're not hurt."

Jennifer was still screaming, but it sounded like Eric was trying to shut her up. Ward turned Joey, who was now clawing and twisting, in an attempt to free himself, to face him. "If you don't stop trying to get away, I swear I'll drop you," he growled. The boy went dead still, eyes wide, mouth open. "That's right. Just hang on. It looks like your dad's on his way."

Tommy and Hildy were paddling for all they were worth, inexpertly, but giving it everything they had. Eric was holding Jennifer, casting quick looks over his shoulder at Ward. He looked scared, but in control.

As the raft slowly approached, Ben and Frank edged theirs close to it, and added their momentum to the kids' efforts. Ward reached out and caught a rope along one sidetube when the raft got close enough. He let it carry them closer to shore. "Grab hold of that branch," he told Hildy. "Hold steady."

She did, while Ward made his way to where the water was just above his waist. He pried Joey's hands loose from his shirt and tossed him into the raft. "Shut up." he said, when Joey yelled again as his mother's arms closed around him. "Where's his life vest, Eric?"

Eric opened his mouth, but Jennifer beat him to it. "You don't have to yell at him. He's just a little boy."

"He's a little boy with fools for parents. Where the hell is his life jacket?"

Jennifer sputtered.

Eric leaned past his wife. "Look, Ward, there's no need to make a fuss. Joey's fine. There was no need for you to go after him. I'd have pulled him in."

"Where's his life vest?"

"He was so hot and uncomfortable, I let him take it off," Jennifer said. She held her son close, stroking his hair. "You said the water wasn't deep."

"Didn't you hear what I said? That no kid under twelve was to be without flotation of some sort?"

"Well, of course I did. You said it loud enough. But I'm Joey's mother, and I believe I know what my child needs better than you do."

"Eric, did you know she'd let him take off the jacket?"

Eric hesitated, then nodded. "I was right here. He was in no danger."

Ward opened his mouth, then shut it again long enough to grind his teeth. "Fine. Get out." He motioned to the shore.

"What?"

"I organized this float trip. That means I make the rules. If you're not willing to abide by them, you can't participate. Get out. We'll pick you up on the way back."

"You're kidding."

"I am not kidding. Take your kids and climb out onto the bank." He looked again. Yes, Angela and Norman had their jackets untied.

Eric bristled, then deflated. "Fasten your life jackets, boys. You too, Angela."

"But you—"

"Jennifer, I have no intention of sitting here in the hot sun for two hours. If the kids get too hot, we'll splash them with water."

"But—"

Eric looked down at Ward. "That suit you?"

"As long as they keep 'em fastened. Hildy, Tommy, you two look like you've got some sense. If those kids don't keep their life jackets fastened, you let me know, okay?"

"Ward, doggone it—"

"Eric, you used to have some sense. Not anymore, so I'm giving the responsibility of keeping the passengers in this raft safe to the folks who will follow orders." Not allowing Eric a chance to say any more, he struck out toward his raft, which by now was a good hundred yards down the river.

How the hell did a son of Ben's get so damn dumb?

Annie was sick. Just sick. Seeing poor little Joey thrashing about in the river brought back all the mental images that had haunted her this past year. There had been a broken water lily stem twisted around one of Calvin's chubby little legs, floating pads torn and displaced. He had struggled for his life. He had tried to escape his watery trap, but to no avail.

If she had heard the splashing, she might have saved him. But she had been inside, gossiping and laughing with the other women. Trusting Walter to watch her darling, precious son.

I hate him. He let my baby die.

The mantra no longer comforted, No longer alleviated the pain. No longer let her forgive herself.

She had been equally responsible for Calvin's safety. She was equally at fault. She had helped to kill her son.

When her mother's hand reached for hers, she grabbed it and held on for dear life.

"Thea!" Gran's cry broke her self-castigation. Annie's mother huddled against the rounded side of the raft, face buried in her hands and knees pulled tightly into her chest.

"Great god!" her father crawled across the center of the raft, took his wife in his arms. "It's okay, Thea. Joey's all right. He's safe."

Gran crawled across the raft. She pushed between Annie's parents. "Thea," she said, her voice sharp. "Thea!" When there was no response, she swung her arm and slapped her daughter's face.

Shocked, Annie cried, "Gran!"

Thea turned into her husband's arms. The awful blankness was gone, replaced by an expression of such unutterable grief that Annie wanted to cry without knowing what she was weeping for.

"Are you back with us, Thea?" Gran said, "or are you still hysterical?"

Annie stared, wide-eyed, at her parents. "What's wrong, Mom? What—"

"Flashback," Ward said, from behind her. "It reminded her— Never mind. She'll be all right. She just needs a minute."

"She needs to unburden herself, that's what she needs," Gran said.

Thea's head snapped up. "You always know what's right for everyone, don't you, Ma? You have no idea—"

"Oh, no? Let me tell you—"

Annie stared at her mother, at her grandmother. In all her life she'd never heard them exchange a cross word. Her stomach tightened. How could they, who had always been the perfect mother-and-daughter pair, suddenly attack each other?

"Stop it! Stop it!" she cried. "You mustn't fight. You can't fight. Oh, please." Someone's arms—Uncle Ward's—went around her. She sank back against him, sitting stiffly at first, then relaxing when her mother and grandmother stopped glaring bullets at each other.

CLAY FISHED BELOW COFFEE POT RAPIDS FOR A COUPLE OF HOURS after he and Annie parted. He wasn't sure why he hadn't gone rafting with her. Maybe because he couldn't trust himself. It was getting damn hard to keep his hands off of her.

Who'd have thought it? He'd been more or less content with his life without a woman since Meredith moved to Dallas. First he'd been too busy winding up his parents' estates. Then he'd had to get his own affairs in order so he could escape the bank. So what was the first thing that happened when he found himself free?

Annie.

He wanted her, pure and simple. So what? Easily handled. Trouble was, she was taking up more and more of his time, his thoughts, and not just his lustful thoughts either.

I haven't got time for a woman. Not now. Not until I take care of all the other changes in my life.

At least that's what he kept telling himself.

Nonetheless, when the shadows spread across the river in the narrow north-and-south canyon, he called it a day. If they'd started soon after lunch, the rafters should be getting to Macks Inn pretty soon.

A raft was just coming into sight when Clay walked down to the landing. A closer look and he recognized the redhead—Hetty, and the bearded fellow Annie had introduced as her uncle...Bill? No, Ben. Before long another raft appeared, then two more.

He was in time.

Clay stood back while the first two rafts unloaded, but when Annie's eased up to the landing, he made sure he was there to grab the hawser and pull it in. He greeted the rest of the party. Her mother looked like she'd gotten seasick and Annie looked a bit wan herself. "Are you okay?"

"I'm fine," she told him, as they walked up the slope toward the parking lot. "Too much sun, maybe."

She didn't look sunburned. "Have dinner with me?"

She stopped walking. "Oh, gosh, Clay, I don't know. I should—"

"You should have dinner with him," Cecile said from behind her. "This is your last chance. Don't waste it."

A quick frown, as if she was not quite sure what she wanted, then she smiled. "Okay. I'd love to. What time?"

"Why don't I drive you back to the ranch now? I'll bet you'd like to get out of those wet clothes."

"Oh, I don't know. They feel pretty good, now that we're off the river. It's hot!" She fanned herself as they left the chattering group behind and walked toward his pickup.

Clay wondered why she was so quiet once they were on the road. After a couple of miles he said, "Did you have fun?"

It seemed to him she had to think about her answer. "Yes, I think so," she said after a moment. "Most of the time, anyhow. What did you do this afternoon?"

"Fished."

Her laughter relieved his mind. "Now why didn't I know that? Catch anything?"

"Enough to feed us both. I hope you like fresh trout."

"You kept them? I thought—"

"They're legal, not to worry. That stretch is open fishing." He signaled his turn. "Your grandmother said it was your last chance to have dinner with me. When are you going home?"

"Sunday. I'll have to be on the road by noon."

Damned if she didn't sound disappointed. Clay couldn't hide his grin.

THE BENTLEY WAS PARKED BESIDE THE BIG HOUSE WHEN THEY returned. "I can hardly wait to hear what Frances thinks of shopping in Idaho Falls," Cecile said to Ward, after Thea and Gib had gone inside. "Although why on earth she thought she'd find anything worthy of herself is beyond me."

Ward handed her the tote bag containing the water pistols she'd contributed to the afternoon's fun. "Ma, your tongue is getting sharper every year." He walked slowly, stayed at her side as she climbed the front steps. "Want some iced tea?"

"I want a bathroom first. Then a nice, quiet time on the porch, with my feet up."

"I'll fix the tea."

When Cecile returned to the porch, Ward was sitting in one of the Adirondack chairs and had padded another with cushions for her. "Every year I mean to replace these," she told him as she lowered herself into the chair's embrace, "and every year I forget until we get here. I have never sat in anything so uncomfortable."

"Pa liked them." He set a small table beside her and put her iced tea within reach. "Never could understand it."

"Neither could I. Never mind. After more than fifty years of sitting in them, I suppose I can manage a few more. Now, did you check your phone messages?"

Ward looked over his shoulder, saw no one within listening distance. Nonetheless, he kept his voice low. "Ed talked to Champion's agent who is apparently playing guard. Explained the situation. The agent agrees with us, that Hildy should have a chance to say goodbye, but he's worried that seeing Champion's condition might be traumatic."

"It would be more traumatic if she didn't get the chance," his mother said. "She needs the closure. What arrangements did your investigator make?"

"Champion's not going to last long, so the sooner we get her down there, the better. Ed got the impression it's just a matter of days."

"I'll speak to Frances, then." His mother pushed herself out of the chair. Grimaced. "I'm not looking forward to this."

"I'll do it."

"No, I'm her mother. It's my job." She went into the house.

Ward stayed on the porch. If he knew his sister, ma would need some cheering up after their confrontation.

Ben and Louisa came walking up from the Blue House while he waited. "Hold on," he told them. "I don't think you'll want to go in there right now."

Louisa took the chair his mother had vacated while Ben perched on the railing nearby. "Oh? Why not?"

"Ma's having a talk with Frances. Not exactly secret stuff, but best kept between them." He looked over at Ben, wondering if he should keep his mouth shut. Decided against it. "What's the deal with Eric? He used to have better sense."

"Beats the hell out of me." Ben shook his head. "I would have said he knew better. God knows, I taught him water safety."

"It's Jennifer," Louisa put in. "She's got him so convinced that she knows the only way to raise those kids... I wanted to slap her today. She won't let them have swimming lessons, wouldn't take my advice to stay behind. 'Oh, no, Mother Armstrong' she said. 'My children are very well-behaved. They'd be so disappointed to miss the raft trip.' Shit! Her children are the most spoiled little brats I've ever seen. I can't believe Eric doesn't see that."

Ward couldn't resist a small chuckle. "I take it she's not your favorite daughter-in-law."

"Oh, lord, Ward, I shouldn't have said that. Jennifer is a good wife, an excellent mother, I'm sure. It's just that her idea of how to raise kids is so different from mine, from anyone's in the family. We get along a lot better when we're six hundred miles apart." She leaned her head back and laid a hand over her eyes. "This week's been a real strain. My tongue's sore, from me biting it to keep from speaking out."

Raised voices from inside forced Ward to his feet. "Well, don't hold your breath. The week's not over, and there's more family fun ahead. Stay here. I'll be back."

His mother was standing just inside the library door, leaning against the wall. She looked every day of her age. Across the room, Frances was dragging her fancy luggage from behind the sofa bed. When he entered, she looked up and said, "Come to back dear old mom? Don't worry. I'm not going to hit her, even if she does deserve to have that busy nose smashed all over her face."

"The child's hurting, Fran. She needs to see the man who's been a father to her before he dies."

"Don't tell me what my kid needs. Ma never knew what I needed, did she? It was always you, the first-born son, or precious little Althea. Sweet little Thea, in whose mouth butter wouldn't melt. Never Frances, the odd one. The plain one. The dumb one, who barely graduated from high school.

"Well, I showed you all didn't I? Showed you I could make something of myself. Hell, I'm so far ahead of the rest of you it's pitiful."

"Frances, this isn't about you. It's about that poor girl. She needs to see Champion."

"No way!" Frances zipped the first suitcase shut on the clothes she'd crammed inside. "He sent her back. Said if I didn't take her in, he'd tell... Never mind. She's not seeing him, and that's the end of it."

"Serhilda is nearly seventeen. Seems to me she's old enough to decide for herself," Ward said, keeping his voice calm and unchallenging with an effort.

"You think so? I don't, and I'm her mother."

"I never thought I'd hear you admit that, Frances," Cecile said. "Serhilda told me you always introduce her as your assistant."

The zipper stuck on the second lipstick pink suitcase. Frances jerked it until it came free, stuffed fragile-looking fabric inside, and zipped it closed. "This is bullshit. Okay. Okay!" She turned to face Ward and their mother, hands on hips. "You don't like the way I'm taking care of her, you do it. I've had it. You hear me? I've had it!" The last words came out as a shriek.

"Will you make that legal?"

Ward looked at his mother in surprise. He knew she'd been worried about the quality of life Hildy had with Frances, but he hadn't expected her to go this far.

"Hell, yes. Have your lawyer draw up the papers. As long as it doesn't cost me anything, she's all yours. The sooner the better. Now get out of here. I want to finish packing."

As his mother turned toward the door, he thought he heard her murmur, "Good riddance."

"Are you going to say goodbye to Hildy?"

"Why? She doesn't care any more about me than I do about her." She paused before dropping a pair of fancy-looking high heels into a pink duffle. "Ward?"

"Yeah?"

"Keep in touch, will you? Let me know how the old lady is now and then?"

He studied her, wondering, as he had many times before, what made his sister tick. "Yeah," he said. "I can do that."

He followed his mother to the front porch, where Louisa said, as she relinquished her seat, "Anything I can do?"

"No, nothing."

Ward hadn't heard Ma sound so defeated since Pa died.

ANNIE WAS GRATEFUL TO CLAY FOR BEING THE MEANS OF HER escape from the Families this evening. Her mother's peculiar behavior this afternoon had upset her. Even more upsetting had been the sudden argument between Mom and Gran. She'd never seen them fight before. For a little while, she'd felt almost like her world was wobbling on its axis.

Now she was wondering if it had been a wise move. As if reading her mind, Clay reached across the wide bench seat and caught her hand. "You're too far away. There's a seat belt in the middle."

She let him pull her closer. Despite the air-conditioning, she could feel the heat of him beside her. She was all too aware of her bare arm pressed firmly against his.

"Now, isn't this more cozy?"

"Yes," she whispered, not entirely in command of her voice.

She willed herself to relax, took several deep, calming breaths in an attempt to push the events of this afternoon to the back of her mind. This was the last time she'd have to spend with Clay, and she wanted to enjoy every minute of it.

Soft music played on the sound system. The tires sang on the hot asphalt of the highway. Clay's unique scent filled the pickup cab, a mixture of sweat and fresh air, with a subtle undertone of wood smoke. He smelled like a man should—no spice, no musk, no fake outdoorsy aroma. The combination, along with his companionable silence, succeeded in draining the remaining tension from her. She felt her mind again drifting aimlessly, like a raft on a lazy river. When Clay's arm slid lower, to rest lightly along her shoulders, she sighed softly and leaned into his embrace.

Chapter Twenty

ERIC SPEARED HIS FINGERS THROUGH HIS HAIR. HE WAS TRAPPED. Caught between a rock and a hard place. "No, Jennifer, we are not going home tonight. Not tomorrow, either. You're just going to have to tough it out until Sunday. I'll be dam...doggoned if I'll disappoint Ma and Pa by taking off early."

"Well, just don't expect me to go to the cookshack tonight. I've done my best all week to get along with your family, Eric, but today was just too much." Her chin quivered in the way he'd always thought charming.

"Damn it, Jennifer. Don't you start crying!"

"Eric!" she wailed. "You swore at me!"

He clamped his mouth shut, biting back words he'd done his best to banish from his vocabulary. "I'm sorry. It's just that... If you'd only listen to reason—"

"Reason? What's reasonable about the way your uncle threatened us? He would have cast us ashore with no water, no shade? What's reasonable about being made to feel that you're endangering your children, just because you want them to be safe? To have good manners? To live godly lives?" Her tears had disappeared now, and her cheeks were splotched with red, a sure sign she was losing her temper.

He knew he ought to take her in his arms and kiss her, but right now all he wanted to do was slam out the door and go for a long walk. He'd known this week would be difficult, but it hadn't. This week had been as close to impossible as he'd ever experienced.

From the very first day, Jennifer had been determined to show the Families how good a mother she was, how good a wife. He'd been amused at first, until he saw how she was getting under Elaine's skin. He might not entirely approve of how his sister and Stew lived their lives, but he'd never try to tell them so. One thing Pa had taught him well was to mind his own business.

"Isn't part of living a godly life to show tolerance for others?" he asked, doing his best to keep his voice mild.

"Tolerance? What about their tolerance for me? What about the way your mother drops broad hints about I'm turning my sons into sissies, how I've spoiled my daughter? Is that tolerance?" The quivering chin was back, along with a tremor in her voice. "Would you really want your sons to behave like that awful Tommy, the way he's always trying to be the center of attention? Or like Serhilda?" Her tone made the girl's name into a swearword.

"Tommy's just lively," he said, while admitting privately that the kid needed some strong discipline. Someone ought to take him in hand, seeing as how his father didn't seem likely to. "And you have to remember that Serhilda wasn't raised by anyone in our family. As far as I can tell, she never has had what you'd call a real family."

"She's a bad influence. Yesterday Angela asked me if she could get her ears pierced."

"What's wrong with that? Haven't a lot of the girls in her class?" Most of the girls—and some of the boys—who brought pets into his office wore earrings. Some wore nose rings, and even eyebrow rings. While he didn't think the latter particularly attractive, he saw no harm in a girl having pierced ears.

"She's only seven!" Jennifer plopped down on the edge of the bed. "Eric, that's not the point, anyway. What I'm trying to make you understand is that your family, nice as they are, are just not the sort of people I want my children emulating. I don't want the children exposed to drinking or licentiousness or—:"

"There's no harm in a drink or two before dinner—"

"Your aunt Joss is a drunk. Haven't you noticed?"

"Well, maybe she does drink too much, but they left this morning. Look, Jennifer, you know I agree with you about alcohol, but I'm not going to inflict my beliefs onto my family." He forced a chuckle, hoping to lighten the atmosphere. "As for licentiousness, I haven't noticed anyone running around naked."

"Don't you patronize me, Eric Armstrong. Your precious cousin Hetty is sleeping with that man she bought up here. With your Gran's encouragement. When I took Angela's clean underwear over to the Pink House this morning, I heard CeCe and Charlene talking about it. Right in front of your daughter."

"I doubt she understood."

"That isn't the point." She reached both hands out to him, pleading. "Eric, can't you see that your family's values are so completely different from mine—from ours? They're nice people, but they aren't the kind of people I want my children to look up to. Can you honestly say you do?"

Unable to stand still, Eric paced to the far wall and back again. "Jennifer, I can't forsake my family," he said, hearing his voice break as he spoke. "But this week...I've seen how far we've grown apart. Our values, our beliefs." He turned and paced back to the far wall, where he stood, staring out the window. Through the trees between, he could see the Pink House, where his little girl had stayed all week, in a room with Kristi—whom he'd trust with his children any day of the week—and Serhilda, a lost soul if he'd ever seen one. He made his decision.

"We'll stay until Sunday. One day won't make that much difference." When Jennifer opened her mouth to speak, he held up a hand. "We'll stay. But I won't ask you to come to another Gathering, Jennifer. I don't agree that the children have been harmed by this week, but we're not going to risk another one. We'll see Ma and Pa at Christmas or Thanksgiving, like we always have, and maybe spend some time with them in the summer. But no more Gatherings. I promise you."

She flew into his arms. "Oh, bless you, Eric. Bless you."

With her arms around him, her warm body next to his, Eric felt at ease for the first time all week. His wife, his family, his beliefs were more important than spending a week every year with people he had nothing in common with, even if he had known them all his life.

"I HAVEN'T EATEN SO MUCH IN MONTHS," ANNIE MOANED, AS SHE pushed away her empty plate. "What's for dessert?"

"She wants dessert. A pound and a half of trout, two potatoes, an onion, three carrots, a gallon of lemonade and the woman wants dessert." Clay lifted imploring eyes to the sky.

"I'd settle for a cup of coffee."

Clay put her plate and utensils into the waiting dishpan, added detergent, and poured simmering water over them. "Coffee you shall have." He disappeared into the trailer.

Annie stared into the fire. It was barely dusk, but its heat was welcome. At this elevation, the air quickly grew chilly when the sun was gone.

I'm happy. Right now, right this minute, I'm happy.

Clay was good company. Lighthearted, often funny, but gentle and caring also. A definite contrast to Walter, who'd taken life so seriously. Somehow she couldn't see him in a bank. He belonged out here, dressed in jeans and plaids, not fine worsteds and silk ties.

A familiar twinge of guilt sliced into her thoughts. *Should I be happy?*

Gran had said she was wallowing in self-pity. Mom believed she was still grieving for Calvin. Uncle Ward advised her to grab her bootstraps and pull herself back into life.

Clay invited her to go fishing, because it was good for the soul.

She turned so she could see into the trailer. The small window over the sink didn't give much of a view, but she could see him there, moving about, could hear the high whine of a coffee grinder.

He had not kissed her again, had not even tried to. He'd been the proverbial perfect gentleman. Perversely, Annie was a little disappointed. She felt mildly guilty about her eager response to his kisses, but at the same time she wanted more. How good it had felt to be held against his hard chest, to feel his lips, so soft and so sensuously knowledgeable, moving on hers. She shivered.

"Cold?" Clay set a steaming cup behind her on the table. His other hand held, of all things, two fragile brandy snifters, their contents golden.

"No. No, I'm not cold. Just thinking." Absently she took the snifter, sipped its contents. Not the brandy she had expected, but B&B. Her favorite liqueur.

They sipped in comfortable silence. "Something happened today didn't it? Something that upset you pretty badly." Clay said, after nearly five minutes.

Again she shivered, but this time with the remembrance of today's terror, of last year's loss. "My baby drowned." She swallowed, unable to say more.

He reached for her hand. "Do you want to tell me about it?"

"I— I don't think so. Not now, anyway. I'm too comfortable, too content." She turned to face him, forcing the memories she'd dwelt on so often to the back of her mind. "Will we fish tomorrow morning?"

"Will the sun come up? Of course we'll fish. Which means I need to get you home. It's after nine." He released her hand. "Finish your drink while I bank the fire."

She noticed that his snifter still held most of its contents when he picked them up to set them inside the trailer.

"I've never been an early bird," she said, when he emerged. "It seems so strange to want to get up before dawn, like I have ever since I got here." She didn't say that the first morning she'd arisen because of the disturbing dreams that had come again and again through the night.

"It all depends on what the day has in store. Early to bed and early to rise..."

"Catches a lot of fish," she finished for him. "And tomorrow I am going to. I can feel it in my bones."

"I often feel that way. My bones lie a lot." He opened the pickup door for her, but stopped her as she started to climb in.

"The evening's incomplete," he said softly, leaning toward her.

"What more does it need?" she whispered, knowing the answer, wanting the completion.

"This." Clay pulled her gently into his arms. He kissed her gently, briefly. Pulling away slightly, he looked a question into her eyes.

"If a thing's worth doing, it's worth doing well," Annie said, casting caution away. She slid her arms under his, wrapped them around his ribs. She needed his kiss, to reaffirm that she could still feel something besides sorrow and guilt.

Clay took her mouth, still with gentleness, but also with demand. This time her lips parted under his and her tongue slipped between them, to meet and parry with his. When her hips thrust involuntarily against his, his body responded. His arms tightened around her for a moment, before he thrust her gently away.

"If I don't take you home right now, I may never." He chucked her lightly on the chin. Insouciance was almost beyond him, but he did his best. "Your call."

She chewed on her lower lip.

Clay waited, not quite holding his breath.

"May I use your cell?"

It was his turn to hesitate. He could just see it tomorrow morning, when he took her home. Father waiting on the porch of that big house, shotgun in hand. Family arranged all around, itching to string him up to the nearest tree. For a moment he actually considered telling her he'd made a mistake.

Then she moved against him. A small movement, nothing sexy about it. Just enough to bring him to rock-hard readiness. "I'll get it."

He listened to her side of the conversation, finding it interesting that she'd called her uncle rather than her parents. "Well, you're the one who told me I needed to start living again. So if Mom and Dad have a fit, I'll blame you."

She listened, then said, "Yes, I'm sure. I'll see you in the morning. About ten. Tell Gran we'll have that talk she's been trying to trap me into when I get home. Bye." Without waiting for an answer, she turned the phone off. "There," she said, looking up at him.

Why did he feel like he was standing on the edge of a precipice? "Annie."

Her chin came up and she looked him straight in the eye. "Clay?"

He licked his lips. "Let's go inside."

The trailer, roomy as it was when he was alone, seemed crowded. The air, fresh though it was with all the windows ajar, felt thick, stifling. He flicked off the light as he entered, so that they stood in shadowy darkness.

She came into his arms as soon as he pulled the door shut, warm and soft. "Ah, Annie, when I saw you there, poised on the riverbank, all I could think of was that you were too lovely to be real. I wondered if you were some sort of forest sprite. I wanted to touch you, to see if you'd vanish, like a dream."

He skimmed his hands up her sides, not quite touching the sweet fullness of her breasts. Back to her waist, where he clasped her firmly, pulled her to him. Her arms again slid around his waist, but she made no other move. Even though he could feel the rapid beating of her heart, she stood almost passive.

Waiting.

He pushed one knee between hers, until she was astraddle his thigh. Even through two layers of denim, he felt the heat of her.

He covered her face with kisses, let his hands roam as they would over her delicious body. One found the button on her jeans. It slipped free easily, and the zipper slid smoothly. Too smoothly, too tempting.

I'm going too fast. I'll never last—

Her shirt was free now, and he slid his hands under it, exploring with slow, sensuous stroking her soft and quivering midriff. Slowly he advanced his hand upward, seeking, finding the clasp of her bra. It opened easily, despite the clumsiness of hands shaking with need.

Her breasts were full and miraculous. Annie gasped when his fingers teased a firm nipple. She moved restlessly within his arms, but made no other response.

Confused, he forced himself to relax. He slid his hands back to her waist, and held her lightly. Unable to release her completely, he breathed into her hair, drinking deeply of its slightly fruity odor. *Apricots. She smells of apricots.*

Still she stood passive, no longer clinging. Her hands lay lightly on his shoulders. "Annie? Something's not working. What is it?"

"I don't know." Her voice was small, uncertain. "I wanted you...and then I didn't."

"Let's sit down." He guided her to the dinette. Before he seated himself across the table from her, he snapped on the light over the range. It was just enough that they could see each other's expressions, dim enough to hide their thoughts.

"I've rushed you."

"No," she said, not quite meeting his eyes. "Or at least not much. You never pushed. And God knows, I let you know I was interested."

His chuckle was rueful. "You know, Annie, I've never thought of myself as being a slave to sex. Not until I met you." He thought back to their first meeting. "I've never come so close to making an ass of myself as I did the morning we met."

"You did? You wanted me then?"

"I wanted you then. It was the strangest thing, as if I'd been looking for you a long time, and there you were, trying to kill yourself."

"I wasn't!" She looked down at the table, where her fingers were twisting together. "Well, not consciously."

He waited, knowing she had more to say.

Tears welled up in her eyes, ran in streaks down her pale cheeks. "Calvin drowned on August second."

"How long ago?"

"A year ago." The words came out in a broken whisper.

Unable to find words, know there were no that would help, he waited.

"Damn it," she sobbed. "I've talked about it too many times. I've relieved every second. Too many times. I need to get past it all. I need to move on."

"I'm not sure you can get past something like that. Maybe the only way to move on is to accept that it happened, that you can't change it, and to take the next step." He repeated his words in his mind. "I'm not making sense, am I?"

"In a way you are. You've lost someone you love, too, so you understand."

"Understand, yes. But you expect to lose your parents, sooner or later. Mom had cancer. She fought it for two years, through chemo and radiation. Nothing worked." He braced himself against the pain, still fresh, still sharp. "Dad lasted about a month afterward. He just didn't seem to be able to go on without her."

Her hand came across the table and clasped his. "Oh, Clay, how did you survive?"

A deep breath. "Like anyone does, I guess. One day at a time. I buried myself in work for a while, but I still had to deal with their estates. What made it tough was that they'd left me a sizeable inheritance. Far more than I'd ever expected. Enough to make me feel guilty that it would let me realize my dreams much sooner than I'd expected.

"I still wonder if I shouldn't have given the money away. It seems almost criminal to profit by my parents' death."

"Everyone told me I shouldn't feel guilty about Calvin's drowning," Annie said, still holding his hand. "Accidents happen, they said. But it wasn't entirely an accident, Clay. He'd be alive today if I'd been watching him as I should have."

"And you've been paying ever since, haven't you?" Clay asked, with a flash of insight.

"Yes." Annie nodded. "It felt wrong to feel good, to let loose and enjoy myself." She buried her face in her hands. Her next words were muffled. "Tonight... That's what I felt. Guilty, because

I wanted you. And it was wrong. I just couldn't." Her sobs were the more heartbreaking because of their hopelessness.

Clay went to sit beside her. He gathered her into his arms, where she clung to him. After a while he picked her up and carried her across to the sofa where he laid her down and knelt beside her.

He pulled the afghan from the back and spread it over her. Gradually her sobs diminished. Her breathing slowed and became regular. He tucked the afghan around her shoulders, stroked his palm down the curved line of her spine.

She sighed and nestled into the sofa. Again he stroked her back, telling himself to ignore the residual hunger he still felt. Annie needed compassion, not passion, tonight. His body paid no attention, until he had to reach down and adjust himself inside of too-tight jeans. Disgusted, he jumped to his feet and strode into the bedroom.

"Horny bastard," he muttered. "She needs sympathy and understanding, not a roll in the hay." For a long while he stood by the window, staring out at the night. What a beating his self-image was taking. Lure a lovely woman to his camp and what did he get? The questionable privilege of providing a shoulder for her to cry on. Never mind that she needed his shoulder much more than she needed his kisses.

"Not nearly as nice a guy as you thought you were, are you, Knight?" he said to his reflection in the window. Eventually, he felt he could check on Annie without making a total ass of himself. He stepped into the other room.

"Annie?"

There was no answer, just barely audible, even breathing. Tenderly he smiled down on her sleeping body. In the dim light cast by the light over the range, he could see her tear streaked cheeks and matted lashes. He stood for a while, wondering if he should wake her. *No, she needs to sleep undisturbed. Perhaps this time she'll heal.*

As he leaned across her to an overhead bin, he smiled. Freed of the crippling burden she bore, maybe she could resume living. Perhaps in the morning her eyes would be cleared of the haunted, grieving shadow that had lurked in their depths ever since they first met.

"Annie Ogilvie, there's a possibility we might have a future together, someday." Tenderly he slid a pillow under her head, laid a light blanket over the afghan. "Sleep well."

As he stood there, watching her sleep, he promised—or did he pray? "Tomorrow is a new day, one without sorrow or guilt."

Chapter Twenty-one

Saturday

"Hey, can I talk to you?"

"If you'll give me a moment to get another cup of coffee," Cecile said.

"I'll get it. Cream, no sugar, right?"

"Right." *The girl sees what's happening around her. She's not as indifferent to us as she'd like us to believe.*

"Can we go outside?" Serhilda said when she returned with the coffee. "Somewhere private?"

"There should be some sunny spots in the grove. Will that be private enough?"

"Sure."

Cecile snagged a jacket from the line of hooks by the door. She didn't know whose it was, and didn't care. She'd return it soon.

They walked to the grove in silence. One of the split log benches sat in the middle of a bright patch of sunlight and they seated themselves. Cecile's coffee steamed in the cool morning air as she waited for the girl to speak.

Finally she said, "Do I have to go back to L.A. with Frances?"

Oh, dear, she doesn't know yet. "No, darling, you don't, not if you don't want to." *No, I can't lie to her. I have a feeling she's been lied to far too often in her young life.* She reached across and took Serhilda's hand. "I was going to tell you later, but this is as good a time as any. Frances is gone. She left yesterday afternoon."

Serhilda's face went absolutely blank. "She left me?"

"I'm afraid so. But don't worry—"

"I'm not worried. Not anymore. I was scared she was going to take me with her. That's what I wanted to talk to you about. I want to stay with you."

There was such an expression of hope on the girl's face that Cecile wanted to weep. "With me? But—"

"I know you probably don't want me, but I'll help out. I can cook—a little. And I can clean. Walk your dog. Drive you to the store. I'm a good driver. Les and some of his friends taught me, like, defensive driving. And I'm really, really good at keeping track of shit...stuff, like appointments and business lunches and cocktail parties."

Cecile stifled the laughter that threatened to bubble forth. Laughter mixed with tears, for a child who felt she had to pay her way with her own grandmother. *Perhaps she has no idea what a grandmother does, the poor thing.* "We'll have to think about this," she said, "but while we're thinking, remember this. You will have a place, whether it's with me or with someone else in the family. If I'd known about you sooner, I'd have done my best to bring you to us."

Serhilda turned away, as if ashamed of the tears that streamed down her cheeks. After a few minutes, she said, in a thick voice, "How come Frances hates the family so much?"

It was a question Cecile had asked herself too many times. "I wish I knew." She fought to hold back tears of her own. "Part of the problem may have been Kirby. He was a frail child from the beginning."

Serhilda made a sound that might have been a question.

"Kirby was my son, two years and two days younger than Frances. He was a surprise to us all, as I would have preferred to wait until she was three or four before having another baby."

"How come you didn't?"

"There was no pill in 1953. We relied on other methods, and they weren't always foolproof. Kirby caught every bug that was going around. Ear infections, strep throat, one cold after another. I can't remember him being well from the time he was an infant. Now we know it was probably an immune system failure, but back then... Never mind. We were talking about Frances. I know she didn't get the attention she deserved, because I was busy with Kirby.

"She was one of those children who need a lot of attention. A lot of cuddling. And she didn't get it." Cecile shook her head, still feeling the weight of a half century of guilt. "I can't remember the first time she said, 'You love Kirby better than me,' but she couldn't have been more than five or six. I never was able to make her understand that I loved her as much as the other children. Never."

"Jeez, that's awful. She must've been pretty dumb not to see you were busy."

"No, darling, she was just a child, with all a child's needs and hungers. The trouble is, most children outgrow that total self-involvement. I'm not sure Frances ever did." As soon as she'd spoken the words, she regretted them. Frances was Serhilda's mother, no matter how poorly she'd done at it. No one should denigrate her to Serhilda.

255

"I don't think she did, either. Francis doesn't give a damn about anybody else. Never has." Serhilda turned around and speared Cecile with a steady gaze. "So. Can I come live with you?"

Despite the inner voice that told her she was crazy, Cecile opened her arms. "I would be delighted. We'll have a grand time together."

"I LOCKED THE DOOR THIS TIME," HETTY SAID, JUST BEFORE FRANK reached for her. She rolled to her side and met him in the middle of the big bed. "It probably doesn't matter, now that Mother's gone, but I wanted to be safe."

He kissed her long and thoroughly. "Good," he said, when he raised his head. "How are you this morning. Too stiff?"

"Not at all. Are you stiff enough?" She ran a hand down his belly, clasped him. "Just about. Is it my turn to be on top?"

He flung his arms out to either side, spread his legs. "Whatever you want. Have your way with me."

Hetty contented herself with kissing a trail from his chin to his chest. When she raised herself so she could proceed farther toward her ultimate goal, her thigh protested intensely.

"What's wrong?"

"My leg. Hurts," she ground out between clenched teeth.

Frank rose up over her and flipped back the covers. "Good God!"

"What?"

"You've got a bruise the size of a dinner plate." He probed gently. "It's swollen, too. Shit, Het, why didn't you tell me? She hit you, too, didn't she?"

"Uh-huh. Oww!" She pushed his hand away. "It's just a bruise. I'll be fine."

"Oh, sure, Let me see you bend your knee."

She did her best, but had to stop when she started seeing pink spots. "God!" she gasped. "I've never had anything hurt like this."

"You should've had them look at it at the emergency room yesterday." He rolled out of bed. "Stay there. I'll be right back." He disappeared into the bathroom.

Hetty thought about getting up. She really did. She rolled to the side and started to swing her legs over the edge of the bed, then fell back. "Damn, damn, damn."

She was still there when Frank came back. He pulled on a pair of Levi's and a sweatshirt. "Stay," he ordered again, and left her.

"Shit!" He was going to bail. She just knew it. He'd spent a lot of money to come here, taken a week off when he had several juicy jobs lined up. *I promised him a week of fun and great sex. So my mother tried to kill him, and even if I could get out of bed, sex is the last thing I want. Damn, that hurts!*

Frank returned and sat on the bed beside her. "Your aunt will be here in a minute. God, Het, that's ugly." Gently he pulled the sheet over her, leaving her legs exposed.

"Thanks." She laid an arm across her eyes, not wanting to see him trying to figure out how to tell her he was leaving.

Aunt Louisa came in before she'd had a chance to build up a good head of self-pity. "Good grief!"

Hetty's whole body bucked at the touch of cold fingers on her thigh. "Oww!"

"Hold still." More prodding, some of which hurt like hell. "Why didn't you have someone look at this yesterday?"

"It's just a bruise."

"Let's hope that's all it is. Frank, will you go down to the kitchen and get some ice. Wrap a couple of handfuls in a towel. We'll try that first." When he'd disappeared, she said, "Hetty, do you have any aspirin? Ibuprofen?"

"I never touch the stuff. Help me. I want to get up."

"I'll help you get decent, but that's all. I want you to stay in bed this morning, with ice on that for a half hour out of every hour. We'll see how it feels by lunch time."

Hetty pushed her restraining hand aside. "No. I'm getting up." She fought the pain in her thigh as she pushed herself upright. "Hand me my robe."

"Stubborn brat." But she got the robe.

"You bet." Putting the robe on was easy. Then she tried to take a step. Her leg protested vehemently when she put weight on it, but it held her up. One slow step after another took her to the bathroom. Once there she pushed the door closed and leaned on the sink. Her body was soaked with sweat, her knees were shaking, and her stomach roiled. Half a dozen slow, deep breaths calmed her stomach, but didn't do a thing for her knees. When she tried to lower herself to the toilet, her leg gave way and she fell the last few inches.

The door opened and Frank filled the doorway. "You screamed?"

"Go away!" *Oh, God, I don't believe this!* She huddled into herself, pulling the robe close about her.

"Damn it, Hetty, are you all right?"

"Yes. Yes. *Yes.*"

He hesitated, then pulled the door closed. "Call me if you need help," he said, his voice muffled by the door between them.

Fat chance.

She managed to finish, to stand, leaning against the washbowl, while she brushed her teeth. Her stomach was roiling again. *Please don't let me vomit. I'd never get on my knees.*

As soon as she opened the door, Frank scooped her up and carried her to the bed. He laid her down gently, pushed her back when she tried to sit up. "Stay," he said.

"Goddammit, Frank Everard, if you don't stop treating me like your dog, I'll...I'll—"

"Hetty, just shut up." He lifted her robe away from her bruised thigh. "This is going to be cold."

She shrieked when the lumpy cold plastic bag hit the bruise. Not from pain, although even that little weight hurt.

He held the ice pack in place when she tried to shove it away. "Be still. Shit, woman, we're trying to help you. Will you stop fighting us?"

"Here's a heating pad, Hetty. If you get too cold, you can tuck it behind you and turn it on low." Louisa laid a soft, thick towel over Hetty's leg. "And here's coffee. I put it in an insulated cup, so it won't be so apt to spill."

Hetty snatched the coffee from her aunt's hands. She took a hefty sip, then another. The hot beverage warmed her all the way down. "That's good. Thanks," she said, between sips.

Frank pulled the sheet over her legs. As he tucked it gently around her, he said, "I'm going over to the cookshack to get some breakfast. Do you want me to bring you anything?"

She shook her head, then changed her mind. "Can you see if there's any apple juice? And some soda crackers?" Those were the only two things she could think of that might not bounce.

"Right. I'll be back in a bit."

Hetty watched him leave, wondering if he was really coming back.

WARD, BEN, AND GIB WERE LINGERING OVER COFFEE IN THE nearly-empty cookshack. Althea and Louisa had departed for one last grocery run to Ashton. The rest of the Families had scattered after breakfast, most with plans for one last day of play. "This has sure seemed like a long week," Ward mused, trying to decide why he felt that way. "Usually the time seems to fly past."

"Lots happening," Ben said, making it halfway a question. "Seems like every day had its crisis."

"Starting with Frances. Y'know, I never believed she was as bad as Thea said." Gib got up to refill his cup. "I was wrong. She's worse."

"A shame what she did with that girl of hers. And leaving her behind like that." Ben shook his head. "What's going to happen to her now?"

"She'll be taken care of," Ward promised. "I'm not sure what Ma has in mind, but she'll see that Hildy has a home."

"Hildy?"

"Would you name a kid 'Serhilda'?"

"Shit no. Hildy it is. I'll tell the kids," Ben said.

Gib, who was facing the window, stood up. "What the dickens is that kid up to?"

The others turned around. "Looks like he's laying a trail," Ward said. "Bread? No, it's popcorn."

Gib chuckled. "I'll bet he's trying to lure that 'coon we saw the other night. Doubt he has a chance."

Tommy disappeared into the grove. The men went on with their desultory conversation, but Ward kept an eye out. Tommy was a real live wire. Too bad Stephen didn't take more time with him. All that intelligence and energy needed to be channeled into constructive paths.

A week with Ben and Louisa would be good for the boy.

Tommy reappeared inside the Grove several times, always flitting between trees. Playing some kind of solitary war game, Ward decided. Or maybe he was a spy. "No, I don't think Annie's back yet," he replied to a question from Gib. "Does that bother you?"

"I have to admit I'd feel better if I knew more about this Knight fella. But Annie's a big girl. And it wouldn't do me much good to say anything."

"I'll take boys any day," Ben said. "Hardest day of my life was when Elaine told me she was living with Stewart."

"Living together's better than a one night stand. I just don't like—what?"

The shrieks were that of a child in pain. "Tommy—" Ward beat the other two to the door.

"No," Ben said, as he broke into a run. "Norman."

The cries continued as they cut through the grove, ignoring the winding paths. A clump of chokecherry stood at the far edge, a screen between the ring road and the Grove. As soon as they'd circled it, they saw Norman standing at the edge of the road, his shirt and shorts splotched with purple and red, his bare legs splattered with bright green. His voice was taking on a tone of hysteria.

Ward decided to let Ben deal with his grandson. He motioned Gib aside, spoke in a low voice. "I thought you said you'd hid that damn paintgun."

"I thought I had." Gib peered back into the grove. "You see Tommy anywhere?"

"Norman!"

"Oh, hell," Ward said as Jennifer burst from the front door of the Blue House, "that's all we need."

By common consent, they faded back into the trees. Once concealed from the road, Gib called softly, "Tommy, you'd better come out now."

The only answer was a crow's raucous call.

"He's probably long gone by now."

"Won't do much good to look for him," Gib agreed. "That kid can hide better than anyone. Let's just hope he runs out of ammunition soon."

They followed a path back in the direction of the cookshack. "I think it's time to have a talk with Stephen," Ward said, after a while. "Tommy needs more than an occasional father. He's not a bad boy, but he's probably more than any hired nanny can handle."

Gib kicked a pinecone out of the path. "I've been thinking the same. I sure hate to stick my nose in, though. If it were me, I wouldn't want somebody telling me I was doing a piss poor job of raising my kids."

"Let Ma do it. She's real good at meddling, and if anybody's got a right, she does. It's not like Stephen has kin who can help with the boy."

"The problem is what to do with him. I suppose we could take him, but I'm not keen on the notion. Thea's shop takes all her time, and she's not making enough yet to hire full-time help. And I can't take more time off right now, not with Jeff Lamarr still recovering from his coronary." He looked into the distance, and Ward could almost hear the wheels turning. "I wonder if Annie could handle him..."

"I think Ma's got another scheme for her. Let's see how Tommy does with Ben this next week," Ward told him. "We'll figure out something."

"Yeah—" Gib stopped in the middle of the path. "There he is!" He pointed toward the cookshack, where a small boy was hunkered down under a bush. "I'll take care of this."

"Be my guest." Ward watched until Gib squatted down beside Tommy, and then he walked on toward the Big House, all the while wondering what else was going to happen before everyone departed tomorrow.

Crossing his fingers against catastrophe.

Chapter Twenty-two

"OH, SHIT! LET'S GO THE OTHER WAY."

Evan turned at the same time she did, and fell into step beside her. "So are things weird this morning or is it my imagination?" Hildy asked him, once they were far enough away from the crowd surrounding the screaming kid and his almost-as-loud mother.

"Things are definitely weird. I've been to a lot of Gatherings, and I don't think anyone ever took off early before, unless they'd already planned to. Do you have any idea what happened with Aunt Joss and Uncle John?"

"You mean you didn't hear? It was like something out of a Grade B movie. Sex and violence and booze. Joss tried to kill Frank for fucking her precious daughter, Ben said he'd seen Joss downstairs hitting the booze in the middle of the night, and John told Gran he was taking Joss somewhere she'd be safe from all the stress of trying to live up to the family's expectations."

"Tried to kill Frank? You're putting me on."

Hildy held up her hand, palm out. "Swear to God. Didn't you see his cast? She broke his arm. Hit it with a big wood thing."

"Christ! I don't believe it."

"You calling me a liar?" Here she'd thought Evan was as close to a friend as she had in the Families.

"No, of course not. I was just stunned. It's the situation I don't believe, not that it happened. I've always though Aunt Joss and Uncle John were so damn respectable. They were the ones I worried about. Say, Serhilda, do you suppose—"

The name grated on her like it always had. With a curious sense of lightness, she realized she didn't have to put up with that any more. "Call me Hildy."

"Hildy?"

"Can you imagine being called 'Serhilda? Honestly?"

He shook his head, but she could see how he was trying not to grin.

"Les always called me Hildy, but Frances wouldn't. 'Hildy is a girlie name. Serhilda is the name of a strong woman, a warrior.' Yeah, right, as if I'm gonna be a soldier or something."

"You could be, you know. You're fast on your feet and in pretty good shape," Evan said.

"Oh, yeah, like I'm gonna march and carry a gun and maybe shoot at people. No way!"

Evan laughed. "I feel the same way. That's one reason I joined Medic Corps. I figure a good way to avoid situations where I'd have to shoot people is to go in and help those who are in need."

"You're gonna be one of those people who goes in where there's been a disaster, Ward said. Cool! Les used to volunteer with some group like that, before he got sick." She was impressed enough to forget to act bored. "In some foreign place?"

"Africa, but I'm not exactly sure where I'll be yet. They don't usually send beginners there, but I speak Swahili and a couple of other languages pretty well. So I got lucky. My assignment begins on the first of September."

"That is so cool. What made you decide to learn that language, instead of Spanish or something?"

He shrugged. "Nobody else was studying it. I used to work really hard at being different."

"That was before you came out, wasn't it?"

He stopped and glared at her. "I don't want to talk about it."

She grabbed his elbow and pulled him around. "Look at me, Evan. Look me in the eye and tell me you wish you were straight."

He aimed his face at her, but his gaze skittered away.

"See! You can't say it. And you know what?"

He shook his head, his expression reminding her of the bloodhound Les had worked with in one of his films. Sad enough to make her want to cry.

"Les said, once, that the sorriest people he knew were those who wished they were straight. When he first realized he was gay, he went kinda crazy for a while, until he got his head sorted out and decided he could live with it. That's when he stopped being fucked up and started being cool with his life." She caught both of his hands and squeezed. "It's no big deal, Evan."

"Huh?"

"Gay's no big deal. Most people don't care, and those who do aren't worth wasting your time on."

When Annie awoke, she knew immediately where she was. What she didn't know was how she could get out of here without waking Clay. No, that wouldn't be fair. She had to tell him goodbye, to thank him for his patience, his forbearance last night. There weren't many men who would have left her to sleep, not after she'd given him every reason to expect her to go to bed with him.

265

She slipped a finger between the slats of the miniblinds above her head. The cool, blue light of early morning told her it was far too early to wake her host. So what am I going to do until... *Wait a minute. Yesterday the sun didn't come up until I was on my way to the river.* She scooted upright, tilted the blinds to let in the morning. *Bathroom? Where's the bathroom?* Past the fridge, she remembered.

Once she'd washed her face and rinsed her mouth out, she felt halfway human. When she emerged, a narrow band of sunlight was peeking through the window, and it showed her a coffee maker on the small counter. The coffee and filers were in the second cupboard she opened.

Fifteen minutes later the bedroom door opened. "Coffee?" Clay paused in the doorway, scratching his chest and yawning. "Do I smell coffee?"

The apprehension that had been knotting her stomach faded away. She hadn't known Clay Knight long, but she was certain he wouldn't ever insist a woman owed him sex in exchange for dinner. He'd been a comforting shoulder for her to cry on, a sympathetic listener to her troubled tale. She'd been convinced that they didn't make men like this anymore.

She filled a cup and handed it to him. "Are we fishing this morning?"

"Is the sun coming up?"

And just like that, she relaxed.

While he dressed, she filled the Thermos. In twenty minutes they were on their way.

"I thought we'd try a different place today," he said in answer to her unspoken question when he turned off the highway at island Park "Give you a taste of some livelier water"

"Livelier?" She didn't like the sound of that. "What do you mean, livelier?"

266

"A few riffles, maybe even a rapid or two. Not all fish like the slow and easy life. Box Canyon will give you a different experience."

Spiders crawled in her belly. Big, ugly spiders whose sharp legs poked and stung as they scampered along her nerves. "Clay, I...uh...I'm not real crazy about rapids."

"You'll love these. Trust me."

You don't have to get in the water. You can tell him you don't feel like fishing this morning. Maybe he won't insist. Or maybe it won't be real rapids. Just a little swifter water. Maybe he's teasing.

He wasn't.

When Annie refused to get into the water, all he said was, "Fishing from the bank isn't as much fun. Try an emergent nymph. It'll work as well as anything."

The fly must have been attractive to the fish because, within the first half hour, she caught two rainbows, both over five pounds. She had to admit Clay had been right, though. Fishing from the bank wasn't as much fun. A couple of times her line tangled in branches and she had to patiently release it.

There were about fifteen other anglers within sight. When her line caught a fourth time, she decided she was done for the day. She put her gear away in the pickup storage locker and dug a Coke out of the cooler in the cab. Carrying it, she walked back along the bank until she could see Clay, hip deep in the rushing water about twenty feet from shore.

Another woman, clad in waders and wearing the usual many-pocketed vest, was sitting on a rock nearby and she motioned for Annie to join her. "I saw you land that big one. What'd he weigh?"

"About seven pounds. He bit on a Blue-winged Olive." By now Annie had learned what sort of answers all fisherpeople wanted.

"I was using a Pale Morning Dun earlier, and had a couple of strikes. Lost the first one, but the second went about six pounds. Do you fish here often?"

"I've never fished much at all before this week. My friend—that's him down there by that big rock—is teaching me."

"You're doing well for a beginner. Keep at it. Pretty soon you'll find you don't want to do anything else."

They conversed desultorily for a while longer, until the woman slipped back into the river. Annie fought drowsiness for a while, but finally her almost-sleepless night took its toll.

A shout awoke her. Annie sat up and looked toward the river, automatically seeking Clay.

She saw another fisherman wading rapidly downstream, heard him call, "Hang on! I'm coming."

The woman she had talked to was standing on the bank several yards away, half out of her waders. She was staring at the river, her face twisted with apprehension, her body tense.

Where was Clay?

Annie leapt to her feet, frantically scanning the rough surface of the river. Plumes of white showed where angular boulders broke its rapid flow.

Where was Clay?

A third fisherman was working his way downstream, his attention on a foaming cauldron amid a cluster of mid-stream boulders. Annie saw a flash of red within the foam.

Clay's shirt was red.

"Clay!" The scream ripped through her throat. Annie did not see the woman tear off her waders. She did not feel the strong arms that surrounded her waist. All she knew was that Clay was drowning and she would not—must not—let him. She struggled to free herself, to keep him from being swept away as Calvin had been.

"He's on his feet!" Annie felt herself being shaken. "Stop it! He's safe!" The shouted words penetrated her panic. She quit trying to escape as she saw Clay's head, hair dark with moisture, appear in silhouette against the largest rock.

He waved and his would-be rescuers waved back. Annie watched while he fought the current, hardly breathing until he was back in smoother water. Smoother, but no less rapid. She had felt the river's relentless pressure against her legs in a slower reach. She knew how much strength it took to oppose it. The occasional emergent rocks told her what treacherous footing there was on its rocky bed.

Slowly, cautiously, Clay worked his way to the bank. Cursing the loose rock that had turned under his foot, his own ineptitude, and the loss of his rod, he finally reached a break in the steep, rocky bank where he could climb out.

"God damn it!" Feet squishing in water that had seeped into his waders, he plodded upstream, condemning to perdition each fallen tree, every angular chunk of basalt that blocked his path back to Annie.

She was huddled against a tree, arms around her shins, her forehead resting on her knees. A middle aged woman was patting her shoulder and murmuring reassurances.

Clay flashed the woman a grateful smile and fell on his knees beside Annie. He spoke her name.

The face that lifted to him was tear-streaked and tragic.

"She thought you were drowning." The woman gave Clay a sympathetic smile before rising and walking away. He was torn between following, to give thanks for her solicitude, and staying, to hold Annie close to his heart. He stayed.

Annie's hands clutched convulsively at his shoulders when he pulled her against him. He whispered her name again and again until the blankness of panic left her eyes.

"I thought... I was so afraid..." she stammered.

"I know, sweetheart." He cupped her wet cheek in his hand. "But I was never in any real danger."

"You could have..."

"Shhh." With one finger, he wiped the tear streaks from her pale skin. "Not a chance. I'm half fish, you know." Her expression broke his heart with its desolation. "Annie, Annie, I've taken a lot worse dunkings than that. I'm still here, aren't I?" He felt a tremor go through her fragile body. "You're cold. C'mon, let's get you home. It's almost noon."

Her hoodie was damp where it had been pressed against his still wet waders. Clay pulled her to her feet and guided her to the truck. He unearthed a jacket from behind the seat and draped it over her shoulders. Intermittent shivers still shook her, but she seemed less distressed.

"The worst thing," he said, as he turned into the ranch entrance after a short, silent trip, "is that I lost the fly rod. And it was my favorite." He grinned across his shoulder at her, but she was still staring at him as if she couldn't get enough of the sight. A little humor, maybe? "Maybe it's just as well I lost it. A fly rod that lets itself get dropped is a pretty poor tool."

She didn't laugh.

Oh, well, it wasn't very funny anyway.

"The worst thing?" Annie croaked, after a moment. "The worst thing?"

Was that a note of hysteria?

Clay pulled into the parking area in front of the Pink House. Tumbling from his seat, he ran around and pulled her from hers.

"That's enough, Annie, sweetheart. I'm safe. Stop crying." She clung to him, sobs shaking her body. He stroked her hair, her back, her cheeks, wetted by new tears.

Gradually her sobs quieted and the tears ceased. Clay continued to hold her, marveling at how right she felt in his arms and on his lap.

"Better?"

Annie wiped her eyes with the backs of her hands, sniffed a couple of times, and nodded. How endearingly childlike she was.

"You okay now?"

She nodded and sniffed again.

"Look, Annie," he said, forcing her to look at him, "all fishermen fall sometimes. Nothing happens, except you get wet, unless you panic." He took her face between his hands, holding her, forcing her to accept the truth in his steady, calm gaze. "I had a little trouble getting my feet under me out there, but I was never in any danger. None."

She didn't believe him. Doubt drew her brows together, was written in the downturn of her mouth.

"Even if I hadn't been able to get to my feet, I'd have been okay. I was wearing my wading belt, so I'd have floated. All I had to do was let the river carry me along to a calmer stretch." He chuckled. "It would have been a long walk home, though."

Annie was patently unconvinced, even after he repeated, over and over again, his reassurances. No smile broke the tightness of her mouth nor did the shadows leave her eyes. Time to change the subject.

"You did well today. I saw one of those whales you caught."

The corners of her mouth twitched.

"How many strikes?" He set his foot on the bench beside her and rested one forearm on his thigh.

"Two." Her voice was lackluster and flat.

"I knew when you caught a big one. I heard you whooping and hollering, even over the noise of the river." He made a face, pretended disgust. "Whatever you did, I wish I knew your secret. I got only one strike, all morning. I tried everything—nymphs, hoppers, even a woolly worm. Nothing."

"I was excited." Annie seemed almost reluctant to admit it. She avoided looking at him.

Just as well. It was too soon yet for her to see just how much he was coming to care for her. She wasn't ready.

Damn it all! If we only had more time.

Chapter Twenty-three

GRAN WAS SETTING UP THE COFFEE POT WHEN ANNIE ENTERED the cookshack. "I hope you're planning to spend some time with your family today," she said, but her smile contradicted her tart tone.

"Good morning, Gran." Annie kissed a papery cheek. "Yes, I've done with fishing. I'll be here the rest of the day."

"Humph. Well, I guess I shouldn't complain. At least you're not mooning around here like a sick calf."

"Gran, I doubt you've seen a sick calf since you were a kid." She resented the implied criticism, but was determined to avoid letting Gran irritate her this morning.

"You don't know what I've seen, miss. Your grandfather and I lived in some strange places in the early years. I've not only seen a sick calf, I've doctored one."

A far off expression came into her face. "It was while we were at Grand Coulee. The only place we could find to live was a little farmhouse, and I kept chickens and pigs as well as a milk cow." She smiled, as at some lovely memory. "Your mother was on the way then and Ward wasn't much more than a toddler. Tom was so busy working on the dam that we didn't have much time together, but what we did was grand."

"Do you still miss him?" She had good memories of the grandfather who had died shortly after her marriage to Walter. Wrapped up in her new life, she had not given much thought to how Gran was taking her loss. How had she been able to survive losing a husband who had so obviously been the center of her existence?

"Child, I'll always miss him. When Tom died, it was like a part of me went with him. But he would have wanted me to keep on living, and so I did. It was hard, at first, until I realized that I had to take myself in hand and find something to occupy my time and thoughts. Then I got involved with the Red Cross and the Library Guild, and each day got a little easier to get through."

She had never before thought about the tragedies her grandmother had survived. Gran had always been generous, sharp-tongued but loving. When Annie was a small child, Gran and Gramps were still moving about to the dam construction projects where he was chief engineer. They came to Portland every year or so, always laden with exotic gifts. A few weeks, and then they would be off again, bound for some distant part of the world. Annie remembered Gramps as a tall, silent man who had always listened to her with intense concentration, but who had been somewhat intimidating—not like Grandpa Ogilvie who was a jolly, loving clown with his grandchildren.

"That young man you were with yesterday. He seems a nice sort."

"He is. I feel comfortable with him." She caught the gleam in her grandmother's eye. "Now look, Gran, don't start thinking those thoughts. I'm learning to fish from clay Knight. I'm not falling in love with him." *Not in love maybe, but I sure like him a lot. And I want him.* She ignored the treacherous thought. She wasn't ready to examine her feelings toward Clay.

"Tomorrow we're leaving here and I'll probably never see him again." Even as she spoke, she knew that tomorrow was too soon to say goodbye to him.

"I'm not thinking anything," Gran said, "except that you ought to invite him to dinner this evening. "

"I was going to ask if I could."

"Well, then, there's something we agree on." The coffee pot gave a last burp and fell silent. "Here's the coffee, finally. The turkey's in the oven and everything else is done until about four. I was going to meet your mother and Louisa out in the Grove. Why don't you join us?"

"I might. After my shower. See you later." She grabbed a half empty package of cookies. When Gran raised an eyebrow, she said. "Well, they were just sitting there in the cupboard. Somebody should eat them."

"I brought them for the children, but with all the other goodies that were here, they were overlooked. Scoot, now! And don't forget to invite Mr. Knight to dinner."

As Annie walked toward the Pink House, she thought, *That's totally strange. Gran didn't say a word about my being out all night. Maybe she's finally realized I'm an adult.*

Hetty was stretched out in a chair in the living room when she came out, feeling fresh and awake after her shower. "Where's Frank?"

"The men went hiking up to the ridge. A male bonding experience, I guess."

"Either that or they're grilling him about his intentions."

Hetty made a face. "After the last two days, I rather imagine that Frank's major intention is to get out of here as quickly as he can. You haven't heard the latest."

A quick glance at the clock told Annie that Gran and the others were surely in the Grove by now. To her surprise, she wanted to join them. "Let's get some sodas and walk over to the Grove. Gran's there. You can tell me on the way."

Hetty maneuvered herself to her feet with difficulty. When she was erect, she caught hold of a cane that was leaning against the chair. Her mouth tightened as she swayed for an instant.

"Good grief! What happened to you?"

"Mother's aim was better than I realized," she said. "Deep muscle bruising, possible bone bruise."

"My God!"

"Yeah, that's what I said, too. Let's go. It's going to take me a while."

In a few terse sentences, Hetty told Annie what the ER doctor had said about deep muscle bruises. "So walking around San Francisco isn't in the cards. We haven't talked about it, but I imagine we'll fly back to Seattle tomorrow."

"Fly? What about your car?"

"I'll have to leave it here. There's no way I can drive it, not that far. And I can't believe Frank will want to be cooped up with me for a couple of days. Not after what he's gone through." She swatted a pinecone out of the path with the tip of her cane. "Damn it, Annie, I thought he might be the one. I could kill my mother!"

Annie liked Frank, what little she'd seen of him. Hard to get to know someone when he's under the influence of painkillers. "So he blames you?"

"Wouldn't you? Look, let's talk about something else. Did you enjoy yourself last night?" She did her best to leer, but the lines of pain around her mouth made it a poor attempt.

Annie shrugged. "We talked. I started thinking about... I started thinking, and got emotional. He was a perfect gentleman. I'd rather not talk about that, either, if it's okay with you."

"Did you invite him to dinner? Gran said she was going to tell you to."

"Oh, no! I forgot. I was going to call him. I've got his cell phone number—" She dug into her pocket, knowing she'd transferred the slip of paper when she'd donned clean jeans. "Yes, here it is. Look, can you wait while I—"

Hetty held out her own cell phone. "Call him."

They traded, cell phone for the two sodas Annie held. She punched in the number, let it ring and ring. She was about to give up, when Clay answered. "Hi, this is Annie. Will you come to dinner tonight? Gran wants you."

"Sure," he said, at last. "What time?" the words had that peculiar disjointed sound that meant he was in an area with poor coverage.

"Seven. Bring an appetite."

"So your fisherman's coming to dinner," Hetty said when Annie handed the phone back. "Does that mean it's serious?"

Annie took several steps before answering. "I don't know. I think I'd like it to be, but I don't think I'm ready. Last night... Well, let's just say I wanted him to make love to me, but I wasn't sure I wanted to make love to him." As soon as the words were out of her mouth, she felt the truth in them. She'd wanted him to take the decision out of her hands. If he'd pushed her, she would have cooperated. Instead, he'd been kind and understanding and patient.

Damn him for being so noble.

And thank goodness he had been. She knew with certainty that if they'd had sex last night, it would have been the only time.

"I'm not sure it was a good idea to invite him. Somebody is sure to say something that will embarrass me—or him."

"Oh, I don't know. They've been pretty easy on Frank. Besides, he looks like the sort who can hold his own, even in this bunch. Don't worry."

Six women were gathered in a rough circle under the pines. Two old aluminum folding chairs sat empty, at opposite sides of the circle. One was between Gran and Aunt Louisa, one between Jennifer and Elaine. "I'll flip you for the one by Gran," Hetty muttered, while they were still far enough away to be unheard.

"Since you're hurting, I'll be nice." She angled toward the left side of the circle, Hetty toward the right.

"Annie, come here by me," Gran said. "I've an idea I'd like to discuss with you."

Annie shot a quick glance at Hetty. "Play nice, now."

"I will if she will." She hobbled to the chair between Jennifer and Elaine.

Annie took the other empty chair. "You ought to be ashamed, Gran. The last thing Hetty needs today is a dose of Jennifer."

"Hush! She'll hear you." Cecile could just imagine how Hetty and Jennifer irritated each other. Two more unlike women she'd never seen. "You're flushed. Are you feeling all right?"

"I forgot my sunscreen this morning, and I fell asleep in the sun."

"You do know better, don't you?" Cecile said, examining the glowing pinkness of Annie's nose and cheeks. She was seeing something else, too, something that satisfied her. "Your color's better. When you got here a week ago, you looked pale and sickly."

"I was, Gran. Inside and out. I think I'm better now."

"It's about time." Her attention was caught by something Jennifer was saying. She cocked her ears but couldn't make it out. The trouble with getting old—one of the troubles with getting old—was that you couldn't eavesdrop worth a darn. She sent a mental order. *Behave yourself, Hetty.*

"Well? Are you going to converse with me, Annie, or are you going to nap?"

Annie started, blushed.

The girl's in love, or very close to it. Good. Means she's healing.

"I was just thinking... Why did I marry Walter, Gran?"

"You're asking me? You should know better than anyone."

"But I don't. I've been thinking about it the last couple of days. I can't remember what it was that attracted me to him. Even before he convinced me to stop working, I think I'd stopped loving him. But you know me." Her small laugh was a little bit rueful. "I hate to give up on anything."

Cecile thought back to the times she'd seen Annie and Walter at family get-togethers in Portland. He'd always seemed to be on the outside, and not particularly interested in looking in. As if he was uncomfortable with the often boisterous family he'd somehow married into. Or as if he'd disapproved of them.

She'd had bad feelings then, but had said nothing. Mostly she managed to mind her own business, no matter how great the temptation to interfere with her children's and grandchildren's lives.

"Gran?"

"Wha— Sorry, I was woolgathering. As for Walter, would you have listened if anyone had tried to tell you he wasn't the right man?"

"I had a feeling you didn't like him, that you didn't think he was good enough for the noble Blankenship family."

"Pooh! Nothing noble about us. Hard work and canny investing is what's brought us to where we are. Walter didn't see that, though. All he saw were the trappings of success. The ranches, Ward's firm, your father's business."

She held up her hands when Annie seemed about to interrupt. "I don't mean he married you for your family's money. He's not a bad man. But I do think the Families' outward appearance of success made him see something in you that wasn't ever there.

"To make matters worse, you were in love and completely blind to his shortcomings. I knew—and I told your parents—that

279

he would be a wealthy man someday. But he would always be poor in spirit. My reservations were because I could see that he lacked some quality that would have made him the husband you need. Walter Abbott is one of the most completely self-centered people I have ever met. I don't think there's an ounce of empathy in him."

"Even more self-centered than Aunt Frances?" As soon as she said it, Annie clapped her hands over her mouth. "I'm sorry. I shouldn't have said that."

"Why not? It's the truth. And that reminds me. Have you seen Serhilda this afternoon?"

"She was asleep in the other bunkroom. I didn't want to wake her. Why?"

"Just curious. I hadn't seen her since breakfast. What do you think of her?"

"Once I got past the body piercings and the bizarre clothes, I liked her. Poor kid. I can't believe what kind of life she must have had, growing up without a mother."

"Do you think she would have been better off with Frances?"

"Good heavens, no. From what she said, this Les was a good father to her. But still—"

Cecile nodded in satisfaction. "There comes a time in a girl's life when she needs a mother."

"Absolutely." Annie bit her lip, then smiled, although tears pooled. "I'm so lucky. I had Mom and I had you. Did I ever say thanks?"

Cecile reached over and took her hand. "There's no need. It's all part of the job." She had to blink her own stinging eyes.

She gave herself a moment to calm, and then said, "You know, Annie, I always wondered why you let Walter convince you to give up your job. You had a promising career. Couldn't you have taken a leave of absence, or worked part time after Calvin was old enough to put into a good daycare?"

"I loved being a stay-at-home mom. I really did. What I hated was the social stuff. Once I was at home all the time, he wanted me to entertain. Elegantly." She made a little moue of distaste. "Would you believe I even signed up for a class in napkin folding."

Cecile couldn't contain her laughter. "You didn't!"

"Oh, yes, I did. I should show you. I do a perfectly elegant Lady Windemere's Fan. And my Cockscomb is *trés elegante*." Her smile faded and she fell silent, staring into the distance. "Why did I do that? I'd never envisioned a life like that for myself."

"Sometimes we slide into patterns without realizing it." Cecile hesitated, reached once again for Annie's hand. "May I be frank?"

"Sure." Annie's voice had gone flat, with the earlier humor gone.

Here goes nothing. "When you remained devastated for so long after Calvin's death, I feared you'd never recover."

"He was my child. Do you ever recover?"

"The Annie Ogilvie of years past would have, as your grandfather liked to say, grabbed her bootstraps and gone on. You gave yourself up to grief and sat around waiting to die."

"How did you... Oh, Gran, you're right. I did. I felt so guilty and so lost. I even resented all the support the family gave me."

"Aside from the natural guilt any mother would feel at the accidental death of her child, what had you to feel guilty about?"

Annie buried her face in her hands. Haltingly, with many long silences, she confessed.

After she sat down between them, both Elaine and Jennifer ignored her. Hetty could understand Jennifer's behavior. "Elaine," she said, after a good five minute's silence, "have I done something to offend you?"

They'd never become fast friends as children. At Gatherings, Annie and Evan had followed Hetty everywhere, and she'd enjoyed their company despite the wide spread of their ages. Elaine had been more interested in playing with her dolls than in hiking and horseback riding, and Eric had even then been something of a dork. Hetty had missed several Gatherings while she was in college, and then Elaine had gone East to college, where she'd met and married Stewart. This was only their second trip west together.

"No, nothing. I'm just—" Abruptly Elaine stood and walked away.

Hetty looked over at Jennifer. "Obviously I walked into the middle of something. Care to enlighten me?"

Jennifer leaned down to pick up the tote bag at her feet. "It really isn't any of your business. Excuse me."

Hetty grabbed her arm before she could leave. "No you don't. I've had my fill of your holier-than-thou attitude this week. In this family, we air our differences, we don't let them fester. Now tell me what's going on between you and Elaine."

Jennifer set her chin, glared at Hetty.

Hetty glared back. "You're not going anywhere until you tell me."

"Mother Armstrong—"

"Aunt Louisa will not come to your rescue. Haven't you caught on yet that she stays out of family feuds?"

"Oh, all right." Hetty had never seen anyone flounce before, especially not sitting down. "It's Evan."

A sick, sinking sensation filled Hetty's middle. "What about Evan?"

"Something Elaine said. And then she denied it. But I know. I know it's true."

"God damn it, Jennifer. What about Evan?"

"Don't you swear at me!"

Hetty held her down, or she would have leapt to her feet and run away. "I'll say anything I damn well please to you. Now, what about Evan? Tell me!"

"He's..." She looked all around. Lowered her voice to the barest whisper. "I think he's queer!"

Hetty laughed, and hoped she sounded genuinely amused. "Is that all? I thought it was something serious."

"Need some help?"

CeCe looked up, but she already knew who was there. Owen had just a little bit of a southern accent, which she found really strange, since he'd told her he'd been born and raised in Columbus, Ohio. She almost refused, but then changed her mind. Once he'd accepted that she really was serious about her cycling, they'd gotten along pretty well. "You can hand me stuff, if you want." She gestured toward the toolkit, unrolled on the grass beside her bike.

He picked up her Allen wrench set and inspected it. "I've never known a bicycle racer before." With one finger, he eased the biggest wrench out and wiggled it back and forth. "What's this for?"

"Adjusting stuff, mostly. Handlebar height, brakes, you know." She unscrewed the pedal and dropped it into a heavy-duty plastic bag. "You want to move so I can turn this over?"

He duck-walked out of her way. "I can't imagine Char knowing which end of a wrench to take hold of."

When she had the other pedal off and stowed, she handed him the bag. "There's a piece of Styrofoam that this fits into. It should be right at the end. Can you pull it out?"

He did, and was impressed with how the pedals just sat into the plastic foam. Interested now, he upended the big box. Four more pieces of foam fell out, along with a humongous plastic bag. "What's this for?"

"To wrap the bike in. At least it was. It's not important for this one. A few more scratches and dust won't hurt it." She heard the little tremor of self-pity in her voice, and took a deep breath to get it under control. *My beautiful bike. I could wring that little brat's neck.*

Eric and Hetty's dad were going to replace it, but that would take weeks. The Bridgestone just wasn't up to what she needed and she knew there wasn't a bike in Denver that would fit her right. If only her arms and torso were a little bit longer. *I'll do all right in the Criterium, but I wanted to win. Darn it, I wanted to win.*

Owen stuck around until she had her bike packed. He followed her into the cookshack and waited while she washed her hands. "You want to go for a walk?" he said, when she came out of the bathroom.

"Sure. Where to?"

"It's only four. We've got time to walk into to town and get an ice cream cone."

"That sounds great. I'll tell Gran."

"Don't." He caught her wrist. "She'll tell you not to spoil your dinner."

"The rule is—"

"Yeah, Okay. But remember, I warned you."

He stayed in the dining room while she ducked into the kitchen.

Gran was sitting at the big table, cutting celery into sticks. "Got your bike all packed?"

She snatched a celery stick. "All done. I left it leaning against the back wall." The celery was nice and crisp. "Owen and I are going into town for ice cream. We'll be back in an hour or so."

"Whose car are you taking?"

"We're not. I need to walk. Tomorrow I'll be sitting all day." She snatched another celery stick.

"Dinner's at seven," Gran called as she escaped.

She waved in acknowledgement. "Let's go," she told Owen, "before somebody puts us to work."

They jogged all the way to the highway, slowed to walk single file along the shoulder. It would be nicer if they could walk side by side, so they could talk, but maybe this was better. She wanted to ask him to write to her, and didn't know how.

The little settlement of Last Chance was less than three miles by road and trail from the houses at the Floating Nought. There was plenty of time for them to sit at a picnic table behind Abe's Fly Shop and eat their ice cream. CeCe had made friends with the old man in the fly shop on Wednesday, when she'd picked up a nail as she rode through town. He'd invited her to sit in the shade behind his shop to patch her tube. "Not so noisy as out on the road," he'd said, "and a lot less dusty." She knew he wouldn't mind if they used his table.

"I didn't want to come," Owen said, once they were settled, "but now I'm glad Mom made me."

CeCe licked up an icy drip that threatened to run across her thumb. "Me too. Not want to come, I mean. My dad didn't give us a choice."

A fish jumped in the river, sending ripples across the shining surface. "They're your relatives. I never figured out how, but at least you belong."

"Gran actually is my grandmother—my mom's mother. But it doesn't matter. She's yours too, now. I heard her telling Aunt Louisa how glad she was Peter brought you. She's really something else."

"Oh man, isn't she? When I told her what I wanted to do, she said she'd see what she could do to help me. Later Ward...uh, Uncle Ward said he had a friend in the Navy who might write me a letter of recommendation. That is so cool." He paused, looking uncertain. "I hope they remember."

"I think if Gran makes a promise, she keeps it. Even my dad thinks she's special, and he doesn't trust most people." Lifting her cone high, she bit off the tip and slurped out the last of the ice cream. Her dad hated it when she did that. "I call him Ward. He doesn't fit the uncle picture. So what's this about the Navy?"

"The Academy. I really want to go there. In June I went back to a week's show-and-tell. It was great. My great-grandfather was an admiral. Nobody else in the family has ever been on anything bigger than a rowboat, I think. But I know I'd like it."

He leaned back and stared across the river at the Tetons, shining brightly in the late afternoon sun, but he seemed to be looking at something much farther away. "An aircraft carrier. That's what I'd like to serve on. Or maybe a battleship. Something big. I'm good with electronics, and..."

He told her about his electronics hobby, and she was impressed, even if she understood maybe one word in ten. In return she told him of her dream to race professionally. "I have to prove myself as an amateur first. And Dad says I have to go to college. That's okay, because I like school. And I've got a long way to go before I'm good enough."

"No wonder you were so bummed when your bike got wrecked. I'd've been totally pissed."

"I was. But there wasn't anything I could do about it. And at least I'm getting a replacement." But not for a month or more. Not until the summer cycling season was over.

Neither of them said anything more for a long time. The river gurgled and the birds swooping close to its surface let out high-pitched little squeaks. Traffic on the highway was a constant growly sound behind them, but somehow it faded away and left nothing but peaceful sounds.

She was perfectly content to sit here with Owen. If only they'd gotten to be friends earlier in the week. Maybe—

"Shit! Look at the time. We're going to have to run all the way back."

CeCe glanced at her watch. Six-twenty. "You're right. Let's go."

"Wait." He caught her arm before she could take off running. "Write to me, will you?"

"If you'll answer."

His smile was a promise. "Let's go. Bet I can beat you there."

"No way!" She sped off at a dead run.

They arrived at the cookshack gasping for breath and holding each other up. But they were in time for dinner.

Chapter Twenty-four

TWO LITTLE BOYS WERE PLAYING IN FRONT OF THE BUNKHOUSE when Clay arrived at six-thirty, bearing wine and an appetite. They led him to the cookshack, chattering about the chuckwagon ride they'd taken that afternoon, down at the park.

Annie came out of the kitchen to greet him, wearing an old fashioned calico apron over her jeans. She brought with her mouth-watering smells of roasting meat and rich spices. "I'm glad you came. When I couldn't call you back, I wasn't sure if you were."

"You couldn't keep me away. I'm already tired of my own cooking. Will this go with dinner?"

She held the bottle up. "Riesling's always good, but especially with turkey. And this is a good label. You didn't find it here, did you?"

"No, I brought over a case of my favorites, since I wasn't sure just what the wine situation was here."

"Idaho has some excellent wineries," Annie's father said, as he joined them. "Good to see you, Knight. I hope you know what you're letting yourself in for."

Before Clay could answer, Annie said, "Now, Dad, don't scare him off." In response to a call from the kitchen, she gave them both a quick smile and left them alone.

Gib Ogilvie grinned after her. "C'mon. I'll introduce you again. Bet you can't remember most of the names from the other day."

"One or two. But a refresher wouldn't be amiss."

Shortly he had a glass in his hand and was in the middle of a hot debate about the Mariners' chance at a pennant. His years in the bank had given Clay the ability to get along with almost anyone, but he found this family not just congenial, but downright comfortable. He wasn't fooled by the apparently innocent questions about his job, his income, and his political philosophy. What made the not-so-subtle interrogation interesting was that he got the impression that they didn't really care about the answers, beyond curiosity.

Once he'd answered most of the really personal questions, the conversation reverted to the argument that his arrival had interrupted. The lanky, bearded fellow—Ben?—said, "Damn it, Eric, when are you gonna learn that more government just means more taxes? Sure, we need quality controls on drugs, whether they're for people or animals, but every time you ask the government to do it, you raise the price and you give those idiots in Washington one more reason to reach into our pockets."

"And what about those drugs a year or so ago, the ones that turned out to do more harm than good? If the government had been—"

"Bullshit!" One of the younger men said. "Take it from me, Eric, we need less government involvement rather than more. In my business—"

"That's enough!" Cecile's voice cut through the men's deeper ones. "You know the rules. No religion or politics in the cookshack. How in the world you expect to enjoy your dinner when your bellies are tight with tension, I don't know. Now either pick a neutral topic or go outside and do your fighting."

"And don't expect us to call you for dinner," Hetty added.

"Annie tells me you're a steelheader," Clay said to Gib, in the silence that followed. "Ever do any fly fishing?"

"I tried it once," Gib said. "Thought it was too easy."

"Too easy? Let me tell you—"

"I've fished up around Park City," Eric said. "The lakes up there are world class."

Clay bit back his opinion of lake fishing. Just because it wasn't for him didn't mean it wasn't for everyone. "I've never been in that area. I've heard it's spectacular."

"You want spectacular? Ever been back East? I'm not a fisherman, but I've talked to those who are. They say the Upper Delaware is as good as anywhere out here." That was Annie's brother. Peter...Ogilvie? Yes, Annie had said he lived in Ohio.

"So what made you give up your career to become an innkeeper?" Ward said.

Clay hesitated before replying. "Y'know, I didn't think of it that way. What I wanted was a place I could fish every day and make a living at it. The innkeeper thing was just part of the deal."

Ben slapped him lightly on the shoulder. "Good luck with it. You'll find life here a whole lot different from the city."

"Thank God!" Clay said, and everyone laughed.

Annie's last task in the kitchen was to whip the cream for dessert. When it stood in high peaks, she covered the bowl with plastic wrap and set it in the refrigerator. That done, she removed the beaters and went in search of Clay.

"For me, Annie?" Janice, Elaine's youngest said, as soon as she cleared the doorway. Annie held them high, out of the child's reach.

"No! Mine!" Jeremy grabbed her around the knees.

Joey threw himself on Jeremy's back. "Me too! Me too!" he yelled.

Jennifer's voice cut through the noise. "Joseph! Behave yourself."

Annie bit her tongue when the little boy stepped back from the fracas, his shoulders drooping, his lower lip stuck out. She was strongly tempted to hand him a beater, just to get Jennifer's goat.

"Not for any of you. This is for grownups."

"Not fair!" Jeremy protested, but he released her. He ran after Joey and punched the younger boy in passing. Joey yelled and Jennifer glared.

Annie wove her way among relatives to where Clay stood. Without interrupting the conversation—which was about fishing, naturally—she waved one of the beaters under his nose.

Clay stopped his spirited defense of catch-and-release fishing and grabbed the beater. His other arm slipped around Annie's waist and he pulled her close against his side.

"Are you sure you want to spoil my dinner?"

"Pooh! One little bit of whipped cream won't ruin your appetite. It's just a promise of great things to come. Here, Frank. This one's yours."

Frank's expression of surprise as he accepted the beater tickled her. Hetty had said he'd no experience with a big family. She wondered what he thought of this one. He'd sure had a memorable introduction to it.

Content to be held at Clay's side, she listened with half an ear to the conversation. Her father was vigorously defending fish as food, while Stewart insisted that they were only edible when red meat was lacking. Evan made a tentative remark about the benefits of a vegetarian diet, and was ignored. Ward listened with sparkling eyes, never saying a thing until Ben commented that it was a shame that overfishing was seriously endangering many ocean species. Then he said, "Whoa. No politics, remember."

"Hell, Ward, conservation isn't politics, it's basic survival."

"Tell that to the damn politicians," Peter said.

Ben grumbled, but he did so under his breath.

Annie, who agreed with him, reached out to squeeze his arm. She wondered what Clay's thoughts were, made a mental note to sound him out on the topic.

And many others. In the last few days, his opinions had come to matter a great deal to her.

A shrill whistle broke into the debate. "Dinner is served!" Hetty said into the sudden silence. "And this time, the adults will serve themselves first. So you kids just stand back out of the way." She glared at Jennifer, who had been the one to insist that her children be served first every previous night. "We didn't slave over a hot stove all day just so you kids could mess up our work of art. Are you ready, Aunt Thea?"

"Ready," came a voice from inside the kitchen.

Annie hurried into the kitchen before her mother could emerge. She was sorry to miss Clay's reaction to the feast.

Clay wasn't sure what to expect, His impression was that this bunch didn't stand much on ceremony, but when Hetty called out "Ta-ta-da" and pretended to flourish a trumpet, he wondered if he hadn't overlooked something.

In a moment Thea came through the door, carrying a huge platter containing an elaborate Viking ship fashioned out of a watermelon. "Don't you lay a finger on that," Hetty cautioned Eric, who was standing close to the serving table with two plates in his hands. "Wait until it's all here."

The next offering was an enormous turkey, followed by a cauldron of candied sweet potatoes, one of mashed potatoes, a third holding mounds of dressing, and a gallon-sized pitcher full of... He took a second look. Yes, it was dark, rich giblet gravy. Numerous bowls of pickles, olives, carrot curls, cheese-stuffed celery, and spiced peaches followed, until one of the long tables was almost completely covered with food.

Clay's mouth had dropped open when the table was about half filled. "I thought you people were roughing it this week," he said to Ward, when Annie emerged for the second time, her hands full of a big, napkin-lined basket.

"This is our Thanksgiving dinner. We always have it at the end of the reunion, because most of us can't take the time off later. It's traditional."

"I like your traditions. But do you think there'll be enough?" he said, still marveling at the great amount of food before them.

"Barely. You haven't seen this crowd eat yet. Come on, grab a plate."

Clay hadn't shared Thanksgiving with a family since his own parents had died. He found himself curiously touched by the sense of belonging he felt with these people. It wasn't that they had adopted him, but more that they had simply opened their hearts to a stranger within their midst. They pulled him into conversations, they treated him like a friend, and they informed him that they expected him to help with the cleanup. "The women cook," Cecile told him, as he accepted a second piece of pumpkin pie. "The men clean up. It's tradition."

He couldn't even regret that he hadn't been able to sit by Annie. She'd found a seat between her Uncle Ward and the teen with all the piercings, while he'd been captured by Owen, who wanted to learn more about fly fishing. CeCe, who'd looked wistful when she explained that their dad hadn't been able to get away from work this week, had sat on his other side, quietly listening to his conversation with her cousin. They were nice kids, the sort he hoped his own would grow up to be.

If he ever had any of his own, that was.

The women all disappeared when dinner was over. "They'll bring up bedding for the littles," Ben explained. "We don't want anyone to miss the show. Here, see if you can find room in the freezer for this." He handed Clay a plastic container of turkey, the last shreds from the ravaged carcass. He wouldn't have believed it, but there were practically no leftovers. Of course, some of the kids had eaten like there was no tomorrow. Clay was sure he had seen the littlest boy—Barty, was it?—go back for fourths.

At last scanty leftovers were stacked in the refrigerator and freezer and the kitchen looked as if it had never been used to prepare a feast. Clay followed Evan into the dining room in time to see Ward setting up a laptop and a projector at the far end. *Damn! I wanted to take Annie for a walk.* He hadn't bargained on having no time at all with her.

"I hope you don't mind," Annie said softly into his ear as she slid onto the bench in the place he'd saved for her. "More tradition. We all send Uncle Ward photos of what we've done since the last reunion."

Once again he slid his arm about her waist. This time she leaned into him.

"It sounds like a great way to keep track of each other." Guilt niggled at him. A second cousin had sent him photos of her kids last Christmas, and he hadn't even sent her a card. He dug into his memory for her children's names and found nothing.

"It is. And I love it." Annie leaned into his encircling arm.

Clay, whose body had reacted predictably, welcomed the sudden dark when Ward turned off the lights.

"If you'll all keep it down to a dull roar," Ward said, his voice carrying over the babble, "we'd like to start this with a little surprise. Ma, will you narrate?"

Cecile explained that the first slide, a rather fuzzy black-and-white shot of a shabby farmhouse with a handsome young man standing on the porch, was one of a number of old photos she'd had scanned.

"Some of you have seen my albums, but not for many years. These start with the early years, when our children were small. That's Tom at our house near Grand Coulee. And this next one shows Ward admiring his baby sister."

"Is that really you, Mom?" a young voice called out.

"My sister," Annie whispered.

Clay watched Cecile's family grow larger and older. He marveled at the primitive conditions under which Annie's grandmother had lived and raised a family, and he found himself fascinated at this saga of a family whose members had done such interesting things, but never so much so that he was unaware of the warm armful of woman with him. The light touch of her hair against his cheek reminded his again just how much self-control he needed while he was with her.

Each child's life was shown, each grandchild's. He saw Annie grow from a dainty little girl with long brown pigtails and a sweet smile into a coltish teenager, and then into the lovely woman she was. When a slide of her wedding came up, he felt a deep and burning envy of the slickly good-looking man she had married, He felt her stiffen and rubbed his hand up her spine. "I wouldn't buy a used car from him," he whispered in her ear. She giggled and relaxed.

Annie stiffened again when a slide showed Calvin's first birthday party. She stared at it, waiting for the inevitable tears, but they did not come. Hardly conscious of Clay's stroking hand, she waited for the smothering grief that had, before this, overcome her at the sight of her son. Waited. And waited.

Her heart ached, but she did not dissolve. When the next slide appeared, she sat a little straighter, sure that now she could go on with her life. The pain and guilt were still there, would always be there, but they were manageable.

Maybe she was ready to look to the future again.

The slide show finally ended at eleven and the family dispersed. Parents picked up small, blanket-wrapped bundles and herded yawning children out of the cookshack and down the paths to the houses. Soon only Hetty and Frank, Annie and Clay, were left.

"After two hours of that, I need coffee," Hetty commented. "How about you, Annie, Clay?"

"Decaf for me" Clay said, before Annie could refuse.

"Me, too." She'd rather be alone with Clay, than share him with Hetty and Frank. Maybe later.

They took their drinks out onto the small front porch and sat in the darkness. "This is some family," Frank said. "There have been so many divorces in mine that something like this wouldn't be possible. Hell, I'm not even sure any more where some of them are."

"It'll never happen in mine either, but because there are so few of us," Clay said. "It must be wonderful, growing up in a big, close family."

"It has its points," Hetty agreed, "but believe me, they're not always positive ones."

"Everyone minds your business," Annie said. "Take one wrong step and wham! Gaggles of aunts and cousins are on your neck." She snuggled closer against Clay. "Of course, the same thing happens when you have problems. There's always someone to turn to."

Saying those words made her realize just how true they were. Sure, Clay had helped her over the last of her healing by showing her the peace she could find in the river. But she'd have never made it through this past year without the Families. Just knowing they were there, even though she'd all but rejected them by running away to Boise, had kept her from giving up, from smothering herself in grief and guilt. She admitted, finally, that she'd shut her family out for far too long.

"Too bad you didn't remember that lately," Hetty said, as if to rub salt into an open sore.

How could she know what I was thinking. Is it so obvious? "No, I didn't. I won't make that mistake again. This past year would have been a lot less painful if I had yelled for help, instead of locking all my troubles inside. I was getting better, but still couldn't forgive myself." She smiled at Clay, squeezed his hand. "Then this crazy fisherman taught me how to find a way out of my self-imposed cycle of guilt and blame."

"Hey! All I did was teach you to fish," he protested, moved at her giving him the credit.

"All you did," she contradicted, "was to teach me where to find peace of mind. Thank you, Clay. Thank you so much." She kissed him lightly.

"The whole family thanks you," Hetty said, but her smile softened her words. "Annie was becoming an awful drip. Come on, Frank, let's hit the sack. We've got a long drive tomorrow." She pulled Frank to his feet and they departed.

"I like Hetty," Clay said, "and Frank's an interesting fellow."

"So are you," Annie told him. "And I meant what I said about being grateful to you. Something happened to me, out there on the river, something that made all the difference. I feel like I can take anything the world throws me and live through it, now. I didn't before." She turned, slipped her arms around his neck. "Oh, Clay, you've become so important to me. I hate the thought of leaving you tomorrow."

Clay kissed her lightly. She imagined she felt him restraining his desire, his need to engulf her in his arms, to kiss her deeply.

She felt his chest expand as he took in a deep breath. Felt it flutter her hair as he let it out in a gusty sigh.

"I'm not too fond of the idea myself," he said. easing her arms from him. "But If we're going to get up any time before noon tomorrow, it's time to call it a day. Can you fish in the morning?"

"I shouldn't," she said with regret. *Wait a minute. This is the new Annie.* "Yes, as long as we do it really early. I don't have to be on the road until noon or so, but I do still have to pack." She let Clay pull her to her feet. They strolled across the lawn, hand in hand. There was so much she wanted to say to him. If only he weren't so damned noble.

I hope he's being noble. I couldn't bear it if what I feel was all one-sided.

His pickup was parked by the Big House. He paused, his hand on the door handle. "Why don't I meet you at the fishing access about five-thirty?" he said, as he took Annie into his arms. She raised her face, but forced herself to wait passively. He kissed her deeply this time, his tongue gently exploring her mouth, lightly sparring with hers.

Annie leaned into his kiss, her hands stroking his broad back. When he would have pulled away, she clung to him, sliding her hands down to cup his buttocks. "I wish you didn't have to leave me," she whispered, moving her hips against him suggestively, tempting his awakening body.

He lifted his head and looked down at her. In the deep shadows cast by the yard light, she couldn't make out his expression. "I wish we had more time. There's something between us, but it's still new. It needs time, and that's what we don't have. If only—" He dipped his head and kissed her again, quick and hard, before stepping back and releasing her. Before she'd had a chance to draw even one breath, he was inside the pickup, looking down at her from the window.

"Tomorrow morning,"

"I'll be there," she promised.

Chapter Twenty-five

Sunday

"DAD, CAN I TALK TO YOU?"

Ben nearly dropped the coffee carafe. It was not yet dawn, far too early to expect anyone else to be around. "Sure. Just let me get this started." He filled the carafe, poured it into the reservoir, flipped the switch. *Did I remember to put in the coffee?* Yes, he had. "Okay, son, shoot."

Eric moved the napkin holder to the side of the counter, lined the salt and pepper shakers up next to the butter dish, and picked up a crumb with the tip of his forefinger. "It's Evan."

Ben slid onto a stool at the counter. "What about Evan."

"Is he really...uh...gay?" Now the trivet sat precisely in line with the butter dish.

"Yes. I thought you knew. He hasn't exactly kept it a secret."

Eric opened and closed his mouth several times.

Ben waited, wishing he were anywhere else. This was not a conversation he wanted to have.

"Don't you think you should have warned us?" Eric's tone made the words half a plea, half an accusation. "I mean, you knew, and you didn't tell us before you put him in the Blue House with...with all those little boys."

"Christ, Eric! Are you crazy? Evan? Defender-of-the-underdog-Evan? The kid who followed every rule. Hell, you used to complain because he was too damned perfect."

"That was before—"

"The hell it was. He might not have realized what he was then, but it's not something that happened to him overnight. Evan's gay. He was almost certainly born that way."

The coffeemaker gave its last gurgle. Ben welcomed the sound because it gave him a chance to step back and think about what to say. He pulled out two cups, filled them, and held one out to Eric.

"No thanks, Dad. You know I don't drink coffee anymore."

He'd forgotten. Ben lifted his own cup to his lips, inhaled the aromatic steam. He eyed his elder son over the rim. *Shit!*

"Eric," he said after a moment's reflection, "I respect your beliefs and I admire you for living your faith. You're a good father and, I presume, a good husband. You're everything a parent would want a child to become. Except for one thing."

Eric's lips had widened in a smile. "What's that?"

"You've become a sanctimonious prig." Ben took a big swig of his coffee, mostly to keep himself from saying any more.

"Da-a-a-d!"

He sounded exactly as he had when he was five or six. Ben's throat tightened at the memory of how Eric had been so protective of his little brother. How he'd rarely complained about the way Evan followed him everywhere. Even in high school the two boys had been virtually inseparable, despite the nearly three years' difference in their ages. He'd always counted their closeness a particular blessing, considering the sibling rivalry he saw frequently in his classrooms. "Sit down," he said, weary already and the day was scarce begun.

"No, I can't. I've got to get back. What I really came over to say..." Eric's hands covered his face, his fingers speared into his hair. "Dad, Jennifer's really upset. She doesn't want Evan anywhere near the boys. So I don't know what we'll do about Christmas..."

The weariness became a terrible weight upon his soul. Ben couldn't think of a thing to say, couldn't think of a way to close this sudden chasm. He shook his head. "Do what you have to, Eric. Your first loyalty is to your wife and children."

Eric just stared at him for a long time. At last he said, "Yeah, I know." His shoulders slumped and he turned away. At the door he paused. Without turning around, he said, "I'm sorry, Dad. So... sorry." As if every step was an effort, he crossed the sun porch and went down the back steps. The morning twilight swallowed him.

So am I. Ben blinked several times, in a futile attempt to hold back tears.

WHEN THE ALARM UNDER HER PILLOW BEGAN ITS INSISTENT BEEPING, Annie almost shut it off. She brought it close enough to read the time and wondered if she'd somehow set it wrong. The lines of light between the closed miniblinds were gray, not the pale, soft gold she'd expected for this time of morning. She rolled out and went to the window. A finger between the slats showed the reason for the dark. Raindrops raced each other down the glass. She could see the tops of the nearby trees swaying in the wind.

"Pooh. I can't imagine any self-respecting fisherperson to go out in this." She got dressed anyway. Her suitcase was packed, and naturally her raingear was on the bottom. She'd never taken it out. While she was digging for it, Gran turned over.

"Annie? Are you going fishing this morning?"

"I doubt it," she whispered back. "It's raining. But I'm going down to meet Clay, just in case."

"Well, whatever you do, can you be back by ten? I want to talk to you and your mother."

Mystified, but not particularly surprised, she nodded. Gran was always wanting to talk to someone about something at the last minute. Nobody started for home without last words of advice from her. She managed to pull her rain parka from the case without making too much of a mess. "I'll see you later."

The house was silent as she tiptoed through the kitchen. The coffee maker called to her, but she didn't want to bother this morning. Maybe she could persuade Clay to go into Island Park for breakfast. They might as well take advantage of their last few hours together.

Maybe you should persuade him to take you to his trailer. Anything could happen there.

"Not yet," she told herself as she climbed into her car. "He's right. The timing's all wrong. Who knows if we'll ever see each other again?"

Clay's pickup was at the fishing access parking lot and he was inside it. When she drove in, he flashed his headlights and turned on his dome light. She interpreted the light as an invitation.

She climbed in and pulled the door shut. The cab was warm and dark, comfortably intimate. "Do fish bite in the rain?"

"If you've used the right lure. But I didn't figure you'd want to learn the joys of fishing in the rain." His teeth flashed white in the shadowy light. "The café was just opening as I came by. Are you interested in breakfast?"

"Sure. I haven't even had coffee this morning."

He started the engine. "Neither have I."

As he guided the pickup out into the road, she watched his face, now barely illuminated by the dash lights. His jaw was set and his brows lowered.

"Clay? What's wrong?"

He didn't answer until they were on the highway. "Is there any way you can stay longer?"

"I wish." She watched the wipers, not sure what else to say. *Swish, swish, pause...swish, swish, pause...*

"I suppose I could come over to Boise—" He said it like it was about the last thing he wanted to do.

"No, don't do that. Not this summer, anyhow. I think—" She closed her mouth on her thoughts because he'd turned into the café's parking lot. "Coffee first."

"Right." He started around to open her door, but she was already sliding out.

The café was already mostly full, but they got a small booth near the back. A good thing, because it was one of the few quiet places in the café. At least they wouldn't have to shout at each other. She hid behind the menu until the waitress came to take their orders.

"I've got to be home by ten," she said, when they were alone again.

"No problem." He stirred his coffee, even though he'd put nothing into it. "Tell me what you're thinking."

"I'm thinking I need more time before I make any major decisions about my life. Not to heal. I think I've done the biggest part of that, and the rest will come naturally. This week—" She took a deep breath. "Clay, am I wrong in assuming you might like more than a one night stand?"

For the first time since they'd sat down, he looked her straight in the eye. "I think so." He exhaled, a gusty sigh. "Hell, that sounds like a copout, doesn't it?"

She had to laugh, even if she didn't think his question particularly funny. "Yes, but I know how you feel. I want you." Butterflies swarmed in her belly when his expression went from rueful to hungry. "I want you, but—" The words eluded her and she shrugged.

As they stared at each other, both silent, she wondered why she was so reluctant to take the last step with Clay. She'd been feeling twinges of desire, unfocussed and elusive, for a while now. They had come as a relief, because she'd felt nothing sexual for a long time, had wondered if she ever would again. Then she'd met Clay and the twinges acquired a target, became focused. It hadn't taken long for desire to become demanding, distracting her while awake, invading her dreams, until thoughts of Clay intruded on all she did.

The waitress set bottles of ketchup and hot sauce on their table as she passed. Clay pushed them aside. "Do you write? Letters, I mean?"

She moved her coffee mug when the waitress returned, carrying two big platters. "I'd rather do email. Good grief, I'd forgotten how much food you get here."

He picked up his fork. "Look at the bright side. You won't need to eat lunch."

As if by mutual assent, they dug into their food, limiting their conversation to moans of pleasure, the occasional "Yum!" and "Pass the ketchup."

Clay swabbed up the last of the golden yolk with a toasty crust. "I won't have a computer until sometime in September. Will you write?"

She heard a plea in his tone. "Of course. Often." She pushed her plate aside, unable to finish her hashbrowns, leaving a slice of crisp toast untouched. "I won't promise every day, but I'll make sure I send you something at least once a week. You'll probably be bored, though. My life is anything but exciting."

He reached across and took her hand. "You don't have to amuse me. I want to get to know you, Annie. To know who you are when you're not on vacation, when you're living an ordinary life, not surrounded by family. The trouble with summer romances is that the people involved in them aren't who they really are. And that's who we need to get acquainted with. We need to see if those two people fit together as well as we have this week."

His hand was warm and strong, wrapped around hers. Annie clung to it. "That's pretty scary, Clay, when you consider that we're both in transition. You're starting a whole new life. I'm trying to put mine back together." Scary indeed. So scary that she blurted, "Maybe we ought to forget the whole thing."

"Or maybe we just need to be patient." He released her hand. "Look at that line. Let's let some hungry people have this table."

Back in the pickup, she resisted the urge to babble just to break the silence. If she'd opened her mouth, she would have pled for him to take her to his trailer, to make love to her. Just this one time. In case they never saw each other again. How could she bear to lose him now, when she'd only seen a glimmer of what they might have together?

Just a glimmer. Not a promise.

When he turned south, she knew where he was taking her. It was just past eight o'clock.

"Well..." he said when he pulled to a stop beside her car.

"You'll need my address." Annie dug in her purse. She found a dog-eared business card from her insurance agent, scribbled her address on the back. "What's yours."

"I don't have one yet. Not locally. I'll have to—"

She couldn't bear this one moment longer. "Here. If you decide to write to me, I'll know where to reply. I've got to go." Jumping to the ground, she stabbed her key into the lock on her car's door. It was a wonder she could see the slot, through her tears.

As she skidded to a stop at the highway, she looked into her sidemount mirror. He hadn't moved, hadn't started his engine.

Only when she was approaching the compound did she happen to look back and see his red pickup turn onto the highway.

THE USUAL CONFUSION REIGNED IN THE COOKSHACK AS EVERYONE gathered up scattered possessions and sorted out the children's toys. Cecile sat at the back table, sipping coffee and feeling relieved that she had no one to worry about but herself. One of the best things about having the property management firm deal with the houses was that they didn't have to clean before they left. She remembered how the last day used to be, before the old house had been torn down. The two families and all their children had crammed themselves into four small bedrooms and counted themselves lucky that they had such a nice vacation home.

"Smartest thing we ever did was remodel the old barn," she mused aloud.

"Talking to yourself again, Ma?" Ward slid in beside her. "Isn't that a sign of senility?"

"Not at all. It's what one does when one wants intelligent conversation."

"Of course. I should have known."

"You look extremely pleased with yourself, this morning. Did you hear from Mr. Champion?"

"I did, yes. He's agreed to see Hildy." His brows came together in a fierce frown. "I sure hope this isn't a mistake. He says he refused to see her before because he doesn't want her memories to be of him as he is now. Maybe he's right."

"Perhaps. But I believe she'll find it far easier to deal with his death if she can say goodbye to him. Have you told her?" Cecile worried about Ser—*Hildy's* reaction to seeing her stepfather's condition more than she would admit. There was no doubt in her mind, however, that they were doing the right thing. It would be the first step in closure for the child.

"Not yet. I talked to Ben, though. He'll drive you back to Portland. I'll turn the car in at the airport."

Wade stood and waved. "Hildy? Over here."

The tough kid with a shell of steel was back. Hildy sashayed across the room, as if she didn't give a damn about anyone in it. Her tighter-than-skin jeans barely concealed her pubic hair, the ring in her navel gleamed, her hair had red, purple and green streaks this morning. She detoured to pick up a mug of coffee, more, Cecile was sure, to prove that she answered to no one than because she needed it.

"Yeah? Whatcha want?" She hiked one foot onto a bench and leaned on the knee. The gaze she turned on Cecile was somewhere between *Damn your eyes* and *I need a hug*.

"Are you packed?" Ward said, as if her appearance and attitude was the most natural thing in the world.

"Sure. When do we leave for Grandma's House?"

What she needs is a good spanking. Trouble is, it should have happened ten years ago. Cecile took a second look. *No, what she needs is a hug.* Unfortunately Hildy was far too prickly this morning to accept a hug willingly.

"We don't," Ward said, his tone mild. "You and I are driving to Salt Lake City, where we'll catch a flight for L.A. Tomorrow we'll go see Les Champion."

Just like a man, Cecile thought, as Hildy's face went perfectly white. *No delicacy at all.* She caught the girl's arm and pulled her to the bench. She was shaking as if she'd caught a chill.

"Oh, hell, Hildy, I didn't think—" Ward scooted over to sit beside her and closed her into a tight embrace. "I thought you wanted to see him."

"I do," she sobbed into Ward's shirt. "I do. I do. Oh, God, is this for real?"

Cecile waved everyone away. She'd satisfy their curiosity later. "It's for real, child. Ward's been trying to get through to Mr. Champion for several days. This morning he finally succeeded."

"When?" Hildy said, on a hiccup.

"Today. As soon as we can get away, in fact. But first you've got to change clothes."

That brought Hildy's tear-stained face out of the shirt. "Huh? I *am* dressed."

"And I'm old fashioned enough not to want to be seen with someone who looks like an invitation to rape. Go put on something decent."

"Ward," Cecile said, warningly, "don't—"

"No, it's all right. Les would have a cow if he saw me like this." She stood up, smiling tremulously. "I'll hurry." She cut through the crowd. By the time she passed the window, she was at a dead run.

Cecile smiled at her son. "Hmmm."

"Hmmm, indeed," he replied. "It should be an interesting trip."

Chapter Twenty-six

THE BUNKROOM LOOKED SAD, SOMEHOW, AS IF IT NEEDED the clutter and color of women to bring it alive. Ben had already picked up Gran's suitcase and tote bag. CeCe's duffle and backpack sat on her bed and Charlene's suitcase stood beside the door, next to some muddy sneakers with her iPod tucked into one. Annie knelt to look under the beds, knowing that at least one shoe or sock had migrated there. Sure enough...

"Annie, are you still here?"

"In the bunkroom, Mom." She rose to her feet, dusted off her knees. The striped sock she'd found must be CeCe's. Charlene wouldn't be caught dead in anything pink and orange. She tucked it into a pocket on the backpack.

Her mother appeared at the door. "Don't you just hate the last day? It's so sad, somehow, saying goodbye to everyone all at once. I'd much rather stretch it out over several days."

"Oh, I don't know. This way it's like pulling off a bandage. Ripping off the tape doesn't hurt nearly as much as pulling it off a little at a time."

Her mother stepped aside, motioning Annie into the hall. "I saw the girls heading out on one last hike, and thought we might have a place for a quiet visit before you go."

A visit? Annie eyed her mother with suspicion. When she was a teen, 'visit' was Mom's word for a lecture. Unable to think of a good excuse to disappear, she said, "I heard Elaine promise Jeremy they'd go say goodbye to the horses, so we're alone here. Shall I make coffee?"

"No, thank you, darling. I'll just get myself a glass of water."

Annie looked in the fridge. There were two Cokes and a pint bottle of orange juice. She went for empty calories and caffeine. Settling herself in one corner of the sofa, she said, "Well, mother?"

"I never could fool you, could I? Yes, I want to talk to you." Her mother settled at the other end. "Your grandmother has convinced me that you need to know—" Her mother bit her lip. "Oh, dear, this is going to be difficult. I've kept it a secret for so long."

"Good heavens. A deep dark secret? Who did you kill?"

To her complete astonishment, her mother burst into tears.

She scooted down the sofa. "Don't cry. Please." Arms around her mother, Annie patted her back and fought tears of her own. "Whatever it is, it can't be that bad. Please, don't cry."

Her whole family was prone to sentimental tears. The women wept at children playing, at beautiful sunsets, at sentimental poetry. Everyone loved to wallow in the bathos of a sappy-happy ending to a movie. Even Uncle Ward, the compleat engineer, was apt to choke up at the final scene in *Bambi*.

This was different. These harsh, choking sobs were for real. Annie took hold of her mother's shoulders and shook her. "Stop it! Stop this right now! Whatever it is you want to tell me can't be that bad."

Thea made a conscious effort to halt the flood of tears. She gulped, sniffed, and hiccupped. Patting her pockets, she failed to find a tissue, so she used the sleeve of her sweatshirt to wipe her eyes, something she'd always scolded the children for doing. "I'm sorry."

"So am I. You know how I hate it when you cry."

Annie did look truly distressed. She'd always been the worst of the children about seeing her mother upset. That was why Thea had learned to hold in the real tears until she could shed them when everyone thought she was being sentimental.

When Annie started to move back to the other end of the sofa, she reached out and caught her hand. "No. Stay here, where I can touch you. I...I need to."

"Mom—"

"Please. I have to tell you this. Maybe it will help you. I've never talked about it." Her inhalation fluttered, as if something was catching the air before it got to her lungs. "You were not quite two, and on the go every waking moment. I had a terrible time keeping up with you."

She held up a hand when Annie would have spoken. "Your father had been called to a construction site. Some question about the electrical system, I think. We were supposed to go to Oxbow Park with friends. He told me to go ahead, that he'd come if he got the problem solved before it was too late.

"There was a little beach near our tables, perfect for children. A log lay at an angle to the shore, so that there was no current to speak of. The water was shallow, no deeper than a foot, even by the log."

Behind her eyelids, Thea could still see the sun flashing off the rippling water, still smell the steaks cooking on the grill set into the ground. The laughter of children came from all around, for many families had come to the park to celebrate an unseasonably warm Mother's Day, an unusually sunny Sunday. Even the river was warm that day, for all it drained the slopes and glaciers of Mount Hood.

"You were younger than the other children, but determined to play in the water just as they were. You had on a little yellow playsuit. It hung to your knees without a diaper under it. Those old gauze ones got so heavy when they were soaked. Yours drooped lower and lower, until I finally took it off."

Annie returned her smile. "I should think so. Thank goodness for disposables."

"I got caught up in a discussion—something about Vietnam, I'm sure. I held pretty strong opinions about it, even though Ward and poor Harald were both in the Army. Some of the others were staunch supporters of Johnson's policies, and I was being pretty vehement about how wrong they were." A good thing she hadn't seen the future. She might have argued even more passionately. "I was so wrapped up in what I was saying that I forgot to keep my eye on you."

"I know how easy that is to do," Annie said, her mouth twisting in a grimace of regret.

"We all do it, darling. That's why I'm telling you this now, so you'll see that you're not the only mother who...who failed. And because...well, I saw how you reacted to Joey falling into the river the other day. You're still frightened of water, aren't you?"

"No really frightened, but certainly not entirely comfortable in it, or on it. More so now, since Calvin..." Again that remorseful twist to her mouth. She shrugged. "I had some trouble getting into the river to fish, but it didn't seem as frightening as if I was in a boat. Or swimming." She gave a shaky little laugh. "You don't have to put your face in the water when you fish."

She leaned forward, caught Thea's hands, which had been twisting the tassels on a cushion. "What do you mean, I'm not the only mother who failed? Do you know someone else who let something terrible happen to her child? Who?"

Thea returned the pressure, until their hands were so tightly clasped that her fingers tingled. "Me. I failed you, darling. I almost killed you."

"That can't be true."

"Oh, it is." She untangled one hand, held up a finger. "Listen to me.

"I'd just finished a fervent little speech about how we had to stop minding everyone's business but our own, how we needed to bring our soldiers home before they all died in a war that we shouldn't be fighting. I'd really been caught up in it, to the exclusion of all else. Then I looked down at the river—"

In that instant she was back there, seeing the little beach, where her baby had been only a moment before....

She told the story in broken sentences, describing the scene she'd relived so recently. "You'd swallowed a lot of water," she said finally, "and for a while we were afraid you'd suffered some lasting effects, but you were fine, thank God. Later you seemed to have no memory of what happened, except that you were afraid of water. So we never spoke of it."

Annie sat for a long time, her hands clenched in her lap, breathing in short gasps. Thea was afraid to say anything, afraid of what her daughter might say to her.

"I remembered. I thought they were nightmares. I fall into the water and float. The water carries me away. It's nice at first, because it feel like I'm on the softest, nicest bed. It sings to me, too.

"Then water splashes in my face. I choke. Gasp, and instead of air, I inhale water. It hurts. I choke again.

"The water won't let me go. It's like some awful monster, clinging to me with cold fingers, sucking all the warmth out of me, filling my nose and mouth so I can't breathe. Something hits me on the head. It hurts. A monster scratches me with its sharp fingers. I roll over and scrape my face on a sharp thing. When I open my mouth to cry, I swallow more water." She buried her face in her hands. "My God! Is this what Calvin felt? Were these his last thoughts?"

Mentally cursing her mother for advising this confession, Thea embraced Annie. "No, darling. *No.* Calvin's death must have been peaceful. He was in a quiet pond, not a rushing river. I think it must have been as if he went to sleep."

"Bullshit." Annie pushed her away so hard that she almost fell off the sofa. "You didn't see the water lily stems wrapped around his little legs, the bruises on his little arms and shoulders. He fought to escape, Mom, and he died fighting.

"No," she said, holding up a hand when Thea would have embraced her, comforted her. "Don't touch me. I have to think about this. I have to think about how much more careful I might have been if you'd told me this a long time ago."

"But darling—" Once again Thea reached out.

"I'm not blaming you for...for Calvin, Mom. But I do need time to think about this. Can we just leave it for now? Someday I'll be ready to talk about this, but not now. Not today."

Although her heart ached for Annie, Thea nodded. "I'm sorry, darling. It's just that I was afraid..." How could she explain that she'd feared that Annie might not forgive her negligence? And later, when Annie's fear of water had become apparent, she'd truly believed that there was no connection with her near-drowning.

Ma and Gib had disagreed, but she'd been so certain, had even spoken to a child psychologist about it. He had supported her opinion, and so the secret had been kept.

"I'm sorry," she said again. "I only did it for your own good."

Slowly Annie stretched out a hand and touched her knee. "I know that, Mom. And I do love you. It's just that right now I'm angry and hurt and upset and...and I don't know how I feel. Give me time, will you? Time to sort this all out?"

Knowing she had no choice, Thea said, "Of course, darling. Call me when you're ready to talk."

Annie merely nodded before rising and returning to the bunkroom.

With an aching heart, Thea walked to the Big House, glad the week was over.

This has been the damnedest Gathering. Nothing has gone the way it was supposed to.

HETTY STOOD ON THE PORCH OF THE BIG HOUSE, WATCHING FRANK load their luggage into the 'Vette. She'd filled its meager cargo space with her stuff on the trip from Seattle, planning to ship the suitcase full of outdoor clothing home on a bus. Since they were headed for Seattle, instead of their licentious week in San Francisco, it seemed silly to ship anything. It was a good thing he'd packed light. His single duffle was crammed on top of her suitcase, behind the passenger seat. She'd insisted on having the top up for the trip home, despite Frank's request that it be down. Two days of windburn would leave her looking like hell.

She jumped when an arm went around her waist. "He doesn't hold it against you, you know," Gran said softly. "He's really very fond of you."

"If you say so," she replied, knowing that this time her aunt was wrong. How could Frank help but blame her for putting him in a cast for the next month? She figured she was lucky that he'd agreed to drive her home, much as she hated to let anyone else hold the wheel of her baby.

Ben pulled the Land rover up beside the 'Vette. "Let's get you loaded, Gran. Louisa is over there, giving Eric's kids one last hug."

"I'll give you a hand," Frank said. He came up to the porch and picked up the two suitcases Gran indicated.

While the men were debating how best to fit them in, Hetty said, "Will you do me a favor? Will you talk to my father again? Try to make him see that Mother's drinking really is out of control."

Gran sighed. "I'll do my best. But it may not be good enough. John has a tendency to see what he wants to see, no matter what the evidence is otherwise."

"I know. But try, okay?"

"Of course. Yes, I'm coming," she said, when Ben held the door open. "I am so not looking forward to this trip," she said, *sotto voce*, "but I'd never tell him that."

Hetty followed Gran down the steps, and climbed into the passenger seat of her 'Vette. "This feels strange."

Frank closed the door on her without replying.

Oh, this is going to be a great trip. A bitchy passenger, a surly driver. What fun!

THIS WAS THE PART SHE HATED. CECILE WANTED TO GO AND HIDE, so she wouldn't have to say so many goodbyes. In some ways it would be easier if they'd all trickle away over two or three days. This way it was almost a shock when everyone left at once.

She was glad Tommy and CeCe were going home with Ben and Louisa. Stephen was doing his best, but those children needed more than a loving housekeeper. *I wonder if Ben... No. Not yet. I'll see how this works out.*

Peter was checking the tires of the tent trailer and Kenna was settling Emma into her car seat. Inside the minivan, Owen was pretending not to look at CeCe, who was leaning against Ben's dusty Land Rover. *They were good for each other. Not quite a summer romance, but more than just friends.* Even if they never saw each other again, she knew that they'd stay close. Something they both needed right now.

Eric closed the door of his monstrous SUV behind Jennifer and came around the back end. He hesitated, then climbed the steps and put his arms around her. "Gran, I'm sorry. Jennifer's just not...she's not used to..." He cleared his throat. "Take care."

As he turned away, Evan came out of the house, pulling a suitcase and carrying a box of books under his other arm. Frank was right behind him, a lumpy duffle in his good hand. When Evan stopped suddenly, Frank plowed into him, all but throwing him into Eric's arms.

The brothers sprang apart, wearing equally appalled expressions.

"Eric, I—"

"Evan, I—"

They stared at each other for a small eternity. An uncanny silence surrounded them, as if the whole family was waiting to see what would happen.

Eric stepped back. "Take care, Evan. God be with you." He turned quickly and all but ran down the steps. Before anyone could do more than stare, he was in the SUV. The roar of its big engine drowned any comments that might have been made.

Cecile saw Eric's mouth move. All the children and Jennifer dutifully waved, but they didn't look like it was their idea. Then they were gone, a rooster-tail of dust marking their passage.

"Hetty? Let's go." Frank sounded impatient.

Hetty came out the door. She stopped to hug Cecile. "I wish you were my mother," she whispered.

"I'd've been proud to have a daughter like you. Now you take care of yourself. And of that man, too. He's a keeper."

"I wish." From her tone, Hetty had already given up on Frank.

Well, no wonder, after what Jocelyn did. That woman is a danger to herself and others. If only Frank has the gumption to blame her, and not Hetty.

Ben finished tying the box containing CeCe's bike on the top of his Land Rover. Cecile wasn't looking forward to the journey across Idaho in that big, boxy thing. *I should feel guilty letting Louisa sit in back with the children, but I don't. My bones are just too old for those back seats.* A good thing she'd let Ward talk her into renting that big car for the trip over. At least this way he wouldn't have to leave her car parked at the Salt Lake City airport for God only knew how long.

"Ready, Gran?"

"As I'll ever be." She picked up her tote and went down the steps. How strange it felt not to be the last to leave. She paused. "Ward? Don't forget to turn off—"

"The water heater, the ice maker, and the attic fan," everyone on the porch and in the driveway chorused.

"Well, pooh to all of you," Cecile said with a sniff. "Next time I won't remind you, and see where you'll be then."

"Helpless, hopeless and stuck with a big electric bill," Thea said with a smile. "Mother, are you sure you wouldn't rather ride with us? We really wouldn't mind taking you back to Portland."

"Not a bit. I'm looking forward to having Tommy and CeCe entertain me all the way home." Nothing could be further from the truth, but Thea and Gib had been planning their trip to Glacier for a long time. How could she be so selfish?

Annie stepped up to hug her. "You were right, Gran. It does get easier."

"In time," she agreed. "And with the right sort of help."

Annie blushed, but said nothing. With a final squeeze, she let go and opened the Rover's passenger door, offering a hand to help Cecile up the high step.

All the car doors closed, sounding like an out-of-tune steel band. Suddenly Elaine's popped open and she scrambled out. "Jeremy left his teddy bear on the porch. Be right back."

Everyone laughed, but they all seemed to share her feeling that it was time. Ben pulled slowly away from the house. Cecile looked back and saw Annie doing the same. *Maybe I should have asked her to take me as far as Boise. No, I shouldn't have. She needs the time alone, to think, to sort her feelings.*

Driving had always been for her a contemplative experience, and Annie had once said the same thing. She'd let all the thoughts and memories and experiences of this past week stew in her mind as she drove. By the time she got to Boise, God willing, she'd be ready to pick up the frayed edges of her life at last.

And by next year, she'll be the Annie she used to be. Cecile was sure of that, particularly when she saw the slicker-clad man watching from the opposite roadside as they turned onto the highway. Clay Knight had been a strong force in Annie's healing. Only time would tell if he was to be something more.

Clay parked at the fishing access and walked along the secondary road past Osborn Bridge. The rain had started again, but it was more like a heavy mist, instead of the fat drops that had freckled the surface of the river this morning. His slicker sat on his shoulders like a portable steam bath and his sneakers squished with every step.

"You're crazy," he muttered. "You've got a nice, dry trailer, and a good book." Instead of returning to them, he leaned against a fencepost and fixed his gaze on the gate to the Floating Nought, about a quarter mile away.

Annie had said she was leaving about two, and it was nearly that now. He wasn't sure why he wanted to see her one last time, but it had seemed important an hour ago.

Two vehicles emerged from the wide gate. A Dodge minivan and that big SUV the veterinarian drove. Had he missed her?

No, here came another. Even in the rain, its bright yellow paint gleamed. The vintage Corvette. A small pang of envy went through him. He'd had a chance to buy one, once, but as with everything else, he'd counted it less important than saving toward his dream.

No more vehicles appeared for a while, and then the Land Rover came into sight, leading a convoy of three. The middle one was a green Accord. Clay stood upright. Stepped to the edge of the road. He raised his arm.

Each of the cars came to a full and complete stop, then turned onto the blacktop. The Land Rover passed him. So did the Accord, then the Volvo. At the highway, they all turned south.

Had she not seen him? Or had she deliberately ignored him? Feeling like he'd been gut-kicked and left to die, Clay turned to walk back to his pickup.

He'd crossed the highway and was only about a hundred yards from his pickup when a vehicle approached from behind. Slowed, then sped up and turned into the parking area.

Even in the rain, its color and make were unmistakable. A green Accord.

Her window was down when he stopped beside the car.

"I wasn't sure it was you," she said.

"I wanted to say good bye."

"So did I. If it hadn't gotten so late..."

He reached through the window, touched her cheek. It was warm, soft. He wanted to kiss her, but knew if he did he'd want more. *Too late. Too damn late.* "Annie, please write."

"I will. And you'll answer?"

"Absolutely. Cross my heart." He did so.

She bit her lower lip. "I've got to go."

"Yes, I know. Drive carefully."

"Clay, I..."

"Me, too." He stepped back. "Go. Now."

Without another word, she rolled up her window and drove away.

Chapter Twenty-seven

Autumn

"THERE. THAT'S IT." ANNIE DUSTED HER HANDS, HAPPY TO BE done loading her car at last. Poor thing, It was stuffed so full she was going to feel claustrophobic. All she had to do now was drop the Boston fern off at The Bakery and give the keys to her landlord, and she'd be on her way to the Floating Nought.

Knowing she'd locked all the windows and turned off the water heater, she went inside for one last check, anyway. The rooms seemed smaller now, with her furniture gone, and dreary. She'd been comfortable here, if not happy, but it was time to move on.

"But am I moving on to the right place?" she wondered aloud as she locked the door for one last time.

"Where am I gonna sit?"

The keys dropped from her hand when she jumped. Although she recognized the voice, her stomach didn't stop fluttering as she turned around. "What are you doing here?"

Hildy, looking every bit the punk, leaned nonchalantly against the side of her car. A well-stuffed backpack sat at her feet. "I'm going with you."

Annie held on to her temper as she descended the stairs. "Since when?"

"Since Gran fell last week. She didn't break her hip, but the doc said she could have. Ward's looking for a place where she doesn't have to climb stairs. I figured he didn't need to worry about me too."

Biting back the questions, Annie did her best to match Hildy's cool. "You told him, of course."

"Nah. He and Gran were already in bed. I left a note." She peered into the well-packed car. "So, where do I sit?"

"Do you mean you just walked out without saying goodbye? What is wrong with you? Don't you ever give a thought to anyone but yourself?"

Hildy pushed herself upright, the light of battle in her eyes. "Hey, I left a note. Told 'em not to worry, that I can take care of myself. What's the big?"

Her hands itching to shake the girl, Annie stepped nose-to-nose with her. "The big, you thoughtless brat, is that Gran loves you and is probably sick with worry. Ward too, if he's not thinking of ways to kill you."

At the flash of fear that crossed Hildy's face, she added, "Figuratively, anyhow. He'd never lay a hand on you, I promise. Look, I know you've never had any reason to learn this, but you need to know that one thing a family does is worry about each other. Even if she didn't care about you, Gran would worry. As it is..." She shrugged. "Let me get my phone."

When Gran answered, she said, "She's here. She's fine. Just a minute." Holding the phone out, she said, "Your turn."

Hildy recoiled as if it were a venomous snake.

"Talk to her. You owe her."

Hildy slowly reached out for the phone, put it to her ear. "Gran?" Her voice was thin, uncertain.

She listened, her body tight, her mouth soft and trembling. After a while she said, "I know you told me... No, I didn't really believe—" Tears streamed down her cheeks. "I'm sorry. I'm really sorry. I—"

Her mouth worked and she looked pleadingly at Annie. "I can't—"

Annie took the phone. "Gran, can I call you back? I have a hunch she'll make better sense when she's had breakfast."

"Make sure she understands that I want her back with me. Oh, Annie, I thought... I was so afraid."

Annie knew exactly what Gran had thought. She got mad all over again. "I'll take care of her. Let me talk to Uncle Ward."

When her uncle came on, she said, "I've got an idea, but I want to talk to Hildy first. Is Gran really all right? Why didn't you tell me she'd fallen?"

"Because she wouldn't let me. If she'd had her way, I wouldn't have been notified. Thank God her neighbor had better sense."

"She's all right, though?"

"She's fine, but still pretty stiff and sore. The fall was a good wake-up call for her. I've been telling her for months she needed to get out of this house, into a place with no stairs. Now she's listening."

In the background Annie heard Gran say something, It sounded like a denial.

"Yeah, Ma, I know you're still able to take care of yourself, but wouldn't it be easier if you could do it all on one floor? Annie? Be gentle with Hildy. She's been through hell, these last couple of months. Once she got back to Champion, nobody was going to pry her loose. She was with him until the end."

All Annie had known was that Hildy had been in California until last week. "Oh, no," she breathed, but bit back the words of pity that the girl would have hated. "We'll look at options and I'll get back to you," she said, in as even a tone as she could manage. "Give Gran a hug for me."

"Will do."

She turned off the phone. "Set that fern on the porch. Then let's see where we can cram this other stuff. You'll have to hold your pack."

"You're taking me with you?"

"I'm taking you as far as The Bakery. We'll have breakfast and talk about what we're going to do."

"Cool." Hildy had obviously regained her aplomb.

Clay picked up Annie's latest letter from where it lay on the table and read it again while he sipped his coffee. What the hell was she saying anyhow? He was confused as hell.

> I've decided we're not getting anywhere this way. You're going to be too busy to come to Boise this winter, and I can't get enough time off to come over there. Getting to know each other by mail isn't working. I need to talk to you, Clay, to see your expressions while you say things off the top of your head. If you're like me, you plan each sentence in a letter, and so you only write what you've given considerable thought to.
>
> I'm reasonably sure about my feelings for you, but reasonably isn't enough. I want to be absolutely certain before we take that next step. I'm just not a person who can be casual about sex. Sorry, but I've realized I need a commitment

before I go to bed with anyone. It doesn't have to be lifelong, but there has to be some prospect of a relationship based on more than how good the sex is between us. I'd like to say that we've got that, but I can't. A week just wasn't enough. I was still too wrapped up in my own grief and self-pity, and you were stretching your wings and feeling out your new freedom. Those aren't good bases for life-altering decisions.

I'll let you know when I've got it all together. Until then, believe that I do care for you, that I want to explore what we have, and I truly believe that we'll be more than friends for the rest of our lives.

The last paragraph had obviously been written in a hurry, as if she was rushing to get it into the mail. He wished she'd taken her time and been more clear about what she was considering.

Maybe he should take some time off and go to Boise. Trouble was, he wanted to get all the cabins' roofs fixed before winter. The more money he could save by doing it himself, the better he'd like it.

Six weeks into his new life and he was sure it was what he was meant to do. Despite the difficulty of finding dependable housekeeping help, he was enjoying the whole experience. Of course, this time of year, most of the visitors were hunters, and spent little time in their cabins or shooting the breeze with the innkeeper.

Life was as close to perfect as he'd ever known. The only thing missing was someone to share it with.

Annie?

The longer they were apart, the more convinced he was that she was indeed the missing element.

And the more he asked himself if it wasn't just loneliness speaking.

"HAVE YOU NOTICED HOW QUIET IT IS AROUND HERE LATELY?" Louisa set the piece of pie before Ben. "Almost spooky."

He picked up his fork, but didn't dig in. "Are you telling me you miss that scamp?"

"I do." She leaned across him to refill his coffee cup. "I was relieved when we sent him back to Stephen, but now..." She sighed and sat down across from him. "Ben, what if...?"

Used to her convoluted way of saying things, he leaned back and waited.

"CeCe said something last summer that got me to thinking. According to her, Stephen would like to sell the house, get away from Denver. He's only stayed there because he believes it's best for the kids. But CeCe would give anything to move here. She says Portland's the best bicycling city in America. Trouble is, Stephen won't listen to her. He thinks it's best for Tommy to stay there with his friends."

Ben snorted. "He's got a bunch of friends here, now. That kid makes friends like a puppy does. But I don't know about CeCe. She probably wouldn't like living out this far."

"No, probably not." She poked at her pie, took a small bite. Made a face. "Not sweet enough," she said. "I'll get the ice cream."

Since Ben liked nothing better than Louisa's apple pie with ice cream on it, he just smiled.

They ate in silence, except for Ben's occasional hums of appreciation. When he'd scraped the last bit of good from his plate, he shoved it aside. "So, shall I write to Stephen and see if he'd like to board Tommy with us?"

"Let's call him instead. I've got his cell phone number."

"Don't you think you'd better see what Tommy wants first."

"Already have." She reached into her pocket, pulled out a letter. "Here. You read it."

> Deer Ant Luoise and Unkle Ben,
>
> I reely miss you guys. I wish there was a way I cood live with you all the time. Dads' gone again. This time until almost Thanzgiving. CeCe says she wants to live in portlin too, and Dad says maybe one of these days.
>
> Missus Jorgensen says shes going to quite at Chrismus, becuse she's gonna have a grandbaby. I dont want Dad to get somebody else. I want to go back and live with you. I miss Snickers and the kittens and Puff and even Rootsie.
>
> Luv,
> Stephen Thomas Lewis (thats my whole name)

Ben cleared his throat, which had inexplicably acquired a frog. "Somebody ought to teach that boy to spell."

"Shall I call Stephen?"

"Yeah. Let's hope he's west of us and not east. I'd hate to wake him in the middle of the night."

"I wouldn't. Serve him right, going off and letting someone else raise those children." She consulted her phone list and punched out a number.

WHILE THE WATER FOR TEA WAS HEATING, HETTY CHANGED INTO sweats and pulled on a pair of thick wool socks. This damn cold had her firmly in its clutches. Her head was stuffed, her chest was tight, and her throat felt as if someone had sanded it. The worst part was that her nose was running a stream, and no amount of blowing seemed to help. Not for the first time she wished her reaction to most cold medications wasn't so extreme. One dose of anything available over the counter and she was out like a light. She had about ten minutes to get herself settled before she went into her usual drugged stupor.

She wiped her nose again, and tossed the tissue in the general direction of the kitchen wastebasket. "Damn! Missed again." If she hadn't grabbed the counter, she would have tipped over when she kicked it nearer its target.

She poured tea into a heavy stoneware mug and made her slow way into her living room, keeping one hand on a wall as long as she could. *Why am I so dizzy?* Tea slopped over the mug's rim when she managed two unsupported steps to the sofa. Fortunately the drips fell on the tile floor and not on the pale green Chinese rug.

Once the mug was safely set upon the glass-topped coffee table, she piled all the small pillows at one end before letting herself collapse into the sofa's embrace. With one foot, she snagged the afghan that lay along its back and pulled it within reach.

A shiver went through her before she got herself covered, and again when the afghan was tucked under her chin. She reached for the mug and brought it to her mouth. Miraculously, she managed to take several sips without raising her head higher and without spilling.

The tea warmed her from within, but shivers still shook her every few minutes. When the mug was empty, she thought about getting more, but the kitchen was too far away.

Sometime later the doorbell rang. "Go away," she muttered, without moving. It rang again, and again, until she'd lost count of the times. After a while the irritating clamor ceased and she slept again.

She woke to paralyzing fear as an earthquake shook the house.

No not an earthquake, she realized when she forced her eyes open and looked up into a fierce, frowning face. Frank.

"Wake up, damn you! What's wrong?"

Shit, I hate it when I hallucinate. She tried to clear her mind so she could sleep again, but hard hands held her upper arms and shook her.

"Hetty, I swear if you don't wake up, I'm going to get a pitcher of ice water."

She peered at the blurry face above her. "F-f-frank?" *Now I know I'm hallucinating.* She hadn't seen him since he'd brought her home after that hellish trip back from Idaho. Two days of chilly politeness, broken only by fist-clenching tension every time he shifted gears at the wrong RPM.

"Are you sick?" he shook her again, not as gently this time. "Talk to me, Hetty. What's wrong with you?"

"Cold, just a cold. I took...took..." for the life of her, she couldn't think of the name of the medicine she'd taken. "Always makes me sleepy." Her mouth was dry, her lips cracked and sore. "Thirsty."

He was gone, then back again, raising her head so he could hold a glass of cool water to her lips.

"'Nuff. Good." She fought the clinging fingers of sleep, felt herself losing. *How did you get in?*

When she awoke the first thing she did was look at the clock. Eleven-thirty. Just like always, the med's effect had lasted a bit over four hours. In a minute she'd get up and make herself another cup of tea.

In a minute.

Unable to decide whether she preferred a streaming nose or more drugged stupor, Hetty groped on the floor for the tissue box she'd left within reach. It wasn't there and she turned to look for it.

That's when she saw him, sprawled in her overstuffed leather chair, stockinged feet at the ends of long legs propped on the needlepoint cushion of her Queen Anne footstool. He wore his usual faded Levi's with a plaid flannel shirt. A billed cap decorated with a Porter Cable logo lay on the table beside him, next to a coffee cup and an empty plate.

She hadn't been hallucinating. "Frank?" It came out a whispery croak. Hetty licked her lips, sucked saliva into her cotton-lined mouth. "Frank?"

He lurched upright. "What?"

All she could think to say was, "May I have some water?"

He picked up the empty glass from the coffee table and carried it to the kitchen. In a moment he was back, kneeling beside her. "Do you need help sitting?"

"No, I can manage." She pushed herself upright, scooted back so the sofa's arm supported her.

He ignored her reaching hands and held the glass so she could sip from it. "What the hell did you take to knock you out like that?"

"Antihistamine." Again she looked for the tissue box. There it was, under the coffee table. "Hand me a tissue, would you?" She blew her nose, dropped the soiled tissue into the fused-glass bowl on the table. "It always hits me like that. But at least I can breathe when I take it." She snatched another tissue and held it to her nose. "Sorry. Can't help it."

Frank set the glass on the coffee table and went to sit beside her feet at the other end of the sofa. "When you didn't answer your door, I got scared. I was parked across the street, waiting until you'd had a chance to change your clothes." His big hand wrapped around her calf, squeezed. "You scared the shit out of me, Het, when you didn't answer the door."

She knew she'd locked the door behind her. "How did you get in?"

"I remembered you telling me you left a key with your neighbor, so she could keep an eye on the place when you're out of town. I convinced her you might need help."

Hetty couldn't decide whether to be touched at his solicitude or mad as hell. What business of his was it if she— "Why are you here, Frank? I got the feeling you never wanted to see me again."

He swiped a hand across his mouth. She heard the rasp of his whiskers against the hard callus of his palm. "I was pissed. A lot of stuff seemed to be wrong for us. You really didn't want to show me off to your family—"

He held up a hand when she would have argued. "Hey, I'm no rocket scientist, but I can tell when I'm being kept a big secret. You kept saying I wouldn't like your folks, that they weren't my kind of people, and I read it that you thought I wasn't *their* kind."

"Oh, no. You're such a good man. I was afraid you wouldn't like them."

"Can't say I do, not your mother, anyhow, but they're not your fault. The way you're always flying off somewhere glamorous sort of got to me, too. I'm not much for travel, y'know. And when I do, I'd want to see the U.S. first. There's a lot to see without ever leaving home."

"There is, indeed," she agreed. So many places in this country she'd never seen, because her job was leading tours to exotic foreign locales. "Do you know I've never seen the Grand Canyon?"

"Me, neither. So when do you want to go?"

Hetty's heart did a somersault. "Frank?"

Once again he went to his knees beside the sofa. This time it was to puller her close. "Hetty, this last couple of months has been pure hell. I've missed you, missed you a lot. Can we give it another try?"

When he leaned to kiss her, she held up a hand. "Don't come any closer. You definitely do not want this cold." Patting the place he'd been sitting, she said, "I've missed you too. Oh, shit!" She snatched another tissue, barely got her mouth covered when the sneeze took her. Another and another, until she lost count. The tissue was in tatters, the elbow of her sweatshirt soaked. And the tissue box was empty.

"You may not want to have anything to do with me if you catch this cold."

"Yeah, I will. Where are your pills?"

"My pills?"

"Yeah. I want to dose you up good so I can get a good night's sleep. We can talk about the rest of our lives tomorrow."

Hetty was so stunned that she let him help her to the bathroom, pour another glass of water down her, and poke an antihistamine into her without protest.

The rest of our lives? I must be hallucinating again.

Chapter Twenty-eight

Eric, your mother has invited us for Christmas again. I thought you said—"

Eric lowered the newspaper and peered over it. "I said we wouldn't go to any more Gatherings." His mouth worked, as if he were testing his words before he spoke them. "We went to your folks' last Christmas, and we're going to have them here for Thanksgiving. I think—"

"Those children will be there. Your cousins. CeCe and that terrible little boy. Tommy."

He'd raised the paper, so she couldn't see his expression. It did dip a little, but then he raised it more. "Oh? That's right. Pa did tell me they're planning to take Marcia's kids in. Stephen isn't making much of a home for them. Always on the road."

Sometimes she could just scream. He *knew* she didn't want the boys exposed to Tommy. He was such a little monster. Totally undisciplined. And such a smart mouth. For a month after they'd come home from the family Gathering, Norman had sassed her back at least once a day. He'd even sounded like Tommy sometimes. "Eric, I really don't want to go to your folks' while those children are there. Can we—"

"No." This time he didn't even wiggle the paper. "Jennifer, they're my parents. I love them, even if they do make me crazy sometimes. And Evan's in Africa, so you don't need to worry about him."

"Well, that's a relief. To think they'd let him be around all the little boys."

Eric crushed the newspaper between his big hands. "Jennifer, Evan is my brother. I don't like how he's living his life, and I'm not comfortable around him. But he *is* still my brother. He's no pedophile. Our sons would be as safe with him as they are with your brothers."

"But...but..."

"But nothing. I over-reacted last summer, and I've regretted it ever since. I'll still keep my promise. We won't go to a family function if Evan's going to be there, because I promised you we wouldn't. But if he comes to town, or if I have a chance to see him some other way, I will."

She knew Eric well enough to know when she could argue with him and when she couldn't. "As you wish. Will you tell your folks we'll be there for Christmas, or shall I?"

"I will." The paper came up, and she felt like it was a wall he was building between them.

"I WON'T GET IN YOUR WAY, YOU KNOW. I MEAN, WHEN YOU AND Clay want to get it on, I'll get lost. I'm not totally clueless."

Annie stared across the table at Hildy. "You think—" she took a deep breath. "Hildy, I am not going to the ranch so I can have an affair with Clay Knight. I'm going there because Gran asked me to. Ever since the fire she's been worried about no one being there to keep an eye on things. If Charlie hadn't gone up to make sure the houses were all locked up, we might have lost them all. She doesn't want to ask him to stay all winter. He's getting old."

"Yeah, right. But you're gonna see him, aren't you? Last summer you two were so hot for each other it was funny."

"Yes, I'll see him." Annie remembered what Clay had said in his most recent letter.

> Before you left, I'd started to wonder if we might have a future. I kept telling myself it was the wrong time, that I already had too many balls in the air, but I still hoped. I wish I could get away. Maybe after winter sets in. We need time together.

Common sense warned her to distrust the idea of love at first sight. One of the many counselors she'd talked to had warned her about falling for the first man who came along. "It's easy to look for a substitute," she'd said, "so you need to be sure that's not what you're doing. Don't rush into any relationship."

"Clay is not the issue here, Hildy. What makes you think you and I can live together in any reasonable harmony?"

"Hey, I can get along with anybody." Hildy said, folding her hands together in an attitude of prayer. "I lived with Frances for nearly a year, didn't I?"

"If I'm supposed to see a halo, you need to work a little harder." She waited while the waitress replenished their coffee. "I don't even know what the school situation is up there. And speaking of, did you go to school while you were in L.A.?"

"Uh-uh."

Annie imagined little yellow feathers in the corners of the girl's mouth. "And why not?"

Her expression became, if possible, more angelic, an interesting contrast with the nose and eyebrow studs. "Nobody brought it up. Hell, Annie, I've only got one more year. I can do it anytime."

"First rule." She held up a finger. "If you're going to live with me, you'll clean up your mouth."

"Sure. What else?"

"I haven't said I'll take you yet." She knew she was going to, but wanted the advantage of uncertainty for a little longer. "You know, Last Chance will be a major difference from what you're used to. Aside from the lack of a mall to hang out in—"

"I never did. That's for dorks."

"Let me finish. Aside from the lack of stores and theaters and whatever else you've always taken for granted, the people in Idaho are not like those in L.A. You've no idea how different it is to live in a small town, particularly in an area that's fairly conservative, both politically and socially." She looked pointedly at the streaks of red and lime green in Hildy's now-platinum hair, at the oversized t-shirt drooping off one bare shoulder. "I think you'll find that Levi's and turtlenecks with fleece vests are more the style than what you're wearing. Think you could handle that?"

"Hey, I can adapt. So, when do we leave?"

Annie gave up. She knew better than to beat her head against a brick wall. "Tomorrow. If you're going, I'll need to take care of some things." Like some sort of legal papers so she could enroll Hildy in school, give permission for medical care... What else? Gran would know. Or Ward. "Look, is there somewhere you'd like to go while I do some errands, make some phone calls?"

Shortly they'd agreed that Annie would get a motel room where Hildy could zone out on TV. "I sort of got hooked on the soaps when I was in L.A.," she admitted.

Once she was settled, Annie went to the lobby, where she punched out a familiar number on her phone. "Help!" she said, when her grandmother answered.

"You look enormously satisfied," Ward told his mother when she'd hung up.

"I am. This couldn't have turned out better if I'd planned it. Now if only Frank— Never mind."

"Ma, are you meddling again?"

"Of course I am. Hetty is refusing to see how much that young man loves her." She reached for her walker, silently cursing the weakness that forced her to use it. The doctor said her ankle would probably get stronger with the proper exercise, but she wanted mobility now, not six months from now. "Come. We need to find those notes I made when we set up the guardianship. Annie needs to be able to enroll her in school and to get any necessary medical care."

Once the appropriate papers had been faxed to Annie at the motel, Cecile suggested Ward stay for lunch. "I believe there's some oxtail soup left from last night."

He followed her into the kitchen. "Hard to resist. Besides, I want to hear more about Frank. Have you talked to him?"

"He was here last week, the day before Hildy arrived. Poor man. I don't know how many times he apologized for disturbing me on my bed of pain." She sat when Ward motioned her to do so, hating the fact that walking the length of her own home wore her out.

While Ward put the soup on to warm, she watched him. At sixty, he was still a handsome, vital man. Without thinking, she asked a question she'd always bitten back. "Why didn't you remarry after Alice's death?"

The lines in his cheek showed how his mouth had tightened. "Never found a woman like you, I guess."

"Don't give me that. A woman like me would be the worst possible wife for you. We're too much alike."

Ward set a lid on the pot with unnecessary force. "The truth? Pure, unreasoning fear, based on past experience." He kept his back to her.

"That bad? I wondered, you know. I always thought there was something missing between you. Not passion, but something more basic. Trust, perhaps? Was she unfaithful?"

"Probably. Not that I cared."

"Oh, Ward—"

His expression, when he turned to face her, was savage. "Drop it, Ma. It's old news, and not something I particularly care to discuss. Besides, by the time she died, I was too old to adapt to another woman. Too set in my ways."

"I'm sorry. You're a good man, Ward. You deserved happiness."

"Happiness doesn't hinge on being married. I've had a good life."

She should have resisted temptation, but she simply could not. "And not a celibate one, I imagine."

His cheeks went red. "God, Ma! I can't believe you said that."

"Well, you don't have to tell me. It wasn't a question."

"Thank you for that. Do you want crackers with your soup?"

"No, there's some ciabatta in the breadbox. Let's have that." Once she had distributed the plates and silverware he handed her, she propped her chin on one hand and watched him as he sliced the bread. "Ward, I think instead of buying a smaller house, I want to go into one of those places where I'll be able to move into assisted living when it becomes necessary."

He dropped the knife. "Ma! What haven't you told me?"

"Don't worry, Aside from this confounded ankle, I'm fine. But the day is coming..." She paused, before making sure there was no trace of self-pity in her voice. "The day is coming when I won't be able to do for myself. Marilyn Wicks moved into an apartment at the Apple Blossom Estates last spring and she is very happy. I visited her not too long ago. Her place is comfortable and quite roomy. They provide a bus to take residents on excursions, so when she decides to give up driving, she won't be housebound."

Ward set the soup bowl on her plate and the breadboard in the middle of the table. Once he was seated across from her, he said, "You're serious, aren't you?"

"Let's just say, I'm giving it serious thought as one of my options. Now, do you want me to tell you about Frank's visit or not?"

His eyebrow went up and he stared at her for a moment. "Right. Frank. What did he have to say?"

She tore off a chunk of bread and dipped it into the olive oil Ward had poured onto a saucer. "That he wants to marry Hetty, but isn't sure how to approach her. I told him that the cave-man approach might be best."

Ward sputtered a bit before breaking into a full-throated laugh. "As in he should toss her over his shoulder and carry her off to the nearest preacher?"

"Not exactly, but close. I said if he was sure in his heart that she was the woman for him, he should not give her a chance to say no. You know Hetty. She'll want to look at all the sides of an issue. And likely as not, she'll end up convincing herself that it would be unfair to Frank to marry him. She's so concerned she'll turn out like Joss."

"Not a chance. She's a Blankenship through and through. She's so much like Aunt Elizabeth it scares me."

"That's what I told Frank, that if he could live with a woman who isn't bound by tradition, who does exactly as she chooses once she makes up her mind what she wants, and who needs a man who will love her in spite of her parents, then he should go after her with all the forces at his command."

Ward finished his soup and sat back, relaxed. "I hope you told him that underneath the tough exterior, she's a pushover for romance," he said, with a chuckle.

"Oh, I did, but I warned him that he'll have to get her attention first, before he gives her flowers and chocolate." She tapped her chin as she thought. "Perhaps he should sling her over his shoulder. That would certainly get her attention."

"Ma, you are incorrigible."

"Not at all. I just want the people I love to be happy."

TOMMY SLAMMED THE DOOR BEHIND HIM. "DAD GOT A LETTER," HE called from the mud room.

CeCe finished typing the paragraph. When she'd started researching this history report, she'd been really bummed. Then she got into the groove. Lots of cool stuff had happened in the Yellowstone area before it was a park. She'd read way more about it than she needed to. She was gonna ace it. "Who from?"

"Uncle Ben"

She turned around and looked at him, her breath tight in her chest. Aunt Louisa hadn't answered her email last week, but real letters usually got where they were going, didn't they? If they didn't answer soon, she just didn't know what she was going to do.

Tommy was picking at the flap on the envelope he held.

"Hey! Cut that out. Dad'll have a fit if you open it."

He stopped, but his bottom lip was sticking out a mile. "It's about us. Why shouldn't we see what it says?"

"'Cause mail's private." She eyed the envelope, wishing she had X-ray vision or something. *Steam it open? No, that only works in the movies.* Dan had an uncanny knack for catching her and Tommy at stuff they shouldn't do.

She snatched it from him. "I'll put it on his desk." Dad was due in late tonight. He hadn't been home since just after school started. Sometimes she wondered if he'd come home at all if she and Tommy weren't here.

Tommy plunked himself down in a chair and stretched his legs out. He'd grown a lot this past year, mostly from the waist down. He was now taller than her by a couple of inches.

"It's probably really for me," he grumped. "I wrote a real letter. You only emailed."

Since last summer, CeCe had learned to recognize signs of Tommy's loneliness. Once they'd seen what real families were like, she knew theirs wasn't even close. If only Mom hadn't died. Or if Dad had gotten married again.

No, that wasn't such a good idea. Her best friend had a stepfather and he was awful. With her luck, she'd get a stepmother like Cinderella's.

"Well, maybe Dad will let you read it when he's done. Go start your homework. I've got to finish this report tonight." She shouldn't have put it off. The weather had been so great though, warmer than usual. The best fall she could remember. Usually the last good rides had been in September, but the club had held something every weekend in October, including an impromptu Century.

Her homework had suffered, and if Dad knew, he'd be royally pissed.

She was looking for the right words to give her conclusion some punch when the incoming email bell rang like an old-fashioned cash register, a sound she got a kick out of. It was from OKO@blankenshipfamilies.com. *Owen? Yes!*

Hey CC!

everything's been crazy with changing schools and stuff. this one's way different from where I went last year.

congratulations on winning a bronze in the Criterium, that's awesome :D i was telling one of the guys about you and he said those are really hard races. he's a cyclist, and is trying to talk me into riding with him. says 'I'm built for it' whatever that means. (???) i think i'd rather fence. can't you just see me in a long black cape, fighting off a villains and saving some pretty chick's life? ROTFLMAO :)

i was really surprised when i got your email. :O i figured you'd go back to Colorado and forget about me. :(it's not like we're real cousins or anything. but it was great, being like in a family for that week. i've got a couple of cousins on my mom's side, but nothing like that. maybe someday i can go back and see everybody.

gtg, but i wanna stay in touch. isn't it sweet, Gran's family having its own domain?

Owen :)

She typed out a quick answer, promising to write more later, when she finished her report. Even though she still believed her future and Tommy's were hanging by a thread, she was feeling a lot better than she had an hour ago.

I don't exactly have a crush on Owen any more. But he's really, really nice. And not quite a cousin.

And kinda hot.

"JEEZ. WHAT A MESS."

Annie couldn't think of better words for what they were seeing. The Blue House was gone, replaced by a tangle of charred timbers, fallen walls, and shattered windows. She shifted into reverse and backed to the parking area in front of the Pink House. The journey had been tiring, with heavy rain and gusty wind all the way from Mountain Home. Hildy had offered to drive, but Annie had refused, not knowing her skill level. "Let's do it." She dreaded the prospect of unloading the car in this weather.

"You go unlock and start some coffee. I'll get stuff."

Surprised, she looked over at Hildy, who shrugged.

"I know which suitcase has your nightgown in it. Do we need anything else tonight?"

"I guess not." Annie reached back of the passenger seat where she'd put the sack of groceries they'd picked up in Ashton. Making sure she had a good hold on it, she opened her door. "Here goes."

She dashed to the house and managed to get the key into the lock on the second try. The air inside had a clammy feel to it, as if the place needed a good airing. She wasn't surprised. The last renters had left three weeks ago, just about the time the couple who were taking care of the houses in the compound had quit without notice. The renters had left the kitchen clean, at least.

She reset the thermostat, got the coffee started, before unpacking the rest of the groceries, enough to last them a few days. Hildy came in with a second load as she put the last cans into the pantry. "I put your stuff in the big bedroom. Okay if I take the little one?"

That was the one Annie had been in last summer. "It's awfully small. You'd probably be more comfortable in the other one."

"Yeah, but I wanted to give you some space. You know, for when Clay sleeps over."

Annie turned around and stared, warmth suffusing her face. "When Clay...? Hildy, we're not..."

"You don't have to pretend. I'm cool with it. Hell, Frances had herself a couple of boy toys while I was with her. Talk about air heads, both of them. But they were sure bulked up, real muscle men." She posed like a body builder. "Clay's okay. He talked to me."

Deciding denial would only convince Hildy that she was indeed sleeping with Clay, Annie indulged her curiosity. "Your mo— Frances brought men into the house? She didn't try to be discreet about it? That's terrible."

"God, Annie, you are totally medieval. Frances goes through men like a knife through butter. She told me that she'd had seven lovers last year. This year she was going to beat that, or die trying."

Curiosity overcame good manners. "What about your father. About Mr. Champion? Did he have lovers too?"

"Les? No him and Brian were together a long time, since I was five or six. We were, like, a family." Her lips creased together and she blinked rapidly. "Brian promised he'd come see me sometime, when he's not hurting so much."

The coffee maker gurgled out the last of its hot water. Annie took down two cups and filled them, all the time castigating herself. Had she ever taken time to ask anything about Hildy's life? No, she'd simply looked at the hair and clothes and all the piercings and decided the girl was a punk—or whatever current street slang described her. Now she looked closely. Under the tough exterior, she saw pain and loneliness and a desperate need for love and stability.

There was a place in her heart that had ached with emptiness for more than a year. Could Hildy fill it?

Was she strong enough, healed enough to give Hildy what she needed? A real mother, for as long as necessary.

Only time would tell. But she was going to do her best.

She swallowed the lump that had crept into her throat. "How do you feel about tuna sandwiches for supper?"

"As long as you've got chips to go with."

Chapter Twenty-nine

A S HE ALWAYS DID, CLAY GLANCED UP AT THE HOUSES ON THE knoll as he passed. Even knowing it was futile, he clung to a small hope that Annie would be the one who came to oversee the cleanup. Charlie, the elderly wrangler, had said the Families were sending someone, but he didn't know who.

There were lights in the Pink House. Chances were it was rented. Several nearby areas were opening to hunting this coming Friday. He'd had half a dozen calls from hopeful hunters wanting lodging. He'd hated to tell them he was closed for remodeling, but none of the cabins was in any shape to be rented, not by his standards, anyhow.

Calling himself six kinds of fool, he pulled over into the next wide shoulder. He still had the number on his phone.

The voice that answered on the third ring was unfamiliar. "I'm calling for Annie Ogilvie. Did I dial the right number?"

"Oh, sure. Hold on." He winced at the clatter when the phone was dropped on a hard surface. "Annie, it's some guy," he heard the woman yell off-mike.

"This is Annie."

His voice caught at the sound of hers. After a second, he found it. "This is Clay. I wondered... I hoped... Where are you?"

"I'm here. I mean I'm at the Pink House. Oh, Clay, I was going to call you as soon as we were settled."

"I'll be there in five minutes."

THE COLD LASTED THREE DAYS.

Frank stayed four. For the first three, she was glad he was there, because she felt like hell.

When the alarm went off Monday morning, Hetty hit the snooze button, needing a minute to decide how she felt.

Much better, she decided. Her throat was still a bit sore, but nothing she couldn't live with. Her sinuses were clear and her ears no longer rang. She sat up and reached for her robe. It wasn't across the end of the bed where she always tossed it.

"How d'you feel?" Frank stood in the doorway. His chin was dark with two days' beard and his morning hard-on tented his boxers in the most interesting manner.

Omigawd! Her thighs tingled, her mouth went dry. *I must be well.* "I thought you'd gone home."

"Nah. I'm staying. Feel like coffee this morning?"

"Sure." She went to the closet, had her hand on the knob. "Wait a minute! What do you mean, you're staying? Here?"

His answer was unintelligible. She pulled the robe on and stormed into the hall. The kitchen light was on, so she stomped in that directions. "You're not staying here!"

Much to her regret, he'd pulled on Levi's. "Yeah, I am. Do you want hazelnut vanilla or toffee mocha?" He pulled the grinder from the cupboard. "You're out of real coffee."

"Frank? Did you hear me? You're not staying here."

"Hetty, I let you chase me away last summer. This time I'm in for the whole game. I'll stay as long as it takes."

Her fists clenched in her robe pockets. It was that or pound on the counter. "Chase you away? I did nothing of the sort. You left because my mother tied to kill you."

With a savage gesture, he switched the coffee maker on. "I didn't leave. You dumped me."

"Oh, sure, and you kept coming back for more, didn't you. No, Frank, you didn't. When I let you out at your place last August, you didn't even say goodbye. You just grabbed your duffle, said, 'Thanks for the ride,' and disappeared. Until the other night."

She swiped a hand across her face, wiping away the tears. Obviously this argument was giving her a relapse. "So what made you show up? Did you forget something? Like your copy of *The Two Towers*? Don't worry. It's in the rack."

She could see he was holding on to his temper by a thread. Good. The sooner he was gone, the better. "I've got to get ready for work. Lock the door behind you." She whirled and headed back to the bedroom. Now her nose was running too. There were no tissues in her pocket so she wiped it with her sleeve. *Gross! Gotta remember to put it in the laundry.*

She set the water as hot as she could stand it and stood directly under the shower head. *God! Why did he have to come back? I was learning to handle it, and now I have to do it all over again. If only—*

The door slid open and he stepped inside. "Conserve water. Shower with a friend," he said in her ear as he slid his arms around her. His hands cupped her breasts, his cock nestled between her buttocks.

"Go away."

"Can't. I'm stuck for life." As if she was small and weak, he turned her in his embrace. "Quit fighting, Hetty. You know I'll win."

"Only because you'll out-stubborn me," she muttered against his dripping chest. She didn't resist when he cupped her mound, slid one finger into her. But she wasn't ready to stop fighting. Not yet. "Damn it, Frank, don't you know any better than to get mixed up with a family like mine?"

"No worse than mine. You ought to meet my Uncle Hadley. He's been in and out of jail since he was nineteen."

His hands were busy stroking her tender, delicate tissues, driving her wild with wanting him. Hetty lost the rest of her arguments in a surge of pure rapture. All she knew was that he was lifting her, opening her, sliding inside. Her body was still singing when he drove her up again, higher, freer than before. His exultant shout pushed her over the edge and they clung together, panting, as the steaming water washed over them, slowly cooling their fever.

"Let's get out of here before we catch pneumonia," he said, an eternity later. The water had gone completely cold. He untangled his legs from hers, sat back so she could rise to her feet. "Las Vegas or Portland?"

"Huh?"

"Do you want to get married in Las Vegas today, or have a big shindig in Portland? I vote for Las Vegas, but my sisters all say that every woman wants a big, fancy wedding."

Her mind seemed incapable of thinking more than one word at a time. "Sisters?"

"Three of 'em. And a brother. Two parents and a grandmother. They want to meet you. I told 'em I'd bring you to dinner next Sunday."

She stared at him, horrified. "Do they know who broke your arm?"

His shrug answered her question. "My mother says it was my own fault. I shouldn't have been sleeping with you at a family reunion."

A shiver reminded Hetty she was sitting naked under a cold shower. She reached up and turned the water off. "I'm freezing." When he offered his hand, she pushed herself to her feet. She opened the door and reached for towels. Once they were both swathed, she leaned against the counter and watched as he briskly toweled his hair dry. "My mother's a drunk, Frank. That means I have a chance of being one too."

"So? Life doesn't give guarantees. I'm willing to take the chance." He came closer, caged her within his arms when he leaned both hands on the counter. "I love you, Harriet Elizabeth Armstrong. I want to father your children and sit beside you on the rest home veranda someday, rocking in the sun and looking back on a long and misspent life."

Hetty searched his face, wishing eyes were truly the windows to the soul some poet had called them. "I'm scared, Frank."

"As you should be. Marriage is a scary step. I had to really psyche myself up to mention it. That's why I haven't called you since August."

"I want to..."

His shout of triumph echoed off the tiles. "That's all I needed to hear. We'll sort out the details later."

His kiss, passionate and tender at the same time, somehow dissolved all her doubts and hesitations.

"IF WE DON'T GET OUT OF THIS CHAIR, WE'RE GOING TO BE TIED into such a knot that it'll take three men and a boy to get us undone." Annie slipped from his lap onto the soft Chinese rug at their feet. "There's more room down here." She patted the space beside her. "And it's closer to the fire." The living room of his cabin was small but cozy. There were still unpacked boxes stacked against the walls, and the furniture was shabby, all except for the thick rug that gleamed like a jewel on the scarred old wood floor.

Instead of joining her, Clay reached forward and took her face between his two hands. "Annie, I have never wanted a woman the way I did you, that night last summer. But I'm glad we didn't... That we waited. I don't think either of us was ready then for any kind of lasting relationship. I think we are now."

Annie returned his gaze squarely. "I think so too. In fact, now that you mention it—" She reached up, grabbed his belt, and tugged him toward her. "Now, it's a whole different ball game. Are we going to finish what we started then, or am I going to pine away while you sit there philosophizing?"

"I'm done with philosophy. It's time for action." He slid down beside her, bearing her to the floor with him. His hands cupped her buttocks, pressing her against his aching need. Her hands tore at his shirt, pulling it free of the pants waistband and slipped underneath to caress his broad back and cling to his shoulders. She nibbled at his neck, pushing the loose collar of his wool shirt aside with an impatient chin.

As Clay's hands ranged over her back, Annie let her lips drift lower, stopping to free each shirt button, one at a time and with innumerable tiny nibbles and feathery kisses on his smooth skin above each one. She loved the feel and the scent of his broad chest, lost herself in the sensations his hands were causing on her back and at her waist. When his shirt was completely open and free of his waistband, she nibbled one last time, just above his belt buckle, and pulled herself up onto her elbow. Her fingers traced the line of his breastbone, hovered above the buckle. She smiled teasingly into his eyes, whispered, "Are you sure we aren't rushing things?"

Clay groaned, pulled her against him, covered her face with kisses, and worked her sweater up, baring her back to his caresses. Again she pulled free, but this time only so that he could slip the sweater free of her arms and unhook her bra. She watched the wonder grow in his eyes as he reached to cup her breasts, lowering his lips first to one then the other, sending the blood bubbling through her veins like champagne released from its cork. His teasing tongue, against erect, pulsing nipples, brought a whimper to her lips. Her hands ached to stroke his body, but she could not move them. Her entire being was concentrated upon the delicious sensation his tongue was evoking as it toyed with her flesh.

When one of his hands found the closure of her jeans, she shuddered with the brush of his fingertips against her bare midriff. She wanted to cry out to him to hurry, to bare her body so she could experience the almost tactile sensation of his eyes upon her skin. But Clay seemed to be intent on taking his time, driving her into a frenzy of anticipation. It took him forever to open the zipper.

She closed her eyes, the better to concentrate on the sensations of his fingertips against her belly, even through the silkiness of her briefs. Feeling his hands pushing against her jeans, she rolled from side to side, letting him slide them down over her hips. It therefore came as a complete surprise when the elastic of her briefs snapped against her waistline.

"Open your eyes, lovely Annie. I want to see your soul," Clay whispered. He was sitting beside her, watching her.

His hands, gentle again, slipped under the elastic, ventured downward. Annie felt herself spiraling down into the warm depths of his eyes as his hands stroked along her now bare legs. When he reached her feet, he looked away from her face and to where his hands were tracing each of her toes. He drew one finger across the sole of her foot, causing her to jerk, not because it tickled, but because it sent indescribable feelings coursing up her leg and into her abdomen. She writhed, every nerve ending in her body alert to the touch of his hands, the warmth from the fire, the scratchiness of the thick rug under her.

Clay's lips replaced his fingers. He kissed the tip of each toe before nibbling at her instep and nuzzling one ankle. She closed her eyes again, but was entirely aware of the progress his mouth and hands made up the length of her leg. When she felt his breath on the soft skin of her thighs, she drew her knees up, let them fall open.

"Touch me! Touch me!" her mind cried, but she was unaware that she had voiced her need until she heard Clay whisper.

"Yes. Oh, yes, my love." His seeking fingers found the small bud of pleasure wherein her need was centered.

At his touch, waves of heat suffused her body. Whatever magic he held in his hands was nothing compared to that he wielded with his tongue. Carefully, with frequent retreats to let her passion ebb slightly, prolonging the delicious agony she felt, Clay brought her closer and closer to peaks she had never scaled before—had not even been aware of. The waves of heat crested, carrying her with them into a paroxysm of pleasure that left her mindless and limp.

She came to herself to find Clay's head resting on her abdomen and one hand gently massaging her breasts. "Oh, my," she said softly.

"Exactly," he said, grinning. He sat up.

Annie saw that his slacks were still in place, realized that he had not shared her ecstasy. "Oh, Clay, I was so selfish..."

"You were not. I love you, my darling Annie. That makes your pleasure special to me, even if I don't completely share it."

"But..." She heard his words of love, but a niggling guilt at her selfishness kept her from awareness of their implications.

"Hush," he said, ensuring her silence with a kiss. "I've wanted you for so long that I'll probably explode the first time you touch me." He stood up, quickly stepped out of the slacks. Annie watched as his erect penis sprang free from the confines of his boxers. Pulsing need returned as she let her eyes move over his body, broad shouldered, barrel chested, slim hipped, and altogether dear to her.

Clay dropped to his knees and framed her face with his hands. "Did you hear me, lovely Annie? I love you. I fell in love with you last summer, and it's grown every day since."

This time the words made sense. The last of her doubts evaporated. The hopes and dreams she had almost been afraid to entertain had not been built of air. "And I love you, Clay Knight. Let me show you just how much."

She reached for his shoulders, pulled him down to cover her body with his. His erection against her belly brought her to full readiness. She could feel his aching need for her in the tension of his spine and the hard grasp of his arms around her. Opening herself, she gasped as he entered, then gave herself up to incredible experience. His climax was imminent, but her own was as close. This time, when Annie reached the peak, Clay was around her, beside her, within her.

Chapter Thirty

Summer Again

THE NEW HOUSE WAS GRAY, BUT EVERYONE STILL SPOKE OF IT as The Blue House. It was larger than its predecessor, with four bedrooms instead of three. Gran had staked her claim to the largest one and ruled over the men and boys like a queen. "They're more rambunctious than the little girls," she confided to Annie during one of their rare quiet moments, "but more interesting too. I'd forgotten how linear their thinking is."

A tiny twinge of sorrow arrowed through Annie, and was quickly gone. She'd miss Calvin every day of her life, but the pain was no longer sharp, no longer insistent. "Maybe that's why we have so much trouble understanding them." She gathered the bows she'd made into a basket and picked up the staple gun. "Are you sure it's okay to staple these to the walls?"

"This old place is so full of holes already, what harm will a few more do?" Gran swept scattered petals and trimmings together and tossed them into the waiting garbage can. "I've always wanted a wedding here," she said, looking around the big room. "It's not fancy, but it's ours. So full of memories." Her voice wobbled a little.

"I remember one Christmas... It was the second one after my father hired on as foreman here. I couldn't have been more than twelve or thirteen. We'd had a big storm that had lasted a week or more. The hands had strung ropes between all the buildings, because the snow was blowing so hard you couldn't see five feet in front of you.

"They were hauling feed to the herds when they could, but Pa was sure we'd lose a lot of cattle. Everyone was worn to the bone, working fourteen hour days under impossible conditions. Folks didn't talk much about wind chill back then, but I'll bet it was twenty or thirty below. The thermometer on the side of the barn registered ten below on Christmas morning."

Annie shivered just thinking about it. They'd had mornings that cold this past winter, but she and Hildy had been cozy and warm inside the Pink House, with its electric heat and pellet stove. "That was during the Great Depression, wasn't it?"

"It was, and a more difficult time to be a rancher I can't recall. We were more fortunate than most, though, because we had meat, and Ma and Tom's mother had put up everything they grew in the kitchen garden."

Recalling a conversation about the difficulty of growing tomatoes at this elevation, Annie guessed that her grandmothers' garden had held more root vegetables than anything else. She pulled the ladder into place in the archway between the kitchen and dining room. "Put the big one here, I guess." She climbed, and held up the largest bow.

"With the tails dangling. Yes, that looks fine. Then a couple of the smaller ones at the corners, with long tails on them." Gran carried the largest bouquet to the cloth-covered altar the uncles had constructed.

With the window behind it, framing the Tetons glowing in the morning sun, the altar hardly needed flowers. Annie hoped the fine weather would hold until tomorrow. She attached the side bows and pinned tails to each, When she turned around, she saw that Gran must have agreed about the flowers, because they were sitting on the floor in front of the altar. "Tell me about your snowed-in Christmas." She'd heard many of her grandmother's stories, but not that one.

"Not much to tell," Gran said as she returned to the table where a dozen small bouquets waited. "There never was much ready money back then, but Ma and Pa always made sure we had something to open on Christmas morning.

"That year the Blankenships invited all the hands to join them for Christmas dinner, since most of them had volunteered to stay and help take care of the livestock. None of the boys were married, as I recall, and only a couple had family in the area. They were bunking in the barn loft."

"Brrr." Not like sleeping up there in the summer. Annie and Hetty had done that once, and discovered that sleeping in hay, even with a good strong tarp under you, was vastly overrated.

Gran chuckled. "That was the first time I heard the saying 'Cold enough to freeze the balls off a brass monkey.' I was shocked."

"I was really disappointed when I learned that it doesn't mean what it sounds like," Annie said. "What did you get, that Christmas?"

A distant, soft expression came over Gran's face. Her eyes looked into an unseen distance. "Socks, I think. Yes, Red socks, with blue heels and toes. Lizzie's were blue, with red toes and heels. She thought they were too gaudy and refused to wear them." Another chuckle. "I do believe she's where John got his stuffiness."

"Your mother made them, I'll bet." The ladder wobbled, as Annie set it next to one of the side windows. She moved it slightly and saw a spoon on the floor. "How is Uncle John? He looks older, more troubled. I wasn't sure I wanted to ask Hetty." The spoon went into her pocket and she went on with her decorating.

"Doing well, he tells me. I'm not sure he is, but at least he's coping. It's just too bad that it took a tragedy to get him to face the truth."

Annie looked down at Gran, who was sitting again. She was not nearly so robust as she had been last summer, and a frisson of fear when up Annie's spine. There would come a day when Gran wasn't here. What would she... What would the Families do then? She swallowed a lump. "At least the bicyclist she hit will be all right. DUII is a lot better than vehicular homicide." *Why did I say that?* "Oh, darn. I'm sorry."

"My thoughts exactly, so don't apologize. Now, where shall we put the table for gifts? It just doesn't work against that back wall. There's not room, not with all the loot that's here already."

"Loot? If I'd called it that, you'd have had a fit." Annie looked around the room, the big tables were shoved against all the walls, the benches set in rows behind half a dozen rows of rented folding chairs. The aisle between led from the kitchen arch to the altar. "It's starting to look like a chapel," she said with a smile. "Oh, Gran..."

"A far cry from the fancy church wedding you and Walter had, isn't it?"

"Don't remind me. I've never been so strung out in my life. All the parties and social stuff. And his parents had very definite ideas what a proper wedding should be. They tried to blackmail Mom and Dad into paying for it, but Dad put his foot down."

"As well he should Ten thousand dollars for a wedding. Ridiculous! Thomas and I paid two dollars for our marriage license, gave the minister twenty, and Ma made our wedding cake."

"And you stayed married," Annie said, wondering if this time she would, too.

"Enough reminiscing. I need a nap." Gran put clippers and wire and floral foam into a basket. "You can walk me back to the Blue House, and then I want you to go relax."

At the archway they paused and turned to look back at their handiwork. The dining room, with its stark white walls, worn linoleum, and wide windows, wasn't exactly transformed, but the flowers and wide ribbon bows gave it charm and a welcoming warmth. Definitely a proper place for a wedding.

Or two. Hers and Hetty's.

"May I play Mother-of-the-Bride?"

Hetty saw Louisa's reflection in the mirror over the dresser. "Of course. Come in." she'd been feeling a little sorry for herself, she admitted silently. Annie had her mother with her, but no one was here to mother Hetty.

Well, you could have had someone. All you had to do was ask.

She had to admit she'd rather have her aunt than Joss, who hadn't acted a mother for a long time. Not since she'd stopped drinking socially and started losing herself in alcohol.

Louisa sat on the bed. "Nervous?"

"Scared shitless. I'm not ready for this. What if I—"

"Hetty, we all ask those questions at times like this. I doubt anyone has ever felt adequate to life's big challenges. The day before I married Ben, I almost ran away."

"No way!"

"Way. And when I discovered I was pregnant with Eric... Well, let's just say I spent nine months trying to convince myself I was capable of being a good mother."

"You're a great mother," Hetty said, sitting beside her aunt. "The way you've taken CeCe and Tommy in. They aren't the same kids they were last summer."

"None of us is the same as we were last summer," Louisa said, her voice breaking. "So much has happened..."

"Oh, God, Louisa, I'm sorry. I never thought—"

Louisa took a couple of deep breaths, and gave Hetty a small, wobbly smile. "It's okay. I'm coping. In fact, having CeCe and Tommy around has helped a lot. I can't give in to grief when I have to get Tommy to his karate class, or drive the pace car for CeCe's cycling team. It's helped Ben, too, having kids in the house. They keep him from brooding."

"It's no solace, but at least Evan was doing something he believed in, something that made a difference. Gran sent me a copy of the letter from his team leader. It was—" Her voice broke.

They clung together, their tears wetting the collar of Hetty's robe, the neck of Louisa's t-shirt. The storm lasted an interminable time, but at last it passed. Hetty pulled away, groped for the tissue box on the bedside stand. "Here. Blow."

A watery chuckle. "You sound like a mom."

"Yes, well, I need to get in practice. I'll be one before Christmas." The wonder of her pregnancy drove the last of her tears away. "Oh, damn. I wasn't going to tell anyone. Keep it quiet, will you?" She sniffed, wiped her wet cheeks.

Louisa hugged her tightly. "You sound happy. Are you?"

"Yeah, I am. Much to my surprise. And Frank's over the moon. He's already started building a cradle. We just don't want to broadcast it until after the wedding. Not that anyone will care." She pulled back, looked at her aunt uncertainly. "They won't, will they?"

"Everyone who matters will be thrilled. Omigosh, look at the time!"

Hetty did, and scrambled to the bathroom. Her eyes were red, her cheeks blotched. She wet a washcloth and buried her face in it. After a couple of applications, she looked halfway decent. Makeup would cover the rest.

Louisa helped her into the lacy slip, with its froth of a skirt. Hetty had planned to buy a sleek, stylish wedding gown, until she'd seen this confection. Strapless, with a dropped waist and a full satin skirt, it had a scattering of lush satin roses across the skirt and a short train that would pick up every piece of dirt and lint in sight.

She didn't care. She loved it.

"I feel beautiful," she said, when Louisa had finished zipping her into the dress. Stepping back as far as she could in the confines of the bedroom, she looked at her reflection in the pier glass. "Just look at me. I look like a bride."

"You are a bride, love. And you are beautiful." Louisa sniffed, but this time Hetty knew the threatening tears were happy ones. "Let's go. It's time."

ANNIE CHOSE NOT TO WEAR WHITE. SHE WANTED A DRESS SHE could use, not something that would go into a garment bag to be looked at occasionally but never worn again. Clay had agreed, saying he'd never had any strong feelings about traditional weddings. The floaty skirt of her deep rose dress swirled around her legs as she and her dad followed Hetty and Uncle John up the aisle. Framed by the window, with the Tetons shining in the afternoon sun behind them, Frank and Clay waited, both serious, both looking a little nervous.

Last night she'd asked herself if she was doing the right thing. Today she had no doubts. This time she'd picked the right man.

Hildy reached the front of the room and stepped to the left as Ward went to the right. When she turned to face the room, Annie wanted to cheer at the happy smile on her face. This past winter and spring, she and Hildy had grown as close as sisters, but in some way they were also mother and daughter. Hildy was no longer a rebellious child, although she would never conform to what the world expected. She was unique.

Frank opened his arms to Hetty and she stepped within them. And then Clay was holding out his hand for hers. She looked into his eyes and saw a welcome, a promise.

Saw forever.

Descendants of John Blankenship

1 John Blankenship 1900 – 1976
+Althea McCray 1904 – 1981
..........2 Thomas Blankenship 1923 – 1997
..........+Cecile Heyward 1925
...............3 Heyward Blankenship 1946
...............3 Althea Blankenship 1949
...............+Gilbert Ogilvie 1950
....................4 Peter Ogilvie 1975
....................+Kenna Chesney Kendall 1969
........................5 Emma Ogilvie 2003
........................5 Charlene Kendall Ogilvie 1990
........................5 Owen Kendall Ogilvie 1988
....................4 Albert Ogilvie 1978
....................+Sha Li Sung 1975
........................5 Gilbert Sung Ogilvie 2005
....................4 Anna Cecile Ogilvie 1983
....................+Walter Abbot 1970 (divorced)
........................5 Walter Calvin Abbot 2002 – 2004
....................4 Kristine Ogilvie 1985
...............3 Frances Blankenship 1952

...............+Manfred Rosenfeld 1944 – 1988
.....................4 Serhilda Rosenfeld 1989
...............3 Kirby Blankenship 1954 – 1964
...............3 Marcia Blankenship 1958 – 1997
.... +Stephen Lewis 1955
.....................4 Cecile Lewis 1990
.....................4 Stephen Thomas Lewis 1994
..........2 Elizabeth Blankenship 1926 – 2002
..........+Robert Armstrong 1920 – 1995
...............3 John Armstrong 1947
...............+Jocelyn Dunne 1952
.....................4 Harriet Armstrong 1978
...............3 Joanna Armstrong 1950
...............3 Benjamin Armstrong 1954
...............+Louisa Hansen 1956
.....................4 Eric Armstrong 1975
.....................+Jennifer Anderson 1975
..........................5 Norman Armstrong 1997
..........................5 Angela Armstrong 1999
..........................5 Joseph Armstrong 2001
..........................5 Bartram Armstrong 2003
.....................4 Evan Armstrong 1978
.....................4 Elaine Armstrong 1981
.....................+Stewart O'Neal 1975
..........................5 Jeremy O'Neal 2000
..........................5 Janice O'Neal 2002
..........2 Harald Blankenship 1931 – 1968
..........2 Harriet Blankenship 1935 – 1941

About the Author

ON HER WAY TO A CAREER AS A WRITER, JUDITH B. GLAD MADE a lot of detours—into motherhood, short-order cooking, accounting, management, graduate school, botanical consulting. Eventually she decided she had to write those books that had been growing in her head for years—romances all. She believes every story should have a happy ending, even if it requires two or three hankies to get there.

After growing up in Idaho—the locale of several of her books—Judith now lives in Portland, Oregon, where flowers bloom in her yard every month of the year and snow usually stays on the mountains where it belongs. It's a great place to write, because the rainy season lasts for eight months—a perfect excuse to stay indoors and tell stories. Judith has four children, all grown, three granddaughters and a grandson.

Visit Judith's webpage at www.judithbglad.com to learn more about her other books. While you're there, take some side trips to view early 20th century picture postcards, read about 5,000 ways to earn a living, and see what a *Mentzelia* really is.